Her M[illegible] Secret

Jan Baynham

Ruby Fiction

Stories that inspire emotions!

www.rubyfiction.com

Published 2020 by Ruby Fiction
Penrose House, Crawley Drive, Camberley, Surrey GU15 2AB, UK
www.rubyfiction.com

A CIP catalogue record for this book is available from the British Library.

EPUB ISBN: 978-1-912550-21-0
PRINT ISBN: 978-1-912550-58-6

For Alan, with love.

Acknowledgements

There are so many people to acknowledge along my journey to publication. Firstly, I'd like to thank my husband, Alan, who has supported me at every turn. He read the first draft of the novel and made constructive suggestions on how to improve. He loves our holidays in Greece as much as I do so I've always been able to do my research in his company!

Thanks are due to the wide range of writing friends for their never failing support, especially Sue McDonagh, Catherine Burrows and Vanessa Savage, the Cowbridge Cursors. Thanks, too, to the RNA, especially to the wonderful New Writers' Scheme, the local Chapter and Sandra Mackness, my co-organiser. I've learned so much from the conferences, workshops, talks and, above all, from the fellow writers I've met at RNA events.

Special thanks are due to my daughter's friend, Victoria Nicolaou, for help with the incidental Greek that runs through the book.

I am very grateful to the Ruby Fiction team for believing in the book, the cover designer for capturing the essence of the story and especially to my lovely editor with whom I have enjoyed working. The team also includes the panel of readers who passed the manuscript and made publication possible: Katie Fussneger, Lauren McCafferty, Donna Morgan, Hilary Brown, Kirsty Thys, Alma Hough, Cordy Swinton, Carol Fletcher, Carol Dutton, Karen Mace, Shona Nicolson and Jo Osborne.

Thank you, all!

Prologue

1969, The Peloponnese, Southern Greece

Sofia Simonides let out a scream and tottered backwards. Her pulse struggled to force blood around her veins. The body was slumped against the gnarled trunk of an ancient olive tree, head hanging to one side and resting on the left shoulder.

The man had a blue-grey pallor, his skin a candle-wax translucency. Sofia bent over and touched his cheek. It was icy cold; she gasped, drawing back her hand. Blood from a gash on one wrist had seeped over his thigh and there was a deep red stain in the sand. A long-bladed knife caked in dried blood lay by his side. Sofia eased out the piece of paper he clutched in one fist, unfolded it and read the message.

Falling to her knees, she sobbed.

'Andreas, no-o-o! No! What have you done?'

A piercing howl from deep inside her shattered the cool, still air of the dawn.

Chapter One

Alexandra

1991, A market town in the heart of rural mid-Wales

The sky was lead-grey, heavy with blue-black rain clouds threatening a downpour. The dreariness of the day reflected my mood as I turned the Mini into the cul-de-sac. A shiny red two-seater was parked in the drive behind my father's Audi. I pulled up alongside the kerb, took a deep breath, trying to avoid a downpour of my own, and entered the house. There was laughter coming from the kitchen.

'What's she doing here?'

My father and his friend turned to face me. His mouth gaped open.

'Alexandra. Apologise, straight away. Sally, I'm very sorry. She has no right to speak to you like that.'

'It's all right, Richard. Alexandra's upset. I'll go now. The food's almost done, anyway. You just need to serve it straight from the oven once the timer rings. Shall I call Claire down on my way out?'

I glared at the woman who stood there taking off Mam's apron. My heart quickened. *Mam?* My mind was playing tricks on me. *It wasn't Mam, was it?* She should be the one standing there, greeting me, cooking dinner. Not her. I struggled to breathe. How dare she? How dare *he*?

My father accompanied Sally outside, and I heard the throaty roar of the sports car signal that she'd gone. I braced myself for the row that would ensue, but I wasn't being unreasonable, was I?

Claire entered the kitchen first. She was four years younger than me, tall and slim with long auburn hair and sage-green eyes. She took after my father's side of the family and he idolised her.

'What was all that about and where's Sally?' she said.

By then, my father had joined us and they both stared at me. 'Well?'

'That woman's here all the time, wheedling her way in. She's even taken to wearing Mam's things.' I twisted the cotton apron into a ball in my hands and heard my voice rise.

Claire moved to switch off the timer and reached for the oven gloves.

‘All I know, sis, is that she’s a damned good cook and we’re eating better than ever.’ She looked at Dad and laughed.

But he wasn’t laughing. He stood there in silence, glowering in my direction while he let Claire prattle on.

Eventually, he said, ‘I cannot believe a daughter of mine could be so rude and ungrateful to someone who’s only being kind.’

My father’s voice shook and for a moment I thought he was going to break down. It would be the first time if he did. Why was I the only one who couldn’t help dissolving into floods of tears whenever I heard her name or thought of something we’d done together?

Claire placed the casserole dish on a mat in the middle of the table.

‘Come on, tuck in.’

I wasn’t hungry.

‘Can’t you see what she’s doing, you two?’ Claire ignored me and spooned the steaming food onto the plates. ‘Not for me,’ I said.

‘Alexandra! She’s just a friend, doing friendly things. She was your mother’s friend, don’t forget. She’s doing it for her.’

I wanted to think that too, but it was something Sally had said after the funeral about Dad needing her more than ever. An innocent enough remark maybe, but something didn’t seem quite right and I couldn’t put my finger on it.

‘Don’t put any out for me,’ I said again. ‘I’m going.’

I grabbed my car keys and left the house.

‘Why did you have to go, Mam? I can’t carry on without you. You had no right to leave. You should have kept fighting.’ My voice resounded in the enclosed space of the car as I gripped the steering wheel.

Tears streamed down my face and my whole body shook. I put the car into gear and drove away as fast as I could. I didn’t know where I was going. It didn’t matter. The rain that had threatened earlier was now coming down in torrents and the windscreen wipers were having a job to clear it. The streets were deserted, and I was soon driving away from the town. The imposing grey stone building of All Saints’ church loomed into view and I parked next to the kissing gates flanked by two giant yew trees. The weather had been the same on the day we’d laid her to rest and the stone in my chest that weighed me down that day was still there. I remembered feeling like a bystander watching anonymous faceless figures dressed in mourning black, heads bowed down under dark-coloured umbrellas, ambling behind her oak coffin towards the gaping hole in the earth. She wouldn't have wanted that, I'd wanted to yell. She'd have wanted us all to wear her favourite bright colours. But I didn't have a say. Nor did my nan, Sadie. Even my small rebellion of wearing a psychedelic scarf of Mam's, a relic from the 60s, was frowned upon but Nan had smiled.

I got out and walked to the left of the church towards my grandfather's polished marble headstone. In sharp contrast was the nameless mound of bare earth lying alongside. I hadn't seen my mother's grave since it had been stripped of the floral tributes. They'd be dead by now like her, I supposed. I hadn't been prepared for the starkness of it. I stifled a sob. Rain was pooling on the top of the mound where the earth had been flattened, and miniature muddy brown rivers trickled down the sides.

I knelt down on the wet grass and let the tears flow. My hair clung in wet strands to my neck and I could feel dribbles of cold rain pour down inside my collar. Once the sobs came, they wouldn't stop.

On my return home, I'd decided to make a real effort with my father and Claire. After all, Mam wouldn't like the atmosphere in the house at all. Anything for a peaceful life, she'd say.

As I let myself into the house, it was all quiet except for a drone of the television in the sitting room. The kitchen was immaculate, all dishes put away and surfaces clear of clutter. I hardly recognised it as the place where my mam and I had chatted about my pottery. Even the first wonky bowls I'd thrown on the wheel had gone. Mam had treasured them. They were always overflowing with bits and pieces that she'd found strewn around the place and never got sorted any further. *Makes the place look lived in,* she'd said. Not like this. Everything on the notice board was pinned in neat rows. It was then I noticed. Mam's array of coats and jackets that hung from a row of hooks on the far wall had disappeared. On my bad days, I used to pick one to wrap around me, with its familiar and comforting scent, and go out into the garden to the place she loved best. It was only a coat or fleece, I knew, but to me it felt as if I was in my mam's arms once more. I felt sick and barged into the hallway, nearly falling over the black bags piled on the cream rug.

'Oh, hi, Alexandra. You're back,' said Claire appearing from her bedroom.

'What have you done? Where's all of Mam's stuff?'

'Dad says it's upsetting everyone to see it lying round – especially you. I've packed it up for the charity shop to save you having to do it.'

I felt my heart thump, and I started sobbing again. 'But it's too soon.'

'Dad,' called Claire, putting her arms around me.

My father came out to see what she wanted. 'What is it?'

'Alexandra's upset.'

'Look, Alexandra. You have to pull yourself together. You're not the only one who's missing her, you know.'

Claire's face crumpled and she ran back upstairs.

'Now look what you've done. I don't know what your mother said to you when you two were huddled together those last few hours, but now she's gone, you do as I say. Understand?'

I pushed past him and ran upstairs. I flung myself on the bed and clutched my pillow tight. My eyes pricked with tears and I thought back to those last few days when I'd slept in the chair at my mother's bedside. That last night she'd fought and struggled, raging against the dark night. She'd tried to tell me something but had been rambling. It was something about my father.

'... your dad ... doesn't want me to ...'

She'd tossed and turned and her face became distorted.

'What doesn't Dad want you to do, Mam?'

Her breathing quickened.

'To say ... Richard ... did a ... generous thing. Good man ... really.'

I held her bony hand, stroking the papery skin and told her not to be afraid. But *I* was afraid. Afraid of what was inevitable. By daylight, she was calm. There was no struggling then, just breathing softly in a tranquil sleep. Sleep, like a baby's, foretelling that her life's circle was nearly complete. We were all there, by then. Dad, me, Claire and Nan. Mam's breathing changed. Nan knew what was coming, she said. I called the nurse. It won't be long now, she told us.

And soon it was over. Dad took Claire out straight away, but Nan sat with me. I wanted to sit and talk as if Mam could still hear me. It was far too soon when we also had to leave the room. Once outside I heard a deafening howl, a howl that came from the emptiness deep inside me.

'Alexandra!' my father had said, embarrassed as always at such a show of emotion.

'Leave her be, Richard. She's in pain. Like us all. She's just lost her mother.' Nan enveloped Claire and me in her arms and then she sobbed, too.

Having drifted off to sleep, it was late when I woke up, cold and stiff, still hugging my pillow. My tears had dried, but the emptiness was still there. And then I remembered the row I'd had earlier. The house was in darkness. Silent like a grave. Dad and Claire had gone to bed. I couldn't stay there, a stranger in my own home. Without Mam, it was just a building with four walls. I had to get away. There was only one place I could go. I tiptoed down to the hallway. Picking up the handset on the telephone, I dialled. It took what seemed like ages for the phone to be picked up the other end.

'Nan? Can I come over? Yes, I know it's late, but I can't stay here a moment longer.'

It wouldn't take long to get there. Maybe I shouldn't have woken my grandmother, but hearing the soft lilt in her voice so like my mam's, I knew I was doing the right thing. I packed a case, filling it with all the mementos I could find of my mother; the things that hadn't been packed away yet anyway. Photos, the locket she'd given me that belonged to her great-grandma that was handed down to every eldest child, her apron that the awful Sally had been wearing, the psychedelic scarf I'd worn to the funeral that still had her scent on, my wonky pots, they all went into the case, wrapped in between the clothes I'd need for a day or two. I'd come back for the rest when my father was at work and Claire was back in school. They'd be all right, I told myself. They had each other.

I let myself out of the house quietly and rolled the car down the drive before starting the engine. No lights snapped on in the house and I knew they would be none the wiser until morning when they found my bed had not been slept in.

I'm doing the right thing, Mam. Let Sally Cooper take your place for all I care! But I did care, a lot. Nan would be the only one who'd understand what I was going through. She'd lost a daughter and that wasn't the right order of things, was it?

Chapter Two

As I drove out of the town leaving the amber street-lights behind, the country lanes to the next village were still wet from the earlier rain and glistened in the full moonlight.

My grandmother's detached house, solitary at the end of a long drive and bordered by wide expanses of lawn, was the only one illuminated in the street. The gravel crunched under the car tyres. As I got closer, Nan flung open the front door and stood on the step waiting for me.

'Whatever's happened?'

She held out her arms to give me a *cwtch*, squeezing me tight, and guided me into the house. As soon as I felt the cosiness of her fleecy dressing gown, I sobbed until there were no more tears left.

'It's awful, Nan. They're wiping away every trace of Mam. How could they?'

'There, there. You've had such a tough time of it. First, Stuart and Lucy and then your mam.' I stiffened at the mention of my ex-boyfriend and my so-called best friend. 'I'm sure they don't mean it as it looks to you. I'll go and get you a drink of hot chocolate before you go up.'

I looked around the large sitting room where my mam had played when she was a little girl and where she'd brought Claire and me to stay every school holiday. Photos of my mother at each stage of her life were displayed on every surface of furniture. I rose from the settee and picked up the silver frame that contained a large close-up photo of Claire, me and Mam just before I left for art college. As I traced a finger over my mother's face, my eyelids burned once more.

'Here, drink this. I love that one of the three of you.' Nan brought the drinks into the room. 'She was very proud of you, Alexandra. Anyway, time for this in the morning. While I was waiting for you, I've made up the bed in your mam's old room. There's so much clutter in there, you'll feel her close, I'm sure.'

'Oh, Nan. Thank you.'

'And promise me, we'll ring your father first thing in the morning to tell him where you are. It will all work out, *cariad*.' She hesitated and then added, 'He's not a bad man, you know.'

Exactly what Mam had tried to tell me in the hospital. Why would they think that? And why did Dad want to know if Mam had told me anything when it was just the two of us?

I followed my grandmother up a second flight of stairs to a tiny bedroom in the eaves of the house. Like all the bedrooms in Nan's house, it smelled of lavender.

'I've never been up here.'

'I know, *cariad*. Your mother insisted the door was always locked and it was out of bounds to you children.'

'But why? I don't understand.'

'She made the excuse of saying she wanted it kept just as it was when she left home. Just lately, though, she'd visit me on her own and spent some peace and quiet time up here sorting out her old things. You get some sleep, now, and we'll talk in the morning.'

I hugged my grandmother and let her get back to bed. As she'd said, the room contained many of Mam's bits and pieces and it did make me feel closer to her. Closer than I'd felt since that awful day in the hospital. This room was a part of her life I knew nothing about.

I unpacked my case and tried the door of the heavy oak wardrobe on the wall opposite the window. It was locked. Next, I placed a photograph of Mam on the table next to the bed. I quickly undressed and snuggled down into the candy-striped flannelette sheets that were a trademark of every bed in my grandmother's house. Smiling to myself, I put out the bedside lamp and curled up under the heavy blankets. I thought back to all the times Claire and I had shared the twin-bedded room on the floor below and had written messages to each other with our torches shining onto the ceiling once the lights had been turned out. The attic bedroom was bathed in a silver glow as a shaft of moonlight peeped through the gap I'd left in the curtains. The bright light caught the glass of a small watercolour painting hanging above the chest of drawers, and it filled the room. I got out of bed to look at the painting closely. It was of a solitary olive tree and in the right-hand corner, I saw that it was dated *1969*.

I tossed and turned for ages. My head was spinning. I re-lived the row I'd had earlier, remembering the look on Sally Cooper's face as I barged in on her and my father. Whenever I closed my eyes, I saw the gnarled bark on the trunk of the olive tree in the picture looking like an old woman's wrinkled face, grey-green leaves cascading down around it like un-brushed hair.

'*Nos da*. Nos da,' it seemed to whisper, in a voice like my mother used when she wished me goodnight.

It wasn't *her* face, I knew that. Hers was beautifully smooth, right to the end, but it sounded like her. That soft sing-song voice had often soothed me to sleep as a child and hearing it again up in that tiny attic bedroom was enough to send me into the first deep sleep that I'd had since she'd died.

The next morning, I was awoken by a gentle tapping on the bedroom door. The room was filled with morning sunlight and for a few moments, I couldn't remember where I was.

'I thought you'd like a cuppa.' My nan held a floral bone-china teacup and saucer, full to the brim with steaming tea, and placed it on the bedside cabinet. 'I've made it weak, one sugar, just as you like it.'

I rubbed my eyes and propped myself up on the two feather pillows.

'You're too good to me, Nan. What time is it? I've slept like a log. The first good night I've had since …'

'You can talk about your mam, you know. I'd like you to. Everyone's afraid to speak Elin's name round here. It's nine o'clock. I looked in on you when I got up, but you were fast. It will have done you good.'

My nan's eyes filled with tears and I knew that losing her only daughter had had a devastating effect on her, too. I wasn't the only one grieving. The dark shadows under her eyes told me that she hadn't had the luxury of uninterrupted sleep that I'd had. I bet everyone told her the same as they told me. It was for the best, Mam was at peace, no more pain. All the old clichés, but they didn't help that physical ache inside, that feeling that there was no point in getting up in the morning. I put my arms out and Nan sat by me on the bed. In silence we hugged each other.

'Thank you, Nan. I know I can talk to you. You understand. Nobody else does.'

My grandmother pulled away gently.

'I know, *cariad*. But I do think you should ring your father. He'll be worried. And after breakfast, if you like I'll come with you to talk to him. In any case, I'm worried about Claire. Bottling everything up isn't good for her.'

She turned to leave.

'Before you go, Nan, I love that painting of the olive tree.'

My grandmother sat back down.

'Your mam painted it, *cariad*.'

'Gosh, I didn't know Mam could paint! It's very good. I wonder why she didn't say.'

Nan broke eye contact and fidgeted.

'Look. We'll talk more over breakfast and you must ring your father.'

She went downstairs to let me drink my tea, wash and get dressed. Before leaving the bedroom, I looked at the picture again. It made no sense. *Why had Mam not told us that she could paint? Yet another family secret.* By the time I joined my nan in the kitchen, the table was laid with the best china and she was standing by the Rayburn cooking bacon and eggs.

'Thought we'd have a treat this morning. Fresh from the farm, the eggs are. I think we can both do with a bit of feeding up. Your mam wouldn't be very happy if we let ourselves get ill fretting over her, would she?'

It was good to spend time with my nan. She'd lived on her own for as long as I could remember. My grampy had died before I was born.

'This is delicious, Nan. I can't remember when I last had a cooked breakfast. In college, it would just be a quick bowl of cereal or, more often, nothing at all. And at home lately, I just haven't felt like eating. Especially anything cooked by that Sally.'

Nan put her knife and fork on her plate and sighed.

'Look, Alexandra. I think you're blowing this out of all proportion. Sally Cooper was a friend of your mother's. They used to help out at the Golden Age lunches. Elin told me she was very kind to the old folk in the village. She was never happier than if she was helping somebody out. You know how useless your father is in the kitchen. I wouldn't mind betting Sally promised your mam she'd make sure Richard and you girls would be all right. Okay?'

I felt my cheeks burn. Was I imagining things? What if she was just a kind woman like everyone said?

'Sorry. But it's just the way she's taken over Mam's place. It's just me being paranoid, I expect. Claire loves her cooking. Says it's better than Mam's.'

'Well, she was never exactly Delia Smith in the kitchen, was she? Much preferred to have her head in a book, I'd say,' said Nan. We both laughed.

'You promised you'd tell me about the painting.'

'It's beautiful, isn't it? She was extremely talented.'

My mother had never said a word. Art had been my favourite subject in school. Not once had she said anything about being a painter herself.

'And, to think she never said a word when I was applying for art colleges or all the time I was painting and sketching.'

Nan put her cup down and her face became serious.

'Your mam painted it in Greece. She went there the summer after she finished art college.'

My mouth gaped open. 'She went to art college? And didn't say a word when I did?'

'Yes, she went to Cardiff. Now, when you've finished, you *must* ring your father.'

Obviously, the matter was closed as far as my nan was concerned. There was something she wasn't telling me.

The rest of the meal was eaten in silence. Knots formed in my stomach and, as I drank down the last dregs of coffee, they tightened. I knew I couldn't put it off any longer.

I went into the hallway and dialled our number.

'Hello, it's me. Yes, I know I should have let you know. I'm sorry. I'm at Nan's.'

I held the receiver away from my ear as my father ranted. Didn't I realise they were all worried? Worried that I'd do something stupid given the mood I was in. Didn't I know the effect it was having on poor Claire? She was very upset and had refused to go to school.

'Okay, okay. I've said I'm sorry. I'm coming back this morning to collect some things. Nan says I can stay here for a while. It's best for everyone.'

'Alexandra? Everything all right?' Nan asked.

My hand shook. 'Charming! He put the phone down on me.'

Nan put her arm around my shoulders and led me back into the kitchen.

'Look. Let's clear away the breakfast things and I'll come with you to talk to your dad face to face. And while we're at it, why don't we take some flowers for your mam and grampy's graves?'

I nodded. 'I went there yesterday. Mam's is very bare. It's horrible.'

'I know, *cariad* I thought we could take the wooden cross I had made for grampy's before we had a proper headstone. It's still in the shed somewhere and a flower pot holder to go in the ground.'

'You kept them after all these years?'

'Never throw anything away, your grandfather always said. You never know when it'll come in handy. Force of habit.' My grandmother smiled and then added wistfully, 'I never thought I'd need them for my own daughter, though'

Tears formed in her eyes. She left me drying the dishes and when she reappeared, she held a plain wooden cross covered in dusty cobwebs and a black container with a tarnished brass lid with holes for flowers.

'Here, they are. While I clean them up, why don't you go and cut some foliage from the garden? We'll call at the shop to get a few flowers to go with it.'

As I indicated to turn into the cul-de-sac leading to our house, I caught a glimpse of bright red car speeding away in the opposite direction.

'Did you see that, Nan? Sally Cooper driving out of our road.'

'Alexandra, you have to stop this. It could have been any red car and even if it was Sally, she may have been dropping something off. You've said yourself how kind she's been making meals for you all.'

I gripped the steering wheel. Why was I the only one who doubted her?

'Now, no more thoughts like that before we go in and talk to your father.'

By the time I'd gone around the car to let my nan out, the front door was thrown open. Claire rushed out, flinging her arms around me.

'Alexandra. Where have you been? I've been imagining all sorts of awful things.'

I realised then how much I loved my little sister despite her being my father's obvious favourite. She missed Mam, too, and I'd just gone and made it worse. I would stay, for her sake.

We walked into the house, arm in arm, with Nan following behind. My father stood in the sitting room, his face as black as thunder clouds.

'The wanderer returns, then? Hello, Sadie. Thank you for bringing her back. I'm sorry you've been bothered by all this, but Alexandra's place is here with Claire and me. It's not fair on Claire, her going off like that.'

'Look, why don't we all sit down and talk about this? We're all missing Elin. It's just that we show it in different ways, that's all. Alexandra knows she was wrong to go off without telling you, don't you, Alexandra?'

My eyes pricked and tears trickled down my cheeks. My father glared at me. 'That's right. Turn on the waterworks, again, why don't you?'

'Richard!' My nan came to sit beside me. 'That's exactly what I'm talking about. You may be able to hide what you're feeling but some of us can't. I came here to persuade Alexandra to come back home but if that's how you're going to react, well, perhaps she will be better staying with me after all.'

I hadn't heard my nan raise her voice before and my father's face blanched. Normally, nan's voice was gentle and calm, soothing like Mam's had been whenever my father had been angry.

'Please, Alexandra, stay,' said Claire. 'I need you here.'

'Claire, you're welcome at my place too, any time,' said Nan, 'but I think it's only your father and Alexandra who need some time apart.'

'And we all know why, don't we?'

'What's that supposed to mean?' I said. 'What have I done?'

My father stormed out of the room, leaving the three of us open-mouthed.

Chapter Three

Claire came with us to All Saints' church. We walked from the house and the fresh air did us all good. The atmosphere in the house had been so tense that even after my dad had driven away, his final words hung there unanswered. What did they mean? Claire and I looked at Nan, searching her face for answers, but she shrugged her shoulders. We called at the village shop for some chrysanthemums to go with the variegated foliage I'd picked earlier. The sun shone through the clouds making such a difference to the graveyard, no longer the bleak desolate place I'd visited the day before.

'Here,' said Nan, handing me the trowel. 'Dig a hole for the cross and then Claire can do the same for the flower holder. I must treat you both the same!' She laughed.

I knew she was referring to what Mam always said. And she did. Whatever she did for me, she did for Claire.

Once we'd checked that the cross was firm in the ground and the flowers arranged in the pot, we all stood back and admired our handiwork. I placed my arm around Claire and felt her shudder as she stifled a sob.

'Oh, Alexandra. Why did she have to leave us? She was so young.'

'I know but we'll make her proud, you and me. This will always be where we can come and remember her.'

Neither of us had spotted Nan walking away, her shoulders hunched and head down. We caught her up and linked arms.

'Come on, Nan,' I said. 'We'll look after you now. You looked after us enough times when we were kids. Now it's our turn.'

As I walked through the kissing gates, I looked back at the graves, the flowers and foliage a sign that someone cared very much about the loved ones buried there. We strolled back in the sunshine in silence. I wondered if Claire and Nan were thinking of Mam, too. I felt more at ease now I'd visited her grave in the sunshine.

'Is it just me or do you two feel better after visiting Mam's grave?'

Nan smiled. 'I'm glad you feel like that. Don't forget, girls, you can go and sit on that bench not far from her resting place any time.'

Claire didn't say anything.

'It helped me no end when your grampy died,' continued Nan.

My father's car was parked in the drive when we arrived back, and I knew I'd have to eat humble pie if I was going to stay. Spending time with Claire had been good and it was selfish on my part to leave her on her own. I was the big sister, after all, and I was sure Mam would have wanted me to stay and support her.

'I think I should stay with Claire, Nan.'

Claire beamed and my grandmother patted my hand.

'Good girl. You'll be fine and if there are any more rows, you know where I am. Call and see me any time.'

We entered the house and joined my father in the sitting room. Claire spoke first.

'We've been to the graveyard, Dad. We've put a cross and some flowers on it. It doesn't look as bare now.'

'I don't want you getting upset. You should have waited for me,' he said.

'Richard, she was fine. We had a nice chat and we all feel better, don't we girls?' Nan smiled. 'I'll go now then and Alexandra's something to tell you before she runs me home.'

'I'd like to stay, Dad. I'm sorry about last night.'

'All right. We'll forget all about it. Goodbye, Sadie. And thank you.'

Nan gave Claire a hug. 'See you soon, *cariad*.'

'Bye, Nan.'

I drove Nan to her house and although I collected my toilet bag and a few essentials, I left most of what I'd taken with me the night before up in Mam's bedroom in the attic. Perhaps I wanted to leave something to come back to when I visited Nan. Now I knew about that room, I could get close to Mam at any time.

'I'll call and see you in a few days, Nan. Thank you for last night.'

Nan held out her arms and gave me a big *cwtch*.

'Bye, *cariad*. Don't worry. It will all work out, I'm sure.'

'Anyone fancy a cuppa?' I called, from the kitchen.

'You're an angel.'

Claire's voice sounded distant, so I knew her bedroom door was closed and I hoped she'd returned to her swotting at last. The exams were in just a few weeks and I worried that she'd not be able to do herself justice after what had happened. There was no answer from my father.

I walked into the sitting room and asked again.

'No, I'm fine, thank you,' he said. He didn't raise his head from the newspaper he was reading. I clenched my fists into tight balls and returned to the kitchen. Sulking was always how he dealt with things. Mam always told you what she thought, but not him. How she'd put up with his cold silences I'd never know.

I took the tea up to my sister and knocked on the door.

'How's it going? Managed to get back into it?'

Claire's eyes were red and puffy.

'It doesn't seem important now, does it?' she said. 'When Mam was ill, I didn't stop working. I just assumed she'd get better. Dad kept telling me that she would want me to keep working hard. Looking back, he kept it from me how ill she was. What if Mam thought I didn't care?'

I put my arms around her and pulled her close.

'Of course, she knew how much you loved her. He did the same to me. Kept saying Mam didn't want me to stop preparing for my finals and I wasn't to come home to see her. I didn't realise how ill she was either. Look we must stick together. You're still his little girl in his eyes and you'll be fine. I'm the one who's getting the silent treatment. Things will get better, I promise. Have a break and drink this. I'll get supper on.'

'Thanks, Alexandra. You're so like Mam, you know.'

I closed the door behind me.

The next few weeks passed without incident. My father and I were civil to each other and I tried to forget about the rows we'd had. Claire spent all her spare time revising and I began working at the Welsh Craft shop in the town. I still didn't know what I wanted to do.

Handling other potters' work, arranging it for display and talking to customers about how the stoneware or earthenware was produced was the next best thing to selling my own pots. That's what I'd really like to do, open my own studio. Mam had been my biggest fan and we'd talked about waiting until I finished art college, getting my qualifications and then looking for somewhere to rent. All those dreams were gone.

'No money in art,' my father had said. 'You need to get a job that pays good money.'

Unless a career was paid well, my accountant father didn't see it as a successful one. He didn't understand the feeling of satisfaction I had when I made something that was aesthetically beautiful. Holding a silky smooth pot in my hands straight from the kiln was something I never failed to marvel at, especially when the mystery of how the glaze would turn out had just been revealed. Mam understood.

It wasn't long before I visited Nan again. Thursday was my day off. I arrived at her house and as soon as she opened the door, I felt tears forming again. That was all I seemed to do at the moment, crying one minute and shouting and screaming the next.

'Hello, Alexandra. This is a nice surprise.'

'I just wanted to see you,' I said, giving my grandmother a *cwtch*. 'The house is too empty when Claire's in school.'

I followed her into the kitchen where there was a familiar smell of baking.

'I was just about to cook some more Welsh cakes I've just rolled out. Why don't you make us both a nice cup of tea?'

I watched Nan grease the bake stone and, once it was hot enough, she placed each creamy circle down carefully. It took me back to the times when she'd let Claire and me cook them, telling us how to wait for the sugar to turn transparent as the sign for when we should turn them over with the flat palette knife.

'You make the *best* Welsh cakes, Nan,' I told her, placing a mug of tea down next to her. 'Everyone in college suddenly became my friend when the parcel arrived from you.'

We both laughed. It was good to relax again. She piled the finished Welsh cakes onto the rack and filled the griddle with more to cook.

'Is it all right if I go up to Mam's room and sort some of her stuff?'

'Of course, it is, *cariad*. You and Claire can have whatever you want. You never know what you'll find up there.'

I downed my tea, pinched another Welsh cake and went up to the bedroom. The door was unlocked. On entering the room, my shoulders became less tense and I felt close to Mam again. As before, my eyes were drawn to Mam's painting, with its luminescent sea colours so different from the grey of the Bristol Channel we saw locally.

As I reached over the chest of drawers to get a better look at the brush work, I knocked the bowl of dried lavender flying onto the floor. Luckily, the bowl didn't break but the seeds went everywhere. A heady perfume filled the room. I started to scoop as much as I could when my fingers felt something cold. It was a brass key.

'Everything all right, Alexandra?' Nan called up the stairs.

'Yes, I've just knocked the lavender over but nothing's broken.'

Filling the alcove, the wardrobe was the only piece of furniture in the room with a lock. My hand shook as I turned the key in the lock and it clicked open.

I hadn't heard my grandmother enter the room.

'So, you've found her secret treasures, then?'

I looked at my grandmother and then to a suitcase on the top shelf of the wardrobe.

'Here, let me help you. It's heavy! I used to tease her because she kept the wardrobe locked, just like her room, and I had to promise not to unlock it for anyone … especially your father. It's from a part in her life he told her she had to leave behind when he married her.'

'I don't understand why she didn't just stand up to him, for God's sake. He wouldn't tell *me* what I could or couldn't keep.'

'Alexandra, I won't have you speak like that. No matter how difficult your father is.'

'Sorry, Nan. It's like I'm walking on egg-shells all the time.'

We placed the small brown leather case down on the bed. The lid was covered with a collage of colourful postcards, held in place with sticky-backed plastic.

'Here it is. All her worldly goods. As I told you, your mam went to art college like you. In her last year, her dad died. She was heartbroken. Sound familiar? She was exactly the same age as you are now. She took it very hard.' Nan wiped away a tear.

'I still can't believe Mam went to art college like me and didn't tell me.' My eyes filled with tears, too. 'And I'll never be able to ask her why now, will I?'

I stifled a sob and Nan gave me a *cwtch*. Confused reactions to the revelation tumbled inside me. How was I supposed to feel? Was Mam ever going to tell me? Part of me felt hurt that she'd kept such a big secret from me and yet perhaps that explained why we'd been so close. I hadn't got my love of art from my father!

Nan smiled. 'I know, *cariad*, but she did. It's just that you did pottery and she specialised in painting and fine art. Open up the case. Your mam decided to spend the money her dad had left her on studying at a painting school in Greece that specialised in oils. She said it was in honour of your grampy who loved the country from his time studying archaeology. She wanted to visit some of the places he'd told her about.

Sliding each end of the metal locks, they sprang open and I lifted the lid. On top was a full-length dress made from delicate silk, swirled in the colours of the sea. I held it against me and then brought it up against my cheek.

'Oh, Nan. Isn't it beautiful? Do you think she wore this?'

I placed it on the patchwork coverlet next to the case.

'I expect so, *cariad*. All the things in that case she brought back from her time in Greece. She showed me when she first arrived back and then said she was going to lock it away in the wardrobe and that part of her life was behind her. I wasn't to mention it again, she said. Next thing, she and your dad were getting married. It was all very sudden but once your mam made up her mind, there was no changing it.'

It didn't make sense. I took out the items one by one and laid them out on the bed. A handful of postcards addressed to Nan showed azure crystal waters, pine fringed golden beaches and olive groves. Lots of olive groves. There was a silver ring with the Greek key pattern. I tried it on my right hand and held it out in front of me to admire it.

'You can keep that, *cariad*. Wear it to remember your mam.'

I smiled and carried on taking things out of the case. I picked up a bright royal-blue glass disc. It had an opaque white centre with circles of light sky-blue and dark blue in the middle. There were a few photos mainly of views of the island but some of groups of people with names written on the back. One was of a young dark-haired man, smiling and pointing at a sign over what looked like a shop of some sort. The sign was written in Greek letters and it meant nothing to me. The man wore a long brown apron and in his other hand he held a piece of wood. On the back of the photo Mam had written '*S.S. 1969*' in her distinctive italic handwriting.

'Who do you think this is?'

'I don't know, *cariad*. All I *do* know is that something happened out in Greece that summer but your mam wouldn't talk about it.'

A tiny box was tucked in the far corner of the case. Inside, wrapped in yellowing tissue paper, was a small wooden heart threaded onto a fine leather necklace. The grain of the wood formed swirls of different shades of brown from the palest ochre to a deep tan. Carved in the centre of it was the letter 'ε'. It felt cool and silky smooth in my hands.

'Wow. Look at this. It's handmade by the look of it. Do you think it was made especially for her? That looks like an "E".'

My grandmother took the heart from me and examined it closely.

'I haven't seen that before, Alexandra. It's exquisite. It's as if she'd hidden it right away, tucked in the corner. She certainly didn't tell me anything about anyone making her a special necklace. And it does look special, doesn't it? The old romantic in me wonders if she met someone out there and her only way of coping with coming home alone was to deny that time ever existed.' Nan sighed. I squeezed her hand.

'We'll never know now, will we?' I looked at my watch. 'I'd better get back, Nan. Claire will be home soon.'

I started to put everything back into the case. We heard a noise from downstairs.

'That sounds like the post,' said Nan. 'I'll go and have a look.'

I placed the suitcase at the side of the dressing table and stood back to take one last look at Mam's painting of the olive tree. The delicate brush work of grey-green foliage draping down over the ancient gnarled trunk, and set against a background of an ultramarine sea, took me to a country I'd only seen in travel brochures. But my mother had been there. The tree seemed to whisper to me that there were secrets she'd left behind.

I rushed downstairs and grabbed my car keys.

'Must dash, Nan,' I said. 'I don't want another ear-bashing off Dad.'

'Here, I nearly forgot. The only post was a letter for you. I don't know why it's come here … and it looks official.'

'Strange! I'll open it when I get home and give you a ring. Thanks,' I said, pecking my grandmother on her cheek.

Chapter Four

I needn't have rushed. The house was deserted when I got back. There was a note from Claire on the kitchen table saying she'd gone out with some friends. She'd signed off with a P.S. 'Dad's having dinner round at Sally's.'

With no one to nag me, I started replacing all the knick-knacks I could find that were tucked away out of sight. First to come out were my wobbly attempts at pottery I'd brought back from Nan's. Next, I delved deep into the cupboard under the stairs and took out Mam's scarlet fleece. Bringing it up to my cheeks, I *cwtched* into it and inhaled lily-of-the-valley. It was her favourite scent and still lingered. In protest, I hung it on a hook behind the kitchen door.

I kicked off my shoes, leaving them strewn across the floor, and made myself a cup of coffee. I took it into the sitting room and settled down to read my official looking letter. It was addressed to *Miss Alexandra Sarah Davies c/o Ambleside House, New Church* and instead of a postage stamp, it had been franked *Carson and Sons Solicitors, Cardiff.* For some reason, my hand shook as I slid my finger under the gummed seal. I took out the letter.

Dear Madam
We have been instructed by our client, Mrs Elin Rose Davies (deceased), that a month after her death, we should request that you attend a private meeting with the member of our team dealing with Mrs Davies's estate, Mr Charles Carson. That meeting has been arranged for Monday June 1st, 1991, at 11 a.m. Please confirm that you are able to attend on that day.

Mrs Davies stressed that you should not be accompanied by any other family member. In order for her wishes to be carried out in full, it is imperative that you agree to do this.

Yours faithfully
J. P. Thomas, Secretary
pp. C. Carson

I sat back in the chair and placed the letter down on the coffee table, my head spinning. What could the meeting be about? Why did I have to go alone? It didn't make sense. I went to the hall. The first thing I needed to do was ring Nan but just as I was about to dial her number, something stopped me. No other family member, it said. If I told Nan she'd insist on coming with me. No, I had to do this on my own and I wasn't going to tell a soul.

I returned to the sitting room, gathered up my letter and went up to my bedroom.

It wasn't long before I heard my father's car pull up outside on the drive. I peeped out of the window and saw him rush around to the passenger side to open the door for Sally. She beamed as he held his hand out for her. Did she look like that at all her friends? Then, I remembered what Nan had told me. I shouldn't jump to conclusions.

My father looked up at my bedroom window and dropped his hand. I heard the two of them come into the hall.

'Alexandra, I'm home. Where's Claire? And what's all this mess? It looks as if your …'

By that time, I was at the foot of the stairs.

'… mother's still here. Yes, don't you wish she was?'

My father didn't make eye contact with me and collected everything on the surfaces and placed it in cupboards.

'Claire left a note to say she was going out with friends.'

'You should have been here.'

'Leave her be, Richard. Don't you want to see any of your friends, too, Alexandra?' said Sally. 'Not much fun for you staying in.'

'I'm fine, Sally. I don't know anyone here my age, anyway,' I said. 'All my friends are either in Birmingham or in Cardiff.' I didn't voice what I was thinking. I'd lost touch with all my friends, spending all my waking time with Stuart. I felt my throat constrict. His betrayal after three years had hurt. Coinciding with finding out about Mam and trying to finish my exam pieces for my exhibition, the vision of finding him and my best friend, Lucy, in our bed was what haunted me when I thought of my final weeks in college. I was off men and I didn't have the energy to seek out old friends. No, I'd be all right on my own.

'I forgot you'd already left home when your mam and dad moved here. I can't believe it's only a couple of years, Richard.'

Sally was still talking.

'Sorry, what were you saying?' I asked.

'I was telling your father that it seems longer than a few years since the family moved here.'

'Mmm,' he said.

He was busy spraying the surfaces. Mam's lily-of-the-valley had receded back under the stairs with her fleece and the chemical pungent smell of kitchen cleaner reigned again. I returned to my cluttered room upstairs. At least that had an air of normality. Perhaps Sally was right. I did need friends. If I was going to the meeting in Cardiff next week, that would be a good opportunity to get back on the social scene. I started to write a letter to my old school friend, Catrin, asking her if she'd like to meet up. For the first time in ages, I felt like I was doing something for me, and it felt good.

Catrin had been pleased to meet up again and we chatted as if we'd never lost touch. She walked with me to the end of the street where the solicitors' offices were and we made plans to spend longer together the following weekend.

I walked along the road, looking at the three-storey buildings for number forty-two. Each mellow stone façade had a large bay window on every floor. They exuded Edwardian grandeur that hinted of an era where wealthy families would have lived with servants to wait on them. Nowadays, they'd been mainly taken over as businesses or hotels. I walked up the black-and-white chequered tiled path and entered the reception office.

'Good morning, I'm Alexandra Davies and I've an appointment with Mr Charles Carson at 11 o'clock.'

I handed the receptionist my letter.

'That's fine, Miss Davies. I'll let him know you're here. Perhaps you'd like to take a seat.'

I thanked the smartly dressed woman. My heart boomed in my chest. Perhaps I should have confided in Nan after all. What could Mam's instructions be? Why a month after her death? It just didn't make sense. I didn't have to wait long. A white-haired man dressed in an expensively cut charcoal-grey suit emerged from a door to the left of the receptionist's desk. His brightly coloured silk tie, with its fiery flashes of red and orange, contrasted with an otherwise sober attire and was the only intimation that he was a man of unique taste. My mam would have approved, I was sure.

He held out a hand. 'Miss Davies. I'm very pleased to meet you.'

His grip was firm as he shook my hand.

'Come with me through to my office.'

I followed him down an oak-panelled corridor and ended up in a large light room. In the bay window was a huge wooden desk that was topped in dark green leather and edged with brass studs. 'Sit down, please. Firstly, I'd like to express my condolences for your loss.'

I sat opposite him in the chair that he'd indicated.

'Thank you. I understand you have something to tell me about my mother,' I said, my throat dry. 'I must admit I was a bit puzzled by your letter, Mr Carson. Especially the part that said I had to agree to come alone. What's that all about?'

Charles Carson leaned back in his armchair and placed his spread-out fingers together, his elbows on the desk.

'Let me explain. Carsons have dealt with your parents' affairs ever since they set up home here in Cardiff a few months before you were born. We dealt with the conveyancing when they bought the home where you live now. They came to us to draw up their wills only a few years ago.'

'But that's all been dealt with by my father, hasn't it? Everything of my mother's goes to my father and after his death, to me and Claire. That's what he said after he came to see you after the funeral, anyway.'

Mr Carson smiled and leaned forward. 'What your father has told you is indeed correct but when your mother was diagnosed with terminal cancer, she came to see me alone.'

From the side of his desk, he picked up a parcel wrapped in brown paper and tied neatly with string. 'She asked me to keep this on our premises together with instructions that exactly a month after her death, it should be bequeathed to you. Of course, that was two years ago. She fought long and hard as you know.'

No, I don't know. No one bothered to tell me, my thoughts screamed at me. The solicitor held the package towards me. '*For Alexandra. I hope you'll understand*,' was written in Mam's distinctive print in fine black felt pen across the middle of the parcel. My pulse raced along my veins. I felt as if Mam was there with us in that sunlit office.

'I do-don't understand,' I said. 'What is it? Can I open it?'

'Of course,' said Charles Carson, handing me the parcel. 'It's yours. All I know is that your mother didn't want anyone here when you received it.'

I slid the string over the corners of the parcel and unwrapped the layers of paper neatly folded around what felt like a book of some sort.

'It looks like a diary,' I said. It was about the size of a school exercise book but covered in smooth, fine-grained leather, the colour of golden sand and initialled E.R.M. in gold letters. *Elin Rose Morgan.* Morgan was my mam's maiden name. 'It's beautiful.'

Charles Carson nodded. 'I believe there's a letter for you, too. She said she'd put the key in the envelope so you could unlock it.'

I was touched that Mam was leaving me something as personal as her diary but scared, too, about what I'd read if no one else was to know.

'Don't get upset, my dear. Why don't you take everything now and read the letter and diary in your own time, in private?'

'Thank you. I'm sorry. It's such a shock. I don't know why she's left it to me and not to Claire and me. She always treated us the same.'

Charles Carson passed a form and a pen across the desk towards me.

'I just need you to sign that you've received the gift left you by your mother. I do hope that you will come to understand why she left you her diary. She didn't say anything to me, I can assure you. It was as much of a mystery to me as it was to you until you undid the wrapping paper a few moments ago.'

I placed the letter in my handbag and loosely wrapped the diary with the brown paper. I stood up and shook the solicitor's hand before leaving. Walking back along the street to the main part of town, a feeling of loneliness washed over me. Apart from my mother, I was the only one who was going to know what was in the diary. *And you're not here, are you, Mam?*

I *had* to read the letter straight away and couldn't wait until I arrived home. I walked down a side street towards the river and found a bench a little way off the footpath that ran parallel to it. Seeing Mam's handwriting brought a lump to my throat again. I opened the envelope and searched for the key to the diary. It was tiny and I zipped it in the inner purse of my handbag for safe keeping.

November 1989

Dear Alexandra

I've had some dreadful news that I don't want to bother you with until I have to. The cancer has come back. I'm not going to get better from this, and it breaks my heart to know that I won't be there for you and Claire in future. I don't know how long I've got but I want to get things in order before I go.

I feel you should know about a part of my life that I've never told anyone about, not even your father. He knew I spent the summer in Greece but that was all. We never talked about it. But I owe it to you. I want you to have my diary and sketchbook that I kept in the summer of '69. It will tell you everything. Yes, I was an artist back then, like you. That's why I'm pleased you've gone to art college, too. Student of the year in your first year! That made me very proud, cariad.

Look after Claire for me, and your nan. Your father is a good man. He just likes to be in charge and that's why sometimes you and he have clashed. Keep him sweet, Alexandra. That's what I learned to do. Well, I tried to, most of the time. I shall always be grateful to him.

When you read this letter, cariad, I will already have left you. Claire will be fine with your father, but I worry about you. Once you've read my diary it's up to you what you do then. Whatever you decide, you will have my blessing. Things could have been so different.

Remember how much I love you and have always loved you.

Goodbye, cariad.
Mammy xxx

I stifled a sob. I hadn't called her 'mammy' since I was a little girl. Her letter had thrown up more mysteries for me. A breeze sprang up and the trees along the river bank rustled in whispers, telling me to return home and read my mother's account in the privacy of my bedroom.

The house was deserted when I arrived home after my hour-long return journey. It was two o'clock and I had just a few hours on my own to start reading Mam's diary. My hand shook as I put the small brass key in the lock. It clicked open.

This diary belongs to:
ELIN ROSE MORGAN
SUMMER 1969
GREECE

I thought back to the suitcase of mementos that Nan had shown me and looked down at my hand with the silver ring and its Greek key design. Would the diary give me the answers I wanted? I turned to the first page and began to read.

June 21st, 1969

Athens airport was a nightmare, even at 6 a.m. Long queues at the passport gates. Started to panic when I saw a sea of faces in front of me as I arrived in the arrival lounge. Tanned faces holding up placards with names written on them, most in Greek letters. Men's voices getting louder and louder, shouting out the names of the passengers they were collecting. Bodies everywhere on the floor, backpackers sleeping rough on rucksacks, inside the building and outside on the wide pavement. Found a space and looked at my letter with its instructions. 'A driver from Hellenic Taxis will be waiting for you by the Olympia Car Hire desk.' Made my way there to find someone waving a sign with my name on. He pointed at his watch. Told me I was late and then shouted something about 'traffic'. Took my life in my hands – he raced out of the airport, cut into the queue of traffic and weaved his way from lane to lane, eventually driving down the pavement(!) and blasting his horn all the way only to turn right at the bottom. Very glad to get out of his cab and board the hydrofoil that would take me to Péfka and my adventure for the summer. At last, I allowed myself to get excited!

Chapter Five

Elin
1969, A small island off the Peloponnese, Southern Greece

Elin stepped off the hydrofoil on to the quayside of Santa Marina, relieved to feel solid ground beneath her feet again. Her stomach was queasy after skimming over the water and what had felt like hitting every wave. The journey from Piraeus to the island had only taken a few hours but it was enough for the spray to blanch the faces of the people standing at the back of the hydrofoil white with salt. She smiled at their windswept hair and ghostly pallors and was glad she'd stayed inside. She made her way along the line of suitcases and rucksacks to retrieve hers. A worn path shone through the mottled grey flagstones and led from the water's edge up to the steps of the old town of Santa Marina. It told of thousands of tourists and travellers who had disembarked before her. Her heart thumped in her chest. This was it. This was the start of her adventure. She'd arrived in the Peloponnese to follow her dreams and leave all the heartache of losing her father behind. Richard had made such a fuss but she'd been determined.

Elin slipped her arms through the straps of her canvas rucksack and from her jeans pocket retrieved the card with the details of the taverna where she was to stay for the summer. She'd picked it in the brochures because it was in the centre of the town … and it was cheap. She shielded her eyes and pulled her hat down more firmly over her head. There was only one street leading up from the harbour and the houses were mainly small whitewashed cottages. The blue painted doors and shutters were peeling in places from the excesses of hot sun. Halfway up on the right, the narrow road opened up into a large square, surrounded by olive trees. The hub of the village was framed by shops and bars. On the right she spotted an illuminated red and blue sign displaying a bottle and the words 'AAØA, Alpha Beer'. Over the door 'Taverna Guikas' was written in large painted letters. An array of blue painted wooden chairs and tables covered in crisp navy-and-white checked tablecloths extended from the taverna onto the pavement. Elin stepped into the cool of the bar. It was dark and smelled of a mixture of lemons, garlic and olives. She pictured her father turning up his nose. *Only plain wholesome food for me, my girl. None of this foreign rubbish.* How he'd survived his travels in Greece, she'd never know. A pang of homesickness washed over her. Dear Dad. He may have been set in his ways and been strict with her but she'd idolised him. He'd been her hero, she his little girl.

'Hello?' she called. She walked across the bar and rang the bell.

A heavily pregnant woman emerged from the back. A little girl clung on to her long patchwork flowing skirt and peeped around her mother's legs.

'*Naí?*'

Elin handed her the letter confirming her reservation. '*Kaliméra.* I'm Elin Morgan. I've booked a room.'

The young Greek woman beamed, brushed her floury hands on her apron, and shook Elin's hand. 'Welcome. We expect you. I am Kýria Guikas, Dimitra. This is my daughter. She is Lyra.'

Although heavily accented, Dimitra spoke good English. Every now and then, Elin had panicked about not being able to converse in Greek but she needn't have worried.

'I take you to your room.'

She followed Dimitra and Lyra up the spiral staircase that led from the back of the bar. Every few steps, Dimitra stopped to catch her breath and Lyra spoke to her mother in rapid Greek and hugged her legs.

'Are you all right, Kýria Dimitra?'

'Yes. It is the baby. It is very heavy now. It is late. Lyra worries about her *mamá*. I do not run after her like before.' The Greek woman laughed but Elin could see how much of an effort it was for her to walk up the narrow metal staircase.

'You speak good English.'

Dimitra smiled. 'I try. Vassilis, he spends five years in Athens. He works in a bar. He teach me.'

The room overlooked the square below and when Dimitra opened the shutters, strong sunlight revealed a large double bed covered by a hand-crocheted white cotton coverlet. A bowl of dried lavender on the chest of drawers at the side of the bed filled the room with the sweet restful smell that reminded Elin of her bedroom at home. There was a small wooden wardrobe and a window seat set within the thick stone walls.

'It's lovely. Thank you.'

'You unpack now, eh?' said Dimitra. 'There will be food when you come down. *Éla*, Lyra. Come.'

Elin unpacked her rucksack. It was the largest she could get but it didn't contain many clothes. She'd just have to buy some more while she was there. There was one book she'd had to find room for. Her diary sketchbook. She'd always kept travel journals whenever she'd gone on holiday with her parents but this was going to be special. It was the last present her father had given her before he died. It was a beautiful hand-crafted book with thick vellum pages suitable for her watercolour sketches and plain sheets of paper interspersed for notes. He would have been thrilled to know she was visiting the area. As an archaeologist, he'd loved travelling to the ancient sites in that part of Greece. And then he'd died. A heart attack they said and her world had fallen apart. This trip was in his honour.

She held the diary up to her nose, inhaling the supple ochre leather cover and then she ran her hands over the metal lock. *Typical of Dad to pick one with a lock and key for all my secrets*. She laid the diary on the chest of drawers with her tiny box of watercolours.

Elin returned downstairs to the bar, which was now filling up with people.

'Here, food for you.' Dimitra directed her to a table in the corner where she'd put bread, a simple Greek salad and a sticky pastry Elin didn't recognise, together with a jug of water containing slices of lemon.

'Kýria Dimitra, that looks delicious.'

The young Greek smiled and waddled back to the bar, holding her hand on her hip and stretching to ease her back. Elin became aware that she had company. Lyra's large ebony eyes stared up at her from folded hands on the table. The little girl said nothing but just watched. She was beautiful. As well as having distinctive eyes fringed with the longest black lashes Elin had ever seen, Lyra's glossy dark hair flowed in gentle waves over her shoulders.

'Well, hello, little girl. Come to watch me eat, have you?'

The little girl didn't say a word and looked down at the table.

'Here. Have some of this.' Elin broke off a small piece of the rustic bread and placed it in front of Lyra who snatched it up and ate it. Elin laughed. She hadn't realised how hungry she was after the journey from Athens. The bread was delicious, nutty and oaty, and she suspected had been made that day by Dimitra judging by the appetising smells coming from the kitchen when she arrived. Elin picked out every olive and piece of green pepper from her salad and left them on the side of her plate. Her father's voice came into her head. *What did I tell you? Awful things, olives. Don't know what the Greeks see in them.* The sticky pastry, though, that was a different matter. She'd have to ask Dimitra what it was called.

By that time, her little companion had left the table and sat on the floor nearby playing with a tiny grey and white kitten. A tall stocky man entered the bar and Lyra shrieked, leaving her kitten playmate, and jumped up into his arms.

'Papa.'

That man was Vassilis Guikas. He hugged Lyra towards him and ruffled his face into her little body making her giggle and squeal with laughter. Elin's throat constricted as she remembered her own dad doing that to her and how good it felt when she was Lyra's age. Dimitra spoke to him in Greek and pointed in Elin's direction. She composed herself. He held out a hand toward her, the other was grasped tightly by his daughter.

'Vassilis Guikas. You are Elin Morgan?' He looked at the plates on the table. 'My wife, she looks after you, I see. You don't care for our olives, eh?'

Elin started to say she was sorry when Kýrios Vassilis let out a large guffaw. 'You young British girls do not know what you miss. I say by the end of the summer you will eat so many we think you are Greek.' She felt her cheeks redden and Vassilis patted her shoulder. 'I tease. The taste, you learn to like it. Tell Dimitra to leave them out of your Greek salad in the future. You liked the feta, eh?'

'I loved it. What are the honey pastries called? They were delicious.'

'Ah, Mamá's baklava!' Vassilis pinched his thumb and first finger together and kissed them. He turned away from her to greet a young Greek man who'd entered the taverna. He was casually dressed in denims and a thin cotton shirt and wore a leather workman's apron. Vassilis brought him over to Elin's table.

'Elin, this is Stelios. He is a very good friend of mine. He works at the wood turner's with me.'

The shy young man smiled and shook her hand, letting it rest for long enough for Elin to feel a tingle she wasn't expecting. His dark olive skin was such a contrast to hers and felt warm and smooth. His eyes were the colour of melted chocolate and yet vaguely familiar.

'Elin comes to the painting school with your brother. She starts tomorrow.'

'I wish you luck. Don't take any nonsense from him. Please.'

Stelios spoke in a soft deep voice with hardly a trace of an accent. But he didn't laugh and Elin found that strange. She dismissed the thought and looked back at his eyes. That's where she'd seen them before. The close-up photo of Andreas Simonides beaming out from the brochure advertising painting holidays at his studio.

Lyra joined them. Stelios ruffled her hair and bent down to talk with her face to face. From the sombre little girl who'd sat at her table earlier, Lyra's eyes twinkled with mischief as she became animated and spoke in rapid Greek.

'Big friends,' Vassilis said.

Elin went back up to her room to collect her diary and soft pencils before leaving the taverna to explore the fishing village that was to be her home for the next few months. She walked out of the square and followed the narrow street away from the direction of the harbour. The midday sun had passed and more people were ambling along the street. The white-blond hair and pale blue eyes she'd inherited from her father made her stand out as a tourist. They all looked at her in a quizzical way and she felt uncomfortable. Two young boys nudged each other as she passed and she felt her cheeks flush. She was glad when the street emptied and she didn't have to pass open doors of the terraced cottages. The houses became grander with gardens containing oleander and bougainvillea in full bloom inside tall metal railings sitting proudly on low stone walls. Elin came to one where the cerise papery flowers formed an arch over a wrought iron gate, the centre of which had the name 'Villa Anastasia' in twisted letters along the centre. Peering through the gate, she saw marble steps leading up to a magnificent white house, glistening in the sunlight. As if from nowhere, a large Red Setter came bounding down the steps and barked in fury at her. Elin was glad that the gate was shut and, judging by the padlock, locked too.

She reached the top of the hill and took a left, turning where a footpath edged the cliff top and faced out to sea. She sat down on a bench and got her bearings. Directly below her was the square and she could make out Vassilis and Dimitra's taverna. On its roof was a sun terrace laid out with sun beds and a few umbrellas not visible from below. Perhaps this was where they spent their private time away from the tourists and customers. Elin felt sorry for Dimitra still working and heavily pregnant. Surely, she should have help in the taverna when Vassilis was hard at work at his lathe with Stelios? She took out her soft sketching pencils and her diary. The sketch came to life on the page and she'd soon captured the crowded housing, how the street split the village in two. Dominating the left-hand side of the street was Villa Anastasia and she could see from her position at top of the hill that in its large gardens there was a kidney-shaped swimming pool, the water echoing the same deep turquoise as the sea below her.

Elin made notes about the colours, promising herself to bring a little jar of water and some brushes next time. On the opposite page she wrote down her thoughts about arriving on this beautiful island all alone.

June 22nd

Arrived and settled in after a long journey. My hosts have made me very welcome. Their little girl is lovely. Feeling excited yet homesick at the same time. Looking forward to joining up with the other students and meeting the painting tutor in the morning. Have walked up to find out where the painting school is. Views from the cliff top are amazing. No wonder Dad loved Greece! I wish I could tell him.

She started to doodle and, as if out of her control, the figure of a young man playing with a little girl and her kitten stared back at her from the page. Why couldn't she get Stelios Simonides out of her mind? And why had he warned her about his brother?

Chapter Six

The next day Elin retraced her steps, making sure she stayed on the opposite side of the street when she passed Villa Anastasia. At the top of the hill she turned right and walked along the edge of a single-track road along the headland leading towards a whitewashed one-storey building facing out to sea. It was surrounded by a wooden fence and behind it olive trees formed neat rows. The sign was newly painted in large hand-written letters: *Simonides Painting School*. As she got close, she heard a babble of voices and laughing and above them one distinct deep voice. She followed the arrows round to the back of the house and knocked. It went silent and through the wide open door, she saw everyone turn and look at her.

'Come in. Join us,' said the deep voice. The man facing her from the back of the studio was a taller, more striking version of Stelios.

He put down his palette on a nearby bench and walked the length of the room to greet her.

'Well, hello.' He looked Elin up and down and his eyes settled on her chest area. 'You must be Miss Elin Morgan, all the way from darkest Wales. I'm Andreas.'

There were some sniggers. Elin felt all eyes on her and willed the floor to swallow her up and out of sight.

'I'm not late, am I? You've started already.'

'No, I like to settle each small group in at a time. Some of these vagabonds started last week and like to get here early and make a head start.' He swept an arm aside to include the vagabonds and the students grinned at him, obviously in awe. 'There's just one more student to come and he's coming all the way from wildest Wyoming. Your easel and paints are in the corner there by Elektra.'

Elin smiled at the others and settled herself and her belongings at her place. All the easels faced the same way and one whole wall of the studio was made up of bi-fold doors that had been opened to reveal the view of the sea.

Andreas went back to his easel and pointed to the areas of paint already on his canvas.

'I want you to paint the sea and the sky today. Notice how many colours you can see. I want you to mix the whole range on your palette before putting your brush anywhere near your canvas. And not just turquoise blue either.

That will result in a very flat painting. I want to see teal, I want to see aquamarine. Violet. Pink. I want the colours to make the sea and the sky come alive like sparkling jewels!'

The more Andreas enthused, the more flamboyant his gestures became and Elin noticed a few raised eyebrows from the male students. *Blimey. A bit different from dear old Hettie,* she thought, remembering her sober grey-haired painting tutor in art college.

He stood by the girl named Elektra and held his hands wide. She beamed and had obviously been praised for her efforts in Greek.

'Everyone. Elektra has this just right. Look at the wide range she has here. Not just the blues we talked about but sapphires, lavenders, a little citrus. Well done, Elektra *mou.*'

The morning continued with more colour mixing and Elektra being singled out for praise every now and then. There was a short break for coffee, which Andreas made on the briki stove. It was very strong and sweet and he warned them not to drink it down to the sticky residue in the bottom. They all went outside and sat in the shade of the pergola that covered the flagged courtyard area. Elektra sat on the bench next to Andreas and flirted. She hung on every comment and laughed extra loudly at every quip and joke he made.

He moved away and sat by Elin.

'Once Brad arrives tomorrow, I think we shall have a rule to speak English,' Andreas said so that everyone else could hear. 'You can all speak it and it will be good practice for you.'

Although she'd learned a smattering of Greek before arriving, Elin's command of the language was not good. She hoped to improve during her time there. Unable to grasp what was said, she heard Elektra mutter something in Greek to another student. The glares in her direction told her all she needed to know.

Back in the studio, Andreas demonstrated different brush techniques and asked his students to use the mixed paints to create the sky and the sea. Elin was finding the oils quite a challenge as she was only used to watercolour painting.

'No, no, no,' said Andreas, standing over her. 'You have made the sea look solid.'

Elin felt her heart sink and saw the smirk on Elektra's face as she delicately glided her brush over the canvas.

Andreas put his arms around Elin, one hand underneath the palette and one hand over her hand holding the brush. 'Like this. Like this. Make your brush sail. Think of the waves rippling in the sunshine catching the little glints of sunlight.'

Elin pulled away, nearly knocking over the easel in front of them.

He stepped back, putting his hands up. 'All right, all right.'

She didn't want to start off on the wrong foot so she quickly added, 'Sorry. I think I can do it. I'll try, anyway.'

The sound of a scooter drawing up outside the building broke the silence that had settled and Andreas rushed from the room.

'At last,' they heard him say and there followed a conversation in Greek.

'Our lunch arrives,' said a male student who was in the row behind Elin. He lowered his voice and leaned across to her. 'Well done. You stand up to him. He tries it on with all the girl students. It is only those two who enjoy and encourage him.' He nodded to Elektra and her friend whose name, Elin had learned, was Maya.

Elin smiled at him and whispered back, 'Thanks. He's creepy. Thinks he'd God's gift.'

The Greek boy looked puzzled.

'It's what we say in Wales when people think they're wonderful.'

They both laughed.

'I am Manos. I look out for you.'

For the first time that day, Elin felt she'd made a friend and allowed herself to relax.

'How was your day?' asked Dimitra. She was sitting in the shade, her large frame filling the space between chair and table. Her ankles were swollen and she looked pale.

'Not bad, I suppose. I've a lot to learn,' said Elin, sitting down beside her. 'But what about you? You look exhausted.'

'Oh, I am all right. I am tired, that is all.' She patted her belly and smiled. 'This little one, he kicks for Thessaloniki today.'

Elin laughed. 'Look, why don't you let me help out in the taverna? Once I'm back from the painting school. Andreas says it's up to us how long we stay there after he's finished teaching.' *And I certainly won't be hanging round any longer than I have to*, she thought to herself.

She hoped Dimitra wouldn't ask too many questions. Manos had told her over lunch that the Simonides family was very well respected locally and by opening up his painting school, Andreas was bringing much needed tourism into the little island.

Dimitra's bottom lip trembled. 'We will see. You are very kind but you have come here to paint and to have fun, not to work in taverna. I will speak with Vassilis. He says as it is my first my mamá should come. She must look after me.' The tears spilled over her lids and trickled down her cheeks.

Elin leant across and patted her hand but didn't say anything.

Her thoughts were interrupted. The wooden beads hanging over the taverna door rattled as Lyra ran out chasing her kitten. Elin turned to smile at the little girl and then looked back at Dimitra. *No. It's not your place to ask, my girl.* Elin heard her dad's voice. He was good at stopping her putting her foot in it.

'Hello, Lyra. How's Cleo today? Shall I get you and Mamá a drink?'

Lyra picked up the kitten, cuddling it tightly, and ran to try to climb on her mother's knee.

'Lyra. You say *efharistó* to Elin. That is very kind. There is a jug of lemonade in the frigidaire.'

Elin made her way into the bar and poured the drinks for Dimitra and Lyra. She'd wait until Vassilis came back from work before mentioning helping out again. She went up to her room and wrote about the painting school in her diary.

June 23rd

Hope I haven't made a huge mistake. To look at, A. is stunningly beautiful, tall and dark, a right Adonis (!!) but doesn't he know it? Too touchy feely for my liking. I could practically feel his ribcage – and other things! – when he tried to 'help' me with my painting. How dare he? I've obviously made an enemy with that Elektra, who hangs on his every word. Thank goodness for Manos. And yet A. knows his stuff. His paintings are stunning – have to admit once he showed me what I was doing wrong with my brush strokes, my painting improved no end. I was quite pleased with it. As long as he keeps a distance!

Elin felt better after getting her thoughts down on paper and told herself she wouldn't waste a minute of her time there on the island. She walked along the landing to the bathroom and filled a small jar with water. She packed her hold-all with sketching pencils, a box of watercolour blocks, brushes and her diary before walking from the square down to the harbour. She sat on one of the benches close to the water where shabby fishing boats filled with discarded grubby nets and cane pots bobbed together in silence, their job done by dawn that day. On the opposite side, several large luxury yachts, pristine and gleaming in the afternoon sun and sporting Greek flags, waited in idleness for their owners to arrive at the weekend. Elin began to paint and her free brush strokes quickly captured the contrast between rich and poor in the village that was already evident to her. She remembered the swimming pool at Villa Anastasia, and yet Dimitra had to struggle to keep working at the taverna.

The noise of a scooter interrupted her thoughts.

'Hey, Elin,' someone shouted.

It was Manos from the painting school, followed by another boy who'd been riding pillion. He parked his bike and walked towards her. Earlier that day, she'd been busy warding off the advances and leering looks of her tutor and she hadn't noticed how good-looking Manos was.

'Hiya.'

'You have not had enough painting today, eh? You must not look *very* keen.'

She laughed and closed her diary. That was the beauty of watercolours – they dried almost immediately in the heat.

'This is Brad. The student from America. He is the one Andreas mentioned starting tomorrow.'

Standing next to a deeply bronzed Manos, Brad held out a hand as pale as her own and ran his fingers through long dark hair that reached his shoulders. He grinned and his ice-blue eyes sparkled. He wore a garish open necked shirt swirled with oranges, lime greens and cerise pinks that shouted 'flower power'.

'Elin. Pretty name. Pretty gal. Great to see someone else who hasn't a tan folks pay mega bucks for back home.'

Manos laughed and held his arm alongside Brad's.

Elin immediately felt at ease with both boys and knew the painting school would be better now she had two friends on her side.

Vassilis was waiting for Elin when she arrived back at the taverna. He paced the floor and wrung his hands.

'Whatever's wrong, Kýrios Vassilis? Is it Dimitra?' He nodded. 'Yes. Dimitra, she fall to the floor in the bar. I send for doctor on the mainland. Her friend is with her now. I cannot lose them, I cannot. This is our only chance. We wait very long time.'

Stelios came out from the bar, his face grave. Elin's heart skipped a beat.

‘Can you look after the taverna for us? I’ll take Vassilis down to the quayside to wait for the doctor on my scooter and then we’ll get them back here by carriage. We can’t afford to waste any time.’

Elin thought it strange that the scooters were the only vehicles allowed on the island except for the horses and carriages. Some of the Welsh roads were no more than dirt tracks but you could still drive cars and vans on them.

Vassilis shook her hand and thanked her.

‘What about Lyra? Where’s she?’ asked Elin.

‘She is with Dimitra but she stay with her friend tonight.’ He hesitated. ‘Dimitra’s mamá come tonight from Ermione.’

She took her place behind the bar and familiarised herself with the prices of the drinks, mentally working out how many drachmae there were to the pound. Lyra came down the stairs and entered the bar. Her eyes were red from crying and Elin bent down holding her arms out.

‘Come here for a *cwtch*.’

The little girl said nothing but hugged Elin tight. She spoke very little English but her sad dark eyes no longer twinkled.

‘Mamá sick. Everyone cry.’

‘The doctor will be here soon. He’ll look after her. Let’s go and find Cleo, shall we?’

They found the ball of grey and white fluff curled under one of the chairs outside on the courtyard in the very last patch of warm sun. Lyra ran and gathered the kitten up into her arms. Elin knew that the little girl would be occupied for a while and returned to the bar.

By the time Stelios returned, Elin had served only one customer apart from the group of old local men who seemed to be a permanent fixture in the corner. As long as they were stocked up with their raki, they were happy enough. A cloud of strong smelling smoke from their cigarettes fogged the air and every now and then there was a chuckle of laughter and their deep Greek voices rose higher and higher, the words tumbling out faster and faster. Once it was silent again, Elin heard the rhythmic click of metal on metal as a couple of them twirled their worry bead *kombolói* or let them fall through their fingers. Lyra was throwing a sponge ball along the flagstones to Cleo and was unaware of the occasional scream from upstairs.

‘Thank goodness, you’re back,’ said Elin, relieved.

Stelios smiled. He took her hand. ‘You’re shaking. Oh, Elin, don’t worry. They’re not far behind. She’ll be fine once the doctor gets here.’

Elin felt her eyes burn with tears pricking below her eyelids. She'd only met Dimitra a couple of days before, but she didn't want anything to happen to her lovely Greek friend. She knew fewer women died in childbirth these days, but it did still happen. And they were a good drive away from the nearest hospital. No, this wasn't helping; she had to pull herself together and be of a practical help to Dimitra and Vassilis.

Stelios placed his hand on her arm. 'That's better. That sounds like them now.'

Stelios looked like his brother. The same high cheek-bones, the chiselled jaw and muscular frame but his demeanour and mannerisms could not be more different. How could this calming, caring man be the younger brother of her arrogant art tutor?

Vassilis and a well-dressed man in a dark suit with a bag in hand rushed through the bar to the stairs at the back. Elin knew that Dimitra was finally in good hands. She went outside to sit with Lyra and very soon they were joined by one of Dimitra's friends. She didn't speak English but pointed to a bag of Lyra's clothes. She knelt down and spoke softly to Lyra in Greek. Elin caught a few words – *my house, sleep, Mamá tired.* The little girl stood up and clutched Elin's legs then waved goodbye. She walked hand in hand with Dimitra's friend and carried Cleo under her other arm.

The noises were coming thick and fast from the upstairs bedroom and Elin was glad the little girl wasn't there to hear. She sat in the bar and watched as Stelios tried to calm Vassilis as he paced the floor. She'd only seen and heard women in labour in films or on TV but to hear it up above so close made her scared. 'It's not like that in real life,' her mother would say. 'All for dramatic effect.' Poor Dimitra, she wasn't on a film set, was she? Elin hoped it would soon be over for her but it went on for hours. It was dark outside when she heard the sound of a baby crying, like a cat mewing but loud and strong.

'The baby, it comes at last,' Vassilis said and rushed upstairs, banging the door behind him.

Stelios laughed and went to sit at Elin's table.

'This baby is very precious for them,' he said. 'They've lost so many before. Time was running out. It means much to a Greek man to be able to produce a son and heir.'

Elin couldn't believe her ears. Back at home, men were starting to be present at the birth of their babies and her dad had loved her as much as he would any son.

'But doesn't Lyra count?' Elin asked.

Stelios didn't answer.

'Well?'

'Lyra isn't their daughter,' he said in a whisper.

Vassilis entered the bar with his baby wrapped swaddling style in a white hand-knitted shawl. Tears wet his face.

'It is a boy. A son. The Guikas name goes on. Yiannis Vassilis Guikas.'

There were cheers and the old Greek men rose to their feet and knocked back more tots of raki. A few came over and slapped him on the back.

'Stelios, you pour the drinks. For everyone,' said Vassilis.

He showed his son to everyone in the bar and then returned upstairs.

Stelios opened bottles of retsina and Elin helped him take the glasses to everyone inside and out.

'*Ya mas*!'

Chapter Seven

Stelios guided Elin to a table under the olive tree in the square. The orange lamp-light found spaces in the canopy of foliage, forming shapes that moved in the breeze like glitter balls..

'I hope Dimitra's all right,' said Elin. 'She's had the hard work.'

'It's just the custom here in Greece,' said Stelios. 'Mamá says once a mother holds a baby in her arms all the pain is worth it.'

On hearing music, they returned to the bar.

One of the old men picked up a bouzouki that had been resting on a shelf behind the bar and began to play.

'Let's dance,' said Stelios. 'I'll teach you some Greek dancing.'

Stelios took Elin in his arms and as they dipped and swayed in time to the mournful music, she felt familiar butterflies flutter in her stomach. She'd promised herself that there'd be no romantic liaisons when she was in Greece. She'd had her heart broken a few times in art college by exciting young bohemians. Perhaps that was why she'd settled for sensible, serious Richard. She felt safe with him and that he wouldn't let her down. But his row about her leaving for the summer, trying to control her, had put her off men. No man was going to tell her what she could or couldn't do. He was getting too possessive. Anyway, holiday flings always ended in tears, her mother said. So why did her painting tutor's brother have this effect on her? His warm breath on her neck and earlobe made her knees tremble.

Without warning, Stelios pulled away abruptly, holding his hands in the air.

'What's wrong?' asked Elin.

'I'm sorry. I'm giving out the wrong signals. It's not fair on you.'

Elin pulled her mouth taut and glared at him.

'You were only teaching me Greek dancing, for pity's sake. Huh! Another Simonides who thinks all women will fall at their feet, eh?' Elin's voice rose above the music. 'As if,' she lied.

Elin stormed off away from the taverna and the square and kept walking. *How dare he? As if I'd give him a second look. He's as bad as that brother of his.*

Vassilis was waiting for her when Elin returned a few hours later.

'Where have you been? I am worried. Stelios, he tell me what happened.'

'I just walked down to the harbour and some of the other students from the painting school were there. I'm sorry. I should have told you where I was going before storming off.'

Vassilis's face softened and he took her hand, patting it.

'You are safe, that is good. The island, it looks quiet but we do not know who comes and goes on the boats that are moored along the quay. *The Palinourus,* it was not there tonight, eh?'

'I didn't look at the names. Why?'

'You must take care, that is all.'

Elin didn't tell him about how uncomfortable she felt walking past one of the yachts where the drunken revellers had been cat calling and whistling as she made her way to the taverna at the end of the harbour. She'd been grateful when Brad and Manos had offered to walk her back to the square. She changed the subject and hoped Vassilis wouldn't want to talk about Stelios. 'How's Dimitra and baby Yiannis?'

Vassilis swelled with pride.

'Excellent, excellent. My son, he is beautiful and Dimitra, she does well.'

Elin looked around the bar, glad no one else was there. She couldn't face Stelios after what had happened earlier.

'Before you go up, I tell you about the Simonides family,' said Vassilis. 'Stelios is upset about what happened.'

Elin tensed herself and felt her pulse quicken. She couldn't be rude to Vassilis. After all, it wasn't his fault Stelios Simonides thought she was falling for him. She sat back down and listened to what he had to say.

'Andreas Simonides, the father, he has much money from the ships he owns. He buys a villa here on the island. He uses it when he does not work in Athens. He marries a woman, Sofia, who lives on Péfka. She gives him two sons, Andreas and Stelios. But then, there is an accident and he drowns. The boys are young and Sofia is pregnant with the daughter.'

'That's awful,' said Elin. 'Poor woman. And poor boys.'

'Yes, she is – how do you say? – a broken woman. She never goes in a boat or on water ever again. She moves from Athens, sells her villa and buys a large house for her and the family over on the mainland.'

'But what has this to do with what happened earlier with Stelios? He's a grown man now.'

'In Greece, you understand that families plan who their sons and daughters marry. It is not formal arranged marriage as in some countries but it is agreed often. Stelios is to marry a girl who lives on the island. Kýria Sofia, she depends on it.'

'You mean he has no choice! What if they don't love each other?' Elin couldn't believe that in these more enlightened times of the swinging sixties, customs like this were still going on.

'That is why he did not get close to you tonight and give you the wrong meaning,' said Vassilis. 'Next year, it is all arranged. On his birthday, when he is twenty-three, he marries.'

'Dare I ask who she is?'

'Anastasia. The girl, she lives at the villa halfway up the hill. It is named after her.'

Elin thought of the opulent residence, resplendent in gleaming white marble where the dog had frightened her. Stelios and Anastasia.

'The two families, they are friends for a very long time. Anastasia's mama and papa look after Sofia when Andreas dies and the children are small. It was Kýrios Loukas, he arranges for young Andreas and Stelios to attend good schools in Athens like their papa.'

Elin went upstairs on tiptoe, determined not to wake Dimitra and the baby. The lamps on the square bathed her bedroom with a soft light. She knew she wouldn't sleep so she took out her diary and pencilled in some sketches of her thoughts – new born babies in cribs, dancers and basouki players, brides and grooms and lots of hearts. She wrote another entry in her diary.

June 23rd

Things are very different here in Greece. No way would I let my parents pick a husband for me. Can you imagine? Mam would pick a nice sensible boy who'd have a safe job with excellent prospects, a banker maybe. And Dad, well, he'd want me to follow my dreams and travel the world so that wouldn't be too bad. Perhaps a travelling musician or a sailor who could take me with him. I made a right fool of myself tonight starting to fall for S. Well, Anastasia's welcome to him. After what I've heard today, I definitely don't want to have children. All that pain. No way. In fact, do I need a husband at all? No, I'm definitely off men.

The next morning, Elin walked up to the studio rushing past the wood turner's in case Stelios was already at his lathe. She slowed as she approached Anastasia's villa. The Red Setter was nowhere to be seen so she peered through the iron gates to get a better look. An abundance of scarlet geraniums tumbled out of large terracotta pots standing on each end of every step. The garden was overflowing with flowering shrubs and there was not a weed visible in the earth around them. A white-haired man in muddy dungarees raked the soil, picking up any weeds or stones that marred the perfect flower beds. Noticing her, he rested his rake against the trunk of an ornamental orange tree and descended the steps towards the gate.

'*Kaliméra*,' said Elin, trying to be polite and mask her nosiness.

'*Naí*?' said the old gardener.

'Just admiring your lovely garden,' she said.

He raised his hands to show he didn't understand. He looked back up the steps when he heard someone come out on to the courtyard. A beautiful dark-haired young woman joined him on the steps. Her long black hair was dragged back behind a wide, white headband to reveal a perfectly shaped face with velvety brown eyes and high cheek-bones. She wore a flowing white voile tunic that made her appear to float down the steps towards the gate. Elin's heart sank as she pictured Stelios and Anastasia together: a perfect couple.

'*Kaliméra*,' said Anastasia. 'I have not seen you here before. I am Anastasia. Friends call me Tasia.'

'Elin. Elin Morgan. I'm a student at the painting school. It's where I'm going now.'

'Rather you than me.' Anastasia laughed. 'Do not be swept away by Andreas Simonides's charms, will you? He has a reputation.'

For no reason, Elin felt herself blush. There was no way she'd fall for her tutor's advances, especially after his little display on the first day. No, she was safe in that direction.

'No, I won't. No men for me. I'm here to learn and improve my painting.'

'That is good. Perhaps I will see you around. My friends and I meet at the taverna at the end of the quayside. You are welcome to join us.' Anastasia's smile reached her eyes. 'You can meet Stelios, another Simonides, but he is *very* different from his brother.'

Anastasia turned and left Elin to continue up the hill. Why hadn't she told Anastasia she'd already met her fiancé? She walked quickly along the cliff top and saw that everyone else had arrived before her. They were lined up outside the studio setting up their easels and canvases. '*Kaliméra*, Miss Morgan. Good of you to join us,' said Andreas, looking at his watch. His long dark hair was worn loose that morning and the warm breeze from the sea was blowing it off his face. His crisp white cotton shirt was open just enough to show off his tan and he looked as if he'd come straight off a film set or out of a fashion magazine. *He* was *a very attractive man.*

'I'm sorry. I've been talking to someone on the way here.'

Andreas didn't ask her any details but welcomed everyone. They would continue to work on the paintings they'd begun in the first lesson but to start, Andreas gave a lecture on perspective in colour and how the brightest greens would appear bluer the further back into the distance they were.

As he demonstrated and mixed his greens, Elin and the students saw the effect he was trying to achieve.

'You see your eye is taken into the distance and your painting achieves perspective. Otherwise the shapes are flat, like you say in English, flat like the pancake.'

Elin placed her easel and board between Manos and Brad, away from Elektra and Maya.

'Thanks for last night, boys,' she said. 'Vassilis was waiting up for me.'

Andreas made his way over to her.

'Stunning. My eye is travelling along your greens into the distance. Excellent.' Elin was pleased that she was achieving the effect he wanted but in the corner of her eye saw Elektra whisper to her friend and scowl.

'I called you from my friend's yacht when you passed us last night but you didn't answer. You could have joined us. We could have done with some female company.' Andreas leaned in a little closer. 'Especially an attractive blue-eyed blonde,' he whispered and walked away.

Elin's whole body shook. She'd thought the incident on the first day was a one-off and was willing to start again but now she knew it wasn't.

'You all right, honey?' asked Brad.

Elin nodded, keeping her thoughts to herself, and returned to her painting.

During the break for coffee, Andreas told them about the school's annual exhibition. He waved his arms around and enthused about how successful his students' exhibitions had been in the past.

'In just over two months' time, a few weeks before your time here comes to an end, we will exhibit your paintings in the gallery in the town hall. I shall expect a *minimum* of eight paintings from each of you but it is up to you how many paintings you wish to put on show. Our reputation depends on the quality of the exhibits. Once you have attended the morning teaching sessions, you are free to paint wherever inspiration takes you. Here in the studio, if you wish, you can paint portraits as well as seascapes. I can get people to come and sit as models. Or you can paint down in the harbour. Last year, I had one student who rose at dawn every day and captured the fishermen bringing in their hauls of fish to be sold on the quayside. Another student went over on the boat to the mainland and captured the tourist shops and large yachts moored in the marina. It is up to you, my friends.'

Elin, Brad and Manos sipped the sweet Greek coffee and planned what they wanted to do.

'Do the paintings have to be in oils? I'm just thinking it's not going to be easy transporting wet canvases around if we go further afield,' asked Brad.

'No, you can use sketchbooks and use pencil or charcoal to capture the moment. Watercolours even. They could then be the cartoons for larger pieces in oils for the exhibition.'

Elin had heard Hettie Grainger, her painting tutor, talk about that way of working and she smiled when she thought of how quickly she'd be filling up her dad's diary-sketchbook. *Things are looking up, my girl,* she thought. *Keep out of Andreas's way and get on with what I've come here to do. Learn how to paint in oils.*

Chapter Eight

After lunch Elin excused herself from the rest of the group and made her way down to the harbour to make sketches for her paintings. As she approached Vassilis's wood turner's, she noticed a familiar face.

'Elin, I wanted to see you.' It was Stelios. 'To say sorry about last night.'

'There's nothing to apologise for. Vassilis told me about you and Anastasia. I met her this morning on my way to the studio. She's lovely.' Elin didn't know what else to say, didn't want to admit that he'd been right and that she had been falling for him. It was for the best. 'I hope you will be very happy.'

In his hand he held a delicately turned wooden rattle. There were swirly patterns of different colours in the olive wood and around the tiny handle was a pale blue ribbon tied in a bow.

'I've made it as a present for Dimitra and Yiannis,' he said.

'It's beautiful. I'm sure she'll love it.'

'I hope so.' He paused. 'Can we still be friends?'

'Of course,' said Elin, knowing she couldn't be mad at this lovely man any longer. Why couldn't his handsome brother be more like him? Vassilis hadn't mentioned an arranged marriage for Andreas, had he? Perhaps his mother had more sense than to try to arrange for him to marry one of her friend's daughters. She smiled at the thought.

Elin and Stelios walked down to the taverna together and it was as if the awkwardness of the night before had never happened.

'You'll have to come and meet Mamá,' said Stelios. He pointed across to the mainland. 'See that white house standing away from the others. That's where she lives, all alone when I'm over here and my sister, Thea, is at university in London.'

'I'd love to. She must be an amazing woman to have raised three young children on her own.' Seeing Stelios look puzzled, Elin added, 'Vassilis told me how your father had died in a boating accident. I'm sorry.'

'It was a very long time ago and all I know is having Mamá to look after us. Andreas had to become the man of the house and grow up very quickly.'

Elin smiled at the thought. *And didn't quite succeed.*

'Dimitra's mother has arrived, then,' said Stelios.

In the cool dark bar, an older woman dressed head to toe in black was nursing the new baby. She glared at Stelios and Elin and shouted some words to Vassilis in Greek. He came out from behind the bar and said, 'It's Stelios, not Andreas.'

'Huh,' she said and resumed cooing at her newborn grandson.

'I'll explain sometime,' Stelios whispered.

Vassilis came over to Elin and Stelios, smiling. 'I am happy to see you are friends again.'

'I've only called in to get my sketchbook,' said Elin.

'I've a little gift for baby Yiannis.' Stelios handed him the rattle.

Vassilis took it and ran his fingers over the silky wood and held it up for his mother-in-law to see.

'This is very beautiful. Thank you. I will take it to Dimitra. She sleeps now but she gets up later,' he said.

Elin went upstairs to her room and left the men chatting.

Elin walked past the end of the harbour wall and climbed the steep stone steps until she reached the lighthouse. The flashing light, so visible from any part of the island at night, was manned remotely and only occupied at weekends for maintenance. That day, the doors were locked and Elin felt free to have a look around. The sun was at its highest and there was no shade. Elin peered across to the mainland and the row of white buildings glistened against the deep turquoise water. Perhaps it was in this strait of water that Andreas Simonides Senior had met his death. No wonder Kýria Sofia had not made the journey across to the island since it happened and why she was terrified of water. Elin shivered at the thought of sailing over the place where your husband had taken his final breath.

She opened her diary and began to sketch. She decided that one of the paintings would be of the lighthouse with the mainland in the distance. It would give her an opportunity to get perspective not only in the drawing of the shapes but also in the colours of the sea and the rocky hills behind the town. The shape of the lighthouse building was distinctive; the first two floors were hexagonal and were topped by another floor in a cube shape surrounded by a viewing galley opening out from glass doors. Above this were windows through which the lights flashed to warn sailors of danger. Elin made notes alongside her sketch and then added the watercolours. The more detail she put into the sketch, the easier it would be to reconstruct in oils. Satisfied with what she'd painted, she walked further along the cliff top to where a row of tamarisk trees edged the footpath and gave her the dappled shade she needed to write in her diary.

June 24th

Things are better today. I've met Anastasia and made it up with S. I think they will make a lovely couple. Perhaps arranged marriages do work after all. S. is very talented. The rattle he made for baby Yiannis is amazing. Very detailed with little grooves and tiny balls of wood carved inside the main shape. A bit like the love spoons back home. He told me the wood is then rubbed with olive oil to make it beautifully smooth.

School was bearable. Couldn't believe the letch was one of those on the yacht cat-calling my name. Heard all about the exhibition. Not much time to waste if I'm going to get my paintings done in time. Determined to make a great show. Make Dad proud. Heard from Mam today.

'So this is where my top student is.'

Elin turned, her heart pounding. Andreas strode along the cliff top towards her. His long hair and loose linen tunic flowed out behind him in the warm breeze blowing in from the sea.

'Just getting some ideas for paintings as you suggested.' Elin knew her voice sounded sharp.

'Here, let me see,' said her tutor moving closer towards her.

Elin felt the hairs on her arms prickle. Her shoulders tensed. He wouldn't try anything out here in broad daylight, would he? 'No, it's all right. I'm fine thanks.'

'Hey, relax. I'm here to help. That's what daddy paid all that money for.'

Elin glared. 'You know nothing about my father or who paid for the course.'

'All right, all right. Lighten up. It's just that lots of students have their fees paid for by a rich daddy, that's all.'

Andreas backed away, holding up his hands in mock protest. Elin resumed her sketching and ignored him.

'I'll leave you to it. I can see you don't want any help from me,' said Andreas. The tone of his voice was sharp, then, too.

Elin watched her painting tutor walk back along the cliff top and it wasn't until he was a small dot on the headland that she relaxed and her breathing returned to normal.

She'd made lots of notes about colours and textures and by the time she left the headland she felt confident about transferring her ideas from her sketchbook onto a larger canvas when she was back to the studio in the morning.

... Spoke too soon. He makes my skin crawl. Stunningly beautiful to look at but creepy. I just can't bear to be alone with him. I need his help yet can't bring myself to ask for it. How dare he say that this was paid for by my rich daddy? If only he knew. I'd give all this up if I could have Dad back.

Back down in the harbour, Elin saw two familiar faces sitting at a table under the shade of an umbrella.

'Honey, over here,' shouted Brad. 'Let me get you a cold beer.'

Elin sat down. 'Thanks. That would be great.'

A large sketchpad was open on the table.

'I try ideas for a painting,' said Manos. 'What do you think?'

Manos had sketched the scene from an angle where he had both the fishing boats and yachts in place, simple and grand, poverty and luxury, side by side.

'These are quite something,' Elin said. 'You've captured the essence of the island. Without those rich yacht owners the island wouldn't survive and yet the fishermen and their catches are vital for the tavernas and restaurants. They are the real backbone of life here.'

Brad returned with three beers. 'Looking good, eh? Read his notes on the colours. Should make the whole painting come alive.'

Elin sat back and smiled. 'Cheers, Brad. *Ya mas*, Manos. Here's to a successful exhibition for all of us.'

Elin told the two boys where she'd been and opened her diary on the page where she'd sketched and painted the lighthouse.

'Any thoughts? If I can show the mainland in the distance and get the perspective in the colours right, I've a feeling this could be my best yet.'

Brad let out a long whistle. 'The angles on that building are amazing. You've a winner, there.'

She laughed. She knew her American friend was exaggerating but in spite of her encounter with Andreas, Elin felt she'd had a successful day and, best of all, she'd made it up with Stelios.

Chapter Nine

Vassilis was at the taverna when Elin left for the studio. He was checking everything was fine for the day. Still there after two weeks, his mother-in-law was in charge of looking after baby Yiannis and Dimitra.

Knowing she was going to be late after forgetting her sketchbook, she walked quickly. Stelios was back at his lathe and Elin waved as she passed but didn't stop. As she walked up the hill, she saw a familiar figure leaving Villa Anastasia. She ducked back behind the branches of a large hibiscus bush that had trailed from behind a garden wall. Through the scarlet flower trumpets, she watched as Andreas Simonides and his brother's fiancée embraced passionately for several minutes.

'What on earth …?' Elin said aloud.

Anastasia re-entered the villa and Andreas made his way up the hill without a backward glance. *No wonder you warned me off him. You obviously don't mind his reputation.*

Elin wanted to shout and confront him. She walked quickly and caught up with Andreas. 'Where did you spring from? I didn't see you pass me. The road was clear in front of me when I came out of the taverna.'

For a split second, he became flustered as he seemed to compose his thoughts. 'Um, n-n-no, I've been to see Anastasia.' He was straight back to oozing confidence and charm. 'Just checking if she knew about the party I'm throwing at Mamá's next weekend. I was going to tell all of you about it this morning in class.'

There was no reason why he shouldn't call on her, of course. The two families were old friends, Vassilis had told her that. But would you embrace and kiss your sister-in-law-to-be so intimately if everything was as innocent as Andreas made out? Elin kept her thoughts to herself.

The rest of the students sat waiting on the terrace in the shade of the pergola at the front of the studio. They clapped when Andreas and Elin arrived.

'My little blonde friend here delayed me. She's a little temptress.'

Elin glowered at him but he grinned at the whistles and cheers from the other students. Elektra stared at her with a look that would turn milk sour.

'What is that about?' said Manos after they'd taken their seats at their easels. 'It is not like the master to be late … or you.'

'You don't believe that little speech, do you? It wasn't me being the "little temptress". There's someone else playing that role. I forgot my sketchbook and had to go back for it, that's all.'

Manos raised one eyebrow.

'I'll tell you later. He's coming over.'

'Now then, let's see your sketches,' said Andreas. His eyes bored into Elin's and she felt her pulse quicken. He leaned over her sketchbook, moving close enough for her to catch a musky smell she normally would find attractive. Instead, it repulsed her and she grabbed her book and shut it with a slam.

Andreas grabbed her elbow. 'What the hell is wrong with you?' He hissed the words in a low whisper and spittle shone on his chin. 'You've nothing to fear from me, Elin Morgan. I like a bit more fire in my women.'

He walked away. Elin felt tears burn her eyelids. 'Yes, like the one who belongs to your brother,' she said under her breath.

Andreas returned to the front of the room and demonstrated how to transfer a small sketch on to a much larger canvas by using the grid method. It was as if nothing had happened.

'What I will show you is this. You draw a grid over the sketch and then you draw another grid on your canvas. The important thing is that it must be a grid of equal ratio. All right, everyone, now you try. I have rulers, pencils, charcoal here.'

Andreas explained it again in Greek. A buzz descended on the studio as everyone attempted to put into practice what he had shown them.

'Andreas, you help, please?' said Elektra. 'I cannot do the squares. They do not work.'

'Of course. A good student will always ask for help,' he said and looked in Elin's direction.

She remembered how Hettie Grainger had simply and efficiently demonstrated the technique without the flamboyance shown by Andreas. All her students had been able to do it straight away without any problems.

'How did you get yours done that quickly?' asked Brad.

'He didn't tell us how to get the size right. You can't guess it. If the squares on the sketch are, say, one inch by one inch, then you make the ones on the canvas two inches by two inches and it will be right.'

'Thanks, hun.'

Andreas then showed the group how to transfer each detail from each square onto the bigger canvas. 'Once you're done, you can erase the gridlines. That's why I suggest using soft charcoal lines.'

'This is very good. The painting is now in perfect sizes. Oh thank you, Andreas.' Elektra never wasted an opportunity to fawn in front of Andreas. She looked at Elin and smirked.

The first half of the morning passed quickly and Elin made good progress with her lighthouse painting. Brad and Manos admired the colours that she'd taken so much care to mix.

'You take us into the distance. The perspective is right,' said Manos.

'Yeah, honey. Spot on.'

Andreas was conspicuous by his absence and that was the way Elin liked it. But wasn't she being stupid? She'd paid a lot of money to get there. Didn't she want to improve? There was only one person who could ensure that she did. She couldn't go on as she was. No, she'd listen and take his advice over painting, work hard and put the uncomfortable incidents behind her.

'This weekend marks an important occasion in the Simonides Painting School calendar. Every year after giving you all a few weeks to settle in, my mother throws open her home for a big party for the painting students. This coming Saturday we will go by boat across to the mainland and meet her. It's just a short walk from the marina to her house. You will meet my brother, Stelios and his fiancée, Anastasia, and my little sister, Thea. The party starts at seven o'clock.'

Andreas walked back to the table where Elektra sat with her friends and resumed his lunch. As he passed Elin, he whispered. 'Happy now?'

Elin took a deep breath. 'I'm looking forward to it. It will be good to meet your family.'

'I hear you've already *met* my brother. Just your type. No fun in him either … apart from enjoying a bit of Greek dancing.'

How did he know about that? Memories of how it felt to be held by Stelios came flooding back to Elin and she felt her cheeks burn.

Brad and Manos looked at each other.

'Of course, you have met his brother. He works for Vassilis,' said Manos.

'I don't think he meant "met" like that, did he?' asked Brad. 'You haven't, have you?'

'No, of course not. What do you take me for? Stelios is engaged to Anastasia and I'm off men. Especially Greek men, no offence, Manos.'

Next morning, the early sun was already beating down and heat shimmered along the roadway. Elin was the first to arrive and Andreas was opening up the studio, folding back the doors and letting air cool the room.

'*Kaliméra*, Elin. I've been looking at your paintings since you left yesterday. They really are something, you know. I can help you improve still further if only you'd let me. Why not stay on this afternoon when the others have gone?'

Elin's pulse raced. She wanted nothing more than to realise her dream of becoming a successful oil painter but the thought of being alone with Andreas filled her with dread.

'Um. That's very kind but … but I've promised Dimitra I'd help in the taverna and I need to look for something to wear to your party. Another afternoon perhaps.'

Andreas shrugged his shoulders and glowered. 'As you wish.'

Manos and Brad arrived next.

'You all right, Elin? You look a bit flustered.'

'I'm fine. What time should we catch a boat on Saturday? I don't want to turn up at this party on my own.'

'There's one boat at seven o'clock and it is not far to walk from there,' said Manos.

'Sounds perfect.' Elin left and walked down to the taverna.

'What on earth am I going to wear to the party, Dimitra?' Elin sighed.

No one had seen her in anything other than a mini-skirt or denim shorts. She knew that Anastasia was going to be there and what to wear had already been the main topic of conversation for Elektra and Maya. If she was going to meet Kýria Sofia Simonides, she wanted to look good.

Dimitra stood under the shade of the awning over the tables on the courtyard, rocking baby Yiannis back to sleep. Her mother had returned home and she was back running the taverna.

'You look beautiful always.' The Greek woman looked over to her and smiled. 'But if you want something new, you visit the boutique in Santa Marina Square. Parthenis, it is called.'

'Thanks, I'll try there.' Elin walked over to admire the sleeping baby.

She wandered down to Santa Marina Square. The whitewashed buildings on either side of the street gleamed in the sunlight and illuminated the vibrancy of the coloured shrubs and flowers that were in full bloom. In her head, Elin was imagining and planning another painting that would reflect the character of the beautiful island.

Parthenis boutique was set back from the main square and its large front window glowed with a display of blues and greens. Along the floor were large creamy white conch shells draped with mother of pearl pendants and rows of turquoise beads. Standing behind the shells, three mannequins modelled dresses for sale in the shop. One in particular caught Elin's eye. It was a halter neck, floor length, nipped into the ridiculously tiny waist of the faceless dummy. The fine silky material was delicately woven in shades of turquoise, teal and blues of every hue.

Elin walked through the open door and asked to try it on. She came out of the fitting room to show the shop owner.

'You look beautiful,' she said. 'The colour – it is perfect with your hair and blue eyes.'

'Evil blue eyes,' somebody muttered behind her.

There was a snigger and Elin turned to see Elektra and Maya, smirking in the doorway. Elin rushed back into the changing room.

When she came out, the shop was empty again.

'I'm not sure,' Elin said.

The shop owner smiled and took the dress from her. 'You must take no notice. The two girls, they are jealous. You look lovely. You go have a coffee and think. I keep it here.' The woman pointed to a hanging rail behind the counter.

'*Efharistó*.'

'*Parakaló*.'

As Elin went out through the shop doorway she spotted something she hadn't noticed before. A large glass eye suspended from the frame. She made her way to the taverna on the water's edge. Every doorway she passed seemed to have a blue glass eye hanging freely. They were of various sizes but there was no mistaking the fact that it was a representation of a blue human eye. What could they mean?

She ordered a coffee and saw Dimitra pushing a pram towards her.

'Dimitra, over here.'

Her friend's face broke into a smile. 'Vassilis, he come back early. I like to take Yiannis out for a walk. Do you get the dress?'

Elin told her about her visit to the boutique and what Elektra and her friend had said.

'After that, I keep seeing those blue eyes everywhere. What are they?'

'Do not take notice of the girl. Elektra, you say? The blue glass eyes you see. They are *mati*. They save us from the evil eye curse.'

'What's that?' asked Elin.

'It makes bad things happen or give people bad luck. You look at newborn baby, he has the curse, they say.'

Elin felt her skin prickle.

'I don't understand. Why did Elektra say I had evil eyes? I know they're blue but …'

'You must take no notice. Do not worry. Here on the island, they say people who have blue eyes give the curse. That is what she means. She is wrong. I let you look at this little one, eh? Me, I do not believe it.'

Elin paid for her coffee and walked with Dimitra and Yiannis down to the water's edge.

'You would like me to see you in the dress?' said Dimitra.

They returned to the boutique and Elin tried on the dress for her friend to see.

'Ah, Elin. You look marvellous. You have to buy it. It is why the girls are nasty. No one is as beautiful as you tonight.'

'That is what I say,' said the shop owner. 'You want to buy sandals to go with the dress, eh?'

Aquamarine glass beads and a pair of strappy beaded sandals completed the outfit.

Elin turned and viewed herself from the back in the full-length mirror.

No one to match me? Not even Anastasia?

Chapter Ten

Manos and Brad were waiting at the quayside when Elin arrived.

'You look very lovely,' said Manos. 'The colours in your dress are like your paintings. And your eyes.'

'What he means is, you look hot, babe. Very hot,' said Brad.

Elin laughed as the three of them boarded the boat and found seats under the awning. It was a warm balmy evening and the sky was streaked with apricot and pink by the setting sun.

'Someone's going across in style,' said Brad, nodding in the direction of the opposite quayside.

The Simonides brothers and Anastasia stood along the handrail of the same yacht from where Elin had heard the mocking taunts the night baby Yiannis was born. The engine sounded and the vessel sped off, skimming over the water and leaving Péfka behind. The swell in its wake caused the passenger boat to rock and sway.

'All right for some,' Elin said. In her mind's eye, all she could see was the dashing figure of Stelios Simonides. She'd only ever seen him in his work clothes and dusty leather apron but that night in his linen blazer, crisp white shirt and navy slacks he even put his handsome brother in the shade.

The passenger boat left Péfka harbour dead on seven o'clock and as they neared the mainland, the glistening sugar lump shapes materialised into the buildings and landmarks of Porto Nikos town. It was the first time Elin had been across the strait since she arrived and as they disembarked, she was struck by the number of luxury yachts lined up along the marina walkway. Many of them sported Union Jacks and she heard British voices coming from inside the cabins where groups of people were enjoying drinks.

'This sure is where the mega rich hang out. We won't be able to afford any of these beauties as penniless painters,' Brad said.

Manos laughed. 'Elin might … if she can catch a Greek ship owner.'

Elin made a face. 'Give me the little fishing port over there any day. This money does nothing for me.'

'The men in Péfka must be careful.'

'Warn the women, too, Manos. They won't get a look in,' said Brad.

The three students were completely at ease with each other and Elin enjoyed their leg-pulling and, without expecting it, felt a lump rise in her throat. That banter was what she missed since her father had gone. Everything had become serious at home. The laughter had gone.

They walked away from the harbour.

'Look at that,' said Elin, pointing at a brightly coloured turquoise camper van parked in the communal car park set back from the quay.

Brad beamed at her and Manos and ran over to the battered VW.

He swept an arm towards the vehicle and bowed. 'Let me introduce you to Betsy. I bought her when I visited the UK on my way here and drove down through Europe. Painted by my own fair hand.'

Stylised daisy flowers were dotted between Ban-the-Bomb signs, rainbows, clouds and shooting stars over the surface of the van.

'There is no hiding away for you, my friend,' said Manos, laughing.

'Poor Betsy, I had a shock when I got here and found out no vehicles were allowed on the island. I had to leave her here on her own.'

'So that's why you disappear every few days,' said Elin.

'Yes, I start her up and go for a spin along the coast. I stop and do some of my sketching this side instead of always being on Péfka.'

Manos took out the party invitation from his back pocket and looked at the map drawn on the back.

'We had better go. We are here. We follow the coast road and we will arrive. Andreas said the walk takes about ten minutes, that is all.'

Porto Nikos was soon left behind and the shops and tavernas thinned out. To the right of them the sea shone in the evening sun and it was not long before they arrived at the Simonides household.

'*Ee Eliés*. The Olives,' said Manos, reading the sign carved into one of the creamy white stone pillars that supported heavy wrought iron gates. 'The name, it is correct. Look at that.'

Brad and Elin peered through the railings at a patch of land to the right of the house. Row after row of grey-green olive trees filled the space that led down to the sea.

'Olive trees, they are important to the Greeks,' said Manos.

As if from nowhere, a breeze sprang up and to Elin, the trees were whispering, whispering about her, whispering to her, as if they were trying to tell her something. Her pulse quickened and her breath became shallow. She shivered not with cold but with an unease she couldn't explain. *You're imagining things,* she told herself. *You have Brad and Manos with you.*

They opened the gates and walked down the dusty scree drive to the two-storey villa. Manos knocked on the large oak-panelled door, bleached grey from the sun, and grinned at his two companions.

'Welcome to The Olives,' announced Andreas as he opened the door. 'Come in, come in. Some of them are here already. You look amazing, Elin.'

'Thank you.'

As she walked through the entrance she was confronted by a large glass *mati.* Elin tensed, willing herself to hear Dimitra's reassuring voice. She followed Brad and Manos outside.

Huge ribbed terracotta pots filled with tumbling scarlet geraniums stood at each corner of a stone terrace and groups of people sat at the tables and chairs dotted around. Elin spotted Elektra and Maya chatting to others from the painting school. When they saw Elin, it went quiet and all eyes turned to look at her.

'*E-leen.*'

At the sound of her name, Elin's heart pounded. There was only one person who pronounced her name like that.

'Stelios.'

He stood back to admire her. 'You look sensational. That colour. It brings out the blue of your eyes.'

Elin blushed and saw Elektra and her friend laughing.

Stelios no longer wore his blazer. The top two buttons on his shirt were undone and in the dusk against the dazzling white shirt, his tanned skin looked darker than ever. His eyes sparkled.

'Let me get you and your friends a drink. What are you having?'

He was soon back with cold beers for the boys who wandered off to join the others. He handed a glass of retsina to Elin.

'Come and meet Mamá.'

Kýria Sofia Simonides stood chatting to Anastasia and a striking younger girl with dark glossy hair that tumbled over her shoulders.

'Mamá, this is Elin. Andreas says she's one of his very promising students.'

Elin caught Anastasia's eye and wondered if Andreas had told her about being seen.

Sofia Simonides looked Elin up and down. '*Kalispéra*. I think you learn much. My son is very clever painter. Clever teacher. People of Péfka thank him.'

Her English was slowly enunciated as she worked out each word to say in a strong Greek accent. She was the only one of the family where the words didn't flow easily.

The young girl raised her eyebrows and looked at Stelios. Anastasia smiled and nodded at Kýria Sofia's every word.

'I'm very pleased to meet you, Kýria Simonides. You have two talented sons.'

Stelios's mother 'humpphed' and walked away.

'This is Tasia, my fiancée, and my little sister, Thea.'

'It's lovely to be here. I've heard a lot about you both.'

Anastasia looked as if she'd just stepped out of a fashion magazine in a white figure-hugging designer gown that matched the dazzling white smile she flashed. 'You haven't joined us for that drink yet.'

'You two know each other already?' asked Stelios.

How could Elin tell him that since she'd seen Andreas leave her villa a few days earlier there was no way she wanted to exchange small talk with someone who was cheating on her fiancé?

Anastasia and Stelios moved away to circulate amongst the other guests. *I thought it was Andreas's party for his art students, celebrating the success of his painting school. Surely it's his job to do that?*

'You know I've started studying in London, don't you?' said Thea. 'So I'm not little like my brother said.'

'Yes, Vassilis told me. How are you getting on? No language problem, I can tell. You and your brothers speak perfect English.'

'Tasia's father saw to that. He arranged for us all to go to schools in Athens. After Papa died.'

'It's obviously paid off. Your mother must be very proud,' said Elin.

'Hmmm.'

Elin rejoined Manos and Brad and the evening passed quickly. There was lots of wine and the conversations became louder and louder. Elin tasted all the Greek delicacies and relaxed.

Andreas banged a spoon on a wine bottle.

'I want to welcome you to our family home. As you will have seen, it is called *Ee Eliés* named after the olives that grow in the grove at the side of the house. We hold a party in July every year to welcome students to the Simonides painting school and to Greece. I'd like to thank my wonderful mother for allowing me to hold it here and opening her doors to you all. Please raise your glasses. '*Ya mas*, Mamá.'

There were murmurings of '*Ya mas,* Kýria Sofia' and spontaneous applause. Sofia beamed at her son. '*Efharistó. Parakaló.*'

Stelios and Thea exchanged glances. There was no doubt they knew that Andreas was the favourite and that no one could compete with the chosen one. Stelios moved across to a large wooden radiogram and the sound of bouzouki music filled the air. Elin felt warmth rise along her neck as she remembered how good it had felt to be held close by Stelios as he taught her the intricacies of Greek dancing the night Yiannis was born.

She looked over to him. He caught her eye and smiled. *Are you thinking the same as me, Stelios?* As if reading her thoughts, Andreas and Anastasia started dancing on the terrace, swaying and dipping, holding each other tight and Andreas nestled his head into his partner's perfectly coiffed hair. The students clapped in time to the music and stood to form a circle around the dancing couple. Stelios watched for a while and then came over to where she was standing.

'Come on. Let's join them.'

Elin blushed and protested. 'I'm sure some of the other girls will be better than me. I don't know the steps.'

'Come on. Just follow me.' Stelios took Elin's hand and led her to join Andreas and Tasia.

Elin felt all eyes on her as they moved to the rhythm of the music. She saw the glare on Elektra's face. She was used to that, but there was one other person whose stony face showed exactly what she was feeling. Sofia Simonides.

Elin brushed her thoughts aside and followed Stelios's steps. Whereas Andreas and Tasia were by then flamboyantly moving around the stone flagstones, exaggerating every turn and sweeping their arms in the air, Stelios held Elin tight and she felt as if he was interpreting the music just for her. He looked deep into her eyes and she let her feet follow the pattern of his. Elin didn't want the track to finish.

'There, that wasn't too bad, was it?' he whispered. His hot breath on her ear lobe made her tingle, just as it had done when they'd danced together the first time. Everyone cheered as Elin went back to her seat. As she passed, she thought she heard Sofia Simonides say under her breath, 'You keep away. You hear me.'

'That was some show, honey,' said Brad when Elin joined them. 'Where did you learn to dance Greek style?'

'Oh, I just had to follow Stelios.'

'You are all right? You look upset on your way back to the table,' asked Manos.

Dear Manos. Always looking out for me. You never miss a trick. Why can't I fall for a nice Greek boy like you with no strings attached?

'I'm fine. Come on. I love this.'

Strains of the theme tune from *Zorba the Greek* filled the air and the three friends joined the large circle to dance. They swayed in time to the music, arms outstretched, kicking to the side. As the tempo increased, they linked arms and travelled round in a circle, getting faster and faster. By the time the music reached its crescendo, everyone was laughing and kicking their heels.

'I enjoyed that. A bit different from the Stones,' said Brad.

Manos and Elin laughed. Brad was never far from his Bush transistor.

'We'd better be making a move if we're going to catch the last boat across,' said Elin. 'Let's go and say our goodbyes and thank Kýria Simonides.'

The three friends made their way back into the house and found her talking with Thea and Stelios.

'We've come to say goodbye. Thank you for a lovely party, Kýria Sofia,' said Elin.

'Yeah, cheers.' Brad put out his hand.

Sofia Simonides reached out to shake Manos's hand but ignored the other two.

Manos looked at Thea and said, 'We will see you again soon, Thea? You come over to Péfka, one day?'

Before the Greek girl could answer, her mother interrupted. 'She no go in boat. Two sons on Péfka now. That is bad.' With that, she walked away.

'Don't mind my mother,' Stelios said. 'She's very protective. Why don't you walk along the beach path to the marina? It's well lit and it will save you time. I don't know where Andreas is … or Tasia for that matter. I'll tell him you've left. Just follow the path through the garden as far as the beach and then turn right.'

'Thank you, Stelios. We've had a lovely time. I expect we'll see you tomorrow over in Péfka,' said Elin. Her heart drummed in her chest as he leaned across and his lips brushed her cheek.

'*Kaliníkta oneira glyká.*'

Elin looked at Manos.

'He said, *Good night. Sweet dreams.*'

Brad, Manos and Elin walked along the garden path towards the sea. The still night air brought out the heady fragrance of the shrubs and flowers. They walked under a wooden arch laden with leaves and tiny star-like white flowers. Elin recognised the sweet perfume of summer jasmine and knew that in the daylight, the white would be edged with pale pink. After his travels to Greece, her dad had tried to grow it in their own garden.

As they reached the end of the garden they heard voices. Laughter. Squealing. Splashing.

Manos went first. 'It is Andreas. And Anastasia. You will never guess …'

'Holy shit. They're skinny dipping!'

Elin pushed between the boys. Clothes were strewn along the sand from the gate to the water's edge. Andreas and Anastasia were stark naked.

How dare they? How could they treat Stelios like that?

Chapter Eleven

The swimmers were oblivious to the fact they had company and only had eyes for each other. The sea glistened in bright moonlight and gentle waves rippled a regular rhythm. *A beautiful setting, just right for love and romance ... but not for those two.* The silhouette of a large solitary olive tree cast a shadow on the sand, hiding Elin as she watched. Bile rose in her throat as she thought of Stelios.

'Come on,' whispered Manos.

'The bastard. The bitch,' said Elin. 'To think that Stelios is keeping himself for *her.*'

She picked up Tasia's white designer dress. 'I could hide this, I suppose.' Instead, she stepped on the hem, leaving a dark wet sandy footprint. 'Oops!' She picked it up to examine the damage.

'Leave it,' whispered Brad. 'Manos is right. What good will it do? And we're late as it is. *Come on!*'

The two boys walked away leaving Elin with her thoughts. *He should know about what they're up to. I feel like going back to the house and telling him right now.* She threw the white dress back on the sand. She saw Manos and Brad disappearing along the beach and decided it was best to go, catch that last boat and find another way of letting Stelios know. Better for her to calm down and decide on a plan when she arrived back on Péfka.

Elin hardly slept that night. She tossed and turned, watching the luminous hands on her travel clock pass through hour after hour. Whenever she closed her eyes, she saw Stelios smiling at her as they danced together earlier that evening. When she did drop off to sleep, she dreamt of a blonde-haired girl walking barefoot along the sand, hand-in-hand with a tall, smartly dressed young man on a warm and balmy evening. Everywhere was bathed in silver and ripples of sea-water trickled over her toes. The olive trees inside the fence edging the beach rustled as the couple approached, whispering to her. The girl dropped her hand abruptly and looked up at her companion.

Instead of Stelios, the sneering face of Andreas Simonides looked back. He opened his mouth and let out a low rasping laugh. Elin woke with a jolt. She was soaked in perspiration. Her heart drummed inside her ribcage. Why would she be dreaming of Andreas?

Her bedroom door opened and the light was snapped on.

'What has happened? You are all right?' Dimitra rushed to the bed and placed her arms around her.

'I must have been dreaming.'

'It is – how do you say in English? A nightmare, *efiáltis*, I think. The laugh it wakes me – very bad. And then you scream.'

Elin accepted her friend's offer of a drink. 'I'm fine now, thank you. I'm sorry I disturbed you.'

Vassilis appeared bleary-eyed in the doorway.

'You are sure? Too much of the rich food cooked by Sofia, eh?'

'That'll be it,' said Elin, trying to force a smile.

Once she was alone, she thought about her dream and tried to decide how she could tell Stelios about his brother and Tasia. But was it her place to tell him? What if he despised her? He must have seen how they were with each other at the party. Perhaps he already knew and wasn't bothered. Did he truly love Tasia? Could she confide in Dimitra and ask her advice? With all these questions whizzing round in her head, Elin eventually fell asleep.

When she woke, light seeped into her bedroom through the thin curtains and her heartbeat quickened when she remembered what had happened the previous night. Elin was in no hurry to get dressed and face Dimitra and Vassilis. It was a Sunday and there was no school. Stelios would be at the house on the mainland, perhaps still unaware of how Andreas and Tasia were behaving behind his back. She took out her diary and sketched. A seascape, gentle rippling waves, two figures. An ancient olive tree took prominence on the page, its thick solid trunk proclaiming its age. She accentuated the deep gnarled texture of the twists and turns of the bark to resemble a wrinkled face, framed by branches of fine leaves. The tree saw everything, watched the deceit, watched the bodies intertwine, caress, explore.

July 22nd

Party for the painting school at the Simonides house last night – idyllic, set in an olive grove and backing on to the sea. Kýria Sophia had eyes only for her eldest son … and not the only one (AL.) Stelios left to do all the work while big brother lorded it around. How did they slip away without being noticed? I want to tell Stelios but not sure if it's my place to. I had a strange dream last night. More of a nightmare. Woke the whole household. It was Andreas's face. Why did he unnerve me like he did? Hope it wasn't a premonition of something bad going to happen. At least I don't have to see him for another whole day. But it also means I won't be seeing another face either. I think I'm falling for Stelios. After all I said before coming here.

There was a knock on the door. Dimitra entered with a tray laid with a small cup of Greek coffee, slices of deep pink watermelon and a few sweet honey pastries.

'Last night you do not sleep well. This morning, I think you like breakfast here.'

Elin rose from the chair and took the tray, placing it on her dressing table. She hugged her friend.

'What would I do without you? Thank you,' she said. 'I'm sorry about waking you.'

'I worry, that is all. You are upset.' She picked up Elin's diary that was open on the page showing the beach scene. 'You are very good artist. This is on the island, eh?'

'No, it's the beach behind the Simonides' house last night.'

'The olive trees, it is possible they live for hundreds of years. This one is very old. The trunk, it tells me,' said Dimitra.

Elin nodded. 'Ancient, I think.'

'I leave you. You must drink the coffee while it is hot.'

Elin sipped the sweet black liquid. She hadn't realised how hungry she was and after eating the juicy watermelon, the flaky baklavas that always satisfied her sweet tooth were just what she needed to lighten her mood. She'd made a decision. She would confide in Dimitra. She wanted to know more about the relationship between the Simonides brothers and Anastasia Loukas.

After Elin washed and dressed, she took her tray down into the kitchen where Dimitra was rolling out pastry for the cheese and spinach pies for the taverna lunches.

'You look much better after you eat food.'

'Yes, thank you. Breakfast was lovely.' She took a deep breath. 'Dimitra, can I ask you something?'

'Of course.' She dusted her floury hands on her apron. 'Let us sit down.'

'What do you know about the Simonides brothers?'

The young Greek woman looked puzzled. 'I know both of them well. I do not know what you mean. About them? Something happened, eh?'

Elin held her hands tightly on her lap.

'I thought Stelios was engaged to Tasia. Anastasia. That's what Vassilis told me. But first, I saw Andreas leaving the Loukas villa one morning and yesterday at the party …' Perhaps she'd better not say too much.

Dimitra sighed and rolled her eyes. 'Those two boys, they are like … how did you say? Cheese and chalk?'

Elin smiled that Dimitra had remembered the saying, even if it was the wrong way round.

'I don't like being close to Andreas. He's a bit creepy but Stelios is lovely, kind.' She added quickly, 'A true friend. I can't see him get hurt. I don't know what to do.'

'I tell you about the family. Kýrios Simonides, he dies when the children are young. He is rich and he leaves lots of money. Kýrios Loukas, the papa of Anastasia, is important man and he helps the boys go to good school in Athens. Andreas, he is the oldest. He grows up very fast and becomes the man in the family. His mother, she loves him very much. What he does, sometimes bad things, it is not wrong in his mamá's eyes. But poor Stelios …'

Dimitra held out her hands wide and shrugged her shoulders.

'That was clear last night,' said Elin. 'You'd think it was Stelios's party. Andreas was swanning around soaking up all the fawning from his students … and his adoring mother. She made it very clear she didn't like me. Why didn't she arrange for Andreas to marry Tasia? Do you think Stelios loves her or is he marrying her out of duty?' Elin had to tell Dimitra. 'Last night we saw Andreas and Tasia swimming naked and poor Stelios was up at the house seeing to the party guests. I feel I should tell him.'

Dimitra frowned. 'I say no. Stelios, he sees.'

Elin's eyes widened. 'You mean he knows?'

'Stelios, he waits for the moment. He says nothing. But he does not marry her. Now I must work. The pies, they do not bake on their own. Everyone likes to eat them. Be a good friend to Stelios. You do not worry about Kýria Sofia. She does not like *anyone* who takes her boys away.'

Dimitra returned to the kitchen, leaving Elin to mull over what her friend had said. The best thing she could do was forget all about it. She'd arranged to meet Manos and Brad for another visit to the beach and knew that once she was engrossed in a seascape, Stelios Simonides would not even enter her mind. Or would he? Elin went up to her room to get her diary and box of watercolours and shouted goodbye to Dimitra and Vassilis.

Outside the sun was at its highest and blinded her after the cool shadowy bar.

'*Kaliméra*, gorgeous.'

Elin hadn't seen Andreas walking down the street and practically bumped into him.

'You went early last night,' he said.

'We wanted to make sure we caught the last boat across. We walked through the garden along the beach. You didn't see us.'

Elin waited for a reaction from Andreas. There was only a short pause as he walked on.

'You should have joined us. The water was lovely at that time of night,' he called.

Elin pulled her face taut and walked in the opposite direction. She heard Andreas laughing behind her.

Manos and Brad were waiting for her where they'd arranged sitting astride their scooters.

'Which one of us hunky beasts are you gonna choose? The Greek god with the smouldering eyes or a bearded Yankee hunk with toned abs?' Brad pulled himself up straight and started punching his taut abdomen. 'The one that loses out carries the pannier with all our gear on the back.'

Manos rolled his eyes and Elin grinned, glad to relax after her encounter with Andreas.

'How about I travel behind the Greek god on the way there and with the Yankee hunk on the way back? Fair?'

Manos held open the pannier and they added sketchpads, boxes of paints, jars of water and Elin's diary. He buckled the lid and strapped it on the back of Brad's scooter. It was the first time Elin had ridden on a scooter and she clung to Manos very tightly. Her long blonde hair flowed out behind her in the warm breeze as they gathered speed. She looked as Brad came along side, grinning. 'What d'ya think?' he shouted above the noise of the bikes.

'I love it.'

A horse and carriage was coming towards them so Brad hung back into single file. Soon a sliver of deep turquoise water appeared in front of them as they approached Agios Georgios beach. A gleam of silver chrome flashed from dozens of scooters neatly parked at an angle facing the sea wall. It was a Sunday and the beach was much busier than normal.

‘Over there,’ said Elin, pointing to a space being vacated by a tall, well-tanned young man.

‘That is good,’ said Manos. ‘You look for handsome men and you find the parking space.’

Elin elbowed him in the back.

Brad rode further along but he too found somewhere to park.

As they walked along to the far side of the beach, they heard shouting coming from the terrace of one of large hotels facing the sea. They put their bags down and strained to see what was happening. People had gathered into a circle around two men who were throwing punches at each other. Another intervened and pulled them apart.

‘What are they saying, Manos?’ said Elin. ‘Sounds nasty.’

Manos moved nearer. ‘He says he owes money. He does not give goods until he has paid. Who is it, do you think?’

‘Well, tell us then?’ said Brad.

‘Andreas!’

The shouting became louder and they watched as Andreas marched out the hotel grounds, holding his jaw, his face pulled into a glower. Oblivious to anyone around him, he mounted one of the scooters and left the beach, revving hard so that everyone turned to see what the noise was.

Elin couldn’t get Andreas out of her mind that afternoon. He seemed to get everywhere on the island. He certainly got into her head. Just what was he up to? She found it difficult to concentrate on her painting. Leaving Brad and Manos on the beach, she wandered over to the hotel. She sat at one of the tables under a large parasol and when the waiter came, she ordered a beer.

‘Do you speak English?’ she asked.

‘*Naí*, a little.’

‘What was the fight about earlier?’

‘The artist, he is trouble. First, he beds the man’s woman, now he owes money.’

The young man left Elin to mull over what he’d said. She wasn’t surprised about Andreas messing around with someone’s girlfriend or wife but why would a wealthy man owe money? Vassilis had said the Simonides family had been well provided for when his father died. The fees he charged for the painting school surely brought in a lot as well. It was clear that her painting tutor had other secrets as well as carrying on with his brother’s fiancée.

‘Here you are,’ Brad said as he and Manos joined her. ‘You didn’t last long. A bit of a hangover have we?’

‘No, I kept thinking about what the fuss was all about with Andreas, earlier. I saw him on my way to meet you two. Told him we’d seen him.’

‘What did he say?’ said Manos.

‘He said we should have joined them. Bold as brass.’

Manos looked puzzled and glanced at Brad to explain.

‘Brazen. No shame.’

‘Aah, I understand. No, Kýrios Andreas Simonides has no shame.’

The two men had finished for the day, so they ordered beers too.

‘It is too hot to paint,’ said Manos. ‘The paper dries very fast. It is dry before we can stretch it.’

‘No, we can do with a day off, I reckon. I’ve five paintings ready for hanging. What about you two?

‘I have four,’ said Manos. ‘But I like to get some that are better than my first ones.’

‘I’ve got four, too. The *letch* said a minimum of eight, I think.’

‘You’d better not let him hear you call him that,’ warned Brad.

Elin laughed. ‘He’d probably enjoy it. Like you said, he’s got no shame.’

A picture of his handsome, sensitive brother came into her mind and Elin’s heart pounded. If only she could be sure that Dimitra was right. Stelios would not be marrying Tasia.

She climbed on the back of Brad’s scooter and they returned to Santa Marina on the other side of the island.

Chapter Twelve

Life on Péfka went on at a leisurely pace for Elin. Over the next few weeks, her time was spent attending painting school in the morning, painting and sketching in the afternoons and generally helping out at the taverna. Andreas kept out of her way and, perhaps because she wasn't being singled out as his star pupil, even Elektra and Maya started to become more friendly.

'How many paintings do you finish?' said Elektra.

'Five now. I'm not sure they're any good though. I think I'll go over to the mainland tomorrow and try to get some more sketches done. Do both of you fancy joining me?' Elin was willing to try to put the past unpleasantness behind her and it would be good to have some female company, much as she loved being with Manos and Brad.

'We meet you in the harbour. We catch the boat at 2.30.'

Elin agreed but had a slight uneasy feeling when she caught the girls share a look later. She put it to the back of her mind. *What's the worst that can go wrong? They don't turn up. I'll just go on my own.*

As she walked down towards the taverna, she noticed the door into the wood turner's was open. Her stomach somersaulted. She slowed and stood in the doorway.

'*Kalispéra*. I didn't know you were opening up today. I thought you were staying with your mother and Thea for a few days.'

A big beam spread across his face and Elin felt her cheeks blush. The closest she'd been to this man was when they danced, so why did he have this effect on her with just a smile?

'Oh, hello, Elin. Yes, I'm having dinner with Tasia and her family. They want to talk about the wedding.'

Elin's pulse raced. *But Dimitra said you would never marry her.* She realised Stelios was still talking to her.

'… so I thought I'd get a couple of hours turning done. The island is filling up with tourists now the school holidays are here. Vassilis needs plenty of bowls to sell.'

'Yes, it is busier. I must go. I promised Elektra and her friend I'd meet them to go over on the boat to Porto Nikos.'

'We haven't spoken about the party. I haven't seen much of you in the last few weeks. It was a good party, wasn't it? I take it you find your way along the beach. I gave your apologies to Andreas when he and Tasia reappeared.'

'Then you know …' said Elin.

'Know what?'

'Where they'd been?'

'Yes, they'd been seeing to the other guests who were leaving at the front of the house when you and the guys left through the garden. Mamá, Thea and I were clearing up when they came back in.'

She felt her eyes burn. *Poor Stelios. He didn't know at all!*

'I'll leave you to it. Call in at the taverna when you can. I'd love to see what you've made.' Elin tried to keep her voice light and practically ran out of the shop. *Would it be awful if she told Stelios where they'd really been? How could he not see what was going on under his nose?* She had a couple of hours before catching the boat so she'd see if she could help Dimitra in the taverna.

'You are very quiet today, Elin.'

Dimitra smiled at her as she stood at the bar. She realised she must have been staring into space.

'Sorry. I was miles away.' Elin looked around the darkened room to check that she and Dimitra were alone. 'I was thinking about Stelios. I thought you said he would never marry that awful Anastasia. Well, he's going to her villa tonight, to discuss wedding plans with her parents!' Her mouth pulled into a hard line and she clenched her fists. 'It makes me so angry, Dimitra. He has to be told. He has to know what those two are up to behind his back! They're taking him for a fool.'

'Who is it that is taken for a fool?'

Elin spun around to see Vassilis in the doorway of the bar.

'Elin is sad because Stelios, he does not know about his brother and Anastasia. Now he talks about the wedding. He goes to the Loukas villa. I say to her he will not marry her. I am right, eh?'

The Greek man put his hands on Elin's shoulders and looked her in the eye. 'I tell you something but you must not say a word. You understand, eh?' Elin nodded. 'You come through to the back where no one will hear us.'

Dimitra stayed to look after the bar. Baby Yiannis lay awake in the crook of one arm while in her other hand, she shook the olive wood rattle that Stelios had made for him when he was born. '*Naí*, you go through.'

Vassilis led Elin through to the family's private living room. Unlike the bar, the midday sun shone through the two windows bathing everywhere in bright light.

'Sit down, Elin *mou*. Stelios, he is my friend. We are like brothers. He tells me everything.'

'Why don't you tell him then?' Elin said.

'You must stop. You hear what I say.' Vassilis put up his hand. 'Stelios, he knows everything. He does not love Anastasia. He says he will marry her to get information.'

'I don't understand.'

'Stelios, he gets to know Anastasia to please his mamá. Very soon, he sees she is not very nice. She is unkind to everyone. Her mamá and papa, too. Stelios, he finds she takes drugs and he says to her the wedding will not happen. If he does this, she tells the police that she buys them from Andreas, his brother. Stelios, he does not want this.. So he pretends and she thinks the wedding returns.'

'But does he know that there's more than drugs between Andreas and Anastasia? Surely he wouldn't put up with that?' asked Elin.

'Yes, he knows. He does not love her and he hates what his brother is doing. He will give him a chance to give up the drugs. If he say "no", he wants the proof and then, he goes to the police. Stelios, he pretends so that he catches them with the drugs.' He sighed. 'You know *The Palinourus* that's always moored down in the harbour? That is where the dealings go on. The dealers come in from Athens, they pretend they are – how do you say? – weekenders, and then they disappear by Monday morning.'

It all fitted. Andreas spending time with his rich friends on the luxury yacht. Who else on the island would have money to buy drugs? Elin looked at her watch. She'd have to go and meet Elektra and Maya soon.

'So, you see, Stelios, he waits. Once he has proof, you see he is different. Then, he follows his heart, eh?' Vassilis gave her a look that made her cheeks redden. 'You must not say a word.'

'I promise. And thank you. I'm glad you've told me. I'm going over to the mainland to do some sketches so I'd better go. I'll see you later.'

Elin made her way down to the harbour. As she got closer, she heard giggling coming from *The Palinourus*, moored on the opposite side of the quay from where she'd pick up the passenger boat. She'd know that giggle anywhere. Elektra and Maya were sunbathing on the deck with Andreas. So much for saying they'd accompany her to the mainland. Obviously, spending time with their handsome tutor was much more tempting.

'Elin, why don't you join us?' shouted Andreas. The girls became silent and Elin imagined the inevitable scowl that would have appeared on Elektra's face under her massive sunglasses.

'No, it's all right. I'm catching the boat across to Porto Nikos to do some sketches of the harbour.'

'Have a good *trip*,' he answered. The girls went into fits of laughter

'Not good trip like ours,' added Elektra.

'*Skáse*. Shut up, Elektra,' said Andreas.

Elin thought back to her earlier conversation with Vassilis and wondered.

Although the boat was full of tourists, Elin managed to find a seat at the back. She turned and watched the island disappear into the size of a small rock. She thought of Stelios and his plan to catch his brother and Anastasia taking drugs. She remembered seeing friends in art college take LSD and how they'd described their trips. Her friend, Tim, painted his best pictures when he'd taken the drug, according to him. Swirls of psychedelia in strident shades of orange, lime and magenta flowed into pools of chaos all over his canvases.

Elin sketched several scenes at the harbour. None of the yachts were as grand as *The Palinourus* but then perhaps they weren't owned by drug dealers, she thought. She started to move along the quayside when she heard an English voice.

'Not spying on us, are you, young lady?' A tanned young man, smiling broadly came through to the back of his boat, which stood out as bigger and grander than the rest. 'I've seen you over here quite a bit lately. You're over on Péfka, aren't you? I'm Tom. Tom Reynolds.'

'Elin Morgan. Hi.' She rose her hand. 'No, we've an exhibition coming up in a month's time and I wanted to get some sketches and notes done. I'm at the painting school there.'

Tom's face dropped. 'Not with that Simonides fella?'

'Yes. Why? Do you know him? Why do you say it like that?'

'He's bad news. I hear he doesn't pay up for his ... *purchases*. Let's say it's only a matter of time. And as for that fancy bird of his. Well, she deserves everything that's coming to her. She's a nasty piece of work. I went out with her once. Right snotty cow.'

Elin's mouth gaped open. She didn't want to hear any more from the stranger standing a few feet away from her. How did Tom know Andreas and Tasia? What did he mean by it was only a matter of time? She'd have to talk to Brad and Manos when she arrived back.

'I must go. I've got another hour before the next boat across to the island and I want to get some more sketching done. Nice meeting you.'

She walked on without giving a backward glance to the smarmy good-looking Englishman who had such a disregard for Andreas and Tasia. She felt his stare burning on her back. She had a nasty feeling about that one.

Elin wandered along the beach, retracing the steps she'd taken the night of the party. The water lapped over her toes as gentle ripples broke onto the pale sand. As she approached the solitary olive tree, the trees inside the fence running along the beach rustled in a whisper and she felt uneasy once again. Would Kýria Sofia be there? She'd made it very clear that she didn't like Elin. But she wasn't trespassing was she? She was just out sketching, putting into practice what Sofia's precious son had taught her. What better place than this part of the coast where the light was perfect and cast a myriad of rainbow colours along the surface of the water? The intricacies on the olive tree bark would make a fascinating painting.

Elin sat on the bank by the fence and drew the ancient tree. As she studied and sketched the gnarled bark, it took on the form of a human face, reminding her of Sofia Simonides. The cascades of grey-green leaves framed the face like unruly hair and when Elin added tones in watercolour, the painting resembled a human portrait. She could see how this could form the centrepiece of her exhibition once she'd painted it on a much larger scale in oils. She imagined being back in the studio overlooking the bay. There was nothing like the smell of oil paint and turps in her nostrils, a palette of newly mixed colours and brush in hand, when faced with the proverbial blank canvas. She never failed to get excited as a new image unfolded in front of her. This one would be bigger than any of the seascapes and boat paintings, even bigger than the lighthouse one that everyone had admired and said should be her principal exhibition piece. She gathered up her sketchbook and paints. She couldn't wait to get back to the studio and start transferring her idea onto the largest canvas Andreas had given her. For the first time that day, Elin didn't think about Andreas and Anastasia and their drug taking; she didn't even think about Stelios. All she could concentrate on was a portrait of Sofia Simonides as a face on a thousand-year-old olive tree.

The whispering started again as Elin walked along the fence. Each tree appeared to be watching her and trying to tell her something. She glanced over her shoulder, convinced there was someone hiding behind the squat trees. Up at the house, she saw someone watering the large terracotta urns of geraniums. Sofia Simonides.

August 9th

Met an Englishman today when over in Porto Nikos. Very full of his own importance. Seemed to know all about Andreas and Anastasia and didn't have a good word to say about them. There was something about him that didn't seem right. Seemed to have plenty of money though if his yacht was anything to go on. Not as flashy as The Palinourus but still pretty showy. How the other half live.

Had a good day sketching and painting the olive tree on the beach. Thick oil paint will lend itself to creating the deep textures on the gnarled bark. I can't wait to get started.

Chapter Thirteen

The next morning Elin was the first to arrive at the studio. Stelios had not opened the door of the wood turner's when she passed and Anastasia's villa was in silence. Andreas was opening up and when he saw Elin, a wide grin appeared on his face.

'This is a lovely surprise. What brings you here this early?' he said.

'Oh, I've an idea for a centre piece painting and I just have to start it.'

Elin felt she wanted to put everything behind her and just concentrate on painting. What did it matter what her tutor did outside school hours? As long as it didn't involve her. And she'd made it very clear she didn't want to be involved.

Elin chose the largest canvas that Andreas had and set it up on an easel by the open bi-fold doors. She mapped out the shape of the olive tree and by the time the others arrived she'd become totally engrossed in the painting. The faint smell of linseed oil mixed with the pungency of the turps had energised her and her hands were smudged grey-green.

'Wow!' said Brad. 'That's some size. How are you going to get that across on the boat? Love the colours on the bark.'

At least he sees it as a tree. Perhaps it's only me who can see Sofia in these wrinkles. Elin chuckled to herself. How could one woman she barely knew make her feel inadequate and stir up such an intense feeling of dislike?

Manos and Brad set up their easels next to hers and no one chatted as they painted.

Elin didn't notice someone standing behind her.

'I think I know where this is,' says Andreas. 'It's the olive tree just in front of the house. Fantastic. Here, let me show you how to make the olive leaves stand out from the canvas.'

He picked up a narrow pliable knife and took paint from the shades of grey-green on the palette where Elin had mixed her colours. With the narrow blade, he applied the paint in short strokes and the immediate effect was that the strands of foliage came to life. Elin stood back and admired the canvas.

'Use more colours, perhaps try a little violet, or touches of lime, here and there to add three dimension to the leaves.' Andreas moved in a little closer and Elin backed away.

‘Thank you. I’ll have a go,’ she said. *When will he get the message?*

Elektra walked past and sneered.

‘It is an old woman, I think. Not olive tree.’

Later Elin met Brad and Manos in the taverna at the end of the quay.

‘Fancy joining us for a cold beer, honey?’ asked Brad when she arrived.

‘Thanks. I’ll get that table outside by the window.’

She and Manos sat down and Brad joined them.

‘The girl says she’ll bring them over.’

Elin made sure she sat facing the boats moored along the quayside. She looked for Andreas or Anastasia on *The Palinourus* but the yacht was deserted.

‘Hey, I found out what Andreas was collecting from that bloke at the beach,’ she said. ‘Well, if he’d paid up, that is. I think it was LSD.’

‘Phew!’ said Brad. ‘Not just the odd bit of weed, then. Serious blow your mind stuff. How do you know it’s acid?’

Elin thought back to the conversation she’d had with the girls. ‘I have no proof, mind. They talked about having a good trip and there was something about them that reminded me of this guy in college who took it regularly. They were all chilled out and calm.’

‘That’s not like Elektra,’ said Manos.

The three friends laughed but Elin shivered when she thought of the dreadful night in Halls when it had all gone wrong for Tim. The other students had watched helplessly in horror as he’d been gripped by the fear and paranoia of a bad trip that went on forever.

‘There’s something else, too. When I went over to the mainland yesterday, I got talking to a guy on one of those flashy yachts. An English bloke. Said his name was Tom. All smarmy to start with but once I mentioned I was a student of Andreas, he changed. Didn’t have a good word to say about Tasia . . *at all!* Something about the pair of them not paying up.’

‘It fits with what we saw at the beach, then,’ said Brad.

Manos raised his left eyebrow. ‘He is their dealer, eh?’

Elin looked over at *The Palinourus* again. She hadn’t noticed it before. Along side the name was a logo of stylised blue and turquoise sailing boats upon ocean waves. She’d seen it somewhere before.

‘That’s it!’ she said aloud. ‘Same logo, just different names.’

Brad and Manos looked at each other and shrugged.

‘Tom’s yacht was called *Aurora* and had a Union Jack not the Greek flag like that one over there but the logo is identical. I tell you that Tom’s involved with them. And he’s not happy.’

‘That doesn’t prove anything, honey. It could be the logo for the make of boat, same supplier, same boatyard, ship chandler. Just a coincidence.’

For the rest of the evening, the three friends talked about the preparations for the exhibition but Elin couldn’t get the Englishman out of her mind. What if he was a dealer and owned *The Palinourus*, as well as his own luxury yacht? Could Andreas and Anastasia be in danger?

Normally spectacular apricot and pink sunsets graced the sky above the mainland across the water but that night, once the light had faded, the sky was solid black and only the lamps at the taverna shone dimly.

Elin shivered.

‘I’m going to call it a night, boys. I haven’t been out this late for ages. I need my beauty sleep. See you bright and early in the morning.’

Manos stood up. ‘You want us to see you home? It is very dark tonight.’

‘No, I’ll be fine, thanks.’

Elin made her way along the harbour wall and tried to keep out of the shadows. Once she’d walked up the steps to the street, only an occasional light from the narrow cottages illuminated her way home. Elin shivered in the humid night air. She heard whispers behind her. Sinister, menacing whispers. On turning around, she saw no one. The whispers stopped. Her heart thumped.

‘Who’s there?’ she said, shouting into the murkiness.

A ball of grey fur scuttled across from the shadows in front of her and snuggled around her ankles. Elin let out a long sigh.

‘Oh, Cleo! What are you tangled up in?’ She knelt down and freed the tiny cat from a stem of leaves caught up in her long fur.

Elin carried on walking. It wasn’t long before icy cold prickles of alarm were back, seeping into her bones again. She quickened her pace. She heard footsteps behind her. They echoed in her head, matching hers step for step. When she slowed, they slowed and when she stopped, they stopped. This was the quiet fishing village of Santa Marina, she reasoned, so why did she have the sour taste of fear on her tongue?

Every door was shut for the night. It got darker and gloomier the further up the hill she went. *Not far now*.

‘Who’s there?’ she shouted again. Silence.

Her heartbeat drummed in her head. She turned on her heel. And gasped.

'Andreas! What the hell are you doing scaring the shit out of me like that?'

Her painting tutor stood about three feet away from her, smirking. He stepped forward and put his hand on her cheek.

'Just thought my favourite student could do with a little company.'

Elin backed away. She could smell alcohol on his breath.

'I don't need any, thank you. I'll see you at the studio in the morning … perhaps you need to sober up before then.'

Elin turned away, determined not to get into an argument with him. She walked on. Andreas grabbed her by the hair.

'Why you, little minx …'

'Get off.'

He turned her around and shoved her against the rough stone wall of one of the cottages.

'Think you're too good for me, do you? Well, I'm telling you, little *Despinis* Frigid, no one says no to Andreas Simonides.'

He brought his mouth down onto hers and forced his tongue between her lips. Elin struggled and tried to push him away. He grabbed her batik shirt and tore it off her shoulder, exposing bare skin. She felt the stone scrape her flesh. She dug her nails into his cheeks as hard as she could and dragged them down causing him to release his grip.

'Help, someone help.'

'No one will hear you, you bitch. You might as well give me what I want,' said Andreas, wiping the blood from his face. 'I can tell you want it, too. Just playing hard to get …'

Elin managed to free herself enough to knee Andreas hard between the legs. He doubled up, clutching his groin. She ran up the hill past the taverna and hammered on the door of the wood turner's workshop. A light snapped on and Elin heard Stelios muttering in Greek as he came to open the door.

'Elin! What on earth?' He opened his arms and pulled her close. 'What has happened?'

Once Elin felt the warmth of Stelios's body around her, she wept.

'It was Andreas. He followed me. He'd been drinking.'

''What! My brother did this to you?'

Elin nodded. He guided her into the cramped living room and sat with her on the sofa, holding her until she had stopped shaking.

‘I tried to push him off. I kicked him where it hurt. I don’t know what he’d have done if I hadn’t been able to get away.’

Her eyelids burned and she forced herself not to let the tears fall again. Her heart drummed in her ribcage. She flinched when Stelios placed his arm around her shoulders, her back sore from being forced against the wall. She looked up at gentle Stelios and saw the shock in his eyes. He clenched his fists.

‘I’ll kill him! I’ll kill him!’

His mouth contorted into a hard straight line and his eyes fired with anger. Stelios stormed out of the apartment, slamming the door so hard it ran through the tiny house like a gunshot.

‘No, Stelios. Leave it!’ Elin said, but her words dissolved into the air of the empty passageway. She hoped Stelios wouldn’t do something he’d regret.

It wasn’t long before he returned.

‘He won’t try anything like that again in a hurry.’ He punched his fist into his open palm and twisted it back and forth. Blood was spattered over his pale blue shirt.

Elin gasped and put her hand over her mouth. ‘Aah! You didn’t …?’‘Let’s say I think he got what was coming to him. I did hit him … hard. But the blood is just where he knocked his head when he fell. Now, let’s get you cleaned up, shall we? And then we’d better get you back to the taverna. Vassilis and Dimitra will wonder what’s happened to you.’

Stelios ran upstairs, reappearing with a clean white linen shirt and a small towel.

‘Here, have this. It will be a bit big but we can’t let Vassilis see the state of your shirt and the bruises on your shoulder, can we? Otherwise my brother will get a second beating from him.’

For the first time since she’d got there, they both smiled. Elin took the shirt and went up to the bathroom where she washed her face and her bare shoulder where indeed the bruises from Andreas’s rough handling were starting to show. She looked in the mirror at the young girl looking back at her. She knew for certain that Stelios was the man she loved, the one who’d avenged her honour earlier that evening. She wondered if he loved her too. But he was not free to love her back, was he?

She went back downstairs and Stelios came over, pulling her towards him. He nestled his head into her neck and his warm breath on her skin made her tingle with arousal.

'Stelios, we can't.'

Elin pulled away, knowing that once she gave way to those sensations, there would be no going back.

'You must know how I feel about you, Elin. How I've felt ever since Vassilis first introduced us. Perhaps it's taken that brute of a brother of mine to give me the courage to tell you.'

Still, Elin held herself taut a few feet away from Stelios. His eyes fired with longing.

'But what about Ana—?'

Before Elin could finish her sentence, Stelios kissed her lips very softly and her insides tingled. She responded by kissing him back urgently until they both pulled away.

'You look very sexy in my big shirt and I want to go on kissing you but you are right, you should go home. I will walk you back and we will talk again tomorrow.'

They walked hand in hand down the short distance to the Guikas Taverna that Elin now thought of as home. As they kissed each other goodnight, Elin whispered in Stelios's ear. 'I have so much I want to say to you.'

August 10th

The worst and the best things happened today. The letch showed his true colours. He has no respect for me. It's obvious he doesn't like having his advances rejected. I really thought he was going to force himself on me. Thank God I got away and S. was still up. I just hope S. hasn't done something stupid. I've never seen such rage. And there was a lot of blood. Andreas's blood.

But afterwards. I thought my heart would melt. Now, I know he feels the same way as I do. How can I pretend we're just friends after that kiss? How can I sleep tonight?

Chapter Fourteen

Elin couldn't get to sleep that night. Every time she closed her eyes, the leer on Andreas Simonides's face as he forced his repulsive kisses on her filled every corner of her mind. Her heart hammered in her chest as she relived the groping, the slobber, the panic of what could have happened. She remembered running away and knocking on the wood turner's shop door, willing Stelios to open it, to help her, to protect her. Only when the image in her head changed to another handsome Greek's face, one that was tender, loving even, was she able to drift off.

Light trickled into her room as dawn broke and Elin woke with a jolt. As she rolled onto her side to get out of bed, her shoulder was sore and grazed. The bruises were blue-black reminders of the night before. How could she go to the studio after what had happened?

Just as Elin was thinking about what to do, there was a gentle knock at the door.

'Come in.'

The door opened and Dimitra entered.

'You are all right, Elin *mou*? Stelios, he tells us what happened with his brother.'

Elin nodded and her cheeks flushed. 'Yes, *efharistó*.'

'I am sorry you have that from a Greek man. Most of them learn from their mamás to respect women. But Stelios is a lovely man, eh?'

'I know. They couldn't be more different,' said Elin, smiling.

'Ah, yes, I see it.'

Elin let out a long sigh. 'I don't think I can face going back to the studio today … or any day for that matter.'

Dimitra crossed the room and took Elin's hands in hers.

'You must not let him spoil your studies. You pay a lot of money for him to teach you. You must continue, for your papa. You must never be alone with him. Now, you dress and I have breakfast for you before you walk up the hill. Andreas Simonides, he is – how do you say? – a bully. You must not let him be the winner.'

As she turned to leave, Elin thought she heard her mutter. 'Not like my poor sister.'

As Elin left the taverna, she couldn't help but look back down the street towards the harbour and the place where Andreas had pinned her up against the cottage wall. She knew exactly which cottage it was, the one with the wrought iron filigree window box. That morning in the bright sunlight, it looked picturesque with its whitewashed stone wall and the blue painted window box full of trailing vermillion geraniums. The door was open wide and she could see the wooden beaded curtain moving in the breeze. Last night, the street had been deserted and inky black shadows gave the place a sinister feel. She wished it had been a moonlit balmy night, the windows open, so the occupants would have heard her cries.

Further down the hill, she saw Brad and Manos striding towards her with sketchpads under their arms. She wouldn't say anything about what had happened to the boys. The fewer people who knew the better.

'Hi, honey. Get home okay, last night? Never known it that dark. Storm never came to much, though.'

'I didn't hear anything,' Elin said.

'You didn't see Andreas, did you? We saw him stumble out of the taverna. He did not look happy. There was an argument in the bar. The next thing we knew, the man we saw him arguing with down at Agios Georgios came out and boarded *The Palinourus.*'

Elin didn't answer.

'There's something dodgy going on, I tell you,' Brad continued. 'Sounds as if our beloved tutor is up to his neck in it.'

'Up to his neck? The drugs, they cannot be up to his neck.'

Elin and Brad laughed at their Greek friend. 'He's in deep trouble,' they said in unison.

For the first time since it happened, Elin felt she would be able to face Andreas with her two friends at her side. Dimitra was right; she owed it to her dad.

'Blimey,' said Brad. He was the first to enter the studio.

Elin gasped when she saw Andreas, too. His left eye was nearly closed and the skin around it was a deep purplish red. On his forehead was a large dressing where crusted blood had seeped through.

'Here she is, little Miss Tease.' All eyes turned to Elin and she felt warmth creeping along her neck. 'This young lady is the cause of this, ladies and gentlemen.' Andreas pointed at his injured eye.

Elektra stood up and glowered at Elin. 'She did that, eh? She is very bad woman.'

'Well, not her exactly but as good as.' Andreas walked the length of the studio and he stood facing Elin. She could feel his breath on her face and shuddered. 'No, this young temptress leads me on and then goes whining to her lover boy – *my* brother! – that I was coming on to her. My brother did this and left me bleeding on the floor!'

Andreas placed his hand on his forehead and Elektra rushed to his aid. 'You sit down, Andreas.'

Elin knew it had been a bad idea to go to the school that day and turned to leave. Elektra blocked her way. 'You and Stelios? I tell Tasia. You are sorry what you do.'

'Yes, my mother is not going to be happy either. Stelios and Tasia were destined to get married ever since my father died and now you've ruined that. Come on, everyone. Let her go. We've an exhibition to prepare for.'

Elin dug her nails into her palms. She wanted to shout, *What about you? Carrying on with your brother's fiancée? Getting involved with drugs.* Instead, she quietly turned on her heel and left the room, her dignity intact. What had her dad always said? *Don't stoop to their level.*

'If you leave this studio today, that's the end of your time at my school, Elin Morgan!'

Andreas's words resounded in Elin's head as she strode away along the cliff top.

She had to warn Stelios. On her way back to the taverna, Elin stopped by the wood turner's shop. The door was open and she stepped inside to the fruity smell of freshly turned olive wood. With his back to the door, Stelios sat behind his lathe skilfully turning a large grained block. She watched for a few minutes without being noticed. Soon, the rough wood evolved into recognisable bowl shape. Judging by the beautiful finished pieces on display, Elin knew that there would be much more time spent refining it. Stelios would sand the bowl and polish it with olive oil until the subtle array of yellows and ochres in the wood came to life and its surface was silky smooth. Her stomach fluttered when she thought of his soft hands as they'd caressed her the night before.

'Hello,' she said, in a barely audible whisper.

Stelios stopped the lathe and looked up.

'This is a surprise. Are you feeling better this morning? How is your shoulder?'

'It's still sore but I'm okay. Look, can we talk?'

'Of course. But I thought you'd be at the studio. The exhibition is only a month away. Didn't you say you still had a lot to finish?'

Elin nodded. 'I did try. But there's something you should know before Anastasia hears.'

Stelios stood up, shut the shop door and turned the sign to 'Closed'.

'Come on up. We can talk in the flat without being interrupted.'

Elin followed him upstairs just as she had done the previous night. He patted the sofa and indicated for her to sit down. She took a deep breath.

'I'm afraid going to the studio and facing Andreas may have made it worse for you. That was the last thing I wanted to do.' She willed herself not to break down. 'Andreas announced to the whole class that I was responsible for his injuries, or rather you were.'

'Well, I think we both knew he wouldn't let us get away with it by saying he walked into a door, did we?' He laughed and took Elin's hand. 'Look, he deserved everything he got. Don't worry. I'll deal with him.'

'He looks dreadful. You gave him a real beating. He said I asked for it. He called you my lover boy. Now, that awful Elektra has threatened to tell Tasia *and* your mother!'

Stelios pulled her towards him and stroked her hair.

'Don't worry about Elektra. Or Tasia. It was over between us long before I knew she'd been cheating with my womanising brother. I don't suppose he told you that some of the punches were for that, too. I bet he didn't announce *that* in public.'

Elin sat upright. 'You knew? But how?'

'I'd suspected something for a while. One night, after a drop too much raki, I asked Vassilis and he told me about the rumours. I had my proof the night of the party. You weren't the only one who saw the display in the sea, you know?'

So Vassilis was right. Stelios knew all along. Elin stood and paced the floor. 'I don't know how you can stay that calm. Aren't you upset about Anastasia?'

Stelios beckoned for her to sit down again. 'Annoyed at being taken for a fool, yes. But you have to understand the way some things are done in Greece. It was always assumed that Tasia and I would get married as our families had planned but we didn't really have a say in it.'

Elin frowned. 'That's ridiculous. They couldn't force you! It's 1969, for goodness sake.' It was just as Vassilis had told her.

'I just went along with it to please Mamá. She'd been through a lot. Anastasia was a nice Greek girl – or so I thought – but we were never in love. So, in a way, I should be grateful to my big brother for giving me an excuse to tell my mother the engagement is off. But I don't want *you* being blamed.'

Elin stood up and made for the door. She knew that, until their kiss the night before, they hadn't done anything wrong but she also realised that Sofia Simonides would not believe that. Not when she saw the state of her older son's face and was told that his brother was responsible. Elin wouldn't call on Stelios again.

'I'd better go. I don't want to make it any worse for you. Goodbye.'

Before Stelios could stop her, she was out in the bright sunshine, her eyes stinging. She felt very alone. What was she going to do?

Dimitra was serving in the bar when Elin entered the taverna. Baby Yiannis was propped on her right hip and she was pouring a bottle of Alpha beer with her free hand.

'Here, let me do that for you.'

'*Efharistó*, Elin *mou*.'

Elin poured the beer and took the drachmae from the customer who then left to sit outside.

Once they were alone, Elin and Dimitra sat at a table in the corner.

'Why are you so soon back?' said Dimitra. 'And you cry. Why is it?'

'It was horrible, Dimitra.'

Elin proceeded to tell her friend everything that had happened earlier at the studio.

'Stelios, he gives him what a lot of people want to do for a long time,' Dimitra said, then added softly, 'my own mama, too.'

'I don't understand.'

At that moment, Lyra entered the bar with Cleo tucked under her arm and joined them. Elin looked at the chocolate-brown sparkling eyes of the eight-year-old sitting opposite.

'I tell you later,' said Dimitra, in a whisper. 'Now I get us all the lunch.'

She placed baby Yiannis on Elin's lap, took Lyra by the hand and they both disappeared into the kitchen.

Chapter Fifteen

Up in her bedroom, Elin lay on her bed pretending to take a siesta but she couldn't settle. The sun had moved around and she knew she'd been there for a few hours. She was desperate to get back to painting. It was what she lived for, what relaxed her, it was who she was but because she had walked out of the painting school that morning, she didn't know what to do next. Should she go back and try to come to an arrangement with Andreas? Would he even want to, or should she just pack up and go home? She re-read Richard's letter that had arrived the previous day. At least, *he* wanted her to return home.

Dear Elin,

I'm counting the days until you come back to me. I know you didn't mean it when you said we were over. I promise I'll forget all about our row. It's just I want to look after you and protect you. You know I don't like you being at art college. You're very beautiful and I don't trust those art students around you. Imagine how I'm going mad with all these miles between us! Let me take over your dad's role – I'll never let anyone hurt you.

Write back soon and tell me I'm forgiven.

All my love,

Richard xx

It would be easy to pack up and leave. As well as putting her father's money to good use, one of the other reasons for the holiday had been to get away and escape the stifling control Richard had over her. In college, he'd insisted on seeing her every day and tried to tell her who she could or couldn't see. No, she couldn't go back. She had to try to reason with Andreas. Perhaps, Brad and Manos would go with her; she couldn't risk being alone with him after what had happened. Her thoughts were interrupted by Dimitra calling her name.

'Elin, there are visitors.'

She ran downstairs to find Brad and Manos standing at the bar. They must have read her mind.

'Honey, are you all right? We were worried when you just walked out like that.'

'We do not understand,' said Manos. 'You have worked too hard.'

Her two friends always made her feel better. Perhaps she wouldn't have to return to controlling Richard for a long while yet. She smiled at them and hugged each of them in turn.

'You're right. I'll go to see him because I can't give up now. You wouldn't come with me, would you? He wouldn't dare try anything if you two were there.'

'Of course. But I think our tutor's feeling very sorry for himself,' said Brad. 'By the way, have you taken your lighthouse picture? When we arrived back into the studio after lunch, it'd gone from your easel.'

As Elin walked along the cliff top with her two friends towards the painting school, she felt her heartbeat increase and she stopped to take deep breaths. What if Andreas wasn't alone? What if Elektra had stayed on? She went to turn back but then remembered her dad's words. *Never give up on your dreams.* She had to give it another try.

'We'll be just out here, if you need us,' said Brad. He and Manos sat at a bench under the pergola.

Andreas stood, looking out across the stretch of sea towards the mainland when Elin walked in. He turned to face her.

'Andreas, can we talk, please?'

'What do you think I have to say to you … after you had this done to me?'

He pointed at his bruised and battered face, but Elin suspected it was his ego that had been damaged the most.

'I did nothing,' she said. 'You received those for cheating on your brother with his fiancée. I've come to talk to you about painting.'

'What about it? When you left this morning, you made it clear you didn't want to paint. Wasted a whole day! And my brother wouldn't have known a thing if a certain someone hadn't told him. Wanted to get into his bed yourself, no doubt.'

Don't rise to the bait. Keep calm. Count to ten.

'There's nothing going on between me and your brother. I've just come to say I'd like to carry on with my exhibition pieces and I'd like your permission to come back to school in the morning.'

Andreas turned to face out to sea again. Elin knew that without her eight paintings the exhibition would look depleted. Andreas relied on the annual show to improve his reputation as a successful art tutor. Reviews would appear in all the upmarket Athens art magazines, and he'd told her and the others that prospective students for the forthcoming year would often enrol because of the exhibition.

'Very well,' he said. 'But you have to make up for today.'

'Thank you,' said Elin. She looked across at her empty easel on the way out and decided she'd look for the missing painting in the morning rather than stay any longer. She'd got what she'd come for. She was going to be painting again the next day. Her dad would be proud of the way she'd spoken up for herself.

'Everything is good?' said Manos, when she came out of the studio.

Elin smiled and thanked her friends. 'I'll be back in the morning.'

'Now we're up here, we're going to work some more on the exhibition pieces. We'll see you later, honey.'

Leaving her friends and the studio behind, she walked along the cliff top path. As she neared a small olive tree growing a few feet from the edge of the cliff, she spotted a creamy white shape resting on the lower branches. It looked like a rolled up ball of paper or card but on closer examination, she could see it was a crumpled canvas.

'No! It can't be!'

Carefully, Elin reached over to the tree and dislodged the canvas. Elin pulled it out and flattened it. Slashed in several places, her lighthouse painting was ruined. Shards of the pale white wooden frame had been thrown further down the bank and strewn along the pathway. Who could have done that to her? The knifing of the canvas skin caused her to feel almost as much pain as if her physical flesh had been punctured. She felt sick and fell to her knees on the scree of the path. She always put her soul into her paintings; they became her.

Her scream shrieked into the clear air but there was no one there to hear.

She rolled up the damaged canvas, tucked it under her arm and strode down the hill. Whoever had done this had not broken her; she'd be more determined than ever to shine at Andreas Simonides's exhibition. But there was one thing that bothered her. What if the person who destroyed her lighthouse painting did the same to her others? She couldn't bear it! She needed to get them away from the studio to a place of safety. *The wood turner's! The space at the back of the workshop would be perfect.*

Stelios was the one person who could help her but she'd vowed she wouldn't call on him again. Yet surely she could ask him to help … as a friend? As Elin neared the workshop, her thoughts were interrupted when she spotted Elektra and Maya walking up the hill towards her. Elin walked past the wood turner's without a sideways glance.

'She does not see lover, today,' said Elektra, with a sneer.

Elin carried on walking but then heard the Greek girl say something that stopped her in her tracks.

'She is no longer the star of Andreas.'

Elin turned on her heel and strode up to the two girls.

'And what do you mean by that?' Her voice rose to a screech.

'You left the school. You cannot come back. Andreas says that.'

Elin unrolled the lighthouse canvas and pointed to the slashes.

'This was you, wasn't it? You ruined my best painting.'

Elektra's mouth gaped open and she looked aghast at Maya. 'That is very bad. Your best piece.'

It was all Elin could do to stop herself lashing out at the girl, but it was what she said next that unnerved her.

'I wish I thought of it first but I know nothing. You do not say I did it,' she yelled.

Elin stared at her. Could Elektra be telling the truth? She certainly did look shocked. But who else hated her so much that they'd destroy her painting? Maya looked away, breaking eye contact with Elin.

'Come we go,' Maya said, quickly.

The two girls carried on their way leaving Elin to re-roll her canvas.

'Someone close to you did it, eh?' shouted Elektra.

The harsh words resounded through the air and Elin rushed up to see if Stelios could help her. There was no time to lose.

The door of the wood turner's was open and as Elin stepped into the cool of the workshop, a bell rang summoning Stelios from the back room. He beamed when he saw Elin.

'Well this is a nice surprise. I thought you were going to keep away from me.'

Elin held up her lighthouse painting.

'What the …? Who did this?'

'I don't know. I found it rolled into a ball shoved into the olive tree on the cliff top. Brad and Manos told me it had disappeared from my easel.'

Stelios came over to her and put his arm around her as she started to cry.

'The first person I thought of was Elektra but she denies all knowledge of it. After confronting her outside, I think she may be telling the truth. She was genuinely shocked.'

'So that's what all the yelling was about. It sounded like your voice but I thought it wouldn't be my gentle Elin so I didn't come out. No wonder you were mad. My poor Elin!'

He pulled her in towards him but she pulled away.

'No we must be friends, that's all. But I need your help. Please say you'll help me. I need to get all my paintings away from the studio. I couldn't bear if this happened again. Could you store them in there?' she said, pointing to the door at the back of the workshop.

'But surely that was a one off.'

'Elektra said to look closer to home. Who could she mean? Brad? Manos? I'm starting to suspect everyone. Maybe even Andreas? He was very angry.'

Stelios took her shoulders and looked directly into her eyes.

'Listen. You have to stop this. We'll go up now and tell Andreas what has happened. He can then decide what he wants you to do with your finished paintings.'

'But what if it's him? Elektra said it was somebody close to me. No, I'll go when he's gone out. He always leaves to go down to *The Palinourus* at seven. I see him every night as he passes the taverna.'

Stelios sighed. 'You haven't thought this through. How will we get in? He'll have locked it, surely.'

'He keeps a key behind one of the terracotta pots on the veranda. He tells us to let ourselves in if he's not there when we arrive in the mornings.'

Elin had it all worked out. She'd call for Stelios once his brother had left, get the paintings to safety and then just return to the studio in the morning and start another painting of the lighthouse. She had all the sketches and this one would be even better.

'I'll see you about 7.30, then. And thank you, Stelios. I knew I could rely on you to help … as a friend.'

He smiled, 'Yes, only as a friend.'

He mimicked a sad face and Elin grinned.

As she looked into his handsome face with its chiselled jaw and tanned complexion, she realised that was not all that she wanted from Stelios Simonides. His features were the last ones she saw when she closed her eyes at night and the first that greeted her when she awoke each morning. But for now, she had to be content with friendship. For his sake, she told herself.

Chapter Sixteen

As Elin and Stelios neared the studio, the night sky blazed fiery red. The sunset on the horizon cast the building into silhouette and Elin fumbled in the shadows to retrieve the key.

'It must be here somewhere,' she said, feeling round the back of the plant pot. 'Ah, here it is.'

'Come on. Let's get what we came for. My big brother's not going to be very happy if he finds out we've broken in.'

Elin opened the door. It was pitch black inside. The familiar smell of turps and paint hit her.

'Shit! I don't know where the light switch is. The shutters block out everything.'

'I don't suppose anyone ever works here at night. I'm sure I heard Andreas say you can only do your best painting in natural light. Perhaps there isn't one,' said Stelios. 'Hang on. What's this?'

Elin heard a click and the light came on. It was true there wasn't an actual switch but there was a pull-down cord instead. In the dim electric light, the studio looked dull and dingy; a complete mess.

'It looks different when the whole of that wall is open. The colours of the sky and the sea are in here, too, then,' she said, sensing Stelios's disapproval.

'It's not that. I don't see how you can all work so closely. He's jam-packed you students in, hasn't he? Anyway, let's get these paintings of yours.'

Elin led him into a small storeroom to the side of the main studio. She pointed out the section of the rack where her five paintings were standing. Each one had been stretched and tacked onto a wooden frame.

'I didn't realise they were this size. We can't just carry them under our arms, can we? And we haven't time to carry them down one by one. Andreas could come back at any moment.'

'But I *have* to get them out tonight. I have to.'

Stelios walked to the far end of the narrow room. 'What's this? Will this do?'

He was tugging at a wooden handcart that had been pushed under the end shelf. Elin had seen Andreas use it to move the bigger paintings from the studio to the storeroom once they were dry. Elin hugged him.

'That will be perfect. I'd forgotten all about that. It's like the one Vassilis uses when bringing supplies up from the boat. We could have brought that if I'd thought.'

'Right, then. I'll wheel it outside and we can bring out the paintings and be gone.'

Elin's heart was racing. If she and Stelios were caught, she knew her time at the painting school would be over for good. One by one they carried the paintings through the studio and stacked them on the cart. As they pulled out the last painting, Elin noticed a brown paper package stuffed in the far corner of her storage section.

'What's that?' she said, stretching her arm in to reach it. 'Look at the address!'

He took the parcel from her and read aloud. '*Thespína A. Loukas, 'Villa Anastasia', Santa Marina, Péfka, Greece.* Hmmm, an Athens postmark. And look, it's been opened and then re-sealed.'

'I don't understand,' said Elin. 'Why has someone hidden a parcel belonging to Tasia in there? In my section.'

'I have no idea. But I think we should be going, Elin. We'll take the package with us. Decide what to do with it after.'

The paintings rattled on the cart as they dragged it along the rough scree pathway. Elin rested her hand on them until they reached the end of the footpath and was relieved when they reached the road.

'Not far now,' said Stelios. 'Let's hope there'll be no one around to ask any questions.'

But the paintings belong to me! We've done nothing wrong! But they had. Elin knew what he meant. All the materials were included in the school fees she'd paid and she'd painted them, so the paintings were *her* property. But she and Stelios had been trespassing and the sooner the paintings were stored at the wood turner's, the better. As if sensing what the other was thinking, they quickened their pace.

'We'll take them around the back,' Stelios said. 'We'll go in through that door.'

He wheeled the cart into the back of the storeroom and locked the door and the wooden shutters before putting on the light.

'There, they're safe. Come here,' he said, pulling Elin into his arms. 'You're shaking. What is it?'

'We've forgotten something. How are we going to return the cart and how am I going to explain why my storage section is empty?'

Stelios kissed the top of her head. 'I'll think of something. Let's go through to the living room.'

He led the way, holding Elin's hand and they sank down onto the worn leather sofa that had seen better days. She rested her head on Stelios's shoulder and relaxed for the first time that evening. In silence, they sat like that for what seemed to Elin a very long time until Stelios stood up suddenly.

'I've just remembered,' he said. 'Let's see what's in the mystery parcel addressed to my fiancée.'

He left the room and returned holding the package aloft. He prodded it and felt all round it.

'You're not going to open it, surely?'

'Why not? Somebody has already. And if it's what I think it is …'

'You know about that, too, then?'

Stelios nodded. 'About the drugs? I'm just waiting for the right time. After I found out that Anastasia was cheating, I found out that she and Andreas are dealing, too. Their supplies are coming down from Athens.'

'And you think that parcel may contain drugs?'

Stelios peeled back the tape that had been loosely pressed back down, careful not to rip the outside packaging. 'Let's see what's inside, shall we? Then we can wrap it back up and post it in the post box outside her villa.'

With great care, he pulled out a small cardboard box and opened it up, placing it on the sofa between them. Inside were phials of colourless liquid and packs of orange tablets.

'I knew it! You know the night of the party you saw me on *The Palinourus*? Well, I guessed something was up then. Andreas kept talking about taking a trip to meet up with a friend and making comments to Tasia that she'd have to keep tabs on him. It was obviously an in-joke because she thought it very funny.'

Elin took out one of the phials.

'Trip. Tabs. This is LSD! The hippie drug. Orange sunshine! I had a friend in college who took it all the time.'

Stelios sat back on the sofa. 'How on earth did they get mixed up in this? It will break Mamá's heart. I don't care about Anastasia anymore but I do care about what happens to my brother. I'll give him a warning that he has to stop or I'll report him to the police.'

'You're a good man, Stelios. After what he's done to you, you still want to protect him. I saw him in a fight with someone. Down at Agios Georgios.

Hadn't seen the man before but he was shouting that Andreas owed him money. It looked nasty.'

Elin felt sorry for Stelios. She had to tell him everything.

'The night Andreas attacked me, Brad and Manos saw him rowing with the same man at a bar in the harbour and then the man went storming off onto *The Palinourus.*'

'*Vlákas!* Idiot. He'll get what's coming to him. Why does he act like this?'

Stelios slammed his fist into an open palm.

'Do you know someone called Tom? He's English I think. He owns a huge yacht moored over in Porto Nikos. I got talking to him. Or rather he talked to me,' she said, remembering the brash yacht owner.

Stelios shook his head. 'There are lots of huge yachts moored over there.'

'No, I know. What was it called? Um, the *Aurora*. Yes, that was it. Once I said I was here at the painting school, his attitude changed. He warned me off. He was pretty scathing about Andreas and Tasia. Said Andreas never pays up. Well, the *Aurora* and *The Palinourus* have the same logo. You don't think he's something to do with the drug dealers, too, do you?'

Stelios stood up. 'Don't get carried away. Having the same logo means nothing. I'm sure there will be lots of yachts with the same logo. The same boat yard, perhaps. But you're right. Something's going on. It sounds as if my stupid brother has some enemies out there so he'd better watch himself, I say.'

He poured them both an ouzo.

'Come on. Let's forget about Andreas. I want to spend time talking with my *friend* and finding out more about her.' He raised his glass. '*Ya mas*. To our *friendship*!'

Elin knew from the way he smiled and emphasised 'friendship' that sometime soon that would change. And she would be ready.

'*Ya mas.*'

Elin returned to the painting school the next day and was determined to produce her best paintings as the date of the exhibition drew closer. Andreas kept a polite and professional distance from her. He helped when she asked for his advice but never reverted to the old familiarity he showed to the others. With the help of the detailed sketches in her diary and another visit there, her new painting of the lighthouse was bigger and better than the one that had been slashed. If Andreas did know anything about who had destroyed it, he never mentioned it. Perhaps she would never know. After confiding in Brad and Manos about what she had done with her paintings, they had stacked some of theirs where Elin's had been stored so no one else knew that hers had been removed.

'Listen, everyone. We have to talk about the exhibition. It's not long. I want to tell you about the arrangements for getting your paintings down to the harbour …'

Elin didn't hear anymore. Her heart thumped. *Shit! I forgot all about the cart. I need to get it back up here before Andreas misses it.*

'But we cannot carry them all the way down to the boat,' someone asked.

'No, I've arranged with the carriage people to come here with three taxis. They do it every year. They take out the seats and we fill the carriages with your paintings. We'll be waiting in the harbour to transfer them onto the boat. No problem the other end. Brad has said we can use his camper van over there.'

Everyone returned to their painting.

'What you gonna do?' Brad whispered. 'We'll talk at coffee time.'

The next hour dragged and Elin went over in her mind how she could return the cart and explain her missing paintings. They may be safe in Stelios's storeroom but what was the point of that if she had to admit she'd broken into the studio … with Stelios? The newly formed truce between her and his brother would be over!

'Time to break for coffee. You've all worked hard. You deserve one. Elektra, that sunset is amazing. I love the way it enhances the silhouette shape of the lighthouse. Well Done!'

Andreas gushed his words and Elektra simpered, looking over at Elin. Everyone walked to the door.

'Bit of a – how do you say? – coincidence that she paints the same scene as yours, eh?' said Manos. 'I still think it is her.'

'Not a patch on yours, though, honey.'

Elin smiled to herself and found a seat in the shade with Manos and Brad away from the others. But then she remembered her problem and frowned. 'I have to get that cart back.'

'Brad and me, we do it. You have worries to get your paintings down to the boat. Andreas, he must not know.' Manos looked at Brad who agreed.

'But what if you two get caught? I can't let you risk that.'

'Look, honey, we'll come to the wood turner's tonight once it's dark and take it back. We know how to get in here the same as you did. Just arrange it with Stelios.'

Andreas stood up and called everyone back to work. His eye was still swollen but the dark red bruising had faded to a bluish-purple, in places surrounded by a yellow tinge. Every time Elin looked at him it was a reminder of what Stelios had done and brought back memories of a night she'd prefer to forget.

'I was saying, just arrange it with Stelios,' repeated Brad.

'Sorry. Yes, I will. I'll call on the way home after class.'

Chapter Seventeen

Elin had been calling on Stelios most evenings. They were still good friends but it was getting harder and harder not to fall into his arms instead of sitting chastely next to him as they enjoyed each others' company. Stelios had made her two promises. He'd go and see Anastasia and officially break off their engagement and then visit his mother to tell her.

'Elin! What brings you here this early in the evening?' Stelios beamed at her as she entered the workshop. 'Nothing's wrong I hope. Go on up. I was going to shut the shop and lock up now anyway. It's nearly 6 o'clock and it's been very quiet today.'

When he joined her in the living room, Elin noticed four deep scratches down his left cheek.

'Oh, no! What's happened? Who did that to you?' She went over to Stelios and gently touched his face. The skin was rough where the blood had crusted over. 'You poor love.'

'Let's say she didn't take it well. I asked her to meet me here last night after I shut the workshop. Telling my mother was worse. Before she heard from anyone else, I went over in my motor launch this morning. Said I was a disgrace to the family. What would the Loukas family think?'

'What! She expects you to still marry that woman when she's carrying on with your brother! In other words, turn a blind eye?'

'Blind eye?'

'Pretend it's not happening. What did Anastasia say? Deny it?'

'She laughed. Said she just wanted some fun before the wedding. She thought there was no harm in it. When I said it was over for good, she went mad. Screaming, kicking and then this,' said Stelios, rubbing his cheek.

Elin clenched her fists. 'What a bitch! Aaargh! I'd like to do the same to—'

Stelios grabbed her wrists. He brought his open mouth onto hers and kissed her hungrily. She pulled away.

'—her face. Wow.'

'I've been wanting to do that for weeks, Elin Morgan. Nothing can stop us now. I just didn't want you involved in the rows.'

He took her face between his hands and kissed her with tenderness. Then he planted little butterfly kisses on her skin, starting at her lips, moving along her neck and finally nuzzling on her earlobe. She caught her breath and moaned softly.

'And I've been *waiting* for weeks, too.'

'Let's go somewhere where I can show you what I've been wanting to do.'

Stelios took Elin's hand and led her into his bedroom. It was cool and shady there and the cotton crocheted curtains shifted in the warm breeze that wafted into the room. He sat on the edge of the bed and pulled her over to him. They fell back together and kissed again, gently to start with but more passionately as their feelings intensified. She felt him harden beneath her.

Stelios slid his hand under Elin's shirt, seeking her nipples, already erect anticipating his touch.

'It is what you want?' He kissed her again on her neck.

'More than anything.' She nodded. She helped him slide her top over her head and lay watching him gaze at her small firm breasts, admiring her pale skin, so different from his own.

'You are very beautiful. Your skin is like alabaster.'

They removed each item of the other's clothing until they were lying naked in each other's arms. She sought out Stelios's lips and they kissed. She felt him gently probe her mouth with his tongue; she'd never experienced such intense feelings before. With Richard, lovemaking had been mechanical. Over before it got going. But lying there with Stelios was sensual, every fibre of her body coming alive. Her skin prickled with excitement. Fine shocks like electricity fizzled along her limbs from the ends of her fingers to the tips of her toes. Their kisses became more passionate, more urgent, until they finally lost themselves in a pleasure they'd both wanted for so long.

Once it was over, they lay together deep in thought. It was Stelios who broke the silence.

'Happy?'

'Couldn't you tell?' Elin giggled. 'What about you?'

He turned his face to hers and kissed her slowly with such tenderness that the now familiar sensations re-surfaced. 'What do you think? But I couldn't tell. Perhaps we need to find out again.'

Elin sat up and grinned. 'No, I'd better be going. Otherwise, Vassilis and Dimitra will be sending out a search party.'

Stelios propped himself up onto one elbow, head on hand and watched her get dressed.

'You didn't tell me why you called in early today. We became a bit distracted didn't we?'

'You could say that. I came to tell you that Brad and Manos are going to call for the cart tonight and return it to the storeroom when Andreas is out.'

She told Stelios of the plans to get the paintings for the exhibition over to Porto Nikos by boat.

'Andreas will know then my paintings aren't there with the others.'

By then, Stelios had dressed and was standing next to the window.

'Leave it with me. I'll think of something. Perhaps tonight I'll confront my brother about his drug dealing and give him one more chance before informing the police. I'll find him in one of the bars by the quay and that will give you and the boys plenty of time to get the cart. I'll put it outside at the back.'

'Thanks, Stelios. Good luck. I know how much stopping Andreas means to you.'

Stelios took her in his arms and they walked down into the workshop.

'Oh, I nearly forgot. While I was thinking about you this afternoon, I made you this. It's only small but made with love.'

Stelios held up a wooden heart pendant, suspending it on its long leather chain from his fingers. Elin took it from him and felt the silky smooth olive wood shape.

'It's beautiful. I love it.'

She stood on tiptoe and kissed him.

'Here, let me' He placed the pendant over her head and stood back to admire it. 'See, my heart resting by your heart when we are apart.'

Elin clutched the wooden heart.

'Oh, Stelios. I'm so happy.'

'Someone looks very pleased with herself.'

Vassilis was sitting by the entrance to his taverna. Lyra was playing with her kitten on the flagstone at his feet.

'Hello, Vassilis. Hello, Lyra.'

The little girl looked up and smiled then resumed playing with Cleo. The bundle of grey fur chased a ball of wool that Lyra pushed away from her every time the little cat got close.

'It is to do with my good friend Stelios Simonides, eh?'

Elin felt warmth flushing up her neck. *Is it that obvious?* She wanted to shout it from the rooftops that she and Stelios were in love.

'I hear he tells that woman who cheats that the wedding does not happen. We say he does not marry her. She is a bad woman. Everyone on the island says the Loukas family is good but no, I say the truth.'

'Who is bad woman, Papa?'

'Oh dear. I forget there are little ears here.'

Elin pulled up a chair closer to Vassilis.

'Lyra, you go inside and tell Mamá Elin is here for her supper.' The little girl trotted off inside with the tiny kitten in tow.

'Yes, he told her. And his mother. He's going to see Andreas tonight and warn him to stop the drugs. Otherwise, he's going to the police,' said Elin in a whisper.

'I wish good luck. Andreas will not change. His mother sorts his mess for many years. You know about Lyra, eh? Shh. She comes back.'

'Mamá say soon.'

Elin looked at the little girl and it dawned on her why those velvety brown eyes of hers looked familiar. She was Andreas's child. It all fitted. Dimitra's comment about not letting Andreas bully her like her sister did. No wonder Dimitra's mother reacted like she did to Stelios when she thought he was his brother.

Lyra went back inside.

'Sofia Simonides say to Dimitra's mamá not to say who is the father of the baby. We thought we could not have children so we say Lyra is our daughter. The Simonides family help us buy this place. Dimitra's mamá say Andreas ruins her youngest daughter's life. In Greece, we say, "dirty goods". Lyra is *our* daughter now and we love her as much as Yiannis. She does not need to know.'

Elin reached across and squeezed the older man's hand.

'Here is the food. Moussaka and plenty of greens, they make you strong,' said Dimitra, placing the plate of steaming food in front of Elin.

'She needs it when Sofia Simonides knows her son loves our pretty art student.' He laughed out loud and Elin blushed for a second time.

'That is very good. You and Stelios, you are made for each other. It is Stelios, eh?'

'Dimitra!' Vassilis and Elin shouted out in unison.

'I tease you. You do not love the other son, the one who chases many women.'

It was dusk when Elin walked down to the quayside and met Brad and Manos in their usual bar.

'You look good tonight, honey. Beer all right for you?' Brad asked.

'Thanks. Have either of you seen Stelios down here with Andreas?' said Elin.

Manos nodded in the direction of the bar at the far end of the quay where the two Simonides brothers were deep in conversation.

'Right, that means the coast is clear. Stelios has left the cart round the back of the wood turner's so you two can get it back up to the studio while he keeps Andreas talking. You know where the key is, don't you?'

Brad and Manos drank their beers and walked away leaving Elin alone. The conversation between Stelios and Andreas increased in volume, and she could soon hear what they were saying.

'It's nothing to do with you what I do!' Shouting, Andreas stood and pushed back the chair. It crashed onto the marble slabs behind him. 'What are you going to do? Beat me black and blue again?'

Stelios kept his voice quieter and Elin was only able to catch a few words. One of them was 'Mamá' and something about the police. Dimitra had been right. Andreas Simonides would never change nor heed his brother's warning. But would Stelios be able to go through with it and inform the police that his own brother was dealing in drugs?

Stelios walked towards Elin's table and sat down. His face was flushed and he clenched his fists.

'Aarggh! He's impossible. I've tried to warn him. If he wants to get mixed up with low-life, he must suffer the consequences. For everyone's sake, he has to be stopped. He deserves everything that's coming to him. Come on, let's see if the boys are back and I'll tell you my plan for getting your paintings across to the mainland.'

Elin and Stelios walked side by side up from the harbour towards the workshop. He took her hand and smiled.

'Are you sure? It will soon get round this place. Everyone knows everybody else's business. Reminds me of back home in Wales.'

'Let them talk away. You're my girl now, and I'm free to love whoever I like.' He stopped walking and pulled her towards him. 'And I do love you, Elin. I want to shout it to Athens and back!'

He took her in his arms and kissed her long and hard. They broke apart when they heard a long loud whistle. Brad and Manos were walking towards them.

‘So you two have got it together at last,’ said Brad, grinning. ‘About time, too, eh, Manos?’

‘You look very happy,’ said Manos. ‘And now we know why, eh?’

Elin felt her cheeks redden and quickly changed the subject back to whether the handcart had been returned to the studio.

‘I’ve been talking to one of my friends who’s been taxiing people and their belongings down to the harbour for years,’ said Stelios. ‘He’s going to collect Elin’s paintings from here and stack them with yours on the quayside as Andreas’s man makes repeated journeys back and forth from the studio. My brother won’t suspect anything.’

Brad looked at Manos. ‘But what if someone sees your friend calling here? The other taxi drivers will notice as they make their journeys to and from the studio, surely?’

‘We’ve thought of that,’ said Stelios. ‘Stavros will say he’s helping Andreas out too as there are many paintings to move. In fact, Stavros did it last year.’

The boys didn’t look convinced but Elin trusted Stelios. Andreas must never know what she’d done.

‘It will work, boys.’ She paused. ‘It will have to.’

She tried to sound convincing but her heart raced as she imagined what would happen if it didn’t.

Chapter Eighteen

The weeks building up to the exhibition were spent finishing the latest paintings and making visits to the town hall building in Porto Nikos where the exhibition was going to take place. During the week before, Andreas allocated wall space and Elin found herself sharing the wall opposite the double doors of the room with Elektra.

'I'm sure that's deliberate. How can two paintings of the lighthouse be displayed side by side … or at least not very far from one another?' complained Elin.

'Don't worry about it. You know who has a lot more to lose than you. Yours is going to make hers look like a school kid's!' Brad soothed.

Elin knew that it would only cause more trouble between her and Elektra but decided she wouldn't say anything to Andreas. *Better not to draw attention to the fact that my paintings are not actually at the studio.*

The day before the opening of the exhibition, Andreas called them all to the centre of the huge hall, and Elektra stood opposite Elin glaring.

'Here are the arrangements for tomorrow,' he said. 'I want some of you up at the studio early.' He started pointing at various students. 'You two will stack the paintings onto the back of the taxis from here and Manos, you and Elektra go straight to the harbour and you will receive them at the quayside.'

Elin's heart raced. *Oh, no. How would her paintings get past Elektra?*

'Are three taxis enough, Andreas?' said Brad. 'It's going to take ages to shift this lot.'

'If you can find another one who's free, the best of luck,' he said. 'Have you seen how many tourists are arriving down there now? But I take your point. I used old Stavros last year. He's pretty slow, though. He may be free. Just charge it to the painting school.'

Elin couldn't make eye contact with either Brad or Manos. Perhaps, Stelios's plan would work after all. No one would suspect that her paintings hadn't come from the studio.

'I shall be over at Porto Nikos to receive the paintings off the boat. Elin Morgan, you'll come with me so be down on the quayside to catch the 9 o'clock boat. On the other side, as I told you, I've arranged for Brad to use his campervan to transport all your precious works of art to the town hall.

You can't miss it. Just remember to wear your sunglasses.' Everyone laughed.

Elin's spirits sank and she felt Elektra's eyes boring into her. Alone with Andreas for all that time was not something she would look forward to but at least he wouldn't be around to see her paintings come from Stelios's apartment and not the art studio.

The rest of the day was spent putting finishing touches to the paintings, checking the cords on the backs of the frames were securely fastened and wrapping them in yards of corrugated cardboard. Andreas floated around the studio like a fussy mother hen, and tempers frayed.

Elin's pulse raced whenever Andreas approached her side of the room and she dreaded him asking her to turn over one of Brad's paintings that she was packing.

'What if he notices these aren't mine?'

'Chill, honey. This is a joint effort, now. We're helping each other, remember? Manos and me have been stocking up on extra card to wrap yours tonight at the workshop. You do the same, okay?'

'Ssh,' said Manos, nodding in the direction of Andreas. 'You must look out.'

She looked up and saw Andreas pointing his finger as if counting around the studio.

'There doesn't appear to be as many pieces as normal. Elektra, check the storeroom is empty, will you?'

Elin felt her pulse race. The call came back that nothing was left.

'Oh, well. We'll soon see when they're hung on the walls of the hall in the morning,' he said, placing his one hand on his brow and dramatically waving the other one in the air. 'I always panic at this stage. Every year I panic. And every year it's a triumph.'

Elektra and several other students laughed.

'Every September, it's the event of the year in Porto Nikos. People travel hundreds of kilometres to see the Simonides Painting School exhibition,' he said. 'And this year will be no different.'

Everyone cheered and applauded but a trickle of apprehension ran through Elin. She dismissed it and returned to the packing. *Tomorrow will be fine,* she told herself.

Elin made her way down to the harbour knowing she'd left her precious paintings wrapped and ready for Stelios to hand over to Stavros. They'd decided that each time the old man passed the wood turner's on the way down from the studio he'd take one or two of Elin's painting and slot them in between the other students' paintings. That way he wouldn't have to leave with a half empty carriage and arouse suspicion.

Andreas was already there with Manos, who took each painting from the parked carriage and walked up the gangplank. Elektra stood nearby watching.

'Well, help the boy, Elektra,' Andreas shouted.

She sauntered over to the taxi carriage and pulled out one of the smaller packages.

'This is one of yours,' she shouted, directing the comment at Elin. She held it over the water pretending she was about to drop it.

'Elektra, stop acting like the fool,' said Manos. 'It is not Elin's. It is mine – the canvas is the same size. If you damage it, you will be killed!'

Elin made her way to the quayside.

'*Kaliméra*, Elin. All ready for spending the day with me?' said Andreas, his eyes boring into her. 'You know, we could make a good team, if only you'd relax a bit in my company.'

Elin glared at him. Even after all that had happened, he was still trying it on.

'I don't think so.'

The journey across to the mainland was uneventful. That morning, the sky was painted a deep cobalt without a blemish of a cloud and the breeze, as the passenger boat chugged over the waves, was enough to cool Elin's cheeks and lift her blonde hair from her shoulders. She wondered how Stelios was getting on, secreting her paintings down to the quayside. She felt her cheeks warm as she remembered their night of lovemaking. How she loved that man!

Her thoughts were interrupted by a very different Simonides brother. They were nearing the busy marina of Porto Nikos.

'I see Brad's van is ready for us when we dock. I'll just start moving the paintings nearer the deck entrance. I may need help with some of the larger ones.'

'Okay. We'll do it between us,' Elin said, but Andreas had organised for one of the crew to help in order to allow him and Elin plus the paintings off the boat first.

'*Efharistó*,' he said to the tanned boatman and spoke rapidly to him in Greek.

Elin's Greek had improved a lot since she'd arrived on the island but Andreas, seeing her puzzled look, told her that he'd explained that they would be busy at the town hall but that two of his students would accompany batches of paintings across from the island on the boat throughout the morning.

'There's Tom now.' Andreas waved at the man standing with Brad by the van. It was the brash Englishman Elin had met before, the one who had warned her not to get involved with Andreas or Anastasia. So what was the connection? Could it be drug dealing from their respective luxury yachts as she and Stelios had suspected?

Tom Reynolds strode over to meet them when the boat docked.

'Hi,' he said offering his hand to Andreas. He turned to Elin. 'And this is Elin, I think.'

'You two know each other?'

'Yes, we met one afternoon when I came to Porto Nikos to do some prep for the exhibition. Tom said he knew you … and Anastasia.' Elin searched Tom's face for a reaction. There was an awkward silence.

'Everyone knows Andreas Simonides,' said Andreas. 'I'm famous around here.'

'Or you could say infamous!' said Tom, and pushed Andreas's left shoulder in a mock fight. Both men laughed.

The paintings were loaded into the back of Brad's van and Elin went with him and Brad to the town hall while Andreas waited for the next boat to arrive with another batch of paintings.

'I thought you didn't approve of my painting tutor. *Or* his partner in crime,' she said.

'I don't know what you mean. He asked me to show your friend, Brad, where to go.'

Elin sighed. Did he think she'd forgotten what he'd said to her? *Nasty piece of work, eh?*

Brad drove down the narrow streets until they came to an open space where a large majestic building stood in a prominent position. The three-storey building had intricate wrought iron railings protecting wooden shutters, opened at exactly the same angles to let in air whilst protecting the rooms from the intense sunlight.

'We'd better get a move on so that I can take the van back for the next load,' said Brad.

One by one they took the paintings into the exhibition hall. They weren't heavy to carry but awkward enough to need the two of them to transport them without fear of damage. Each space of the walls had been labelled with the students' names. Elin unwrapped each painting and stacked them neatly under the appropriate label.

'I don't see anything in your spot yet,' said Brad.

'Mine will be in the next batch, I expect. Look, why don't you two get back to Andreas? I can manage here.'

As they made to leave, Tom held back and went over to Elin, placing a hand on her arm. 'Not a word to anyone but I'm on to Kýrios Simonides and his rich lady friend. I work for the port of Piraeus police and we've had a tip off. Drugs worth thousands of drachmae are moving in and out of the country and we've reason to believe that the two are involved.'

'But I thought you were part of their scene … the luxury yacht, the expensive lifestyle. And you were *very* pally with him back at the port.'

'No way. I'd *never* touch drugs. I've seen too many friends ruined by the stuff … and worse. This is all a cover. Well, that's what I want everyone to think. I'm hoping to get some inside knowledge from the two of them. Remember, not a word.'

Elin warmed to the man who'd annoyed her when she'd first spoken to him. Perhaps he would be the one who could help Stelios get his brother to see sense. But it might already be too late for just a warning. If the set-up was as serious as Tom said, Andreas and Anastasia were already in it too deep.

'You can rely on me. I try to have as little to do with him as I can. He's a creep. A brilliant artist, though. That's the only reason I stay. And as for that woman. What she's done to poor Stelios!

Tom smiled. 'You've fallen for him, haven't you? Hook, line and sinker! I must go. Are you going to be all right on your own?'

Elin nodded. 'I'll carry on unwrapping the paintings. And Tom, please sort out Andreas. I hate what it's doing to Stelios. He says it will break his mother if she finds out he's been dealing.'

'Come on,' shouted Brad.

Tom turned to go.

'Look. I'll do my best but they're devious. You never see them with anything on them. It's all done well away from Péfka apparently.'

Elin thought of the package addressed to Anastasia planted in her locker. Hadn't Stelios said he'd posted it in the Loukas Villa letterbox?

'Maybe try the Loukas Villa,' she said. 'Andreas will be waiting for you; the next passenger boat will have docked by now. I'll tell you when you get back.'

More and more paintings arrived at the hall and finally Andreas entered the large room with the rest of the students. Elin's talk with Tom would have to wait.

'Gather round everyone. We've now to hang the paintings. Remember what I said about the spaces in between being as important as the pictures themselves. Pick one piece to be your focal point for the whole display of your work. Once the exhibition opens in the morning, it's tradition for the Mayor of Porto Nikos to choose one painting as the winner.' Andreas swept his arm around the room in his usual flamboyant, dramatic way. 'This year, I'm glad I don't have to do the judging. It could be any one of you. The standard is very high.'

Elin stood back checking that her paintings were well spaced and she admired the largest painting, her major work. It was of the solitary olive tree found growing out of the sand. She'd painted it first in watercolour as a small version of what she knew she wanted to be her focal piece. It was her best work ever, because it captured the very essence of the ancient tree with its long history, witnessing the saplings behind in the olive grove evolve into trees providing the livelihood of fruit and oils. Elin had travelled across to the mainland to make sketches, knowing that behind that part of the beach was the Simonides' family home where she'd danced with her handsome Greek on the night of the party. Sometimes she'd day-dreamed that Stelios was waiting, sat under the canopy of grey-green leaves and resting his head back on the rough gnarled bark. His face would break into a beaming smile as she approached. He'd stand and lead her up the path alongside the olive trees, through the garden brushing against the fragrant jasmine and into the cool of the house.

'Elin Morgan. Did you hear what I said?' Andreas was walking over in her direction. 'I said you've captured that olive tree perfectly. I didn't know you knew that part of the beach that well.' Elin willed herself not to blush.

When Elin got back to the taverna, she couldn't settle. She knew everything was ready for the morning. Stelios had managed to get all her paintings down to the quayside without suspicion but something wasn't right. Perhaps writing her thoughts about the day in her diary would help.

September 8th

Trying to get excited about tomorrow. I'll be fine once the exhibition opens but my stomach is all in knots. I was just the same before my finals at the end of college and that turned out okay, didn't it? But there's one difference now. Dad was there to support me then. He and Mam were so proud the day they came to see that exhibition. He grew six inches in stature when they read out our names. He'd say it was just nerves. 'Do your best, cariad. That's all you can do.'

Chapter Nineteen

The exhibition opened early the next morning and very soon the town hall was full of people. Andreas had asked all the students to be present and on hand to answer questions about their work. If they were in agreement, people could buy their paintings and a percentage of the sales would be given to Simonides Painting School. No painting could be removed from the exhibition hall until the end of the afternoon but could be reserved with a red sticker. Andreas had called on his mother and young sister to oversee the sales.

'What if they want to talk to me in Greek?' Elin said to Brad and Manos. 'I don't know any technical language if they want to talk about my paintings in any detail.'

'Don't worry. You know the word for "wonderful", *"ypérochos"*,' joked Brad.

'Ha, ha.'

Manos laughed, too. 'Elin, your paintings *are* wonderful. If you do not understand, I stay by you. Brad is right. They will love your work. The olive tree is very beautiful.'

Elin hugged the young Greek. 'Aww, that's lovely of you. I don't know what I'd have done if you and Brad hadn't been here for me. On the first plane home, I expect. Oh no, don't look now but Elektra's coming over.'

The photographic style of Elektra's painting was in complete contrast to the freedom of Elin's. There was no doubt she was very talented. From a distance, the seascapes she specialised in could have been taken with an expensive camera. It was only when you went closer you could see the intricate brush work and her amazing eye for colour that it was clear they were paintings. Apart from one piece. The painting of the lighthouse would not have looked out of place amongst Elin's works of art. The brushwork and the colours of sunlight she'd painted on the hexagonal building were virtually a replica of those on Elin's slashed painting. And yet hadn't Elektra denied she was to blame? 'Many details on the olive tree,' she said. 'You visit many times to study it.'

The girl with her giggled and they walked over to where Andreas was talking to his mother. Elin clenched her fists and her nails dug into her skin.

Why does that girl always have this effect on me? And Andreas would have to have put us together!

As if reading her thoughts, Brad said, 'Don't rise to the bait, honey. The big man has done you a favour putting you two on the same wall. Yours are much better … and Elektra knows it. Oh, and talk of the devil. Here he comes now with the Town Mayor. Good luck, I'd better get back to my paintings.'

Maya stood with Elektra in front of her lighthouse painting, looking up at the picture and then back to Elin. Both girls laughed. At that moment, Elin remembered Maya's flushed neck, the break in eye contact and how she was in such a hurry to get away when she'd confronted Elektra about destroying her canvas. She'd got the wrong culprit! Elektra may not have known anything at the time but Elin was sure she did now. Maya would do anything for her best friend, wouldn't she?

By the end of the afternoon, the Mayor had visited each display and talked to every student. Andreas introduced him to the assembled crowd of people, many of whom had been there for most of the exhibition or had come back and forth during the day. Red stickers adorned many of the paintings and every one of Manos's had been sold.

'Well done, Manos. You deserve to have sold them. You've worked very hard,' said Elin.

'*Efharistó*. I hope I now paint for a living when the course ends. I do not want to return to my father's shop.'

'You will. You're a natural. What are your plans, Brad? We've only got three weeks left now.'

'Not sure. Maybe bum around a few more islands as long as I can take Betsy onto their roads. Definitely not ready to go back to the States. I kinda like this place.'

Before Elin could tell the boys that she was dreading leaving Greece, Andreas called everyone to attention and introduced the Mayor. Manos stood between Elin and Brad and translated what the man said.

'He say it is a big honour for him to choose the winning painting again. He say Andreas is a brilliant teacher. Many visitors come to Porto Nikos every year to see the paintings. The town owes him a lot.'

'Shhh!' said Elektra, glaring at the trio who stood behind her.

Elin noticed Tom Reynolds who was standing to the side of their row. He raised one eyebrow and Elin smiled.

'And now for the moment you've all been waiting for, the student whose painting has achieved the accolade of the gold award.' Andreas repeated the announcement in Greek.

'Mayor?'

All Elin heard was ' ... *elyóthentro* (the olive tree) and Elin Morgan.' The crowd erupted with applause and Brad and Manos took turns to hug her. Elektra looked around and faced her in stony silence.

'Elin come forward to receive your award, *efharistó*,' Andreas was saying. Elin made her way to the stage. As she passed Tom, he shook her hand and gave her congratulations, but there was one man who'd just arrived in the room whose approval would mean more than the whole crowd of onlookers put together. Stelios stood at the back of the room and beamed at her.

The Mayor handed a large golden cup to Elin and shook her free hand, congratulating her. '*Syncharitíria*.'

Elin returned to her place and noticed there was now a red sticker on her winning painting. Sofia Simonides had moved to stand in front of Elektra and Elin's paintings. She glowered at Elin and placed a sold sticker on the lighthouse painting on Elektra's half of the wall, staying to talk with the Greek girl.

Elektra and Sofia Simonides huddled together, speaking in rapid Greek. The volume of their conversation rose until Kýria Simonides turned and shouted at Elin. Andreas and Stelios hurried to where the argument was taking place.

Elin knew that Elektra had said something to anger the older Greek woman and that it involved her.

'Manos. What's going on? What is she saying?'

Manos coloured. 'She calls you – how do you say? a ... whore. You meet her son for love when he is to marry another woman. He takes you to the *Ee Eliés* family home. The painting is proof.'

'But anyone can go on that beach. It's a public place!'

Elin hadn't been into the house alone with Stelios. She'd often imagined what it would be like to make love in a wide king-sized bed so different from the single bunk in the wood turner's apartment, but Elektra didn't know that, did she?

Andreas put his arm around his mother and guided her away. Kýria Simonides was now sobbing uncontrollably and still shouting so loudly that everyone in the hall had stopped their own conversations in order to watch the spectacle. First, Stelios came to Elin's side and then moved on to the stage to make an announcement.

'I think it's best if you all go now, thank you. Thea, my sister, will deal with your purchases for collection and if you pay her, Andreas will settle with the students themselves. I'm sure my brother would want me to thank you for your support again this year.'

He came back to Elin. 'Don't upset yourself. My mother had no right to speak to you like that and especially in front of all those people. I don't know what else Elektra said to her for her to be that vicious. She's had it in for you from the start, hasn't she? Come here, *agapi mou*.'

After calming his mother and leaving her with Thea, Andreas returned to the group.

'Well you two ruined the day, didn't you? Mamá is completely distraught. She says you can go to your little Welsh girl, if that's what you want. She wants nothing more to do with you.'

Stelios went red in the face and made to grab his brother by the throat. 'Why, you …'

Elin screamed. 'Stelios, no! He's not worth it. Let's get my paintings and go.'

Stelios moved back to Elin's side. 'You are right. I will help you.'

There was only one left unsold, but Elin's winning painting remained, waiting to be collected. Who could have bought it? Maybe they'd changed their mind.

Tom Reynolds was waiting outside the building and helped Elin, Brad and Manos put any unsold paintings in the camper van to take back to the marina. Stelios kissed Elin goodbye and told her he'd catch up with her later after he'd helped clear up the hall.

'You're still helping Andreas after all he's put you through?'

'Look, I don't want the people of Porto Nikos saying the Simonides family leave the place in a mess for others to clear up. I'm not doing it for him … Besides, I do it every year. Come up to the apartment at seven. Tell Brad and Manos to come, too.'

Elin sat in the passenger seat alongside Tom.

'That was some scene from Mamá Simonides,' said Tom. 'She can't see any wrong in her eldest son, but poor old Stelios …'

'She's happy to condone Andreas carrying on with Anastasia because she's Greek and her family's well connected,' said Elin.

‘These Greeks, a funny lot,’ said Brad, looking in the rear mirror from the driving seat. ‘Sorry, Manos.’

Manos laughed. ‘I am very cross, too. Elektra is a bad girl and she is very jealous. Her face, it is angry when she hears your name, Elin.’

Elin felt uneasy. She wished she hadn’t won the damned cup. It would be too big to fit in her rucksack when she went home, anyway. And she’d had to leave her favourite painting there in case the buyer turned up.

Brad parked the van and Tom helped the boys unload the paintings.

‘Elin, can I have a word?’ said Tom. ‘What did you have to tell me about Anastasia?’

They walked away from the others. Elin told him everything she knew about the planted package of LSD that Stelios had re-posted to her, the row down at Agios Georgios between Andreas and another man and then the argument where a different man stormed off from Andreas down at the harbour and boarded *The Palinourus.*

‘Stelios has warned him, telling him that it will break his mother’s heart but he just won’t listen. In spite of everything his brother has done, Stelios is still a family man and will do anything to keep that intact.’

‘Even give you up? It doesn’t look as if his mother will accept he’s fallen for you.’

Elin felt her heart sink. She knew what Tom was saying was true. ‘I know that. But I’ll be going home soon. The exhibition is the highlight of the course. Andreas says we can spend the last few weeks painting for fun without the pressure of exhibiting. ’

How could she return to Wales and never see Stelios again? Their love was doomed, over before it began. Nausea washed over her. How she wished things could be different. Richard’s face came into her mind.

‘Are you all right? You’ve gone as white as a sheet.’

‘Yes, it’s just been a long day. The boat’s about to leave. What do you want me to do?’

‘You can tell Stelios it’s not his place to protect his brother any longer. Leave it to us. I shall be on *The Palinourus* tonight and if we can actually catch them handing over the gear or see money passing hands, we’ve got them.’

Elin looked over to Brad and Manos carrying the last of the unsold paintings onto the boat. ‘Understood. Andreas will get what’s coming to him.’

The horn signalled that the boat was about to leave and Elin rushed to get on the passenger boat before the gangplank was raised just as Brad disembarked to drive Betsy over to the communal car park. The van became a dot on the edge of the marina and Elin joined Manos.

'You speak very seriously with the man who is English, Elin. You have met him before today, eh?'

Elin tapped the side of her nose and said, 'All will become very clear very soon. Call up at the wood turner's tonight about seven. Bring Brad with you. Stelios will be back by then.'

The boat bobbed along under the sky, streaked pink and apricot in the low sun, and soon they were disembarking on the quayside on Péfka.

'Thanks, Manos, for all your help today. I'll see you later.'

Chapter Twenty

At the end of the exhibition, only one of Elin's paintings remained unsold. It was the one she'd re-painted of the lighthouse. She wasn't surprised. It had been overshadowed by Elektra's of the same subject; her painting formed the focused piece for her display. But Elin loved her own smaller version and she knew exactly who she'd give it to. It was light enough to carry up to the taverna herself.

'Vassilis, Dimitra. You'll never guess. You won't believe it. I can scarcely …'

The taverna was deserted when Elin rushed into the cool dark bar and Dimitra, baby in her arms, hurried through from the back.

'What has happened? You must slow down. What is it that we will not guess?'

By that time, Vassilis was at his wife's side.

'I won. I won the gold award!' Elin thrust her cup in front of her. She placed the small painting on an oil-clothed table. 'My name is going to be engraved on this cup and I can keep it for a year!'

'That is such good news. You are very clever,' said Dimitra, coming over to hug Elin.

'Well done. You have worked hard and we are very proud of you. Eh, Dimitra?'

Elin remembered the look on her parents' faces when the post had arrived with her A-level results and recognised the same pride in her Greek hosts. Her throat tightened and she felt her eyes burn. She wished her dad was still there to hear her news.

'Look, I won't be in Péfka to give it back next year and I want you both to have it here. Display it where you want to. If it wasn't for you both giving me a home here, I doubt if I would have stayed long.'

Dimitra handed baby Yiannis to his father and took the cup from Elin. 'It will be here in the bar to show we are very proud. When you go home, every time I polish it I think of our lovely Welsh guest.'

Elin's eyes did fill with tears then. She had grown to love the Guikas family as if they were her own.

'Here, I want you to have this …' Elin picked up her painting and handed it to Dimitra. 'This is for you to keep. To remind you of why I was here staying with you.'

Dimitra took the parcel, undid the string and unwrapped the painting from the cloth and corrugated cardboard. She gasped.

'Look, Vassilis. It is the lighthouse. We go there before we marry. To be alone.' Dimitra beamed at Vassilis and turned to Elin. 'It is beautiful. You paint the amazing sunset.'

Elin was pleased that her lighthouse painting hadn't sold. She could never have anticipated how much it would mean to Dimitra and Vassilis.

It was a few minutes before seven o'clock when Elin left the taverna to meet Stelios.

'You look very beautiful tonight,' said Vassilis.

'Thanks. I'm just going up to Stelios. He wants to see Brad and Manos, too. I won't be late back.'

The two boys were walking up from the harbour and Elin waited for them.

'I do not know why Stelios wants to see us,' said Manos.

'Yeah, thought he'd prefer some time alone with his latest love.'

'Shh,' said Elin. 'Look who's coming down the hill. Not a word, either of you.'

Anastasia Loukas looked immaculate as always. Her expertly applied make-up looked natural enough to show the glow of her tanned olive skin while accentuating her velvety brown eyes and full red lips. She wore a white linen tunic that floated behind her as she walked.

Ignoring Brad and Manos, she stared in Elin's direction. '*Kalispéra.* You are calling on my ex-fiancé tonight, I see. I will not tell his mamá,' she said with a scoff. She walked past them.

'That woman! What did Stelios ever see in her?'

They knocked on the door of the wood turner's studio and heard footsteps on the other side.

'*Kalispéra*. Come in, come in.' Stelios kissed Elin on both cheeks. 'I'm pleased you both came, too. I need to tell you something and hope you can help. Go on up into the living room.'

The soft light from two table lamps gave the room a cosiness that Elin loved when it was just the two of them. Tonight, it wasn't right somehow. It was as if Brad and Manos were invading her space, the private space she shared with Stelios.

'Sit down, please. What will you have to drink? Retsina for you, Elin?'

'Beers will be fine, thanks.' Brad answered for them both and Elin nodded.

While Stelios went out to get the drinks, Manos was the first to speak. 'I do not know what he is going to tell us, eh?'

'Me neither,' agreed Brad.

Stelios returned with a tray of drinks and sat on the sofa next to Elin.

'I expect you're wondering why I've asked you here. Elin has told you about my brother and Anastasia Loukas being involved with drugs.'

Elin looked at the boys. 'Yes, I told them about the package that had been planted in my storage area up at the studio and they were with me at Agios Georgios when Andreas got into that argument. And, you know that British bloke? Well, I found out that he's not another drug dealer. He's working under cover for the port police in Piraeus. He's posing as a drug taker to catch Andreas and Anastasia.'

The boys sat back on their seats. 'Whew! So it's not just them supplying a few friends and the awful Elektra with a bit of LSD then. This real dealing,' said Brad.

'But, are you sure that guy, Tom, is genuine, honey? Seems a bit strange to me unmasking himself like that.'

Elin's pulse suddenly raced. What if she'd been taken in?

Stelios put his head in his hands. '*Vlákas*! The idiot is in far deeper than I thought. I've tried talking to him. Pleading with him but it's no good. It will break Mamá. Her precious boy is not the admirable son she thinks he is.' He stood up and started pacing around the room. 'My mind's made up. I'm going to make sure he and that ex-fiancée of mine both get what's coming to them. Before someone gets hurt. Dies, even.' Stelios sat down again, and turned his clenched right fist into his left palm, his knuckles white.

'How do we help you?' asked Manos.

'He won't be down at the harbour tonight. I heard him telling Mamá and Thea he'd be staying with them.'

'So Tom will have a wasted journey, then,' said Elin.

'Yes, but in the morning when he opens up the studio, I want you to ask him to supply you with some LSD.'

'No way. We don't touch the stuff.' Brad shook his head and looked at Manos in disbelief.

'I live near here, Stelios. Please do not forget. I do not want people thinking I take drugs.'

'I know it's a lot to ask but if we know he's coming to meet you, I can tip off Leo about it. They just need to catch them in the act.'

'Who's Leo?' asked Elin.

'Leo Giannopoulos. He's a detective based here on Péfka.'

Elin's pulse raced again. What if it went wrong and her friends were implicated in something they didn't do? But Stelios resorting to informing on his own brother would not be a decision he'd taken lightly.

'It's too risky,' she said.

'I promise you, Leo will know it's a trap. If it's going to pay off, I'll make sure the police know it's all a set-up as far as Brad and Manos are concerned.'

Elin had to trust him. 'We've just seen Anastasia on her way to the harbour, to *The Palinourus* I expect.'

'Yes, and we left Tom down at the quayside, didn't we? How about me and my Greek friend here go down to the taverna and keep our eyes open for what those two get up to? If he's who he says he is, he'll be keeping away from the psychedelic stuff,' suggested Brad.

'Surely, you won't be able to tell by just watching?' Stelios said.

'Boy, I'll know,' said Brad. 'I've witnessed more trips that you've had bowls of moussaka! All the kids back home were tripping. I tried it once. Never again. I had a bad one. Scared the shit out of me. But I'll sure know. Coming, Manos?'

'Thanks, boys. If we can set this up, the whole of Péfka will thank you. It's getting known for the drugs rather than a lovely family place to visit. Just let me know the time and place you arrange with my brother.'

Stelios stood up to let the boys out, locking the door behind them. He came back to the living room and sat down beside Elin. She snuggled up to him and rested her head on his shoulder. Neither of them spoke until Stelios finally broke the silence.

'You know, I can't wait now for Andreas to get what's coming to him. I've given him chance after chance but he thinks he's above the law. He's not. When the police get to him, then perhaps he will be sorry … but Mamá will have her heart broken again.'

For a while, they sat in silence as the seriousness of what was planned sank in. The room grew darker. Shadows from the branches outside the window entered and skittered across the walls, as they blew in the breeze.

Elin turned to face Stelios, took his head in her hands and drew him to her. She kissed him slowly and tenderly and felt him relax.

'Forget about tomorrow. Let's enjoy the moment.'

Their kissing became more urgent and familiar feelings stirred within her. Stelios unpeeled Elin's clothing, piece by piece, until she was lying back on the settee naked. He planted feathery kisses along her neck and down over her left shoulder, along the top of her breast until he reached her nipple. She shivered with pleasure.

'Let's go somewhere more comfortable,' he whispered into her neck. He took her hand and, stepping over the trail of discarded clothes, they went into his bedroom. The bed was scattered with pink rose petals and the curtains were drawn for privacy.

'It looks as if you planned this, you naughty man.'

'I've been planning it all day!' Stelios pulled off all his clothes until they were both lying, skin to skin. Elin sat up suddenly and pointed to the wall opposite the bed.

'It was you! You were the buyer!' She hugged Stelios so tightly he could hardly breathe.

'Hey, you didn't think I'd let the gold award painting go to be hung on any old wall, do you? This way, every time I open my eyes I see the old olive tree that can be our meeting place in future, *agapi mou*. Besides, it's a brilliant work of art.'

Then it was Elin's turn to be held. Stelios moved gently on top of her and they made love with a passion that Elin had never experienced before. Afterwards, they lay in each other's arms, just enjoying being with one another. The sky became dark and the room was bathed with a soft orange glow from the street-lights outside.

'We'd better get dressed,' said Stelios.

Elin planted a kiss on his lips and ran to retrieve her clothes.

They spent the rest of the evening listening to music and talking about what Elin was going to do with the money from the sales of her paintings.

'Once Andreas has taken his cut for the painting school you'll have enough drachmae to buy something nice for yourself. He does have quite a big bill for staging the exhibition over in Porto Nikos, I suppose, but after that it's yours.'

'I don't want you to pay anything for the painting of the olive tree, Stelios. Pay the percentage to Andreas if you have to but that's it. My present to you. I'm flattered that you love it. And I hope that one day soon, I'll be waking up looking at it, too.'

Stelios beamed. 'Stay tonight. We'll wake up to it in the morning.'

'No, not yet, Stelios. I just want Vassilis and Dimitra to get used to the idea. I don't want to be thought of as a loose Welsh woman. They're very traditional, you know, and I wouldn't like to hurt them. They feel responsible for me, I think. But one day, soon. I promise. Oh, no. Is that the time? I promised Vassilis I wouldn't be late.'

Elin kissed Stelios goodnight and rushed back to the taverna.

It was eleven o'clock and Vassilis was about to lock the door.

'You are lucky, eh? Dimitra finds your key on the table by the bar. You put it there when you give us the painting. Otherwise I go up and nothing wakes us.'

Elin smiled. 'Thank you. See you in the morning.'

Chapter Twenty-One

Elin woke with a start the next morning to the sound of loud voices and a motor engine running. Since arriving at the taverna, she'd often heard raised voices outside in the square but in all the three months she'd lodged there the only vehicle she'd heard was the gentler phut-phut of a scooter. She rushed to the window and saw a police van with lights flashing parked on the hill opposite. A man was speaking in Greek to the driver of the van. Elin strained to hear what they were saying but the exchange was so rapid that even if she could have heard more clearly, she wouldn't have understood the Greek. Whatever it was had to be very serious for a motor vehicle to be allowed on the island.

The man crossed the road to speak to Vassilis, who had by then appeared on the street, and pointed up the hill. Vassilis shook his head and seemed to push the man to go, as if there was no time to lose. He rushed back into the van and the driver drove at top speed back in the direction of the harbour. Vassilis sprinted up the hill and went into the wood turner's.

Elin felt nausea mingling with unease flooding through her and she sat back on the bed. Perhaps Tom Reynolds had done what he said he would. Had the police arrested Andreas and Anastasia already? There would be no need for her friends to do anything, after all. She washed and dressed and went down into the bar to see Dimitra.

'Dimitra, what's happened? The police van? And why has Vassilis gone up to see Stelios?'

'I do not know. He hears the noise and goes outside to see what has happened. He does come back here.' She looked past Elin to the door. Vassilis stood there, blocking the light. 'He is here now.'

Vassilis Guikas was spectre-white and his whole body shook. Dimitra and Elin took his hands and guided him to a chair by a table.

'Oh, Vassilis *mou*. I get you a raki to steady the shakes. What has happened?'

For what appeared to be an age, Vassilis just sat there staring into the space in the middle of the bar. He downed the raki and gulped as the burn of the spirit travelled through him.

'It is Andreas.'

'That man! What has he done, now? That is where you have been. He gets his brother to sort out another mess, eh?' said Dimitra, raising her eyebrows.

'Andreas, he has gone.'

'He's left? But what about the painting school? He can't just leave,' Elin said.

'No, you do not understand. Kýria Sofia found him this morning. He is dead. He does not return after he swims at midnight. She looks for him when she sees his bed is not slept in,' said Vassilis. He had a little more colour in his cheeks.

The women gasped.

Dimitra shook her head, wringing her hands. 'That poor woman. She does not cope with another tragedy, eh? How does he die?'

Vassilis walked to the bar and poured himself another raki. 'It is – how do you say? – suicide. He cuts his wrist.'

Elin's eyes widened and her hand shot to her mouth.

'Oh, that is very sad. That is not the Andreas we know. He always enjoys the life. I cannot believe it,' Dimitra said, her voice quiet. 'Sometimes, they hide behind the mask. We do not always know the person. I go to wake the children.'

Vassilis sat back down by Elin.

'Stelios mentioned that Andreas was staying over with his mother and Thea last night. Poor Stelios. I have to go to him,' she said.

'He is not there. He puts the sign in the shop window, *kleistó* – closed. He goes to *Ee Eliés* to be with Sofia and Thea. He does not wait for the boat. He goes in his own motor launch. It is much faster, eh? Poor Stelios. He does not always get on with his brother but … I do not know how to say it in English, "blood is fatter than water"?'

'We say blood is *thicker* than water. Same thing. Stelios is such a family man. He will be heartbroken. I think I'll go up to the studio and tell the others. No more painting lessons for us, now. What a terrible waste.'

Elin walked up the hill and, as she passed Anastasia's villa, she wondered what could have made Andreas take his own life. *If he had*. He'd just had a successful exhibition of his students' artwork. Something wasn't right. The very night the Piraeus police were on to him and Anastasia and then he's found dead. *Who got to him first, I wonder?* Once she turned to walk along the footpath across the cliff top, Elin could see that she wasn't the only one to have heard the news. Her fellow students were congregated on the patio in front of the studio where the shutters remained down. Everyone knew about the key but there wasn't any point in opening up without their tutor.

The mood was sombre and many huddled in groups wanting to talk about Andreas. Elektra sat alone, staring out over the cliff top. Her eyes were puffy and red raw from crying. Every now and then, she would sob. No matter what had happened between them, Elin knew how much Elektra thought of Andreas and walked over to sit beside her.

'I am sorry, Elektra,' she said. 'I know how much he meant to you. No one could have known he was going to do something like this.'

The Greek girl stood up suddenly and pushed Elin from her seat onto the patio.

'I do not want your sorry,' she screamed. 'It is because of you that he is *dead.* You tell his brother about him and Tasia and now he dies. If not, he still teach us. You go back to your country very soon. I hate you, I hate you.' She let out a screeching wail and her friends surrounded her, enveloping her in comforting hugs.

Manos picked Elin up and she rushed to the back of the building where she was violently sick.

'Honey, are you okay? Don't let that bitch get to you.' Brad came over the join them.

'She is kind to her and that is how she is thanked,' said Manos.

'I skipped breakfast, that's all. I'll be fine.' But Elin had a suspicion that she wouldn't. The three friends joined the rest of the group and sat away from Elektra.

'Listen up, everyone,' Brad said. 'We've all had a dreadful shock here this morning. We owe Andreas a lot. I know I'm a much better painter than when I arrived and yesterday was awesome.'

'She makes him die,' shouted Elektra.

'*Skáse*, Elektra.' Elin looked at Manos. 'I told her to shut up,' he whispered.

'As I was saying,' said Brad. 'Why don't we meet down at the harbour tonight and down a few beers, drink a couple of retsinas or tots of raki in his honour? If you'd like, bring flowers in all the colours you can find to float on the water to remind us of how he used to rave about our colour mixing and brush strokes in our seascapes. Until seven o'clock. To Andreas.'

Everyone cheered and applauded just as they had the day before, but that day Andreas Simonides was dead, and killed by his own hand at that. Elin didn't believe that though. She didn't cheer but Brad didn't know what he'd done to her, what he was really like. Andreas *was* a brilliant teacher, popular with his students, and who was she to deny him the accolade Brad had planned?

By the time Elin reached the quayside, most of the art students had congregated along the harbour wall by the water's edge. Brad had appointed himself the organiser of the meeting and stood on one of the stone benches, getting everyone's attention.

'Guys, this is amazing. Andreas would feel very honoured that we've all come here tonight. Before we throw our flowers into the water, would anyone like to share their memories of him?'

Much as Elin didn't want him dead and was as shocked as everyone else that their tutor had taken his own life, the only burning memory she could conjure up was the night he followed her home and attacked her. She closed her eyes and all she saw was an image of his bloodied and bruised face after Stelios had beaten him for what he'd done to her.

Elektra stood up on to the bench next to Brad.

'*Naí*,' she said, her voice breaking. 'Andreas is very good. I come to his classes every year after I leave school. He makes me better painter.' Her voice shook. 'He is the *best*. I … miss him very much.' She sobbed.

Maya helped her down and enveloped her in her arms.

'Thank you, honey. I think we know you two were close. Anyone else?'

In turn, several students shared their thoughts about Andreas. Some were funny anecdotes, others were about more serious moments when they recalled his talent and how he'd helped them improve their techniques. Brad looked over at Elin who was standing at the back of the group. She shook her head.

'Right, if that's everyone, let's form a line along the harbour wall and throw our flowers into the water. Half close your eyes and picture the colours mixed in with the turquoise of the water and imagine it to be one of Andreas's seascapes and his amazing brush work. On the count of three … One, two, three. Throw! To Andreas.'

The low sun caught the vibrancy of the petals as they travelled through the air before landing on the surface of the sea water, a kaleidoscope of colour and a fitting tribute to a man who had inspired his students to take risks with their colour mixing and gain amazing results.

There was a spontaneous applause and the young people broke into small groups, making their way to the various bars and tavernas dotted along the quayside. Elin, Brad and Manos sat at a table in the taverna they usually visited.

'You did well, there, Brad,' said Elin.

Manos agreed. 'Yes, Andreas has many faults – and you know that, Elin – but we owe him a lot. He is a talented painter and a good teacher.'

Elin nodded. 'You're right. My painting has definitely improved and you, Manos, I'm sure you could make a living from your art now.'

Elektra appeared at their table. Elin felt herself tense. What insult was she going to get, she wondered?

'What happens to us, eh?' said Elektra. 'Andreas is dead. Do we go to our house?' Her large brown eyes filled with tears. 'There is no one to teach.' She wandered back to her friends.

'She has a point. What *do* we do? Manos you live just a few kilometres away and you haven't far to go. But me and Elin. We've decisions to make. Change the dates of our flights for a start. Or stay until the end but with no school?'

'It's only a few weeks so I'm staying.' Elin's heart raced. She couldn't leave. Stelios would need her more than ever now. She had to see him. Her thoughts were interrupted by Brad.

'Hey, guys. Haven't you noticed something?' He pointed to the other side of the harbour. '*The Palinourus* has gone. It was definitely there this morning.'

Elin thought back to what Tom Reynolds had told her. He would be on the yacht all weekend trying to get evidence that Anastasia and Andreas were buying and selling drugs from there. And now Andreas was dead and there was no sign of Anastasia. Every time the three friends went down to the harbour, she was always there on the luxury yacht but with *The Palinourus* gone, she was nowhere to be seen.

'Something's not right,' said Elin. 'And where is Tom? You don't think his talk about being undercover was all lies and he was in with them as we thought? You were right, Brad. No *real* undercover cop would tell me, a complete stranger, what he was up to. Aaargh! How stupid can you get? I should have guessed.'

Brad and Manos exchanged glances.

'You don't know anything, yet,' said Brad. 'Let's just wait and see.'

While the friends were speculating about what could have happened, Stelios arrived back at the quayside on his motor launch. He moored the boat in the space left by *The Palinourus* and walked up the hill.

‘I have to see him,’ said Elin. She left Brad and Manos at the taverna and ran after him.

‘Stelios,’ she called.

Chapter Twenty-Two

Stelios turned and Elin ran into his outstretched arms. His face was pale and the sparkle had gone from his eyes.

'Elin, *mou*. It's good to see you.' His eyes were full of anguish. 'It's awful. Mamá and Thea are in a terrible state. I've just come over to get some things. I'll be staying over there now until the funeral.'

Elin pulled him to her and felt his whole body shudder.

'I'm sorry. Everyone says it was suicide. But why? Why would Andreas do that? He was in such a good frame of mind yesterday at the exhibition. It was a huge success.'

Stelios looked at her. 'It wasn't suicide, *agapi mou*. Leo thinks someone murdered him and made it look like suicide.'

'I knew it. I knew he wouldn't have killed himself. It was the drugs, wasn't it?'

They walked together arm in arm and entered the wood turner's.

'We don't know yet. Leo asked me awkward questions for a start.'

'You? Surely not?'

'He knew about the beating I gave him. Said it showed I was capable of violence towards him. I told him I was with you last night. I'm sorry I had to involve you but you are my only alibi.'

'But you *were* with me. I'll tell the police that. And you know *The Palinourus* has gone?'

'Ah, has it? They took my fingerprints and I had to write my address in capital letters like the so-called suicide note was written. Oh, this is such a mess.'

Elin took his face in her hands and kissed him slowly. They stood just holding each other until a knock at the door broke the silence. It was Vassilis.

'Come in, Vassilis. I won't stay long here. I have to get back to Mamá. She's in a dreadful state as you can imagine. I was going to call in later with the keys. I shall have to stay at *Ee Eliés* until this is sorted. I'm sorry.'

Vassilis put his arm around the young man.

'You take as long as you need. What can I do for the family? What do you want to do about the painting school?'

'I hadn't even thought of that. I suppose we should inform the students that it's closed and that they should return home. They must take all their artwork with them. They've paid for all the materials. Elin how many weeks early will it be finishing?'

It dawned on Elin that this was the end for her. She'd have to leave, too. Feeling sick, she ran to the bathroom.

Elin returned to the sitting room and held her arms around herself.

'It is the shock. She does not look well, eh? Elin is at the taverna for another three weeks but she does not want to leave until everything is sorted.'

Elin agreed.

'Are you all right?' asked Stelios.

'I'm fine,' she said. 'I can speak to the other students for you. I'll get Brad and Manos to help. You have enough to worry about. Vassilis, the police don't think it is suicide now.'

'So what do they think happens?' Elin exchanged a look with Stelios.

'They think he was murdered. And we're *all* under suspicion. Leo Giannopoulos is going to be interviewing everyone who had anything to do with Andreas,' explained Stelios.

Stelios disappeared upstairs to pack and left Elin and Vassilis to talk.

'Many people, lots of husbands, want to beat Andreas but kill him, eh? No, *óchi*. It is someone from outside, not local.'

Elin sat closer to the older man and lowered her voice. 'They've taken a statement from Stelios and fingerprints. They asked him to provide a sample of his handwriting, too. I'm his only alibi for last night.'

'But he only needs one, eh? Stelios does not do it. I tell the truth.'

An image of Andreas's battered and bloodied face entered her subconscious. Stelios had been extremely angry that night. She dismissed the idea. No, Vassilis was right and she had to clear Stelios's name.

'It's so unfair. He's mourning the loss of his brother and yet he's under suspicion for killing him. I'll tell the police he was with me all night.'

Stelios entered the living room with a holdall and handed Vassilis the keys to the studio and apartment. 'Here. I don't know when I'll be back, Vassilis. And Elin, Leo Giannopoulos will come to you, I'm sure of it. He told me he'd check out my story with you.'

He pulled Elin towards him and hugged her.

'Don't worry, *agapi mou*. Just tell the truth and everything will be fine. Thank you for helping to sort out the painting school for me.' He shook his head. 'What a mess,' he said again.

Vassilis kissed Stelios on both cheeks and patted his back as he left.

Goodbye, my beautiful Stelios. Elin's eyes burned as she watched the hunched figure she loved very much walk through the door and into the street. She couldn't help but wonder how long it would be before she saw him again. Vassilis locked up the wood turner's and together, he and Elin returned to the taverna.

That night, Elin couldn't sleep. Every time she closed her eyes, she imagined being the one to find Andreas's body. The noise of rustling leaves in the olive trees took on the form of human whispers, sinister and beckoning her to the tree where she'd find him. *He'ssss here, he'ssss here.* Blood dripped down from a gash on his wrist, staining the sand to form a sticky deep wine-red pool at the side of his thigh. His wax-like face was no longer bronzed but had taken on a translucent bluish tinge, his lips almost indigo.

'Noooooo!' she screamed and sat upright in the dark. Her heart slammed in her ribcage. She was bathed in cold sweat.

Dimitra rushed into the room and sat on the bed beside her.

'It is all right. I am here now. You have the *efiáltis* again.'

Elin clung onto her Greek friend.

'Dimitra, I saw Andreas's body. There was so much blood.' She sobbed.

Dimitra continued to hold Elin until her breathing returned to normal and she'd calmed down.

'It is an awful shock. For everyone. The police get who does this. You must not worry. You get some sleep, eh?'

Once Dimitra had left the room, Elin put out the bedside lamp but lay back on her pillow, keeping her eyes wide open. She eventually fell asleep and slept soundly for the rest of the night until sunlight poured in through her curtains. For a moment, she thought it was just like any other day, but then she remembered. A rush of heartache overwhelmed her; sorrow for the Simonides family but mainly sadness for Stelios. She hugged herself tight as she blinked back the tears.

'Elin. Someone, he calls to see you.'

Dimitra's voice echoed up the stairs. Elin was writing in her diary about the events of the day before. She put down her pen and closed the book. Who could be wanting to see her this early in the morning?

She walked into the shadowy bar to see a distinguished looking man, his black hair streaked with grey at his temples, talking to Vassilis.

'This is Leo Giannopoulos. He is the detective who finds out about Andreas.'

The man offered a hand to Elin. 'I am very pleased to meet you, Miss Morgan. My friend Vassilis sings your praises, says you are a very good person.'

Elin blushed. 'Kýrios Giannopoulos. I've been expecting you.'

The detective raised an eyebrow. 'You have, eh?'

Vassilis led the two of them over to a table in the corner. 'You will have quiet time here,' he said.

'Yes, Stelios told me you'd be coming to talk to me.'

Leo Giannopoulos took out a notebook and pen. 'Elin – I can call you that, I hope – tell me everything about the evening of September 9th, two nights ago.'

Elin took a deep breath and began speaking.

'It was the day of the exhibition. We arrived back in Péfka on the 6 o'clock boat. I remember the time because we had exactly an hour before meeting Stelios at his apartment.'

'You say "we"?'

'Sorry, Brad and Manos. They're also students at the painting school. Stelios had asked us all to meet up at seven. He was going to explain the plan to us.'

'Please, you continue,' said Kýrios Giannopoulos. 'What was the plan?'

'Stelios had begged Andreas to give up the drugs. He gave him chance after chance. He was worried about what it would do to his mother. Andreas just laughed in his face. So in the end he was going to inform you about what was going on. He asked a big favour of my friends. The next day, they were going to ask Andreas to supply them with LSD – in the form of orange sunshine tablets and the police could catch him in the act.'

'Why does he ask for those tablets? Why not the other forms of LSD?'

'Because a package of those was planted in my locker in the studio. They weren't mine – I'd never do drugs.'

The detective scribbled away furiously, making a note of everything Elin said.

'The package, where is it now?'

Elin hesitated before answering.

'Stelios sealed it back, readdressed it to Anastasia Loukas and posted in the family's letterbox.'

'What had Miss Loukas to do with all this?'

'She and Andreas were having an affair and dealing drugs together. They were clever and Stelios knew they'd get away with it, unless they were caught handing over the drugs. That's why he asked Brad and Manos to help.'

'Did your friends stay with you and Kýrios Simonides all night?'

'No, they left about 8 o'clock once they had their instructions about what to do.'

'So after that it was just you and Stelios, eh? And you stayed at his apartment all evening?'

Elin nodded, thinking back to the time they'd spent in each other other's arms.

'Does anyone agree with that time? What time did you leave?'

'It was 11 o'clock. I'd forgotten my key and Vassilis was waiting up for me.'

'Thank you. You've been most helpful. Just one more thing.' He pulled out an item from a bag. It was a knife with a long blade that had mud caked on its blade. It was sealed in a transparent polythene bag. 'Do you recognise this?'

Elin felt the hairs on the back of her neck prickle. She clenched her fists. She knew exactly where she'd seen it.

'Miss Morgan?'

'I may have seen one like it.'

'And …?'

'It's like one that Stelios uses to trim the underneath of his wooden bowls.' In horror, she realised that it wasn't mud, but blood.

She dashed to the bathroom and retched.

When she returned to the bar, Leo Giannopoulos was talking to Vassilis.

'I'm sorry about that,' said Elin. 'I must have eaten something that didn't agree with me.'

The two men exchanged glances.

'I tell Leo that Andreas, he attacks you on the way home,' said Vassilis. 'He does not treat women very well. Apart from Anastasia Loukas. She makes him do what she wants. She is a very spoilt girl, eh? And like Andreas with his mamá, she can do no wrong in her father's eyes.'

'I didn't ever want to be on my own with him, but he was a brilliant teacher. You don't think someone killed him because of his womanising, do you?'

Vassilis shook his head. 'I tell Leo that you and Stelios are very close after Andreas attacks you. I say too that you are with him the night of the murder.'

'Yes. Vassilis agrees with your story. You return here at 11 p.m.'

'It was 11 o'clock, I am certain,' said Vassilis, turning to Elin. 'You forget your key and I look at the clock when you come in the door.'

Leo turned to go and after shaking Elin's hand, followed Vassilis to the door.

'Thank you. You've both been very helpful.'

By that time, the bar had filled with several locals and a silence descended on the room as the detective emerged from the corner.

Vassilis came back to Elin. 'There is nothing wrong? You do not seem like Elin, somehow.'

With the painting school closed and Stelios living with his mother and Thea, Elin found it hard to fill her days. She insisted that she helped Dimitra run the taverna and look after the children. Late summer was one of the busiest seasons for tourists arriving on Péfka.

'You go and open the shop, Vassilis. Stelios does not come back but we must not miss the trade, eh? I manage and Elin helps me,' said Dimitra, putting her arm around Elin.

'You are sure, eh? And do not spoil my children, Elin.'

He smiled at them both.

Vassilis opened up the wood turner's again and life on the quiet island returned to normal. Except for Elin. She loved helping with the chores especially looking after Lyra and Yiannis, but her heart ached to see Stelios again. It was as if no one wanted to talk to her about the awful events for fear of upsetting her. Leo Giannopoulos spent most of his time over with the police in Porto Nikos and to the people of Péfka it was as if Andreas Simonides had just disappeared rather than lost his life in such a violent way.

Chapter Twenty-Three

Richard's letter came as a shock, more insistent than the last one. It arrived by afternoon post a few days after she'd spoken to Leo Giannopoulos.

Darling Elin (He's never called me that, she thought.)

I've been to see your mother. She said you're flying home on 29th September. Why didn't you tell me? You know how much I want to be the one to meet you at Heathrow. Well, she's agreed I can. I don't think she likes me that much. She's always offhand with me but she cannot deny how much I love you. And that's why I think you should come home and forget all your silly ideas of becoming a freelance artist. We'll get married and move away. Somewhere where I can have you all to myself, my darling.

I'm counting the hours until the 29th.

With much love

Richard xxxxxx

She didn't want to go home and she certainly didn't want to move in with Richard. She had to see Stelios. She needed to find out how he felt about her. Once the murder case had been solved and the murderer caught, could they have a future together? It was such a mess.

While she was thinking this, Brad and Manos came into the taverna and sat at a table.

'I'll get this, Dimitra,' Elin said.

'Hi. How are things?' asked Brad.

Manos stood up and put his arm around her.

'How do you think things are, Brad? You must look at her. Stelios goes back to *Ee Eliés,* eh?'

Elin nodded. And dabbed her eyes. 'What can I get you, boys? The usual?'

'Yeah, two Alphas, cold and wet.'

When she returned she caught the end of the boys' conversation.

'What is it I may have heard?' she asked, curious.

'We do not know how to tell you.'

Elin's heart raced.

'What?'

Brad placed a hand on her arm. 'Honey, Stelios has been taken into custody. The rumour over in the marina is that it was Stelios. He's the one who killed Andreas and made it look like suicide.'

Elin's hands shook and she dropped the tray, the two glasses of beer shattering on impact with the floor.

'He couldn't have. He was with me. You know that,' she screamed. She burst out crying.

Dimitra came from behind the bar. She comforted Elin and asked the boys what had happened.

'Let us help you clear up the mess, Dimitra. I am sorry that we say to you, Elin, but it is right that you know,' said Manos.

'Yeah, but it's only a rumour,' soothed Brad. 'You know how these things start. As you say, we know he was with you that night.'

Dimitra took Elin to one side and made her sit down. She returned to Manos and Brad with a brush and pan.

'It is all right. I look after her. Elin is fine. It is a shock. You call on Vassilis and you ask him to come here? He shuts shop when you tell him I talk about Elin.'

Brad and Manos left the taverna without ordering any more beers and did as Dimitra had requested.

It wasn't long before Vassilis entered the bar of the taverna.

'What is the problem, eh? You call me home in the middle of the day? It is very busy. Many tourists at the moment.'

Elin had never heard Vassilis be irritated with Dimitra like that before.

'I think it's my fault. I've just had some awful news and I reacted badly.'

The Greek man's features softened. 'What is it?'

'Stelios is charged with Andreas's murder,' Dimitra blurted it out. 'Stelios and Elin, they were here on the island. It does not make any sense.'

Vassilis grabbed the back of a chair. 'There is a mistake. I waited for you myself. I tell the police exact time you come home. I look at the clock.'

'So how can they think he did it?' asked Elin. 'His own brother.'

'I catch the boat across and see Giannopoulos again. He stays in Porto Nikos now until it is over.'

'Can I come with you, Vassilis? Do you think I'll be able to see Stelios? I can't bear to think of him locked up.'

Vassilis put his arm around Elin. 'Of course. I want him out of there as much as you do.'

'What about the shop, eh?' asked Dimitra.

Vassilis moved to take his wife in his arms and kissed the top of her head.

'I am sorry, *agapi mou*. I must not speak like that to you. This is very bad. Our friend is in trouble and he needs our help. The tourists must wait.'

Dimitra smiled and put her face up to kiss her husband.

It was true. Stelios had been arrested for his brother's murder. By the time Elin and Vassilis arrived at the police station in Porto Nikos, Sofia Simonides was there already, demanding to be allowed to speak with Stelios. On seeing her old friend, Kýria Sofia broke down. She and Vassilis spoke in Greek but Elin was able to understand most of what was said.

'Do not upset yourself, Sofia. Stelios is free soon. He has nothing to do with Andreas's death. I am sure.'

'They tell me he says lie.' She glared at Elin. 'If not with her, it does not happen.'

Elin felt her cheeks redden. 'It wasn't a lie, Kýria Simonides. He *was* with me all night until I returned to the taverna.'

'Andreas die at twelve. They say time to come in boat.'

Vassilis spoke to the officer on duty. He came back to the two women, shaking his head.

'There is nothing we can do. No one sees him, only his solicitor. They charge him. Now they build the evidence. The results of the fingerprints and the handwriting come back tomorrow. Now we must go.'

Sofia Simonides marched up to the desk.

'He innocent,' she screamed. 'I lose one son. I no lose another.'

Elin would never forget the image of a mother, wailing in distress. Much as she had no time for the woman who had dominated her family and who hated the thought of anyone other than women of good Greek stock claiming her sons, Elin felt enormous pity for Kýria Simonides at that moment.

'Sofia, I take you home to Thea, eh? If there is news of Stelios, I say Leo comes to tell you.'

They left the police station and Vassilis said he would take Sofia home in a taxi. Elin made her own way down to the marina to catch the boat over to the island.

Elin kept herself busy helping Dimitra in the taverna and with the children. There was no news from Porto Nikos about Stelios. He was still being kept locked up and Vassilis had questioned why his solicitor had not been able to secure bail for him.

'It is very bad,' he said. 'He is not a danger to anyone. He must be home with his mamá and his sister. They help each other with the sadness. They lose a son and brother.'

'I suppose if he's been charged with murder they consider him to be a violent man.'

Vassilis agreed.

'*Naí*. That is right. In Greece, killing the brother is very bad crime.'

Somewhere in the depths of Elin's subconscious, a word surfaced.

'It's the same in Britain. I think we call it "fratricide". Like Cain and Abel in the Bible.'

'The reports, they must clear him, eh?'

Elin decided she couldn't just spend time at the taverna and wanted to be with the one man who was fighting for Stelios's freedom.

'Would you mind if I came to the wood turner's with you today, Vassilis? I won't disturb you. If you let me have a key to the apartment, I'll look around to see if I can find anything that will help Stelios.'

Elin had no idea what she was looking for as she walked up the stairs from the studio. Opening the door into the deserted apartment made her realise that she and Stelios may never enjoy the privacy of the place again. Her heart raced. What if the results didn't clear him? It was his knife, she was sure of it. If he hadn't used it, then who had? Because the trimming knives were so sharp, he kept them secure behind his lathe. It had to be someone who knew they were there. *So had they been up here, too?* Her heart sank. Everything was as it was when she'd left him that night.

Vassilis called up the stairs to her. 'Detective Giannopoulos is here. He looks around the apartment. I send him up, eh?'

Leo Giannopoulos greeted her and began to examine the living room.

'Is this how you remember the room when you left Kýrios Simonides at 11 p.m. the night Andreas was murdered, Miss Morgan?'

She nodded. 'Yes. Yes, it is.'

Vassilis joined them.

'I have put up the closed sign. Why are you here, Leo? And why is Stelios not free, eh? It is clear there is no proof.'

The tall, distinguished figure of Leo Giannopoulos paced the floor.

'Something is not right. Perhaps we get the prints back today. But it takes a long time with the handwriting expert. It is very important I solve the case. They say I must find someone who did this … very fast.'

The two men started shouting at each other in Greek.

Vassilis turned to Elin. 'Sorry, Elin *mou*. I have said "getting someone" is not right. It is like they say anyone will do so that the case closes. It has to be the *correct* someone and Stelios Simonides, it is not him.' Then added, 'Or her.'

Elin crossed to the older man and placed her hand on his arm.

'Don't get upset. We have to hope that the truth will come out.'

'And if either of you remember anything, then please call me.'

'Only that *The Palinourus* and Anastasia Loukas have disappeared.'

'Yes, *efharistó*. We are looking into that. I can assure you, Miss Morgan, we follow every lead.'

Elin followed the two men downstairs and Vassilis saw the detective out.

'I wish these results would hurry up and come back from the lab,' she said. 'Until they clear Stelios, he'll be stuck in that cell all alone.'

'Yes, and it is important that the police finish with the body. Then Sofia puts her son to rest. It is not heard of in Greece to take all this time.'

Vassilis went behind the lathe and took down an identical knife to the one Elin had been shown in her interview at the police station.

'The one they showed me was caked in blood,' Elin said and shuddered. 'Ugh! Andreas's blood.'

'The person who kills Andreas plans everything. Who is clever like that, eh? It is not Stelios.'

If Stelios was proved to be innocent, everyone else on the island and in the painting school would be under suspicion. Someone had murdered Andreas Simonides and they were no closer to finding the real killer than they were on the morning he'd been found. It was such a mess.

Chapter Twenty-Four

There was still no news from the police station in Porto Nikos when Elin met up with Brad and Manos two days later. They were waiting for her at the taverna in the harbour.

'Hi, honey. We thought you'd already caught that plane home. Where've you been? We've got the beers in.' Brad slid a glass across the wooden table to her.

'Oh, just helping Dimitra with the bar and the children. Vassilis has to be at the wood turner's now Stelios is not working there. Cheers.'

The boys looked at one another.

'Stelios has not been released then?' said Manos.

'No, that detective came to the studio when I was there and started asking more questions. He's under pressure to solve the case as quickly as possible and Stelios is an easy target.'

Elin felt a warm flush move up her neck as she willed herself not to cry.

'Do not worry yourself. They do not have any proof that he did it, have they? They must match fingerprints.'

Elin nodded. 'The results are due any day, Kýrios Giannopoulos said.'

'Well, there you go,' said Brad. 'Your Stelios will be out and home to you in no time.'

Elin forced herself to smile but deep down, she knew it wasn't going to be that easy. She needed to see him urgently, and certainly before she left for home.

'We came to tell you about the arrangements. Andreas's body has at last been released for burial. Over at the tiny church on the road just past *Ee Eliés*. We've been talking to the others and we thought we'd all go to pay our respects. Early morning on Friday. He'll be buried in the family grave. Will you come with us, honey?'

Elin's heartbeat quickened. No, she couldn't go. Scenes from her father's funeral came into her mind; raw, fresh. The sea of sombre mourners, moving like an army of black ants. They gathered round the monster-mouth hole in the ground that gaped, ready to swallow up her beloved dad. She gripped her glass tighter.

‘S … sorry. What were you saying? The funeral. Yes, I’ll go if you two are going. But it doesn’t make sense. Having the funeral before Stelios is released.’

There was a pause. Brad continued.

‘Elin, rumour has it Sofia Simonides has disowned Stelios. He’s been charged with Andreas’s murder now. She didn’t believe it when he’d just been arrested but now he’s been charged, she thinks they wouldn’t have done that without evidence. He’s guilty as far as she’s concerned. He wouldn’t be allowed to attend the funeral anyway.’

‘What! Rumours, rumours. This place! You’ve heard her say that have you?’

She stood up and hurried back to the taverna. She knew she was being unfair to her friends. Hadn’t they been right when they told her about the rumour that Stelios had been arrested?

The boat was full to capacity on the day of the funeral. Villagers from all over the island were travelling across to pay their respects to one of their own. If the respect wasn’t for Andreas himself, it was for Kýria Simonides and her family who had lived in the area for generations. Dimitra stayed with the children and Vassilis went alone. Every member of Andreas’s art school was there, looking very out of place in black mourning clothes. The only clue that they had had a special relationship with the dead man was that everyone sported a tiny dash of colour somewhere – a tie, a neckerchief, a scarf, a head band, beads or a belt. It had been Brad’s idea and it worked. The man who had taught them about the intricacies of colour mixing was being honoured in an outpouring of respect for his talents. Elin had borrowed a long black linen dress from Dimitra. She wore rows of deep peacock blue beads around her neck; her sun-bleached hair was held back by a band of muted aquamarines, turquoises and teals, accentuating her deep cobalt eyes.

‘I’m sorry I snapped at you. You didn’t start the rumours, did you? I shouldn’t have taken my anger out on you like that.’

Elin sat beside Brad and Manos.

‘It’s all forgotten, isn’t it, Manos?’

‘Think no more about it.’

Elin tucked her arms through the boys’. She looked across the deck and felt Elektra’s eyes staring at her. The Greek girl stood up and strode across to where Elin and the boys were sitting. Her eyes were red-rimmed from crying and the skin underneath was puffy and grey.

'Mati,' she hissed. 'You, with evil eyes. You are reason Andreas dies. You arrange it. You and his brother together.'

Brad stood up.

'Come on, Elektra. That's enough. Go back to your friends. Elin had nothing to do with it.'

The girl started sobbing and returned to her seat.

'And neither has Stelios,' said Elin, quietly.

A hush descended on the boat as it bobbed its way across the strait to Porto Nikos. Elin felt all eyes watching her. Surely, they didn't think what Elektra had said was true? Yet, whispers suggested that Stelios was responsible so why not believe she was in on it, too?

The walk from the marina to the church took about half an hour. Many of the older islanders took some of the taxis lined up along the quayside. The art students walked together as a group along the road and when they approached *Ee Eliés*, Elin shivered. The familiar whispering of the olive trees she'd heard the night of the party gathered in volume until she passed the Simonides' house. What were they trying to tell her? She dismissed the unease and caught up with Brad and Manos.

'What do you think of Manos's idea?'

'What idea's that?'

'When we get to the churchyard, there'll be a wicker basket full of olive branches. It's an old tradition on Péfka. When the funeral cortege makes its way to the family grave, mourners line the route and wave olive branches, throwing them on the pathway for the coffin to travel over. It's supposed to be a way of making peace for the body before it enters the next world,' explained Manos.

'Very apt in this case,' said Brad, 'after such a violent end. What do you think?'

Elin thought back to the rustling and whispering of earlier. Could the waving of olive tree branches bring peace for Andreas? 'Sounds like a wonderful tradition,' she said finally.

The little church with its whitewashed walls glistened in the pale dawn sunlight. It was full to capacity with friends and family and the art students lined the pathway along the wall. Manos handed out an olive branch to each young person.

'Is it right that the coffin is open throughout the service?'

'Yeah, that's what Manos told me,' Brad said. 'They close it before bringing it out to the grave. Shh, here they come.'

The coffin was held by six pall bearers and the students threw the olive branches on the ground, forming a grey-green pathway over which Andreas travelled on his last journey. Dressed head to toe in black, a lace veil covering her face, Sofia Simonides was supported by Thea, her daughter, and an older man. They followed the Greek Orthodox priest who was chanting and swinging an ornate metal censer filled with aromatic incense. They led the rest of the mourners to the Simonides' family graves. At the graveside, prayers were said by the priest who then put soil on top of the casket, forming the shape of a cross. Each mourner placed one flower on the casket or some spread the soil before it was lowered into the ground.

'I've never seen that before,' said Elin, in a whisper.

As the coffin disappeared into the earth, the haunting wail of Sofia Simonides echoed around the churchyard. A mother's wail for her dead son. Elin remembered feeling bereft at that final act of lowering her father's coffin into the ground and wanted to rush and comfort the Greek woman. But whenever they'd met, she'd made it clear she was not welcome. Elin looked away instead.

The mourners dispersed and the art students made their way back to the marina to catch a boat back to Péfka. Something made Elin look back at the little church. Walking along to the grave was a figure she recognised. He stood, hanging his head with shoulders hunched. She ran as if her life depended on it.

'Stelios! You're free!'

He turned and held out his arms.

'Mamá said I wasn't welcome. But I had to come. Andreas and I may have had our differences, but he was my brother. I didn't kill him. I didn't.'

Stelios's eyes were full of tears and for a moment they stood in silence by his brother's graveside. He crossed himself before taking a flower from one of the tributes laid alongside and pressing it into the soil mound.

Elin squeezed his hand.

'I knew they'd have to let you go. You could no more have killed your brother than I could.'

'But someone did and they're no closer to finding out who it was than the morning when Mamá found him. I'm very pleased to see you. Let's go back to Péfka. Mamá won't have me at *Ee Eliés*, she's made that perfectly clear. In her eyes, if the police say they have proof I did it, I did it.'

'But they don't, do they? They've let you go.'

He turned to Elin and took her head in his hands. He was no longer under suspicion, but his mother didn't know that yet. He kissed her very slowly as if savouring the fact he had been cleared. Elin responded. Her insides tingled with longing. Stelios was free and she had something she wanted to share with him.

'It will be great to have you living at the wood turner's again. Vassilis says the trade has been the best ever. He'll be glad to have you back as well.'

'So, you have missed me, then?' Stelios put his arm around her shoulder and pulled her close.

They walked hand in hand along the narrow road. As they approached the Simonides' family home, Elin felt her heart beat faster. Would Stelios be able to just walk past as he'd planned? Thea appeared and ran towards them, her arms wide.

Stelios and his sister hugged for several moments.

'I've just heard. They've let you go. I knew it couldn't have been you.'

'But what about Mamá? She said she wanted nothing else to do with me. She thought I was guilty.'

He took Elin's hand and walked on.

'No, Stelios, You're wrong. Mamá was distraught at losing her eldest son. She wants you to come home. Come to the *makaria*. They're all there now for the funeral meal. The whole family.'

Thea hurried back into the house.

Stelios looked at Elin. At that moment, she knew that the pull would be too strong. He'd go back to living at *Ee Eliés*. He'd support his mother and his sister through the tragedy, and she loved him all the more for it.

'You go. Your mamá needs you. Our talk can wait.'

She leaned up and kissed him before walking away.

The other students had caught the earlier boat across to the island and while Elin waited for the next one, she pondered over what would happen to her and Stelios. Her heart told her that he would find a way to see her somehow, but her head told her otherwise. The haunting wail of his mother still rang in her ears.

It was with a heavy heart that Elin ambled up to the taverna from the quayside. Dimitra was waiting to greet her.

'A letter arrives for you.'

Dimitra handed her an air mail letter addressed in her mother's distinctive copperplate handwriting. Over the last few months, she'd enjoyed hearing all the news from her local village. Her mother's letters were filled with titbits of family gossip, details of village weddings and new babies, and sometimes long-distance advice on how to avoid summer colds and sore throats. Oh, and sunburn! Dear old Mam.

'*Efharistó*. I'll go up to my room and change out of your dress. I'll tell you all about the funeral when I come down. Vassilis not back?'

'Not yet. Kýria Sofia invites him to the *makaria* with the family and old friends.'

Once in her room, Elin slipped out of Dimitra's 'funeral' dress, changed back into denims and a tie-dye T-shirt and opened her mother's letter.

My dear Elin

I can't believe that your time in Greece is coming to an end at last. I'm looking forward to seeing you again, cariad. Richard Davies called to see me yesterday and said it was all arranged. He'd be picking you up from Heathrow. Are you sure? You know your dad would have done it if he'd been here and I felt it was my job to do it now. But Richard insisted. You know what he's like. Please write back and let me know if this is what you really want.

Nellie's in hospital. She had a fall and broke her hip, poor old dear. I'm calling in every day and they say she should be out of hospital soon. Oh, perhaps I shouldn't say but Sheila Hopkins is getting married, soon ... all of a rush if you get my meaning.

I'll close now, cariad. Just let me know if you want Richard to pick you up from the airport. I'm counting the days.

Love Mam xxxx

She hadn't agreed to anything. Her eyes misted over and she imagined how things might have been. She saw her father's beaming face the other side of the barrier as she entered the arrivals hall. He'd be desperate to know what she'd thought of his beloved Greece. Had she visited any of the amphitheatres he'd told her about? Or any ancient archaeological sites? She'd tell him about the places she'd managed to visit on her occasional days out when she'd allowed herself a break from her painting. About whispering in the centre of Epidaurus and Brad and Manos hearing every word. She'd tell him about how she nearly slipped on the polished well-worn surfaces in

Mycenae and how Stelios had caught her, saving her from falling down the flight of steps. She'd tell him how she'd fallen in love with the kindest man who was very like him. But it was not to be.

She rummaged in the top drawer of the chest and found her Dan-Air return air ticket. Athens to London Heathrow. September 29th, 1969. It was days away. She wanted to see her mother, of course she did. But Richard? Did she want to have all her decisions made for her again? There was one person who could help her make up her mind about getting on that plane, but he was back living in the family home. And she didn't know when she'd see Stelios again.

Chapter Twenty-Five

Péfka resumed its sleepy existence with tourist numbers dwindling as September drew to a close. Families with children and college students needed to get back for the start of term. It was as if the murder hadn't happened.

Elin wandered up to the painting school and sat at the wooden table on the terrace under the pergola. The shutters were locked and an eerie silence had descended on a place that had once buzzed with creative excitement. She wandered over to the stove in the corner and picked up the copper briki from the grey ashes and smiled as she remembered her first Greek coffee.

'Don't drink down to the bottom,' Manos had warned. But it was too late. Her mouth was full of the sweet sticky paste that had settled at the bottom of her cup. They'd teased her about it ever since. She closed her eyes, letting the warm Autumn sunshine settle on her eyelids, and remembered Andreas. Confident, brash, womanising Andreas. The brilliant artist who taught her so much but who'd pursued her to the point of assaulting her. Yet he hadn't deserved to die the way he did.

Damn you, Andreas. You've ruined everything. Broken your mother's heart. And what about your brother? He won't leave her now she's let him back into the fold.

Brad was leaving on his island-hopping adventure the next day and Manos was going home to his parents and to start up his painting business. It was over a week since the funeral and there had not been a word from Stelios. There was nothing on the island for her now. She'd return home on the date planned and work out what to do after that when she arrived home. She stood up, unsteady on her feet. She grabbed the edge of the table and feared she was going to faint. *That's what getting up too quickly and not eating any breakfast does to you,* she told herself.

Elin walked along the cliff path and looked over to the mainland. The sea was a deep azure and she remembered how Andreas had encouraged her and the students to look for the surprise of colours they weren't expecting. No matter what happened when she arrived home, the myriad of vibrant colours in the Myrtoan Sea would be imprinted on her memory. If only she could see Stelios one more time. He was somewhere in one of the white sugar lump houses dotted along the coast opposite.

Turning left, Elin walked down the hill and stopped when she got to the Villa Anastasia. It was deserted. No Red Setter came bounding down the steps as it did on her first walk up to the cliff top. The large wrought iron gates were padlocked and the pristine white shutters securely fastened down over the windows. A card had been stuck to the top of the post box with an Athens address for re-directing mail.

'They leave.' A voice behind her made Elin turn. It was Vassilis. 'They say Anastasia breaks their hearts. She goes without saying goodbye. Very cruel, eh? They have one daughter and they have no idea where she has gone.'

Elin had had no contact with Stelios since he was invited back into the family after the funeral. She understood that he had to support his mother but secretly wondered if one of her conditions for him staying was that he had nothing more to do with her. Sofia Simonides made it perfectly clear that she didn't want her son anywhere near Elin. Kýria Sofia would have loved Anastasia for a daughter-in-law as she and the Loukas family had arranged. What they hadn't bargained for was that Anastasia had other ideas and now she'd gone. And no one knew where.

'Have you seen Stelios since the funeral? I thought he may have come back to help you in the wood turner's,' Elin asked Vassilis. *And to see me*, she thought.

'I speak to him at the *makaria* and I tell him he must not hurry back. His place is at *Ee Eliés* now. In Greece, the family mourns for forty days and he must be there.'

Elin's face gave away the shock she felt at hearing that and a heavy weight filled her chest. *Forty days and I'll be long gone.*

'I am sorry. You love each other, eh? You work something out. You must leave in two days? There won't be much work here on Péfka now the season comes to the end but there is work in Porto Nikos, I am sure.'

Elin shook her head. 'No. Nothing will come of Stelios and me. His mother will see to that. He'll have to find a nice Greek girl to marry and present her with lots of dark-haired, olive-skinned grandchildren. She'll be happy then. Mamá knows best.'

'Oh, Elin *mou*.' He hugged her but didn't correct her.

'In any case, I've written to my mother and told her that Richard my ex-boyfriend will be picking me up from the airport. He'll be there when I step off that plane.' Elin's stomach did somersaults as she realised the consequences of what she'd done. Her life with the one man she'd ever loved was over.

The next day, Richard's letter arrived confirming he'd be in the arrivals hall waiting. One sentence jumped out at her.

I'm counting down the hours when we'll be back together at last. I've booked us into a nice little guest house off the A40. It will be like the last three months never happened.

Elin felt a lump rise into her throat. He was controlling her before she touched down on British soil. But there was no other way. It would break her mother's heart and the gossips in the village would have a field day if her suspicions proved true.

Elin took out her pad of writing paper and put all her thoughts about how she felt about Stelios in a farewell letter to him. Every few lines she stopped and took a deep breath. She wouldn't cry over this. It was a summer romance, but it was over. Surely it was better to have known the true love she felt for Stelios than never to have felt it at all? She'd thought she'd been in love with Richard at the beginning. Yes, she'd just have to learn to love him all over again. He was a good man, wasn't he?

She folded the letter and sealed it in an envelope. She would try to tell him everything in person, but just in case she knew exactly where she'd hide it ready for him to find it. She went downstairs to find Vassilis.

'He is at the wood turner's. He tidies the shop before the season ends,' said Dimitra. 'I do not believe you leave us the day after tomorrow, *agapi mou.*' The Greek woman's eyes misted and she came from behind the bar to hug Elin.

'You'll start me off, but I have to go home. There's nothing for me here.'

'Not us, the Greek family, eh?' Dimitra raised an eyebrow and laughed. 'I tease. You must go to your mamá.'

'Yes, something like that.'

'You come back next year, eh? Lyra and Yiannis love to see you again.'

Elin smiled and knew that when she walked onto that hydrofoil the next day she would never return. She would be leaving a period of her life that would have no resemblance to the one ahead of her with Richard.

'I'm just popping up to see Vassilis. I won't be long.'

The door to the wood turner's studio was open and Vassilis was sorting all the olive wood bowls into sets and different sizes and packing them in boxes.

'This is a good surprise.'

'Do you mind if I pop up to the apartment? I'm packing and think I may have left something there.'

'*Naí*, you go up.'

Once Elin was upstairs and alone, tears trickled down her cheeks. This was where she'd spent her happiest times over the last few months and memories of languorous love-making in the cool of the evening flooded her mind. She walked into the bedroom and faced the painting of the olive tree. Stelios had bought this to remind him of her when she wasn't with him, he'd said. What better place to put her letter of love? He would never get rid of her painting. One day, maybe after the official period of mourning was over, he'd come to get it. She pulled the painting away from the wall, far enough to wedge her letter in the bottom corner behind the diagonal, wooden strengthener. It didn't matter if he didn't read it straightaway. If he ever read it. The important thing was that she'd written it – an outpouring of her feelings, what he meant to her and how the life she was facing would never match up to what they'd had together. She'd give up painting altogether. It would be too painful to carry on. No, she'd marry Richard, find a little part-time job and have a meal waiting for him when he came home from work just as he wanted. She straightened the painting on the wall and left the bedroom for the last time.

Chapter Twenty-Six

It was important that Elin tried to see Stelios before she left. She scribbled a note asking him to meet her on the beach under the old olive tree at ten o'clock the next morning. She'd booked the hydrofoil for two-thirty which gave her plenty of time to get over to speak with him and get back to Péfka.

She walked out of Porto Nikos along the road to Ermione. The heat reflected back from the road surface and Elin pulled her hat down to shield her eyes. She approached *Ee Eliés* and heard the whispers from the olive grove as a cool breeze blew up from the sea. She felt a shiver as she walked down the drive to the heavy oak door. The house looked deserted with the shutters down.

Looking around her to check there was no one else around, Elin posted the sealed envelope to Stelios through the letterbox. She turned on her heels and strode back up to the road. She heard a click as someone pulled the letter through to the other side of the door. Why hadn't she just knocked and handed it to whoever was in the house? Who knew who'd got hold of it now?

That night Dimitra organised a farewell meal for Elin. The bar in the Guikas Taverna stayed open but outside on the terrace opening onto the square, the tables were pushed together. Elin sat by Lyra and baby Yiannis lay contentedly in his pram. Friends of Vassilis and Dimitra arrived with their children and gifts for Elin. The chair to the side of Elin remained empty. The tables were laden with Greek salads, souvlaki and Elin's favourites, cheese and spinach pies. There were plates of every baklava you could think of and carafes of retsina.

'We wait for one person,' said Vassilis, and Elin's heart skipped a beat.

'Ah, he is here.' Dimitra clapped her hands. 'Manos. You sit by Elin, eh?'

Elin smiled at Manos as he sat down next to her. They'd both seen Brad leave a few days earlier and now he'd come to be with her. Without those two boys, her trip here wouldn't have been the same.

'I wondered who the seat was for,' she said.

'You are not sad? You think it is Stelios, eh?'

'No, he wouldn't leave his mother to come here to Péfka. Vassilis says mourning goes on for forty days here in Greece, is that right?'

He nodded as Vassilis stood to announce they could start the feast.

'You must eat all your olives up, Elin *mou*. I say to you on your first day you eat them like a Greek girl very soon.'

Elin laughed. He'd been right. She was going to miss the salty taste of the plump black fruits that adorned every meal prepared by Dimitra. Back to mashed potatoes and boiled cabbage, no doubt, unless Richard had learned some new recipes since she'd been away.

'Calamari, anyone?'

'*Naí. Efharistó*, Papa,' said Lyra.

Manos passed the dish of steaming rings across to the little girl. Elin sat back in her chair.

'I'm sorry.'

Elin dashed from the table to the bathroom and tried to be sick. Calamari had always been another favourite … until then. She returned to table.

'You are all right, *agapi mou*?' said Vassilis. 'You are very pale. You must be well for the long journey tomorrow.'

'I'll be fine. Thank you.'

She looked at Dimitra. She knew.

The meal continued and Elin felt much better.

'You eat lots of baklavas,' said Manos, laughing.

'You must know by now that I've a sweet tooth.'

'Sweet tooth?'

'It means I love anything that has plenty of sugar or, in this case, honey.'

Vassilis stood up and knocked his spoon on the side of a wine bottle.

'Everyone. Elin leaves tomorrow after she stays three months with us. She becomes one of us. She is here when our son Yiannis arrives and makes big friend with Lyra. She comes to Péfka to learn to paint and she does it. She wins the best painting and wins also the heart of one of our friends. The murder of Andreas Simonides spoils the happy times. I am sorry, Elin *mou*.'

Elin couldn't allow herself to think what might have been.

'*Parakaló*, you raise your glasses. We wish Elin a good future. You come back and visit us, eh? *Ya mas*!'

Everyone stood. There was a clink of glasses. '*Ya mas*. To Elin.'

'*Efharistó*, everyone. I've loved being here. I've loved Greece. I shall miss you.'

Lyra squeezed both arms around Elin's waist. 'You must not go, Elin.'

It was then that the threatened tears spilled over. Dimitra led Elin away from the table and everyone dispersed back into the bar.

‘I always knew it wouldn’t last forever,’ said Elin. ‘I don’t know what’s wrong with me.’

Dimitra smiled. ‘I know, eh?’

The next morning, Elin rose very early and packed her rucksack. It was heavier than when she arrived with an assortment of mementos and souvenirs for her mam. Her beloved diary sketchbook bulged with her sketches and watercolours and was packed at the top. What would she get for Richard? She smiled to herself as she imagined giving him some *kombolói*. No, he wasn’t the ‘worry-bead’ type, she decided; she’d buy him something at the airport.

Downstairs, Dimitra had laid a breakfast of fresh fruit and pastries for her. Once she’d eaten, Elin left to catch the boat across to Porto Nikos.

‘*Efharistó*. I’ll be back later, Dimitra.’ She didn’t wait for Dimitra to ask where she was going.

On the journey across to the mainland, Elin rehearsed what she wanted to say to Stelios. She knew they had no future together. Kýria Simonides would see to that. She wanted nothing from him but he deserved a proper goodbye. She wanted him to know that she loved him and would never forget the short time they’d had together. She’d tell him about the letter she’d left behind the painting and ask him never to forget her.

The horn announcing the boat’s arrival in Porto Nikos marina interrupted her thoughts and Elin stood to take her place in the queue for disembarking.

‘I thought you leave today.’ She hadn’t noticed Leo Giannopoulos on the boat.

‘I do,’ Elin said, ‘but not until this afternoon.’

‘If I do not see you, you have a good journey home.’ He shook Elin’s hand. ‘I am sorry you were caught up in the Simonides’ murder business. We have a couple of leads now. You will not be here but I hope it will not be long before we catch who did it.’

‘Thank you, Detective. I hope for the sake of Stelios and his family you do.’

Elin walked down the narrow stony lane to the beach. Stelios’s motor launch wasn’t moored in its place at the side of the jetty but she hoped he’d be at the olive tree as she’d arranged. The sand was hot under her bare feet and she ambled along the water’s edge, cooling her feet in the ripples cascading onto the shore. She was early.

The ancient olive tree loomed into view and she thought of her best painting hanging on the bedroom wall at the wood turner's. How long would it be before Stelios retrieved it and read her letter? As always when she was near the olive grove, a breeze sprang up and the whispering started. She kept walking. Her stomach churned. He wasn't there. She checked her watch. So much for his words about wanting to be together, she thought.

Elin sat down on the sand and rested her back against the rough gnarled tree. Soon, she stood up, horrified when it dawned on her what she'd done. She'd been leaning against the very trunk where Andreas had been found dead. Hadn't they said he was slumped against the olive tree? She felt sick. She imagined the sand stained red from his blood. No wonder Stelios hadn't turned up. How heartless could she be? Asking him to meet her at the very spot where his brother had been murdered. *Oh, Stelios. I'm so sorry,* she said aloud. But there was no one there. She looked up into the garden at the house. All was quiet. She'd try walking around to the front of the house and knocking the door. But deep down, she knew she'd never see her beloved Stelios again.

She walked back along the beach and up onto the Ermione road. The main gates to *Ee Eliés* were shut; a sure sign no one was at home. But she had to try. She looked at her watch. Time was running out if she was going to catch the boat back to Péfka and be in time for the hydrofoil departure to Piraeus. She strode down the wide drive and knocked on the door several times. There was no answer. She tried again. Nothing.

Elin turned and ran back to the marina. The horn was sounding as she reached the boardwalk. She scaled the gangplank two steps at a time and flopped into the nearest available seat.

'You make the time it leaves,' said a familiar voice.

'Oh, Manos.' Elin wept. Tears of defeat, maybe.

'There must be no tears. I come to wave to you from Péfka and say *antio,* goodbye.'

'*Efharistó*. You're such a good friend. I've done the most awful thing. I wanted to see Stelios before I left and I only arranged to meet him at the very spot where his brother's body was found. It was thoughtless. No wonder he never turned up. Why didn't I stop and think? Now, I'll never be able to tell him.'

Manos put his arm around Elin.

'I do not know what you want to say to Stelios. He does not come so there is a reason. You say a time, eh?'

'Yes, ten o'clock. I posted the letter myself.' And then Elin remembered the click of the letterbox. What if Stelios had never received the letter?

Manos stood beside Vassilis, Dimitra and the children on the quayside ready to wave to Elin as she left the island of Péfka for the last time. No one lingered over saying goodbye; the kisses and embraces were deliberately brief. Dimitra's eyes were full of tears and Lyra hugged Elin tight.

'You come here, *agapi mou,*' said Vassilis, physically unpeeling his daughter's arms from Elin's hips.

Elin picked up her rucksack and boarded the hydrofoil. She scanned the marina and quayside, hoping to catch a glimpse of Stelios and his motor launch but he must have long gone. The engine started up and with one last wave to her friends, Elin found a seat inside the cabin next to the window. She opened up her diary and wrote the last entry she'd ever write. This was a part of her life that was now closed. She vowed never to paint again, never to think about Stelios Simonides and never to mention anything about the unsolved murder of his brother.

September 29th

The summer of 1969 has come to an end. I'm leaving Péfka, leaving Greece and a part of my life I shall never visit again. It's the only way. It never happened. Over.

There, short and sweet. Nothing else to say.

She flicked through her book for a final time, reading the entries since her arrival back in June and looking at the watercolour sketches interspersed throughout the pages. Each one brought back memories of a certain day, a special visit or fun event … but she deliberately never mentioned the worst day in detail. September 9th. The murder of her painting tutor was permanently etched on her brain. The most painful to read were the entries where she'd recorded her love for Stelios. She would never look at them again. Wondering what he would have said if she'd been able to tell him what she suspected, she took the key and locked the diary. With care, she slid it down to the bottom of her rucksack and sat back in her seat. She was on her way home … to Richard Davies and a new life.

Chapter Twenty-Seven

Alexandra
1991, Péfka, a small island off the Peloponnese, Southern Greece

The journey from Piraeus on the Flying Dolphin passed quickly. In no time, I arrived at the island of Péfka and took in the view of the harbour and the town behind it. Lemon, pink and white-painted buildings with terracotta ridged tiled roofs glistened in the strong sun. They formed a guard around a pretty stone quayside, filled with every kind of sea-going vessel from luxury yachts to humble fishing boats. A large flag-pole dominated the jetty that jutted out into the water and sported the distinctive blue and white Greek flag. The view was not a complete surprise. I'd read my mam's diary many times, and I knew exactly how Péfka harbour and its quayside would look.

June 21st 1969

Péfka harbour is very picturesque. A mix of marshmallow coloured town houses with balconies and fishermen's stone cottages. Gleaming white motor launches bob on the deep aquamarine water alongside schooners, exuding affluence. Yellow canvas parasols shading the diners at Xante's taverna look like a field of sunflowers. I've arrived in paradise!

When I'd first read the diary entry about arriving on the island, I had been sceptical about the flowery language she'd used but when I stepped onto the quayside, I took a deep breath. Mam had not exaggerated. The parasols were now a bright blue but the taverna was still Xante's. Flowers tumbling in abundant tresses from terracotta pots and urns adorned the fronts of houses and shops, balconies and steps. I spotted the Parthenis boutique where Mam had bought the dress she'd worn to the painting school party. It was as if time had stood still here and through the diary, I felt I was *returning* not visiting for the first time. One thing had changed though. The horse and carriage taxis were still lined up along the quayside as Mam had described but now there was a motor taxi rank on the other side of the marina. Taxi drivers, chatting and smoking, leaned on the blue-striped bonnets of their gleaming white vehicles waiting for their fares.

The sun beat down on my bare arms and legs. I pulled my straw hat further over my forehead. *No wonder you loved it here, Mam. The colours alone make it an artist's heaven.* I stifled a sob and tried to swallow the lump that had formed in my throat. If only Mam had shared her love of painting with me instead of denying this part of her life had ever existed. I didn't know what I was going to find out by coming to Greece, to this island, but I was sure my mother wanted me to come.

I checked the address of the taverna where I was to stay. Taverna Zena, chosen because it was cheap. Leaving one hand free to follow the instructions of how to get there, I pulled out the handle on my suitcase and dragged it behind me. The new-fangled suitcase was a present from my nan. She was the only one who knew about the diary. She'd encouraged me to come to Péfka to find out more about the time Mam spent in Greece during that summer of '69

I walked up the slope from the harbour and found the narrow street on the left where Taverna Zena was situated. The cottages along here were more modest than some of the grander houses along the sea front. The simple doorways and wooden shutters were painted in shades of pale blue and many of their inhabitants stepped straight from a living space onto the stone pavement. On either side of many of the doors, wooden chairs with raffia seats acted as outside space in the intense Greek sun. As I approached one cottage, I heard a rhythmic clicking. As I got closer, I watched an elderly man sitting outside and letting a row of wooden beads flow between both hands, starting at the tassel, one bead to another along the metal chain. I stopped and smiled, remembering the ones I'd found in Mam's secret box.

'*Kalimerá.*' I pointed to the address on the paper.

The old man placed his worry beads on his lap and answered me in Greek. When he realised I didn't understand, he stood up and pointed down the street. He pointed to each finger and the thumb on his left hand and then held up his hand to face me.

'*Pénte.*'

I didn't know if he meant five houses down, or five turnings but I thanked him and carried on walking. I counted the houses then five turnings and, sure enough, there was a taverna, set back from the pavement. A large painted sign with the letters 'TZ' hung freely from a wrought iron bracket. The letters were surrounded by hand-painted olive leaves, silver-grey and green, from which hung clumps of purple-black olives. The words *Ee Eliés* were painted under the initials. My heart skipped a beat. That was the name of the Simonides' family home. Outside, a van with the name *K. Markos* on it was parked to the side of the building, another sign that things had moved on since Mam was here. Then the only sound would have been the clip-clop of the horses' hooves or the phut-phut of scooters on the roads.

I entered through a beaded curtain, hung over the wide doorway, keeping the sun out of the taverna. It was dark and cool inside and the bar was deserted. I walked towards the serving area and pressed the bell.

'*Kalimerá*?'

A beautiful dark-haired girl emerged from the back. She wore a white apron over denim shorts and wiped her hands on a towel.

'*Naí*?'

'I'm Alexandra. I've booked a room with you.'

The girl opened a book on the counter of the bar and picked up a pencil.

'Ah, it is here. "Alexandra Davies". That is you, eh?'

'Yes, that's me.'

The girl smiled and held out a hand.

'I am Zena Markos. I own the taverna with my husband, Kostas. You are very welcome.'

'*Efharistó*.'

'Come.' Zena led me upstairs along a narrow corridor into a small room. It was cool and the shutters shielded it from the blinding sunlight that flooded the room when Zena flung them back.

'There. It is small, yes, but it is our best one because of *that*.' She pointed through the window. 'You see the sea and the cliff covered in pine trees. Péfka, our beautiful island of pines.'

The room was spotless and in spite of being cramped there appeared to be plenty of drawer space and a roomy solid wardrobe that had been made to fit exactly under the slope of the eaves. It reminded me of Mam's secret bedroom at Nan's house, down to the calming smell of dried lavender in a bowl on the bedside cabinet. The coverlet was patchwork, beautifully hand stitched by the look of it, in the colours of the sea.

'This is lovely, Zena. The sea view is a wonderful surprise. I thought I'd be looking onto houses. Thank you.'

'I am glad you like it. No one expects to see the sea. We hide away but we are high and look down to the harbour. You unpack, now, eh? Come down when you are ready. I have food for you then. You are hungry after travelling?'

I sat on the bed and unlocked my suitcase. Laid on top of the clothes was my most precious possession, Mam's diary. I placed it on the chest of drawers. Before I did anything else, I unpacked my case and found a home for everything. I went downstairs and discovered a place laid for me at a table in the corner of the bar. On it was a carafe of iced water, a basket of rustic bread and a Greek salad.

'Come and eat, Alexandra. It is simple food. It is not very Greek for your first meal. You like olives, eh?'

I was about to admit that I hadn't tasted them when Zena laughed. 'I tease you. Plenty of time.'

I had only known the young woman for a few hours but already I felt at ease with her. I had a good feeling that Zena would be the one who would help me unravel the secrets Mam left behind on the island. But not yet. I wasn't ready to tell anyone, not even Zena, the real reason why I was on Péfka.

She left me to eat my meal. I heard her squeal and looked up. She was swept off her feet by a handsome, bronzed man about the same age as her.

'Kostas!'

The two of them kissed and then spoke in Greek so fast that I didn't think they had time to draw breath. I wondered if my mother had learned the language when she was here.

Zena and Kostas walked over.

'Alexandra, this is my husband, Kostas. He helps me run the taverna but he is a fisherman, too. Every day, he catches the fish for the restaurant.'

Kostas beamed a smile that made his bronzed cheeks look even more tanned.

'Alexandra. You are the guest from Britain. I am very pleased to meet you.' He held out a hand and shook mine firmly.

I smiled back. '*Kalispéra*, Kostas. I'm happy to be here.'

I went back to my room and wrote letters to Nan and to Claire. My sister had begged me not to leave her behind but I had promised that once her exams were over, I'd see if she could join me. It was the first time we'd been apart since Mam's death but Nan had promised to look out for her. I told them about the chaos in Athens airport and the taxi ride to the port but the main part of the letters described my first impressions of Péfka. Its beauty, the heat, the vibrant colours of the sea and the warmth of the welcome from Zena and Kostas. All I'd told Claire was that I was tracing our mam's footsteps, following a journey she took twenty-two years before, before either of us were born. I didn't tell her about the diary. Only Nan knew about that. I'd tell Claire when I had unravelled the secrets.

'Zena, I'm going to post these letters. To let my family know I've arrived. I'll walk down to the harbour and find my way around.'

'That is a good idea, eh? There is a post box along this street or there is the main one by Parthenis boutique. Enjoy yourself.'

The old man was still sitting outside his house, still playing with his worry beads. I raised my hand as I passed in the shade on the opposite pavement. He waved back.

That first evening in Zena's Taverna, I read my mother's diary page by page. The sketches of the harbour and the boats, tied to the metal bollards that edged the quay like solid mushrooms, came alive now that I'd actually been there. The tavernas skirting the marina were ones where Mam had drunk beers with her friends and chatted about her painting. I turned the pages and found the sketches of the fishing boats where she'd captured the silver wriggling fish in the nets spilling over the sides. So many thoughts whizzed round my head before I fell to sleep. I couldn't wait to explore some more of the island in the morning.

It was very early when sunlight streamed through the crocheted curtains. I wished I'd put the shutters down and tilted them at an angle, enough to let air in yet allowing the light to filter in gently rather than be woken with a start. Drawing the curtains back, I looked out towards the sea. It was a beautiful turquoise blue-green, and even at that distance I could see it glinting like a jewel in the sunshine. It was six o'clock and the house was silent. I washed and dressed as quietly as I could and tiptoed downstairs, letting myself out into the street. I retraced my steps down to the quayside and found several fishermen arriving back with their catches.

'Hey, Alexandra. It is early in the morning for you to be up.'

Kostas was heaving large plastic tubs of squirming fish from his fishing boat onto the quay.

'Hi, Kostas. The sun woke me up. Anyway, it's good to see someone working hard.' I laughed. Even though there was blood and grime over his clothes and he was wearing a plastic apron, he was still very attractive. For a split second, thinking about handsome men reminded me of Stuart. An image of finding him with Lucy flashed into my mind. *You're definitely off men, Alexandra Davies. Remember!* And Kostas was happily married to Zena.

Mam must have come down here at this time too, in order to capture the fishermen emptying their boats of fish and mending their nets as some were doing then. When I'd flicked through the diary last night, every watercolour sketch was made real by the fact that I was now there visiting the very places where they'd been painted all those years before.

'I'll see you back at the taverna,' I called.

Kostas waved his hand as I left the quayside and walked up the hill along the main street that split the town in half. Households were waking up. Women were opening doors and lifting shutters. As I passed some, the smell of freshly brewed Greek coffee wafted out into the street and my stomach rumbled. I'd return to Zena's for breakfast and then spend my first full day finding my bearings and visiting some of the places Mam had written about in her diary.

'Here you are, Alexandra. I think you are still in your room. Breakfast is ready.'

'I woke early and went down to see the fishermen bringing in their catches. Kostas was there.' I looked at the breads and pastries, honey and thick Greek yogurt waiting for me on the table. 'This looks lovely, *efharistó*.'

Zena continued to boil the coffee on the stove by the bar as she talked to me.

'You have had Greek coffee before? Here, come and watch. See, we put the coffee in this.' She held up a small copper pan with a long handle. 'It is a "briki". We add the water and it boils until there are bubbles.'

She then poured the steaming coffee into my cup and carried it over to the table. I followed and sat back down.

'The coffee will settle but make sure you don't drink it down to the … I think you say in English "sludge", in the bottom.'

I took a sip of the rich sweet drink.

'That's lovely. Zena, have you and Kostas lived on Péfka long?'

'No, we came here from Athens. We moved here about five years ago.'

'You both speak English very well.'

'*Efharistó*. That is kind. I studied it in university, and Kostas learns, too. I like to practise with the guests. We only came for a holiday to start. We loved it so much, we decided to stay. When this place came up for sale, it was in a very bad state but very cheap.'

My heart sank. I'd hoped they were both from island families who would have known what happened in the summer of 1969 when Mam was there.

'The taverna has not always been a taverna. It was the police station for the island. The only policeman on the island lived here.'

'When did it become a taverna, then?'

'1980. It says on the sign, look.'

Zena pointed to a replica of the sign outside that hung on the wall behind the bar. MCMLXXX.

'Ah, I see. Is there anything left of the police station, now?'

'No. It was empty for many years. There was a murder. No one talks to us about it.'

'I can't imagine a murder happening on this beautiful island,' I said.

'*Naí*, I know. I was very scared to sleep in my bed for the first weeks.' We both laughed. 'Sorry, Alexandra. I must work. The bar will fill soon.'

Chapter Twenty-Eight

With the diary packed in my bag, I wandered from the taverna up the hill in the direction of the cliff top. I hoped that, if I followed Mam's instructions carefully, I'd find Andreas's painting school where she had studied that summer. The taverna where she stayed was on the right as I walked up and opened onto a light airy square. It wasn't called Taverna Guikas anymore and I wondered what had happened to the couple who had made my mam so welcome. They would be in their early sixties now, at least. I passed the wood turner's. The name over the door said '*Yiannis*'. I remembered the name being mentioned in the diary, the baby boy, but there must be hundreds of Greek men called Yiannis. A bit like John back home. The shop window displayed a wide array of goods made out of olive wood. The bowls must have been turned on the lathe I could see at the back of the workshop but no one was at work that day.

I carried on walking. I stopped at some large gates set in a white wall on which there was a sign, 'Villa Violetta', fashioned in the same scrolled wrought iron as the gates. I peered through to see sweeping white marble steps leading to the front of a beautiful villa. This had to be the Loukas villa Mam had described. I half expected to see the elegant Anastasia walking down towards me. On either side of each step trailing geraniums in various shades of red tumbled out of terracotta flower pots. They formed a procession to the terrace at the top where enormous ribbed urns held ornamental palm trees and scarlet hibiscus flowers.

'It is very elegant, eh?'

I turned to the direction of the voice behind me. It came from a young man with long dark hair framing a handsome bronzed face.

'English? I am Yiannis.' He held out a hand to shake mine.

'I'm from Wales. One of the countries that make up Great Britain. I'm Alexandra. Yes, the villa is stunning. But it looks deserted.'

Yiannis stood by my side and we peered through the gates.

'They are – how do you say? – weekenders,' he said. 'We call it the Captain's house. His wife, her name is Violet. They come down from Athens. About fifteen years ago, I think.'

'If I owned something as luxurious as this, I wouldn't want to leave it … even for a few days every week.'

Yiannis nodded in agreement and together we walked up the hill.

'I have not seen you here before. You are on holiday, eh?'

'Yes, I'm staying at Zena's Taverna. I'm just finding my way around.' I looked out of the corner of my eye and took in every detail about the person walking beside me. He was taller and leaner than Stuart and he was casually dressed, not in a scruffy way, but impeccably and stylish. Why did I compare his appearance to Stuart's? I hadn't thought about my ex for months before Mam had died. Yet there on Péfka, I'd done it twice in one day. First, Kostas and now Yiannis.

We reached the top of the hill where the road split into two. I didn't tell Yiannis that I knew where both led to. No one need know my real purpose for visiting the island. It was better to find out if people knew anything about what happened on the island twenty-two years ago without letting on who I was.

'It has been good to meet you, Alexandra. Now I leave you. I show you around the island, perhaps? If you want, you ask me, eh? I work at the wood turner's and I finish at six o'clock.'

'*Efharistó*. I'll do that.'

Perhaps I'd ask him about the previous owners and why they'd moved away.

'You learn some Greek, too.' Yiannis smiled. 'I like that.'

The contrast of his even white teeth against his tanned skin made my stomach flip. Yiannis had the most engaging smile and I was annoyed at letting myself be affected by a handsome face … again.

I turned right and walked until I saw a building in the distance. It faced out to sea and I knew this was the art studio where my mam had come to improve her painting. The painting school was boarded up but I could just about make out the name 'Simonides' on the sign where the paint was peeling. I walked round the building and imagined Mam looking out to sea and sketching the little scenes I'd seen in the diary. I sat down at the back of the house on a bench that had seen better days and took the diary from my bag. I found the entry about meeting Andreas and the other students for the first time.

June 23rd

My stomach churned as I got nearer. The olive trees appeared to sense my nervousness. They rustled in the breeze blowing in from the headland like whispers telling me, 'Sshh, now. It will be fine'. I wished I believed them. The noise from inside became louder. People were laughing now. How could I go in? I knew I had to. I entered. It fell silent. Eyes all on me, the new girl.

Poor Mam. Not knowing anyone and studying in a foreign country – yet she did it. But something happened that summer. It was something she was determined to forget and never mention again. The olive trees were still there, planted in rows, and just as they had for Mam, they seemed to whisper to me, too. I shivered in spite of the late morning heat and my heart beat a little faster. Could something have happened there at the painting school that affected my mother? I had to find out.

Walking down towards the harbour took a lot less time than the slog up the hill. I stopped at the large taverna where my mam had stayed and sat at one of the small tables spilling outside onto the paved square. Over the taverna door, there was a sign that said 'Taverna Filia'. Crisp fresh tablecloths in blue and white gingham complemented the blue painted chairs with raffia seats. It was a typical feature of all the tavernas I'd seen on the island, all trying to give themselves a Péfka identity. No one came to serve me so I went inside. Old family photos covered every space on the walls and several pots of ivy filled the window ledges. Most tables were occupied with people eating. There was a strong smell of garlic and lemons. In contrast to the heat on the square, the bar was cool and dark. I found an empty table in the corner.

A young girl with glossy black tied-back hair asked me, in perfect English, what I'd like to eat.

'What do you recommend?'

'The cheese and spinach pie is very good. A secret recipe by Mamá.' The young girl smiled at me, her pencil poised to write on her pad.

'I'll try it. And a small Greek salad and some tzatziki, *parakaló*.'

'And to drink?'

'A small beer. *Efharistó*.'

I didn't know if I'd like the tzatziki or the beer but I remembered reading that was what Mam always drank when she was with her friends, Brad and Manos. It was often Alpha beer and my eye was drawn to the red and blue symbol by the bar. They still served it there.

I looked up at the photos. Some of them looked very old. Sepia ones like the ones I'd seen at Nan's. Perhaps some were of the Guikas family who ran the taverna when Mam stayed here.

When the girl came with the food, I asked her.

'Are these all your family?'

'Some. These here are what we brought with us.' She pointed to the wall behind where I was sitting. 'That is my papa's family. His parents, his eight brothers and sisters.'

'Have you been at the taverna long?'

'We moved here from Corinth, ten years ago. The rest are photos that were here before. I do not know who everyone is but it makes a good display, eh?'

I agreed and the girl left me to eat. As I ate, I looked up at the photos and wondered which of them were of Vassilis and Dimitra, my mam's friends. Even though they'd left the taverna, they may still live on the island. I'd ask Zena when I arrived back. I'd been concentrating on the photos so much that I'd hardly noticed I'd finished eating.

'You like Mamá's cheese and spinach pie?' The young Greek girl was back.

'Yes, it was lovely.' I lied. The taste hadn't registered with me. 'Nothing left anyway.'

'That is good. You were miles away.'

'Sorry. I'm fascinated by the pictures. Are any of them of the previous owners?'

The girl went closer to the photographs. 'This one says "Simonides" in the corner, look.'

I didn't comment but felt the hairs on the back of my neck prickle. Could they have owned the bar at one time? In any case, the family group was of a smiling couple with two young boys, near enough in age to pass for twins.

The girl continued talking.

'But that is not the name of the people who ran this place before. You must ask someone who has always lived on the island. Someone who knows the history of the place. We are still the outsiders, eh?'

I laughed and went to the bar to settle her bill. It was the same where Nan lived. Any trouble in the village and it was always 'outsiders' who were responsible. I'd always joked with my grandmother and asked how long you had to live in the village before you were accepted as a local.

'*Antio*, goodbye. I hope you will come here again,' the girl said. 'I am Filia, by the way.'

'Alexandra. Goodbye, Filia.'

When I walked into the taverna, Zena and Kostas were oblivious to anyone else in the room and locked in an embrace. I coughed.

'Hello, you two.'

The young couple broke apart and I was cross with myself for thinking sexy thoughts about Kostas that morning. The two were devoted to one another.

'You have a good day, eh? Where did you go? What did you do?'

'You must let the girl get in through the door, Zena,' said her husband, laughing.

'It's all right. I walked up the main street as far as the cliff top and found a deserted building. It had a sign but the name wasn't very clear. It was almost worn away.'

Zena exchanged glances with her husband.

'It was a painting school. Something happened but no one tells us what it was. We are outsiders.'

'Not you as well. That's what Filia at the taverna I went to said.'

Zena and Kostas laughed. 'Some families live on Péfka forever. You ask them.'

'I met Yiannis from the wood turner's and he was nice.'

Nice! He was more than nice. As I talked, my heart beat faster. My insides somersaulted. I knew nothing else about him, so why did he affect me like that?

'Our guest is red, Zena. Yiannis is good-looking, eh?'

I felt the warmth creeping up my neck.

'Stop it, Kostas! You must not tease. You go up to your room … and you do not take notice of my silly husband.'

I did as Zena said and took out my diary. The name Yiannis jumped out from one of the early entries. On the night he was born, Mam had danced the night away. Perhaps it was with Andreas, her painting tutor. But it didn't sound like him to hang around to hear about a baby being born. It must have been Stelios, his brother.

If I was going to find out more about Andreas Simonides and the painting school and how they'd affected my mother's decision to give up her painting, I'd need to be more convincing. I'd start to paint again. I hadn't picked up a brush since the end of my first year at art college when I'd chosen pottery as my specialism. Mam's sketches were always finished off with watercolours but I had no idea what her bigger paintings were like or in what medium she'd painted. The small olive tree painting hanging in the secret room in

Nan's house was a watercolour like the ones in the sketchbook. But the description of some of her exhibition pieces suggested that they were very large and the paintwork thick and applied with a palette knife.

I took a long time to fall asleep that night. My head was full of paintings of olive trees, seascapes and sunsets, and beautiful Greek men. One face in particular kept moving to the forefront. It belonged to someone with long flowing black hair, eyes the colour of melted chocolate and a dazzling smile.

Chapter Twenty-Nine

I went out early the next day. I called first on Yiannis. The bell rang when I opened the door and he came into the studio from the back workshop. His face broke into a smile and I felt my cheeks redden.

'*Kalimerá.* You said to call if you could help me. I hope it's all right … I can come back if you're working.'

Yiannis brushed curls of wood shavings from his leather apron.

'Of course. It is good. What can I help you with?'

'After I saw you yesterday, I walked along the cliff top and came to a boarded up building. Zena from the taverna thought it was once an old painting school. The scenery is stunning from there and I'd like to start painting again to capture what Pékfa is actually like. Can you tell me if I can buy brushes and paints here on the island?'

I felt myself colour again. It was such a feeble excuse. I could have asked anyone that. Gone down to the harbour and wandered around the shops.

'*Naí.* You will get some things but there is a – how do you say? – a specialist art shop in Porto Nikos. It depends what you want.'

I moved to a shelf displaying beautiful hand-turned wooden bowls. 'Just some sketching pencils, a pad and maybe a few watercolours to start. Did you make these? They are amazing.'

Yiannis flashed his smile again. 'You pick one up and feel how it is smooth. They are made from olive wood. I then polish them in olive oil.'

The bowl felt like silk in my fingers and a variety of shades of raw ochre, burnt umber and sienna formed twirling patterns against creamy wood grain. Why was I suddenly thinking in artists' terms for colours? Could it be that I was taking up the very thing my mam had left there, her love of painting?

'Where did you learn a skill like this? I'm a potter and it's taken me years. But my bowls are no where near as good as this.'

I placed the bowl back by the others.

'You go down and get your artist things, eh? I close the shop for an hour and I meet you at Xante's for a coffee. I tell you then. Now, I turn this bowl and then I finish.'

Following the road down the hill, I looked for Filia when I passed the taverna but no one was around. I found the shop Yiannis had told me about easily. It was tucked in between the Parthenis boutique and the small supermarket on the corner. He'd been right; the range was small but I bought a couple of soft sketching pencils and a small box of watercolour paints for a few drachmae. When I came out of the shop, I spotted Yiannis already sitting at a table at the water's edge at Xante's.

'You buy what you wanted?'

I sat on the seat beside him and showed him my purchases. 'Yes, I only bought a few things. I'm not sure how I'll get on yet. I'm better with clay.'

Yiannis placed a faded canvas bag on the table.

'It is good you did not buy much. I did not say because I did not know if I could find them. When my father leaves the taverna, he gives me these to keep at the studio. They belong to a British girl who stays there. She leaves them behind.'

My pulse raced. So perhaps he was the Yiannis in my mam's diary! *I expect they had art students staying every year. There's nothing to say it was Mam.*

'What is it?'

'You open it, eh?'

I pulled open the draw-string cord and took out the contents. It was a full range of sable paintbrushes, from the finest tip of a few hairs for detailed work to a thick plump brush suitable for washes and larger areas.

'Wow. These are the best quality,' I said.

I read the initials on each dark red wooden ferrule: *E. M. No, it was wishful thinking on my part. Too much of a coincidence. Lots of painters must have those initials*, I told myself.

And yet my throat tightened and my eyes prickled along the eyelids. I couldn't show Yiannis. I wouldn't. He mustn't know I was convinced I was handling Mam's very own paintbrushes.

'Everything is good, eh? Your face is very white.'

'Yes. But I can't accept these, Yiannis. They're beautiful. And expensive. Look they've someone's initials on them. Couldn't your father have sent them to her?' I tried hard to make myself believe they belonged to someone else.

'She does not leave the address with my father.'

No, I thought. *These brushes were another part of my mam's life she wanted to leave behind.*

'He hopes she comes back the next year. But no.'

'If you're sure, and your father wouldn't mind, I shall treasure them. *Efharistó.*' Little did Yiannis know the depth of feeling in my words. 'I think I'd like to meet your father and thank him in person.'

Yiannis called over the waiter and ordered two Greek coffees and a plate of baklavas. I was glad to change the conversation away from painting, afraid I'd get emotional again thinking about my mother and why she'd kept it a secret. I didn't want to confide in Yiannis yet.

'How did you know about my sweet tooth?' I said, taking one of the honey pastries.

'Sweet … tooth?' Yiannis looked puzzled. 'Your tooth is sweet?'

I laughed. 'I'm sorry. It's just something we say if we can't resist anything sweet or sugary. I adore these already and I've only been in Greece a couple of days.'

'My papa says no one makes baklavas like his mamá, my yiayiá, could. She is dead nearly thirty years and he says it *still*. She is dead before I am born.'

I smiled. 'I say the same about my nan's Welsh cakes. No one makes them like her.'

Yiannis wanted to know what Welsh cakes were and before I knew it, I was telling him all about Nan and the rest of my family. Apart from one person, my mam. The one person who meant most to me. And she was gone. How could I tell him about the very person who was the reason for my visit?

'You do not talk of your mamá?'

I took a deep breath. 'She died … a few months ago.' My eyes welled with tears and I looked away from the handsome face now appearing so concerned opposite me. Yiannis placed his hand on mine and tingles raced through me.

'I am sorry. Do not get upset. I know what it is like. My mamá dies, too. Ten years ago. I still cry when I think of something we do together. They say time heals. But it is always sad, eh?'

We sat in silence, holding hands and looking out over the sea to the horizon and beyond. There was something about the sensitive young Greek man that made me feel at home on the island of pines. He made my heart skip that little bit faster but above all, I knew I'd made a friend. Once I knew him better, I'd tell him how much his gift of the paint brushes meant to me.

I did get to know Yiannis well over the next few weeks and he did tell me how he got into wood-turning, following in his father's footsteps. I'd spend the days finding new places around the island where I'd practise my painting.

Using my mother's brushes made me keener to improve my skills and, although I never showed anyone my sketches, I knew I was getting better. I became fascinated with the shapes and textures of the numerous olive trees growing everywhere. Péfka may have been the island of pines, but olive trees grew in abundance, too. It was wishful thinking on my part and could only be a figment of my imagination, but whenever I unscrewed my water pot and began to paint, the whispering would start. It was as if my mam was there, guiding my hand and talking me through the rustling of the grey-green leaves. I felt her presence everywhere. Perhaps she felt that she'd returned to the place where she was truly happy and she wanted me to feel the same. I made sure I arrived at the wood turner's just as Yiannis was closing each evening and we'd walk to Xante's. He would tell me about his day and I'd tell him about the new places I'd found.

'You are not lonely, Alexandra *mou*? You spend every day on your own.'

I smiled. How could I tell him that I never felt lonely now I'd started painting again?

'No, I'm loving being back with my paints. One of these days, I'll show you my sketches and watercolours. But not yet. They are for my eyes only … until I get better!

'But you paint the olive trees. That is all. Perhaps you come here and paint the boats in the harbour? Or people? You paint me, eh?'

He stood up and, posing, placed one hand behind his ear and the other on his hip. I laughed.

'As I said. When I get better, I'll hold you to that.'

Yiannis looked puzzled.

'It means I'll do what you've suggested.'

We smiled at each other and left the bar.

Each evening, he walked as far as the turning to my taverna and we arranged to meet the next day for an hour or so before dinner. It always followed the same pattern. The same place, talking about what we'd been doing. Nothing more. Part of me was disappointed that he never suggested going out on a date or taking a meal together but hadn't I decided I was off men? In any case, anything else would keep me from the purpose of my visit. No, being friends was just fine.

After a few weeks on the island, I arrived back at the taverna after seeing Yiannis. Zena was waiting for me in the bar.

'*Kalisperá*, Alexandra. I hope you had a good day. This arrived for you.'

Smiling, she handed me an airmail letter addressed to me in Nan's distinctive copperplate handwriting.

'Yes, thank you. I got a lot of painting done.'

'Not more olive trees, eh?' Zena and Kostas had started to tease me when I said they were all that I could paint at the moment.

My mind was elsewhere and I smiled. My hand shook as I held the translucent blue envelope edged in dark blue and red diagonals.

'*Efharistó*.'

I went up to my room and lay back on the bed. Pangs of homesickness washed over me when I realised how much I was missing my nan and sister. Perhaps Yiannis was right. I was lonely.

I ran my nail under the seal, unfolded the letter and began to read.

My dear Alexandra,

Thank you for the postcards, cariad. Your Greek island looks amazing. It took me right back to the summer when your mam used to send them. I'm glad you've settled in and made a friend.

Your last card cheered me up no end. It arrived on the day I'd had some upsetting news. You were right all along. Your father and that Sally woman are getting married. And your mam not dead no time at all! To think I stood up for her. I was taken in like everyone else with all the talk about promising your mam she'd look after you all after she'd gone. While all the time she was carrying on under everyone's noses. And *according to some in the village, it was going on before my poor Elin passed on ...*

How could he? Poor Nan. What an insult to her only daughter. But it wasn't a real shock. It's what I suspected from the start, but everyone said I was being paranoid.

Claire is distraught, bless her. She blames herself for not seeing what only you could see. She says Sally has completely re-decorated the house and wiped away any signs that your mam ever existed. Claire's come to live with me. Richard gave her her marching orders after a blazing row. I'm sorry to bring you bad news but felt you should know.

Your mam was a changed girl when she came back from Greece and I'll never know why she took up with your father again. But she did and once you arrived I had to accept it. She always told me you were the best thing that happened to her, cariad. And then she had Claire and devoted her life to the two of you.

Find out why she left, Alexandra. Claire will want to know, too, I'm sure of it.

Write back soon.

Lots of love

Nan xxxx

Chapter Thirty

I refolded the letter and placed it on the bedside table. *I knew it. I wasn't imagining things.* If I could be in the same room as my father, I wouldn't be responsible for my actions. How could he treat Claire like that? They could have waited at least until she'd had her exam results and was settled in uni. I had to get some fresh air. I ran downstairs, tears streaming down my face. Out of the corner of my eye, I saw Zena standing behind the bar, her mouth open.

'Alexandra, what is it that is wrong?' she called after me.

I kept on running until I was out of breath. I arrived at the top of the street and walked along the cliff top to the old studio. As I approached the row of olive trees, my heartbeat slowed back to a normal pace and I felt calmer, the whispering soothing me. Mam was there. I was sure of it.

'*Sshh,* cariad. *Sshh.*'

'Oh, Mam. How could he? And with her. Why did you leave this beautiful place and go back to him?' I said aloud

I walked round to the back of the former art school building and sat quietly on one of the wooden benches under the old pergola. The air there was still and the silence helped me sort my thoughts. Any loyalty I'd felt towards my father had vanished. There was something about the last entries in Mam's diary that had set me wondering. What had she been desperate to tell Stelios before she left? It made sense – my May birthday, my olive skin and dark colouring that no one in the family had, the fact my father and I were so different. I was more determined than ever to find the man I suspected of being my real father. And I didn't mind who knew it. No more secrets. I'd start with Nan and Claire. *I'll write to them both and tell them what I've learned from Mam's diary.* The crystal-clear sea stretching out in front of me glistened like an aquamarine.

I leaned back on the seat and closed my eyes. Through the slots of the pergola the hot sun warmed my face and I composed in my head what I would say in each of the letters.

'I thought I saw you pass.'

I opened my eyes to see a concerned Yiannis looking down on me.

'Oh, Yiannis. I didn't hear you.'

'You walked past in a hurry. You are very sad, eh? Is everything all right, Alexandra *mou*?'

He came and sat beside me, taking my hand in his. My throat tightened.

'I'm fine now. I had a letter from my grandmother telling me that my father is getting married again. I was just angry. And when I'm angry, I cry. It looks as if my father was carrying on with this woman before my mam died. Can you imagine how that feels? I'll never forgive him for that. Never.'

He took my clenched fist, unpeeled the fingers and brought my hand to his lips.

'I like you, Alexandra. I am sad when you are sad and all alone.'

His lips on my skin sent tingles through my body.

'I'm not alone when I have a good friend like you.' *And what I want more than anything is for you to be more than a friend.*

After arranging to meet Yiannis later that evening, I returned to my room at the taverna and took out the writing paper and envelopes Nan had insisted I pack before I left. I wrote two letters, first one to Nan and then another to my sister.

I wrote everything down about Mam I'd learned from her diary, how she'd spent her summer painting, how she'd fallen in love with a Greek man called Stelios and how she'd left after the painting school closed earlier than expected. I didn't know why the school had closed or why this part of her life was never mentioned again.

But from the way she spoke about Stelios Simonides and the love she had for him, I believe he is my real *father ... not Richard, the man I've always thought was my father. I think she came back pregnant and accepted Richard's offer to marry her and give me a name. I don't know if Stelios is still here on the island but if he is, I intend to find him and introduce myself as the daughter he didn't know he had. By leaving me the diary, I'm sure Mam wanted me to come here and find out about my father for myself.*

I hoped that Claire would understand why I had to find Stelios and that it wouldn't make any difference to us as sisters. It all fitted – why our father favoured Claire, his real daughter, why he'd resented the time I had with Mam alone in the hospital, why she'd never painted again. Was it one of the conditions for him marrying her?

There was a knock on the door.

'Alexandra. How are you?' It was Zena. 'You were upset when you ran out of the taverna.'

I rubbed my hand across my eyes, knowing that Zena would be able to see I'd been crying again.

'Come in, Zena. Yes, I'm fine. *Efharistó*. It was my grandmother's letter.'

'Your *yiayiá*? She is not well?'

I patted the bed for her to sit beside me. It was time to let someone else know the secrets I'd been keeping, especially about the purpose of my visit to Greece and the island. Zena let me talk and the more I told her – about Mam dying, what I'd learned from her diary and why Nan's letter with its news about my father and Sally getting married had upset me – the better I felt. It was as if the heavy weight resting on my shoulders had been lifted.

'So you think your real father lives here on the island? And he does not know he has a daughter?'

I nodded. 'I don't know where he is after all this time. In the diary, my mother said that he didn't turn up as she'd asked him to and she had to leave without saying goodbye or leaving any forwarding address. So how would he keep in touch, even if he wanted to?'

Zena placed her arms around me and pulled me close.

'Well, Alexandra. We help you find this father of yours. We do not know the local families so it will be good for us to find out more. Kostas will ask questions for you. Simonides, you say? We heard that name when we arrived here, I am sure.'

'*Efharistó*. I have many questions, Zena. You are the first person I've told about everything that was in my mam's diary. I haven't even told my grandmother all of it. And tonight, I shall tell someone else.'

Zena raised one eyebrow. 'That is a very handsome young Greek, eh? The *friend* you see every night. He brings a red colour to your cheeks every time you say his name.' She laughed and placed a hand on my arm. 'I tease you.'

I felt a flush travelling along my neck.

'Yes, I'm meeting Yiannis at Xante's later. I'm going to ask him to help me find my father.'

I couldn't decide what to wear that evening. I was meeting Yiannis at seven o'clock and by six-thirty I'd tried on every item of clothing in my wardrobe. In the end, I settled for a short cotton shift. I checked my reflection in the mirror on the chest of drawers as I left the room. *That'll have to do.* I wore little make-up, just a hint of smoky eye shadow and a smear of shimmery lipstick. The sun had done the rest. I'd only been in Greece for a few weeks but already my naturally olive skin had tanned. The shades of blues and sea-greens in my dress looked more vibrant in contrast.

'You look lovely,' said Zena as I walked through the bar. '*Naí*, Kostas?'

Her husband looked over at me approvingly. 'You make the Greek men turn their heads tonight.'

Blushing, I left the taverna and walked out into the evening sunshine. It was still very warm and the air shimmered in a haze. Yiannis was sitting at the furthermost table at Xante's, next to the quayside. He was facing the water and his head was tilted up to the sun, eyes closed. I tiptoed towards him and whispered, '*Kalisperá.*'

He turned round and his face broke into a grin. He opened his eyes wide. 'You look very beautiful tonight.'

I laughed. '*Efharistó*, Kýrios Yiannis. You mean you've only seen me in scruffy shorts and not in a dress before.'

'No, I mean …'

'I'm teasing. Isn't it a beautiful evening? The sunset is going to be amazing.'

Even in the short time it had taken me to walk from the taverna, the sun had turned into a deep fiery orange orb sinking towards the horizon in an apricot and coral sky, streaked with shades of lilac and vermillion.

'Péfka, it is famous for its sunsets. You must bring your paints one evening.'

'I'll do that.'

Subconsciously, I patted my bag. Mam would have seen sunsets as beautiful as the one I saw in front of me and yet the paintings and sketches I remembered were all in her trademark, blues and greens. Yiannis was talking to me and I'd let my mind wander back to Mam.

'Sorry. I was miles away.'

'I say the colours, they suit you. The colours of the sea.'

'They were my mother's favourites.' I took the diary out of my bag and placed it on the checked tablecloth between us. 'Let's get something to drink and I'll tell you all about this.'

Yiannis called over the waiter and we ordered a carafe of retsina, some olives and pistachios. He picked up Mam's diary and ran his hands over the smooth leather cover.

'The book, it is beautiful.'

'I haven't told you the real reason I'm here,' I said. 'You know I told you my mam passed away recently. Well, she left me this – her diary which is also a sketch book.'

'I do not understand. What has the diary to do with you coming to Péfka?'

I took the diary from him. 'This is my mam's account of how she spent her summer on the island in 1969. She studied painting at the painting school at the top of the hill. You know where you found me yesterday. Here, read the first page. She arrived here in this very harbour, where we're sitting now.'

It was quiet as he read and I watched his expression change. He flicked through the book stopping to look at some of the watercolour sketches. 'She is very good, isn't she? But you do not tell me? Why is it a secret?'

'I'm sorry. I thought I'd try to find out what happened on the island that summer and people would hide things if they thought I'd be upset by the truth.'

Yiannis looked puzzled. 'The truth?'

'Something happened that summer. Something my mother never told anyone about, not even her mother. All my grandmother said is that she was never the same after she returned. She never picked up a paintbrush or painted ever again. I didn't even know she *was* an artist.'

I told Yiannis all I knew about my mother's secret life, what I'd found out in the diary.

'I am born here in 1969 so it is a long time ago. I am no help. Sorry, Alexandra *mou*. We move to the mainland when I was a little boy and Mamá and Papa did not talk about the island. When I want to start up my business here, my papa does not at first agree. He says it is best to stay away. Mamá has died by then so that is the reason, I think. He does not talk about it. He never comes to the island since I move here.'

'As far as I can see, everyone living here now is a newcomer. There's no one to ask. But I've never asked what your surname is? It's not Guikas by any chance?'

As Yiannis took a sip of wine, at hearing that, he spluttered. 'How do you know that?'

'Because in the diary, my mother talks about staying at the taverna half way up the hill and that the hosts, Vassilis and Dimitra Guikas, were very kind to her.'

'My mamá and papa.'

‘I thought so. My mam was there the night you were born and you have a sister, Lyra. Am I right? And those paintbrushes you gave me – they were Mam’s.’

Yiannis stood up and came round to my side of the table and took my hands. ‘Alexandra, this means I *can* help you. I take you to meet my father. He must talk about his life on Péfka now.’

That night I couldn’t sleep. The last thing Yiannis said to me was that he would contact his father and arrange for me to meet him soon. I was finally going to meet someone who knew Mam when she visited Greece all those years ago. How much would Kýrios Guikas be able to tell me? Did he know that Mam was in love with Stelios? When I closed my eyes, a picture of a greying man with Yiannis’s face came into my mind. From what Mam had written about him and from the short time I’d known his son, I couldn’t wait to meet Vassilis Guikas. I knew I was going to like him.

Chapter Thirty-One

The next day, armed with a street map of the port Kostas had given to me when I arrived, I took the ferry boat to Porto Nikos. The ferocious midday sun beat down and I was glad of the cooling breeze as the boat sped out into the open water of the strait. The sky was cloudless, a deep cobalt. As the boat got closer to the mainland, gleaming white dots morphed into luxury yachts and motor launches lined up along a pristine stone jetty which looked newly built. Behind them, a line of cars, vans and lorries resembled a shiny snake waiting to slither onto the ferry for its journey to the island.

I placed my bag over my shoulder and walked towards the gangplank. The ferry was full of passengers and I watched as the first group disembarked and formed a line traipsing along the quayside. I followed, not knowing where I was going but hoping that it was the right direction for the port. I stopped at a small café on the edge of the marina, proudly displaying a sign stating 'we speak English'. Wanting to find the beach where she'd had painted the solitary olive tree, I took out my mam's diary. I found the diary entry where she and her Greek friends had walked along the road to the house for the party. Mam had written that the Simonides' house was called *Ee Eliés* and was on the road to Ermione, the next town along the coast.

A young Greek girl arrived at the table to take my order. She smiled and handed me a menu.

'A coffee, *parakaló*.' I pointed at the image of a cappuccino style coffee as a change from the strong Greek coffee I'd being getting used to on the island.

'What a beautiful book,' the girl said, with only a mere hint of a local accent.

'*Efharistó*. It belonged to my mother.'

When the waitress returned with her coffee, I asked her to show me the way on the map. The girl's face lit up and told me that Ermione was where she lived and that it was an excellent base for visiting the small islands dotted along the coast.

'I won't be going that far today, just to a beach off the road to Ermione, but thanks for the tip, anyway.'

I paid for my coffee and walked out of the port.

The heat was a shock as I made my way down the lane to the beach. The air shimmered in a haze. Bubbles of tar oozed, forming black sticky streams that flowed to the gutters on either side. I shielded my eyes and squinted into the distance. Whitewashed buildings appeared out of focus, gleaming like sparkling jewels in the sunlight.

I reached a narrow strip of soft sand and I let the sea water cool my feet, allowing it to wash away the burn of the beach. This was where my mother must have walked. A breeze sprang up and made me shiver, not with cold but with an unease I couldn't explain.

'*Thissss way, thissss way.*' A murmuring came from behind me. The tone was sad and wistful but on turning around, I saw no one. Just like the ones by the painting studio, the olive trees here were whispering to me, too. I heard it again but this time it was more insistent. The whispers gathered in volume as more voices joined in. They were definitely coming from the olive trees that stood like sentries inside a fence which ran the whole length of that part of the beach. But one voice stood out amongst the others, 'Cariad, *thissss way!*'

'Mam?' I said aloud. Silent again, the breeze dropped. I looked down at the sand and saw delicate footprints forming a track in the direction of the olive trees, beckoning me to follow. I stepped on each one with trepidation expecting them to burn my soles but they were damp and cool. The beach was deserted and the footprints came to a stop in front of a single olive tree set away from the fence. I looked up and took a sharp intake of breath, placing a hand over my open mouth.

I had been concentrating so hard on fitting my feet into the footprints in the sand, my crooked little toe fitting exactly into the imprints, I hadn't noticed. The scene confronting me was the one I'd seen every time I'd gone into Mam's secret room at Nan's. This was *her* tree. The ancient gnarled face on the bark of the olive tree, with its thin leaves like dishevelled frizzy grey hair, had stared out from the watercolour painting that hung on the bedroom wall.

As I'd lain on the bed that first time in Nan's house, I'd imagined I could see an old lady's face on the olive tree trunk. If Mam had been alive, I could have joked with her, and made up stories about a wrinkled old lady I'd decided to call Olive.

I felt that mother and daughter warmth again as I stood at the very spot where she must have sat with a pad of thick grained paper, her sable brushes and palette of colours. I moved to sit under the silver-green canopy for shade and, from my bag, took out my mother's diary. The whispers started again, the leaves above me shivering and shaking. I looked behind me and I was sure the wrinkled face on the bark smiled back at me.

I flicked through the diary entries and found the painting of the tree.

I was jolted out of my day-dreaming by the sound of voices. A slim tanned woman was racing two young boys down the path from the house

The children squealed, charged over the sand and hurled themselves in the sea. They were soon splashing each other in a pretend fight.

The young woman turned and walked over to me, stopping a little way from the tree. She spoke in Greek.

'British?' she said when it was obvious I didn't understand.

I nodded. She didn't move any closer as if her feet were transfixed to the spot in the sand. I stood up and walked over to her.

'I didn't see you there. I was busy acting as referee for the boys' race into the water,' she said. 'I haven't seen you here before. I'm Thea, by the way.'

'Alexandra,' I said, shaking her hand. 'This is my first time here.' After hesitating, I added, 'My mother came here a long time ago.'

'It's lovely, isn't it? We live in England but every summer, we come to stay with my mother. But please move away from the tree.'

Before I could ask her why, a strident screech shattered the still air. I turned to see an old woman dressed head to toe in black shaking her fist, heading in my direction and shouting in heavily accented English. I went cold.

'Stay away, stay away. You no good. I hate you!'

Thea's eyes widened in disbelief.

'Mamá, what on earth is the matter?' She held the old woman's arm firmly and led her away, talking to her in Greek.

I was still trembling when Thea returned.

'Standing there under that awful olive tree, I'm afraid you've reminded my mother of something that happened in the past. Her dementia's become a lot worse since we visited last year. I can only apologise. I'm so, so sorry. I've never seen her like that.'

'I think I know what's happened,' I said, but before I could explain more Thea's sons came out of the water and joined us on the beach.

'What's the matter with *Yiayiá*?' the younger one asked.

'She's all right, boys. You know how she forgets things she's just done and then remembers things she did a long time ago. Can you take her back to the house?' Thea smiled in my direction.

The old lady was calm again and took the boys' hands, as they guided her back through the olive trees towards the house.

'Would you like to come up to the house for a cup of tea? It will be nice for you to see Mamá when she's relaxed.'

I hesitated. I knew the old woman thought I was Mam but if I was to get answers, perhaps I should go.

'If you're sure. That would be lovely. *Efharistó*.'

The whispering of the leaves on one side and the sound of the sea surf on the other reassured me that I would not be alone when I went up to the house. I felt my mam would be with me every step of the way. My heart raced.

Thea gathered up the children's towels from the beach and we started our walk through the garden. We came to a wooden archway where a familiar scent washed over me, causing me to stop in my tracks.

'Are you all right?' Thea asked.

'It's just the jasmine. My mother's favourite flower. It always reminds me of her.'

I turned my head as if to smell the tiny pink-white flowers, not wanting Thea to see the tears that were pricking below the surface of my eyelids.

It wasn't long before we reached the house with its bleached walls and terracotta tiled roof. Painted wooden shutters were closed to block out the sun and huge urns, abundant with cascading vermillion tresses of geraniums, lined the terrace.

Thea invited me to sit down in the shade.

'Mamá. I've brought someone for a cup of tea. Come out and meet her.'

By now, my heart thumped so loudly in my chest that I was sure that Thea would notice. What if her mother started screaming at me again? The older of the two boys came through the beaded curtain of the open doorway.

'*Yiayiá*'s gone to have a lie down.'

I felt myself relaxing into the wickerwork chair.

'Milk or lemon in your tea?' Thea asked.

'Milk, please.'

'It's lovely to have some young female company for a change. It's quite lonely around here for the six weeks we're here. My husband never comes.' She placed the cups of tea on the table and smiled. 'You saw what Mamá was like earlier and the boys … well, enough said.'

I wanted to ask why her husband never accompanied her and the boys to visit but she volunteered the information herself.

'My husband is English. We met in uni when I was studying in London back in the late sixties. Mamá's never forgiven me for not marrying a "good, Greek man" and made it so unpleasant for James that he stopped coming in the end. I only visit once a year and feel very guilty that I don't come more often. Six weeks is a long time for us to be away from each other.'

Her bottom lip trembled. Here was a woman torn between wanting to do right by her mother but obviously missing her husband. 'Half way through the holidays me and the boys meet him up in Athens for a long weekend and Mamá has to manage as she does the rest of the time.'

'*Yiayiá*'s up and about. I told her you had a visitor,' said one of the boys. Thea's mother joined us on the terrace. She looked straight at me and smiled, her wrinkles softening.

'Welcome to the house,' she said. There was no recollection of what had happened on the beach earlier.

'See,' said Thea, smiling. 'All forgotten. Tea, Mamá?'

'You have a beautiful home here, Kýria Simonides.'

Thea reappeared with her mother's cup of tea. 'That's strange. How did you know my mother's name?'

I felt my cheeks burn. 'Oh, I thought you told me … down on the beach.'

'No. In any case my name's Cooper now. My married name.'

'Um, it must have been the girl in the café when I was asking the way to the beach. She said there was a single olive tree growing in the sand in front of the Simonides' house.' My pulse raced. Why didn't I just tell her who I was? 'Yes, that's it. She was from Ermione. A local girl.'

Thea went out into the garden to sort out a row between the boys that was getting louder and more argumentative.

'Do you have any other children, Kýria Simonides?'

For a moment, the old lady looked directly at me and I thought that maybe I would revert to being my mother again in her eyes. Instead, she wrung her hands and sucked in a deep breath.

'Dead. Both dead. Only Thea now. She never here.'

At hearing the news, my chest filled with a huge weight. *I was too late. I'd never meet my real father and he died not knowing he had a daughter.* I stood up, wanting to get out of there before the threatened tears fell.

'Oh, Alexandra. You're not going? What's wrong?'

'I must get back. Thank you for the tea. Goodbye, Kýria Simonides.'

The old woman's face changed. She glowered at me. 'I know you. You steal my son. He still alive if you no steal. Get out, get out!'

Thea rushed me out through the front door, closing it behind her. Her mouth became a hard line.

'Look, I don't know what this is about but I think you should go. You were right. First, my mother shouts at you on the beach, then you know her name and now this again. There's something you're not telling me … And I'm sure I've seen you somewhere before.'

I paused. 'My mother was Elin Morgan and she spent the summer here on Péfka in 1969. I think your mother recognises me because I look a bit like her.'

Her face softened a little.

'Of course, different colouring but the same features. I met Elin, too. She was a brilliant painter. One of my brother's best students.'

'Your mother said both her sons are dead. Surely that can't be right?'

'Yes. I'm afraid it is. But Andreas died in 1969. Didn't your mother tell you?'

I gasped. 'No, I had no idea. All I know is what she put in her diary. She's dead too.'

Thea put her hand on my arm. 'I'm very sorry, Alexandra. She was lovely, and extremely talented.'

'Thank you.' There was one question I still wanted answered. 'And your other brother? He's dead, too?'

'We have to accept that he is. His boat was found capsized in one of the secluded bays on Péfka not long after Andreas died. They didn't find his body. Mamá even paid for a private investigator but he found nothing. Stelios was missing, presumed dead. Nothing in the last twenty-two years has made us think otherwise.'

I wanted to scream aloud the thoughts whizzing round inside my head. *No. It's so unfair. I've only just found out that he was my father and now he'll never know.*

'Are you all right? You've gone very pale.'

'Yes,' I said. 'I'm fine. I must go. I'm sorry I bothered you and upset your mother.'

'You must call again. Tell me all about Elin,' Thea called after me.

I didn't look back. I strode up to the main road to Ermione along the front driveway where there were no olive trees whispering and murmuring to me. The reflected heat from the pale lemon gravel was intense and I had to find shade.

Chapter Thirty-Two

I remembered very little about how I arrived back to the harbour to catch the ferry to Péfka. All I could think of was that my father was dead, just like my mam. What was the point of staying in Greece? I would never get to meet him or find out what happened. I fiddled with my mother's silver ring on the third finger of my right hand and wondered if Stelios had bought it for her. *I wish I'd never read the bloody diary. Why did you have to leave it to me, Mam?* My eyes burned and the weight inside me felt heavier than when I arrived in Porto Nikos earlier that morning. But on the boat journey back to the island, I came to a decision. I would cut my visit short. Go home to Nan and Claire. They'd be pleased to see me, at least. Richard and his fancy woman could go to hell! I burst into tears. Once the sobs started I couldn't stop and people stared in my direction.

One of the passengers sitting alongside me looked very concerned. He raised his eyebrows and gestured with his hands as if to ask if everything was all right. It was clear that he spoke no English. I nodded, dried my eyes and smiled.

'*Naí, efharistó*.'

There was only one person I wanted to see when I was back on the island. I walked up the hill to the wood turner's. It was only fair that Yiannis was the first to know I was cutting my holiday short.

'Alexandra. You surprise me. I think you sketch and paint on the mainland. You follow your mamá's diary.' He came over from his lathe and brushed the sawdust and wood shavings from his apron. 'Come, sit down. Something is wrong, eh?'

He led me to the leather sofa where customers would sit while waiting to be served.

I took a deep breath. 'I did go but there's no point in carrying on now. I met Thea Simonides, the sister of Andreas and Stelios. He's dead, Yiannis.'

'Andreas? It is the reason your mother stops her holiday, eh? The painting school closes early because of this?'

I nodded.

'Yes, he died before Mam returned home, Thea said. But no, I mean Stelios is dead, too. The brother my mam fell in love with. The man who I think– I mean I knew was – my father.'

My throat constricted and I couldn't continue. Yiannis put his arm around me and pulled me close.

'You are sure? To lose two sons, it is very sad, eh? Poor woman.'

'There's no point in staying now. There's nothing for me on the island. I just have to accept that the only person who knew why my mam left is dead and I'll never know what happened.'

'You must not decide yet. Tomorrow, I shut the shop and we go to see my papa together. I say a friend. Your mamá, she stays with him and Mamá so perhaps she tells them what happens. We ask him about Stelios dying, too.'

What harm would it do? Before I'd arrived on Péfka, I'd hoped that Vassilis would still be at the taverna and I'd be able to find most of my answers from him and Dimitra. Now she, Mam and my father were dead and he was the only person who held the answers to the many questions I had. Yiannis was right. I wouldn't book my flight or cancel my room at Zena's Taverna yet.

Yiannis took my face in both hands and kissed me very lightly on the lips. My insides somersaulted.

'This is another reason why you must stay. I want to do that since we first meet.'

'Me, too.'

I tilted my head inviting him to kiss me again. This time he held me very close and his kisses became more passionate. All thoughts about Mam and her secrets were forgotten and I knew I wanted more than friendship from Yiannis Guikas.

That night, I read my mam's diary again, looking for clues about what happened to Andreas. Every entry up until the exhibition where her olive tree painting had won the gold award was written with lots of detail and hinted that she was having fun with her friends Brad and Manos. Almost daily, she'd shown she was enjoying her painting and whenever I found one of the places she'd sketched and painted with watercolours, she'd captured the very essence of the scene. But in September, the entries became very infrequent. There were no coloured sketches only occasional charcoal drawings, some very heavily shaded. One, dated 9th September, had a figure lying against the trunk of a tree surrounded by waves and shells. I hadn't thought much about them when I read the diary the first time. The exhibition, towards which everyone had been working hard, was over and she knew it was getting closer to the time when she needed to return home. When Andreas died, all the students must have been affected. The painting school would have closed. But this wouldn't have been enough for her to give up painting, would it?

I put out the light and tried to sleep. I tossed and turned all night. One minute, I was thinking about the father I'd never meet, and the next an image of lovely Yiannis filled my mind. I watched the luminous hands on my travel clock pass every hour until thin dawn light trickled into my bedroom.

The next thing, I was woken by a light knocking on my bedroom door. It was Zena.

'You sleep too long. Yiannis is here.'

I shot out of bed. It was nine o'clock. 'Tell him I'm sorry. I'll be there as fast as I can.'

I washed and dressed quickly. I grabbed my bag, making sure Mam's diary was in there. There would be no time for breakfast. Why, oh why, had I overslept on that day of all days? It was the first time Yiannis had come to the taverna for me and I was late!

He was sitting at one of the tables outside in the shade. He stood and kissed me on both cheeks. The citrusy smell of his freshly showered skin was intoxicating.

'*Kalimerá*. You are ready to meet Papa?'

We hurried to the harbour and heard the horn signalling that the ferry was about to leave. We practically ran up the gangplank and flopped down on our seats.

'Phew! Just made it,' I said. 'I'm sorry, Yiannis.'

He grinned and said, 'You sleep a long time. You dream of me, eh?'

I put my arm through his and he pulled me closer. 'Maybe,' I said. 'Not telling.'

The journey passed quite quickly. Yiannis pointed out the direction we'd be travelling along the coast road to get to his father's house. He told me all about his childhood spent there, where he went to school, who his friends were and how the family had been ripped apart when his mother, Dimitra, died.

'Papa never accepts it,' he said. 'He is a lonely old man now. I go to see him but the house is very sad. He goes out one time in each week to help a friend's mamá. She lives on her own – he shops, he gardens, he helps with the olive trees. He does not talk about it. It is his duty but she is not thankful.'

We disembarked and walked along the quayside admiring the yachts and luxury schooners moored there. Yiannis joked about where he'd take me if he suddenly came into money and could afford one.

'Perhaps Santorini, eh? Have you been there? It is my favourite Greek island. The sunsets are even more – how do you say? – spectacular than here on Péfka. We ride the donkeys up the steep steps to Thira. We visit churches with the blue domes. Then we have dinner on one of the balconies that are romantic, with the candles and with the stunning views.'

He placed an arm around my shoulders and pulled me closer to him. We passed the bar where I'd stopped the day before. The young Greek girl with the perfect English raised her hand. 'Ermione today?' she called.

'Not today. The opposite direction.'

We turned left out of the harbour and walked to the bus stop.

The journey took us along the winding coast road. From high up in the bus, we saw frills of white spume lapping the many inlets and coves. The Myrtoan Sea was a deep aquamarine and glistened jewel-like under the intense heat.

'It is not far, now,' said Yiannis, squeezing my hand.

'Does he know we're coming?'

'Yes. Oh, and I give you a warning …' He laughed. '… he asks you many questions. He marries me to every girl. When I see him, he always says "You found a nice Greek girl yet, eh? I marry your mother at your age."'

I laughed, too, but thought about what my mother had said about Stelios. His mother wanted a 'nice Greek girl' for him, too. It was the Greek way. We sat in silence for the rest of the way. I wondered what Vassilis would be able to tell me about Stelios. I had no proof that he was my father, of course, but I was sure he was. It all fitted. If only Mam had told me.

'*Poli me elyóthentra*,' shouted the bus driver.

'That's our stop.'

I followed Yiannis down the aisle. The blistering heat hit us when we alighted the bus and I pulled my sunhat down over my eyes. Olive trees lined the narrow street, growing randomly in the dusty dry earth. Some with enormous squat trunks and deeply ridged bark must have grown there for hundreds of years.

'Can you see why the town's called *Poli me elyóthentra*?' asked Yiannis. I looked puzzled. 'It means "Town of the Olive Trees". They say there are more olive trees in this small space than anywhere else on the Peloponnese.'

'Everywhere I go seems to be called something to do with olives or olive trees.' I laughed.

The whispering started as we crossed the road and walked the hundred or so yards to Yiannis's family home. The rustling leaves reassured me of Mam's presence. The stone cottage with its terracotta ridged tile roof was set well back from the street and fruit trees, laden with lemons, oranges and figs, grew either side of a crazy-paved winding path. Yiannis took my hand and led me through a rustic wooden archway weighed down with the delicate pink-white stars of a fragrant jasmine. I bit my lip. The sweet perfume had the same effect as it had done when I was with Thea. We reached the front door. Faded blue shutters, tilted at an angle to keep out the glare of the sun, covered every window. My pulse quickened. What sort of welcome would I get from his father? The door was open and a wooden beaded curtain hung from the doorframe like the ones on Péfka. The beads moved in the gentle breeze and made a clicking sound that reminded me of the *komboloi* as they flowed through the fingers of the old men I'd seen in Santa Marina. Yiannis parted the strands and I followed him into the house.

The room was in shadow and cool, the whitewashed walls a contrast to the simple dark wood furniture.

'He is in the garden.' Yiannis walked through to the back of the house and called from the doorway. 'Papa?'

As I waited, I noticed a photograph on the sideboard. It was of a smiling couple with a little girl about seven or eight and a baby in arms. From the faded colour of the print, it had to have been taken some years ago but the good-looking young man with his arm around his wife's shoulder could easily have been Yiannis. When the two men returned, I saw for myself how alike father and son were. Vassilis was an older version of Yiannis with rich brown eyes and tanned skin. His once black hair was streaked with grey and the hair at his temples was snow-white.

'Papa, this a friend of mine. This is Alexandra.'

'I'm very pleased to meet you, Kýrios Guikas.'

The older man took my hand and smiled. 'Welcome, Alexandra.' He didn't release it but continued to look carefully at me. 'You are very like your mama, eh?' His eyes misted.

'Everyone says I look like her. Different colouring, that's all.'

Yiannis invited me to sit down and his father sat alongside me on the sofa.

'Elin. Our lovely friend. Many years ago.'

'Yes, I'm Elin's daughter minus the beautiful blue eyes and blonde hair she had when you knew her, I expect.'

'We do not hear after she leaves. Not a word. I think she must write to Dimitra and me. But no. She goes one day and we do not see her again. It is summer '69, I think. Bad things happen that summer. Perhaps, she wants to forget, eh?'

I didn't know what he meant and before I could ask him Yiannis had returned with three beers and a bowl of pistachio nuts.

'How is she, your mother? She's not with you?'

I hesitated and Yiannis took my hand.

'It's all right, Yiannis.' I turned to his father. 'I'm afraid Mam died a few months ago. She had cancer.'

Vassilis Guikas gasped and covered his mouth with his hand.

'No, not our Elin *mou*. She is so young. It is an awful disease. The same, it took my Dimitra.' His eyes filled with tears. He stood up and walked to the window not letting us see his face. His shoulders hunched and started shaking. He sobbed quietly.

Yiannis put his arm around his father.

'It is all right, Papa.'

Vassilis composed himself and sat down by me.

'She talks about us, eh? She is happy in Péfka. But she does not write to us.'

I took the diary from my bag.

'I never knew anything about her being here. I didn't know she'd been an art student until after she died. She left me this.'

Vassilis took the diary from me and stroked the soft leather cover. 'Ah, it is her beautiful diary. She takes it with her, always. It is a gift from her papa, eh?' Yiannis's father had relaxed and was smiling.

'I didn't know that. But there is much about her I don't know, Kýrios Guikas. I'm hoping you can help me.'

'You must call me Vassilis.'

Yiannis handed the nuts around and his father took a long sip of his beer.

'Tell Papa what you told me, Alexandra,' said Yiannis. 'About what you suspect?'

His father interrupted. 'No, no, she is not a suspect.'

Yiannis and I looked at each other.

'Papa, why would Alexandra think her mother is a suspect? For what?'

'Ah, you do not know about the murder, then?'

Chapter Thirty-Three

I looked first at Yiannis and then his father, who fidgeted in his chair.

'No, she is not a suspect. I think perhaps she says to you, that is all.'

'Papa, you must tell us … everything. We do not know about the murder. Alexandra does not know her mother comes to Greece until after she dies.'

Vassilis Guikas proceeded to tell us how Andreas Simonides had been murdered and that his brother had been the prime suspect. It must have been the murder that Zena mentioned when I first arrived.

My stomach churned. Thea hadn't said how her older brother had died.

'That's awful. What happened?'

'He is on the beach behind the Simonides house. He is against the olive tree. Sofia finds him. His own mamá. It is very bad, eh?'

I couldn't believe what I was hearing. No wonder poor Thea wouldn't come near the tree on the beach. There was no mention of this in Mam's diary.

'When did this happen? Obviously he was alive at the time of the exhibition?' I said.

'September 9th, the date it stays with me forever.'

Of course, the charcoal drawings. The figure slumped against a tree. It had affected her badly. No wonder she didn't want to talk about it. Could that be the reason she never painted again? But why had the man I believed to be my father been accused of murder? He sounded such a lovely man from what my mother had written in her diary.

'I knew Stelios had hit Andreas. Mam wrote that Andreas had come on to her – well more than that, assaulted her – and Stelios was furious. But murder …?'

The older man walked over to the sideboard and picked up his worry beads. He paced the floor.

'No, Stelios does not do it. He is angry, but no, he is – how do you say? – framed. Someone wants the police to think it is him.'

Yiannis looked at me. He raised his shoulders and held out his hands. 'But why? What does Stelios do to make it look like he has done it?'

'It looks like Andreas, he does it himself. But the knife, it is from the wood turner's where Stelios works. There were drugs involved. The drugs, they are in a package addressed to Stelios. The note Andreas holds, it says about the very bad row between the two brothers. Everything looks like it is Stelios.'

'Did he go to prison? Is he still there?' I asked. Perhaps Thea told me he was dead to cover the family's shame.

Vassilis shook his head. 'No. I thank our God. He has the alibi.'

He didn't say any more.

'Well, go on,' said Yiannis. 'Who?

'Your mamá, Alexandra. Elin is with him at the apartment. I take her to the police station. It does not help him to start with. They say he takes the motorboat to the beach after she goes back to the taverna. The times, they do not fit.'

The rhythm of the worry beads clicked into the quiet as we pondered on what Vassilis had told us.

'Stelios is in the police cell for many days. Then he is free. The results, they come back to say he does not kill his brother. His fingerprints do not match or handwriting on the note. But it does the damage, eh?'

'What do you mean? You said he was cleared,' I said. Thea had said her brother was presumed dead. My voice trembled.

'In Greece, there are people, they think there is truth in the lies always.'

I knew what he meant. Richard was one of those who never thought the best of people.

'In Britain, we say "No smoke without fire". Poor Stelios.'

Vassilis sat back down beside me.

'*Naí*, poor Stelios. Even his own mamá has the doubts. She says she believes Stelios does not do it. But he cannot please her. And then when your mamá leaves without a word, he is a very sad man.'

I would never be able to find out from my father what happened. Could he have had something to do with it? Yet, the picture I'd formed of him from reading Mam's diary was of a man incapable of such an act. How could Mam have abandoned him when he needed her? But it was not how she saw it. It was Stelios who abandoned her.

'Do not cry, Alexandra *mou*,' said Yiannis. 'Your mamá, it is not her fault. She is part of a very bad thing that happens.'

I nodded. 'I know but here, if you read this. She did try to meet him and tell him she was leaving for home. But he never turned up.'

I opened the diary on the last but one page and handed it to Vassilis and Yiannis.

'You read it, Yiannis. My glasses, I do not have them.'

Yiannis read out the diary entry.

September 29th

Waited for S. under the olive tree as arranged. Why didn't he come? I wanted to tell him my news. I didn't expect anything of him. I'd tell him I'd manage. Felt he should know before I left. I think she had a hand in it. She was there when I posted the letter, I'm sure of it. My only crime was not being Greek. No, he didn't want to see me. Not even a goodbye, then.

'Ah, so she tries to say goodbye, eh? If only he knows this …'

'He wouldn't have killed himself,' I interrupted. 'Thea said they found his boat by a cove on the south side of the island but his body was never found.'

Vassilis dropped his worry beads and they clattered onto the floor. He became flustered. 'We do not know that.'

'But you say he is a very sad man,' said Yiannis.

'*Naí*, but that is not the reason to kill himself. You look at me when your mamá dies, but you must still live the life, I think. No, Stelios does not take his own life. It is the accident. I am sure of it.'

I was listening to what Vassilis and Yiannis were saying while flicking through the pages of Mam's diary.

'But don't you see? I think the reason Mam wanted to meet Stelios before she left was to tell him she was pregnant with me. She knew they couldn't be together because of his mother but wanted him to know.'

Vassilis put his hand to his mouth and breathed in hard.

'But why now, she says it?'

'She married Richard and he brought me up as his daughter. She told no one but I think before she died, she felt I should know the truth and that's why she left me this.' I held up the diary. 'I came here with Mam's blessing to find my real father. Stelios didn't know he had a daughter … And now it's too late.'

As we stood in the small hallway saying our goodbyes to Vassilis, I noticed an oil painting of a lighthouse over the hall table. My heartbeat quickened. I went closer and saw that, as I suspected, they were my mother's initials *E.M.* written in the corner of the canvas.

'This is one of Mam's,' I said.

Vassilis beamed at me. '*Naí*, the painting, it is our treasured possession. Elin gives the present to Dimitra and me when she goes away. It is the lighthouse where we spend many happy hours before the marriage. She paints it for the exhibition. You know she wins the gold award, eh?'

'She wrote about it in here,' I said, pointing to the diary. 'What happened to the winning painting? The one with the solitary olive tree?'

Vassilis shook his head. 'I do not know. Stelios, he buys it but where it is now, I do not know.'

'Oh, well. It would be lovely to see what earned her that award. But I'll never see it now will I?'

'*Antio*, Papa. I knew you would want to meet Elin's daughter.'

Yiannis kissed his father on both cheeks.

'Goodbye, Vassilis. *Efharistó*.'

He walked with us to the gate and before we left him alone, he grabbed my hand.

'I am very glad you come to see where your mamá is happy in that summer.' He pulled me closer to kiss my cheek and lowered his voice. 'She does not tell us but we know she and Stelios are in love. You look at them together and you know.'

The journey back to Péfka was a quiet one. Yiannis and I held hands but said very little to one another. It was as if my quest to find my real father had come to an end and that the last tie with this beautiful country had been severed.

'I do not know what to say, Alexandra *mou*. Thea tells you Stelios is dead but inside here, I hope my papa has more to tell you. More about your mamá. But the murder, it is all he talks about.'

'Yes, that was a shock. I'd hoped so, too, but he did tell me my mother and Stelios were in love. The fact that I was able to talk to someone who knew Mam back then was comforting. Thea didn't know her properly. She met her a few times but your mamá and papa knew her very well. It sounds as if they were great friends. I knew how much she thought of *them* from reading the diary but Vassilis seemed to be genuinely very fond of her, too.'

'Your mama, she sounds lovely. Now I understand the tears in your eyes from the gift of the paintbrushes. You know they are hers, eh?'

I nodded.

The bus arrived at the port and we walked along the jetty.

'What will you do now? I hope you do not rush home now your search has come to an end.' Yiannis placed his arm on my shoulder and pulled me close.

‘No, I’ve booked into Zena’s for another two weeks so I’ll stay and treat this as a holiday in the sun now. You giving me Mam’s paintbrushes has re-kindled my love of painting. A lot more portable than a lump of clay and a potter’s wheel!’

We both laughed and walked up the gangplank onto the boat.

As we left Porto Nikos, I looked across to the coastline where the Simonides’ villa was. I imagined Andreas lying fatally injured against the olive tree just as my mam had drawn in her diary. Vassilis didn’t say who’d killed him. The late afternoon sun was still hot and yet I shivered. Thea Simonides was alone and had to come to terms with one murdered brother, another presumed dead and a mother suffering from dementia. I decided I would visit her again, admit that I was her niece and say I would be willing to support her.

That night I didn’t put out my light until I’d re-read Mam’s diary from cover to cover. Again. By then I knew it word for word but wanted to check that I wasn’t missing something. Why hadn’t Mam mentioned that Andreas was murdered? She obviously hadn’t intended anyone to read the diary back then. I turned to the date Vassilis had said Andreas had been found.

September 10th

What a shock! So much for our best laid plans. Stelios wouldn’t need Manos and Brad’s help any more. The Simonides family name would be forever remembered for another reason now. Poor Stelios. No one can believe it. He’ll need me more than ever now.

That was all she wrote about it. Cryptic clues were dropped like crumbs throughout the next pages of the diary with monochrome sketches without spelling out what had actually happened to her. All I knew was that everything had changed and it had affected Mam deeply. Maybe that was why she never mentioned that part of her life ever again. Perhaps it wasn’t Richard being controlling, forbidding her to talk about her summer in Greece.

I must have drifted off to sleep eventually with my head full of unanswered questions. When I awoke, thin light trickled through the curtains and gave the room an ethereal feel. I blinked my eyes open and for a second, I imagined that a younger Mam was standing at the foot of the bed, her long blonde hair gleaming in the silver early morning light. My mind was playing tricks on me. There was no one there but could it be a sign? Was Mam trying to get me to delve deeper?

It would soon be time to get up. I'd visit Thea and tell her who I was. Or who I thought I was. Stelios was dead. I had no real proof but the more time I spent on the island, the more I read between the lines of what Mam had written in her diary, the more I was convinced I was his daughter. If I was right, then what remained of the Simonides family should know.

Chapter Thirty-Four

It was overcast when I walked out from the marina in Porto Nikos. Since I'd arrived in Greece, I'd never seen the sky anything other than a vibrant cerulean blue, cloudless. As I passed, the young girl in the bar raised her hand and waved.

'There's a storm on its way,' she called.

The buildings around the harbour looked greyer and the gleam on the paintwork of the yachts and schooners glistened a little less brightly. The dull headache I'd had since leaving Péfka told me the girl's prediction was right. I walked along the road in the direction of Ermione and turned off at the narrow lane that led to the beach in front of the Simonides' house. A strong wind whipped up and I shielded my eyes from the sand. The rustling leaves on the olive trees inside the fence no longer whispered. That day, the noise was more of a howl and I felt Mam's presence strongly as I approached the solitary tree. The howl became a shriek telling me that was the very spot where Andreas Simonides had met his death. No wonder Thea had not come any closer. An old dilapidated motor launch was moored on the stone jetty a short distance away. It tossed up and down on the sea water. The wind died down and returned to whispers.

There was no one about but as I turned to go there was a terrific crash from the jetty. Wind had whipped up the sea and the motor launch had been hurled into the stone wall. There was a gaping hole in the side of the boat and it started to sink. The noise had alerted the people in the house next to the Simonides'. A man and a young boy raced from their garden and started pulling the boat towards the beach by its mooring rope. They spoke in rapid Greek and I understood nothing. They were battling against each wave that threatened to submerge the boat. More people joined them and a young man managed to pull up the anchor and toss it into the boat. They dragged the boat on to the sand and flopped down exhausted. The motor launch rested on its side.

Thea and her boys had heard the noise and had come out to see what had happened. She spoke in Greek to the men who had managed to salvage the boat. All I heard was '*efharistó*' and the word for storm, *'thýella'*.

She turned to the boys and said. 'It was your Uncle Stelios's boat. It's very badly damaged. We can't repair it. The last bit of him.' She began to sob.

The younger of the two boys hugged his mother round her waist. 'Don't cry, Mamá.'

She started to walk back to the house, each arm resting on her sons' shoulders. Then, she noticed me standing under the olive tree, watching.

'What are you doing here?' she said. 'I expect you saw what happened to the motor launch. We never get weather like this. The last time …' Thea's eyes filled with tears. 'The last time we had a storm like this was when they found my brother's boat. Abandoned in a cove and no sign of him. Then or since. We brought it back here.' She turned her head away. 'I always hoped …' There was a deep intake of breath and she turned to face me again.

'I'm sorry, Thea. I was hoping to catch you, to talk. I should have been honest with you when I was here a few days ago.'

The boys had run on into the house. Thea shivered and hugged her arms around her. Large spots of rain fell. It was going to pour down.

'Look, we're going to get soaked. Come up to the house. Just be prepared for Mamá. I never know how she'll react from one day to the next.'

I followed Thea through the garden past the olive trees in the grove alongside. The rustling and whispers started but, rather than feeling nervous about telling Thea about what I suspected, I felt at ease. It was the right thing to do. The rain had started in earnest and when we darted under the arch of summer jasmine, the intense perfume took my breath away. Mam was watching over me, I knew it. I hadn't felt like that in Wales after she'd died but I sensed it here in Greece where she'd been very happy during that summer.

We reached the terrace and veranda of the house just before the heavens opened and Thea took me inside.

'You remember, Alexandra, Mamá.'

The old woman sat in a wooden rocking chair just inside the doorway. She had a crocheted shawl over her shoulders and worked at a cross-stitch picture of an old fisherman. She peered up at me and there wasn't a flicker of recognition in her black piercing eyes.

'*Kalimerá*, Kýria Simonides. I like your picture.'

She stood up suddenly and dropped her tapestry onto the floor.

'You no good. You take Stelios. My son. You evil.'

She pushed me with full force and I went flying. I banged my hip on the edge of a table and fell headlong across the room.

'Mamá!' Thea screamed and ran to help me up. 'Boys, come and sit with *Yiayiá*.' She turned to me, 'I'm very sorry, Alexandra. She doesn't know what she's doing … or saying.'

Her mother sat back down and rocked back and forth, moaning quietly to herself.

'Come through to the front room. Let's see where you're hurt,' said Thea.

Rubbing my hip, I followed her into a large room where the furniture was more formal and luxurious drapes framed the floor-to-ceiling windows. The pink marble fireplace was the focal point of the room, which was in complete contrast to the homely living room we'd just left. On the chimney breast, three portraits of handsome young men looked down with an air of importance.

'Sit down, Alexandra. Where are you hurting? We must get you to a doctor.'

My hip was throbbing but the initial pain had subsided. I knew I'd have a huge bruise there in the morning but it wasn't serious. 'It'll be fine, I'm sure. I should never have come back. Upsetting her like that.'

Thea shook her head. 'I don't know what I can do. She's getting worse. The only person she seems to be like her old self with is the gardener. He comes once a week to help her with her shopping and do the garden. He's a great help, tending to the olive trees too, especially when the harvest comes. I think perhaps it's because he's known her since she was a young woman and they talk about the old days.'

I looked up at the portraits. The one on the left appeared to make eye contact with me and I told myself not to be stupid. All three were looking the same way, the way the artist had painted them.

'Who are the young men?' I asked.

'The one in the middle is my father. I never knew him. He was drowned before I was born. The other two were my brothers.'

Before Thea told me which brother was which, I said. 'That's Stelios on the left, isn't it?'

'You're doing it again. How do you know that?'

I shifted in my seat. 'Oh, just a guess.'

I wanted to tell her that the expression on my father's face was exactly the one I saw in a mirror sometimes and that the single dimple on the left cheek was like the one that formed on mine when posing for a photograph.

‘Mamá never comes in here. It’s only opened up and aired when I come home. She can’t bear to look at the men she’s lost from her life.’

We sat in silence for a few moments and then Thea said, ‘You had something you wanted to tell me.’

I nodded. I reached inside my bag for Mam’s diary and placed it on my lap.

I took a deep breath. ‘I know you met my mother when she was here, but how well did you know her?’

‘I met her at the party and only knew her from what my brother told me. We weren’t friends as such.’

‘Which brother? Andreas?’

‘Of course. He was the one who knew her. He used to rave about her talent all the time. So much so that I think Mamá was worried he was falling for her. She wouldn’t have approved as she wasn’t “a nice Greek girl”.’ Thea laughed and looked puzzled. ‘Why do you ask? I don’t think Stelios knew her very well. But hang on … the night of the party. Yes, they danced together a lot. Tasia was off somewhere with Andreas organising the drinks. Come to think about it, they were together after the funeral, too.’

I opened the diary, turning to the passages I’d marked with postcards where Mam had hinted that she was in love with Stelios.

‘Thea, I think they were more than friends. Here, read the parts I’ve marked. See what you think.’

Thea took the diary and smoothed her hand on the soft leather cover. ‘Beautiful.’ She read each passage in silence and her eyes widened. ‘My God, she was in love with him. All the time we thought he’d marry Tasia.’

‘I think until the engagement was broken off, she kept her feelings to herself. But towards the end, I think things became serious.’

‘He never said a thing. Of course, Mamá would never have allowed him to marry anyone who wasn’t Greek. I know. It was only when I threatened never to see her again did she relent and let me marry James but, as I told you the other day, she makes him feel so unwelcome. Such a stupid rule! But in this household, Mamá’s word is law … so she used to think. And now look at her.’

Thea’s eyes welled with tears. She glanced up at the men looking down at us from the chimney breast.

‘What I came to tell you is that I think Stelios was my father. That’s why I came here. With Mam’s blessing. She knew she was dying and she left me her diary to be read after her death. Thea, don't you see she wanted me to find him?'

Thea gasped and put her hand over her mouth.

'My God. I can see it.' She pointed up at the portrait. 'That expression. It's exactly the same and the one dimple. You may have Elin's features but you're my brother's daughter all right.'

My heartbeat quickened and I felt the hairs prickle at the back of my neck. For the first time, someone else recognised who I actually was. Thea crossed the room and hugged me close.

'You're my niece. My niece, Alexandra. Mamá has another granddaughter!'

I didn't understand at first but pushed the thought away as I wondered how Thea would make her mother understand. Thea grabbed my hand and dragged me back into the living room where her mother was back embroidering her tapestry and the boys were playing a game of dice.

'Boys, I have some news. It will take some getting used to but it turns out that Alexandra is Uncle Stelios's daughter. She's your cousin. Isn't that good?' The boys looked up, agreed and then resumed their game.

Thea smiled. 'Now for the more difficult bit.'

She took her mother's tapestry from her and placed it on the table nearby. She knelt down beside her. Taking her mother's hand, she spoke to her in Greek. I recognised names – *Stelios, Elin, Alexandra*. I knew *'kóri'* meant daughter. The old lady frowned and looked first at Thea and then at me. There was no reaction. For the first time, I was looking at my Greek grandmother and thought how different she was from my vibrant nan, waiting for me back in Wales. As well as never having met my father, I would never get to know my *yiayiá* either.

'I'll tell her again later. Maybe get out some photos from when we were children. That sometimes triggers some memories.'

I didn't know Thea very well, but I could see how the realisation that her mother was slipping further away from her each time she visited was taking its toll.

'I wanted you to know who I was, Thea. You must let me help you with *Yiayiá*.'

She smiled. 'You don't know how good that sounds to hear you call Mamá that. If only she was able to realise what an amazing thing this is. To have a part of Stelios back in our lives.'

Thea wept softly and I led her out onto the terrace so that the boys wouldn't see. They were still engrossed in their game and my grandmother had resumed her needlework.

'It's been very hard,' she said. 'I feel guilty leaving her to go back to London. Guilty when I get frustrated with her when I'm here. Guilty when I take the boys away from their father.'

'Ssh!' I said. 'Don't be hard on yourself. Look I'm only here for another couple of weeks but if you like, I'll call every day. I won't be able to do much for *Yiayiá* on my own but at least I'll be able to give my auntie some moral support. Or maybe take the boys to the beach for you?' I returned inside. '*Antio*, *Yiayiá*. Goodbye, boys. I'll call again tomorrow.'

Thea led me through the house so I could leave by the front door.

'I'll try to find everything I can that belongs to Stelios by the time you come again. And *efharistó*, Alexandra. This is the best news.'

Chapter Thirty-Five

'Are you going to *Ee Eliés* again today?' Zena was clearing away my breakfast things. I still hadn't become used to eating outside for every meal. I was going to miss this when I returned home. I had so much to tell Nan and Claire but for now I was going to enjoy every moment in the Greek sunshine that I could. It may have been too late to meet my father but I had gained an aunt, two cousins and a grandmother.

I'd explained to Zena about visiting the Simonides' home on the mainland and being Stelios's daughter. She'd been thrilled to know I was half Greek and lost no time in giving me more Greek words to practise every time I saw her.

'Yes, I thought I'd take my paints and see if I can paint the old olive tree that grows alone in the sand,' I said. 'If Thea wants me to look after the boys, I'll be just at the end of the garden.'

When I went up to my room to get my things, I heard loud voices in the street below. Two men were greeting each other in Greek, patting each other on the back and laughing. The one with his back to me turned and pointed to the taverna. It was Vassilis Guikas. I rushed downstairs and out into the street.

'Vassilis,' I said. 'What are you doing here?'

'I come to see you.' He turned to the other man. 'My friend, here, I have not seen him for many years?'

The man with Vassilis was the man with the worry beads who had directed me to the taverna the day I arrived. He nodded and his face broke out into a smile. He shook Vassilis's hand again and turned to go back up the street to his house.

'*Antio*,' he called.

Vassilis spoke first.

'You ask why I was here. I tell you something I do not say in front of Yiannis. Today, he is in Porto Nikos getting more olive wood. We go up to the old studio on the top of the cliff. No one disturbs us there.'

I wondered what he had to tell me. I rushed back into the taverna and grabbed my bag with my mother's diary inside. For some reason, I thought what Vassilis was about to tell me would concern her. We turned left at the end of the street and walked up the hill. Vassilis didn't stop when we passed his old taverna and I heard him take a deep breath. Why couldn't he bear to live on the island anymore? Had the murder affected him so much that he'd had to take Dimitra and his children away from where he grew up?

We reached the top of the road and took the right fork, walking along the cliff top. The view across to the mainland never failed to mesmerise me and I paused for a moment to drink in the scene once more.

'Magnificent, eh?' Vassilis pointed to a group of whitewashed buildings on the coastline. 'That is where you come to see me yesterday.' He moved his arm to the right. 'And there is where the Simonides family lives.'

The olive trees whispered as we walked along the footpath to the art studio. Just as it was when I went there the first time, the place was deserted. We went around the back and sat on the bench under the pergola.

Vassilis took my hand. 'Alexandra, I do not tell you the truth.'

I pulled my hand away. *What could he mean?*

'Stelios is not dead.'

I gasped and brought my hands up to my face. I must have misheard. My head started to swim. I stood up, wanting to get away. My legs buckled and I felt dizzy. I grabbed the edge of the bench.

'But you said …' My voice rose. 'Why do you lie to me? Thea said he is dead.' My heart thumped in my chest.

'I *say* the Stelios I know does not kill himself. It is an accident. The boat, it turns over in the storm. But Stelios, he gets out in time. He goes away and lets everyone – me too – think he drowns. He starts again, somewhere new, eh?'

I clenched my fist and felt my pulse race faster. How could Vassilis have done that to me? He knew how much I wanted to meet my father. And what did it say about the man who *is* my father? How could he put his sister through all that heartache? Even if he and his mother didn't get on, Thea was only young when he faked his own death. What kind of brother was he?

'How could he do such a cruel thing?' My voice rose to a screech. Poor Thea.

'Do not get angry. It is very bad for him. All the time his mother say it is better if he dies, not Andreas. Your mamá, she leaves and she says nothing. The boat accident is a way to start the new life.'

My skin prickled. 'Don't try to blame my mother for this! She tried to let him know and he didn't turn up.' I stood and paced the flagstones. 'It sounds as if she had a lucky escape,' I shouted. 'What a selfish man!'

I'd built the image of my real father into being a gentle kind man, adored by my mother. Once I'd found him, I'd imagined a tearful emotional reunion and we'd spend the rest of our lives making up for the lost twenty-two years. I sobbed. That was never going to happen. A breeze sprung up and the leaves in the olive trees standing along the back of the studio rustled and whispered to signify Mam's presence.

Vassilis patted the bench beside him. 'Please, Alexandra. I think this happens. That is why I bring you here so no one sees. Come and sit down. He knows about you now but he doesn't like to see you. I am very sorry.'

'Well, I don't want to see him either if that's the man he is.' My voice cracked.

'I try again, you know. Once he meets you, he changes the mind, I am sure of it. Stelios, he has a shock, a big shock. You must not say to anyone. Not even Yiannis.'

I sat back down and we talked. Vassilis told me how once a week, he worked over at *Ee Eliés* and checked on Sofia Simonides.

'I tell Stelios how his mother is. He is a good man, Alexandra. Still he cares for her but she treats him in a very bad way. I say nothing about him. At first, when she talks about his *death,* I take the care not to say he is still alive. Dimitra says she sees him once and I do not like the lie.'

'So it's you! Thea told me someone helps out and visits her mother when she's back in London. Doesn't *she* ask any questions?' The fact that my father had just disappeared and was living not far away was hard to believe.

He nodded. 'Yes, she is very sad when his boat is found. Not a body is very hard for her. She does not believe it for a long time. Then she is angry, very angry. I tell Stelios it is cruel. I ask and ask to let Thea know the secret but he says no one must know.'

I thought back to the man my mother had described in her diary. The Stelios who was full of life and popular with the islanders. The man who made her happy. How could he live the life of a recluse, cut off from everyone? It didn't make any sense. Vassilis interrupted my thoughts.

'You wonder how he lives on his own, shut away with no friends, eh? Sometimes, he visits very good friends in Athens. They must not tell, like me. He changes once your mamá leaves. No address, no number for the telephone. I try but no one knows. Her friend Manos lives here but he knows nothing.'

Vassilis looked at his watch. 'It is time to go. I get the next ferry across. I am sorry I do not have good news, Alexandra *mou*. But I try again. I do not give up.'

I smiled at Vassilis. '*Ehfaristó.*'

‘Stelios lives in a very big house in olive groves. It is twenty kilometres past Porto Nikos and he needs my help at this time of year with the watering. It is very busy. I go there tomorrow and I ask again. And remember, do not say a word to Yiannis.’

He kissed my cheek and walked away. I opened Mam’s diary and turned to the pages where she’d arranged the meeting with my father. *So somebody didn’t give Mam’s letter to Stelios. Someone who wanted to keep them apart.*

The image of an elderly Greek woman dressed in black and shaking her fist at me came into my mind.

‘Sofia Simonides, my *yiayiá*.’

The door to the wood turner’s was still closed when I passed. I stopped and peered in through the windows to check that Yiannis was not back. If only I could have told him what his father had revealed but, if I wanted to eventually meet my father, I had to be patient and do what Vassilis said. And I did still want to meet him despite what I said to Vassilis earlier. There was still plenty of the day left. I decided to do what I’d planned to do and catch the ferry over to the mainland.

The sun was high in the sky and when I reached the beach the water was a cool relief from the hot sand. The olive tree loomed into sight and I waved to Thea who was sitting a distance away from it on the sand as the boys squealed and splashed in the sea. There was no sign of *Yiayiá*.

‘I thought you weren’t coming,’ said Thea, standing.

‘Someone called to see me and it made me late. The man who ran the taverna where Mam stayed. Why didn’t you tell me he was the gardener who calls on *Yiayiá*?’

‘Vassilis. I didn’t think you’d know him. How strange he went to Péfka, though. I thought he wouldn’t set foot on the island after Dimitra died. Too many memories to start with and then he said it was full of incomers.’

Perhaps I shouldn’t have said anything. *What if Thea asks questions and I say something I shouldn’t?* It was going to be hard enough keeping his father’s visit a secret from Yiannis. I changed the subject.

‘If you want an hour of peace, I’m happy to stay here with the boys. I know this old tree has bad memories for you. Vassilis told me it’s where Andreas died. I’m sorry. Did I tell you there’s a watercolour painting of it in Mam’s old bedroom at my nan’s house?’

She paused ‘It’s just me. I just wish I could make myself sit under it.’ She sighed. ‘I shall never forget Mamá’s scream that morning. It’s been painted many, many times. Your mamá won the gold award at the art exhibition with a huge oil painting of it.' She became wistful. 'Stelios bought it. But I don't know where it is now … or where he is.'

I felt a flush creeping along my neck. *This isn't right, Stelios.*

Thea stood up. '*Efharistó*, Alexandra. I'll not be long. I'll check on Mamá and sort out some of Stelios's things for you.' She turned to the sea. 'Boys, Alexandra is here to keep an eye on you. No fighting now. I'm just going up to see to *Yiayiá*.'

As promised, Thea gave me a bag of Stelios's things when she returned to the beach later. My hands shook as I took the bag from her.

'It's not a lot. Just the personal belongings we found in his apartment after he disappeared. The furniture is exactly how we left it, I expect. Yiannis Guikas, Vassilis's son, lives there now so you could ask him to show you.'

I hugged my aunt. 'Thank you, Thea. This means a lot. I know Yiannis. He was one of the first people I met when I arrived on Péfka. But I haven't been to his apartment, only to the studio and shop. I'll ask him.'

Chapter Thirty-Six

Instead of going to Zena's Taverna when I arrived back on Péfka, I went straight to see Yiannis. The bag weighed heavily on my arm. How would it feel touching my father's possessions? Would there be any clues as to how he felt about my mother in them? The door to the wood turner's was open. Yiannis was back. The bell rang as I entered the studio and Yiannis, dressed in a leather apron covered in sawdust, emerged from the back room. His face broke into a wide smile

'This is a pleasant surprise, Alexandra *mou*. What have you done today?' He took me in his arms and kissed me tenderly on the lips. 'Here, I take the bag. It looks heavy.'

'Thank you. Thea gave me some of my father's things. I haven't had a proper look yet, and hoped I could do it here in the place where he lived. I didn't know this was his apartment.'

'Yes, there is an apartment over the studio. It is where I live now. Surely you knew that, eh?'

I hadn't thought about it before. I'd just assumed it was where Yiannis worked and turned his beautiful olive wood bowls. I thought he lived at one of the many cottages on the main street or down by the harbour. There was much I didn't know about my handsome friend. I looked around the studio and the display shelves forming the shop area. I imagined my father hard at work creating works of art in his beloved olive wood.

'Do you still have the wooden rattle he made you?' I asked.

Yiannis's mouth gaped open.

'The rattle, how do you know?'

'My mother wrote about it in here,' I said, patting my handbag that contained her diary. I described it down to every detail including the number of wooden beads contained in it and the blue silky ribbon threaded through its handle.

'You come with me,' said Yiannis.

I picked up the two bags. He took my hand, locked the door of the shop and led me upstairs to the apartment.

The light and airy room was simply furnished. A large sofa dominated the room and a simple wooden sideboard displayed delicately turned olive wood bowls. Placing my bags down, I walked over and picked one up. The surface of the wood was silky smooth and the colours ranged from a pale yellow ochre through to a deep auburn.

'Did you do these? They are beautiful,' I said.

Yiannis smiled. '*Efharistó*. I am happy that you like them. You show me what you have in the bag.'

I opened Thea's bag and took out the contents one by one, placing the items on the low table in front of the sofa. There were several black and white photographs in ornate silver frames. One was of the same man whose portrait I'd seen at *Ee Eliés*.

'I think this is Stelios's father,' I said. 'They have all inherited their father's good looks, haven't they? Thea showed me the portraits of the three Simonides men when I was over there.' I noticed a single dimple on the left cheek of Kýrios Simonides and smiled. The other photos showed dark-haired children when they were younger and playing together. One was of a happy family group, a strikingly beautiful Sofia Simonides nursing baby Thea with her boys standing either side and her husband behind her. His hands rested on her shoulders whilst she leaned back against him, beaming with happiness. I took in a deep breath. It reminded me of the happy carefree times Claire and I had growing up. Mam may have left the love of her life behind in Greece but she never let it spoil our childhood. She had never painted again but she devoted her time to us girls. And if she hadn't married Richard, I'd never have had a sister. A sister whom I loved dearly.

One piece from the bag caught my eye. My hand instinctively went to the wooden heart pendant I was wearing around my neck. An identical one lay on the table. Whereas mine was inscribed with the initial ε burned into the wood, this one had Σ Σ. I looked at Yiannis.

'It is the Greek letter for "S", sigma.'

'S.S. – Stelios Simonides. A matching pair.'

My eyes pricked with hot tears. If only things could have been different.

'You are all right, Alexandra *mou*?'

'I'm just thinking about what might have been. Stelios and my mother obviously loved each other very much. I have to make him see …'

'What do you mean? He is dead, Alexandra. You hear what my father says. It is too late. I am very sorry.'

My heartbeat quickened. Keeping a secret from Yiannis was going to be harder than I thought. But I'd promised Vassilis. If he was ever going to persuade Stelios to see me, I had to do it his way. I changed the subject.

‘There’s not much in here,’ I said, emptying the rest of the contents of the bag onto the table. ‘Worry beads, an old driving licence, a pair of cufflinks. Do you think they’re gold?’

Yiannis took them and looked carefully on the back of each oval disc. ‘There is a stamp on the metal so I think so.’

‘You’d think Thea would have wanted the boys to have them, wouldn’t you?’

Yiannis nodded.

‘What is this?’ He picked up a faded pale green card and unfolded it. ‘It is a ticket. To Ermione. The date is the 29th September 1969. 10.00 a.m. Why would he keep that?’

‘Don’t you see? That’s the day Mam left. He *must* have gone to see her before she left, thinking she was going by ferry. But he had the wrong time. He was supposed to meet her at the olive tree by his house at ten yet he was down at the ferry port trying to see her before she boarded a ferry.’

This proved that both of them had tried to see each other before Mam went home. If only I could show Stelios some proof that my mother had truly loved him. I took a deep breath to control the tears that threatened again.

‘Come here.’ Yiannis pulled me into his arms and kissed the top of my head. I lifted my face towards him, seeking out his lips and we kissed. At first, the kisses were gentle, tender. Yiannis planted tickly kisses down from my lips, along my neck and across my bare shoulder. I shivered with pleasure. I knew I wanted more from this beautiful man. He pulled me closer and our kisses became more urgent.

‘Is this what you want, Alexandra *mou*? I stop if it is too soon.’

I gave him my answer by undoing his shirt and exploring his taut chest. I kissed the smooth tanned skin revealed as each button was released until I arrived at his belt and the top of his jeans. I slid in my hand and he moaned.

‘Let us go upstairs,’ he said.

Yiannis pulled me to my feet. He caressed my breasts and pulled my top over my head. We left a trail of clothes along the floor so that when we reached the bedroom we were naked and ready to fall together onto the bed.

Afterwards, we lay for a long time in each other’s arms. Happy in an afterglow that I’d never experienced when Stuart and I had made love. I say *made love* but compared to what I had with Yiannis, it was a quick fumble. Never had I felt like that before. I looked up at his beautifully sculpted face with its bronzed skin, crinkly creases in the corners of his eyes that became deeper when he smiled and the soft full lips that had worked their magic on me. Feeling me move in his arms, Yiannis opened his eyes. 'What is it?'

'I'm just admiring the view.' Unable to control my emotions, my voice cracked as I said, 'Thank you. For making me feel that life is worth living again. After Mam … you know.'

Yiannis hugged me tight and kissed me on the lips, long and hard.

I looked around the room for the first time. At the furniture that once belonged to my father. There was simple chest of drawers on which Yiannis had placed a photo of a beautiful dark-haired woman holding a baby in her arms and with a little girl by her side. I recognised it from a similar one in Filia's taverna.

'Is that a picture of your mam with you and your sister?'

Yiannis stood up and dragged the coverlet off the bed and wrapped it around him. He brought the photo over.

'Yes. That was Mamá before she became ill. We all miss her very much.' He took a deep breath. 'Papa finds it very hard to come to Péfka. Too many memories, eh? He has not come to the island since he moves from here.'

I didn't make eye contact with him.

'Where's Lyra now?'

'She marries a boy from Péfka. They move to Athens after the wedding to find the work. When Mamá dies, she finds out she is not Mamá and Papa's daughter. They bring her up as their own but they do not tell her that our aunt is her real mother. Lyra never forgives them. She says she lives the lie.'

I know how she feels. I remembered the shock I'd felt when I read Mam's diary for the first time.

'My aunt, she is very young when she becomes – how do you say? Pregnant. Mamá and Papa are married but they do not have children then. I do not understand why Lyra is so hard on Papa. She is angry that Mamá keeps the secret from her. Even when Mamá is dying, she does not tell Lyra about it.'

But I could understand. Even though Mam left me the diary with all its clues, a part of me felt hurt that she couldn't have shared her secret with me. Maybe by suppressing it far inside and for such a long time, she did think of Richard as my real father.

We dressed and went downstairs.

While Yiannis made coffee, I settled down on the sofa and marvelled at the fact that I was sitting in the room where my parents had spent time in private. I reached for Mam's diary and flicked through to one of the passages where she'd mentioned the apartment.

I love being here with Stelios, away from prying eyes. No Elektra to go tittle-tattling to Anastasia or Sofia Simonides. We can be ourselves. Tell each other how we feel about each other. I was thrilled he'd bought the olive tree painting. It means so much and I know he'll treasure it after I've left. If only I didn't have to go ...

'Here is your coffee,' Yiannis said, placing the small cups on the table along with two tumblers of iced water. 'It is strong and sweet made the way the locals drink it. You are soon one of us, eh?' He laughed.

I remembered how sickly and thick I'd found Greek coffee when I arrived but he was right, it had grown on me.

'I'll always be an outsider. Even if Yiayiá Simonides understands what she's been told, I'm only *half* Greek. That wouldn't be good enough for her.'

He smiled. 'Well, it is good enough for me. I am very sad that your Greek father never meets you.'

I looked away and changed the subject.

'I don't suppose you found any paintings in the apartment when you moved in?'

Yiannis raised one eyebrow.

'It's just that my mam's painting of the olive tree was bought by Stelios. I wondered if it was still here.'

'There are no paintings on the walls when I arrive. But now I think, there are marks where paintings are for many years. I paint over them.'

My heart raced. 'Do you think someone has taken them? Thea said she only left furniture. She never mentioned any paintings, other than to say she didn't know where the winning picture was.'

Yiannis was quiet for a moment, deep in thought. He stood up and went back through to the kitchen.

'There is one place I do not open up. It is the store in the courtyard. I do not need more space. We go and see, eh?' he said, holding up a key ring from which hung a deep blue *mati*. Its evil eye stared out at me from above a bunch of rusty old keys of various sizes. 'I found the keys everywhere when I come here. I put the ones I do use on this. Perhaps one of them fits, eh?'

My heart thumped. If I could find Mam's painting, I could prove to Stelios that she did love him and that leaving without seeing him had been a huge mistake.

The courtyard behind the studio was cool and under shade. Tubs of geraniums like the ones at the Simonides' house glowed fire-like against the whitewashed walls. A wooden slatted table, with benches attached, was placed under a pergola. Papery magenta bougainvillea hung in vibrant clouds, its colour jarring with the scarlet of the geraniums. Yiannis led me to a door at the far end of the crazy-paved area. The pale blue paint was peeling and a small window to the right of it was obscured with grime and cobwebs.

'You pick one of the keys,' said Yiannis, offering me the bunch. I picked a heavy brass one that would be right for opening a traditional lock. The key went in but wouldn't turn.

'I think it's going to be a case of trial and error,' I said.

On the seventh attempt, one key opened the door and Yiannis pushed the swollen wood along the flagstones inside.

'There is something here.' Thin flat shapes wrapped in thick corrugated card and plastic were stacked on their ends.

'They have to be paintings, surely,' I said.

Yiannis handed me one shape at a time and I laid them on the table. My hands shook as I carefully removed each one from cardboard and inner layers of cotton muslin.

'Do you have luck?' called Yiannis, from inside the shed.

'Not yet. They are paintings but not Mam's.'

By the time all paintings had been unwrapped, it became clear that the painting of the solitary olive tree was not there.

'I am sorry, Alexandra *mou*. It is very important that you find it, eh?'

I nodded. If only I could take it to my father and show him the letter Mam mentioned she'd hidden in the frame. 'Can I have one final look? Please. Sometimes, a second pair of eyes and all that.'

Chapter Thirty-Seven

I took the bunch of keys from Yiannis, leaving him to re-wrap the paintings. Inside the shed, it was gloomy and dusty. I brushed cobwebs away from my face and tapped each of the walls. The back one sounded hollow. I made out a small lock about half way down. I stepped back outside into the sunlight and searched for the smallest keys.

'There's something behind the main space. There's a lock in the wall. Have you a torch?'

Yiannis came back into the shed with me, illuminating the space as I tried each of the keys in turn. After several attempts, the false back wall of the outbuilding sprang back into the place where we were standing. Yiannis shone his torch inside. A very large package rested against the stone wall. My pulse raced and my ears filled with familiar whispers. There were no olive trees in the small courtyard but the effect was the same. Mam was there with us.

'Here, you help me lift it, Alexandra. We must take care. You have that side and I go out backwards.'

It was bigger than all the other paintings we'd found. It had to be Mam's. I knew before peeling back the cardboard and extra protective layers of cotton muslin. Excitement prickled along my neck as I anticipated seeing my mother's famous painting for the first time.

I lifted the last layer of loosely woven cotton and stood the painting on its end, standing back to admire it. I saw an olive tree with the textured wrinkled bark that had been thousands of years in the making, the deft brushstrokes creating grey-green foliage that cascaded down to provide a shady canopy on the sand. Solitary, standing proud, solid, against the transparency of the turquoise water. I gasped. 'Oh, Mam.'

Yiannis placed an arm around me.

'Alexandra, it is beautiful. I see why it won an award.'

'I know. It's much better than the little watercolour in Nan's house. But why is it hidden away?'

'We take it inside.'

Together, we lifted the framed canvas into the sitting room and rested it against the sideboard while Yiannis went to get a hook and tools. I felt around the back of the frame and found what I was looking for. The letter was where Mam said she'd hidden it. No one had read it. I placed the envelope in my bag, intending to read it later. I'd tell Yiannis about it once he found out that Stelios was actually alive. But not yet.

Yiannis hung the olive tree painting on the wall over the sideboard and it faced us as we sipped another cup of coffee. It was big enough to take pride of place in the room but not so big that it dominated the space. The delicate shades of the brush work had a calming effect against the cool of the white walls.

'Every time I visit you here, I feel Mam is here, too. I'm so happy.'

Yiannis placed our cups down on the coffee table and pulled me towards him, leaning back against the soft sofa cushions. We began kissing. The kisses became more passionate. He felt under my T-shirt and my nipples were erect knowing what was to come. Feelings became more intense and my insides somersaulted.

'We go back upstairs if your mamá is in the room with us, eh?' said Yiannis, pulling me up to standing.

I grabbed him around the waist and followed him to the bedroom.

'I think she'd definitely approve of what I'm going to do with a handsome Greek,' I said, laughing. 'She did the same with her Greek lover or I wouldn't be here. I love you, Yiannis Guikas.'

Later that evening, in the privacy of my bedroom at Zena's Taverna, I peeled back the gummed seal of the envelope. The paper had yellowed with age but my mother's distinctive italic handwriting brought a lump to my throat. The last letter she'd written to me was the one giving me her blessing to follow her journey to Greece. Without that, I would have never found Yiannis. I blushed when I remembered telling him I'd loved him earlier. I'd only known him for such a short time. I knew very little about him but because of what Mam had written in her diary I felt I'd known him since he was that tiny baby born on the night when my parents had danced closely together. It had been the beginning of them becoming aware of their feelings for one another.

I unfolded the letter and read.

I had to see Vassilis. He'd said he'd broach the subject again with Stelios but I couldn't wait. I'd found the painting, found the letter and had the proof I needed that Mam had loved him. Perhaps that would be enough to soften my father's feelings towards my mam and me.

The sky was uncharacteristically overcast as the ferry left Péfka harbour. There was a sultry feel to the morning and a storm threatened. I hoped that Vassilis would be in and my journey wouldn't have been in vain. I waved to the girl as I passed the bar at the edge of the quayside.

'Looks like rain,' she called.

I raised my hand. I didn't have long to wait for the bus and once I arrived at the town of the olive trees, the sky was streaked with indigo and violet clouds. Vassilis's Toyota pick-up was parked alongside his house. I was in luck. I felt happier that I was about to tell him about Mam's painting and the love letter. I walked up to the door and knocked.

'Alexandra, it is a lovely surprise!' He looked past me. 'You are on your own?'

'Yes, I haven't told Yiannis I was coming to see you. It's getting very hard not to say anything about Stelios being alive.'

Vassilis's face became serious. 'You have not said to him, have you?'

'Of course not.'

Vassilis asked me in and it was strange entering the house without Yiannis. Before he could ask me why I was there, I blurted out that I had the proof that my mam did love Stelios.

'It wasn't just a summer fling. She truly loved him … and I can prove it! I want you to take me to Stelios. You don't have to come in with me, just tell me the address.'

I was gabbling. The words tumbled out but I knew I had to see Stelios that day. As soon as I'd found the letter, I wanted my father to read it. 'Please, Vassilis.'

'You slow down the words, Alexandra *mou*. Still, he does not want to see you perhaps? You are ready for that, eh?'

I clutched the letter my mother had written. 'He won't refuse to see me. You can give him this first if you like,' I said, waving the letter aloft.

'All right, but you do not say it is my fault if you cry at the end. Stelios, his will is very strong.'

Vassilis went to get his keys.

But he's also kind, and gentle and loving. Mam would never have fallen for him otherwise.

I got into the passenger side of the truck, my heart thumping. I was finally going to meet my real father.

The sky was still overcast but the further we went, the more blue appeared. Vassilis followed the coast road for a while before turning off up into the hills. The road became no more than a dirt track, dusty and pot-holed. He tried dodging the worst of them but every now and then, I was thrown forward in my seat as he braked hard to avoid them.

'I am sorry, Alexandra *mou*. The holes in the road, they get bigger every time I come up here.'

After a few more kilometres, we reached a viewing point where Vassilis stopped and we both got out.

'You see the villa, there. That is where your father Stelios lives. It is in the middle of nowhere. He is all alone.'

I followed the direction of where his arm was pointing. A large house, the colour of pale cinnamon, stood surrounded by a large expanse of land populated with trees. The terracotta ridged tiles were clearly visible in the clear air. The threatened storm had blown over completely together with my dark frame of mind. I had a good feeling. Perhaps my father was going to accept me after all.

'Olive trees, I presume.'

'Of course. It says how rich the man is in Greece. Your papa is very rich, Alexandra. Come, we go there.'

As the truck got close, my heart beat faster. Knots in my stomach tightened. Vassilis drove up to a post on which there was a speaker. It flashed red.

'*Naí*?'

'Vassilis.'

The enormous wrought iron gates opened slowly and Vassilis drove the truck through and began the long drive up to the house. Four chocolate-brown Dobermans bounded alongside the car, barking loudly.

'Do not worry. They are safe, harmless. Very gentle.'

The tyres of the truck crunched on the lemon gravel as it came to a halt at the shady side of the house. We got out and I was glad to feel terra firma under my feet again. As well as the bumpy ride, Vassilis was a very fast driver. A stocky man in faded navy-blue overalls and wearing a battered straw hat appeared from behind the house. That was my father. Upright and tall, he sauntered towards Vassilis, shielding his eyes from the glare of the sun with one hand.

'Stelios!'

My father's voice was mellow, deep, as he emphasised his friend's name as if to ask what he was doing there. 'Vass-ee-lis?'

Vassilis and Stelios spoke rapidly and loudly in Greek. They gestured with their hands and I picked up a few words – *Elin, kóri, Alexandra*. It was obvious that the conversation was becoming more and more heated. Stelios gestured for Vassilis and me to go and walked away.

I took my mother's letter out of my bag and held it firmly. The olive trees whispered around me, quietly at first, then building to a crescendo the nearer I got to Stelios. Mam would approve of what I was doing, I knew that.

Tears fell silently down my cheeks. 'Kýrios Simonides. Stelios.' I called after him. 'Papa.' On hearing that, he turned to look at me. I walked towards him, holding out the letter in my outstretched hand.

'Here, read this. My mother wrote this before she left Greece. This proves how much she loved you, how much you meant to her. You are my father. She suspected she was pregnant when she had to leave. She would never have left without seeing you. Someone tricked you.'

My father took off his sunhat and wiped his brow with his hand. He took the letter and I sobbed. I couldn't do any more; it was up to him now.

I turned and walked back to Vassilis who was waiting for me by the truck.

'You must give him the time, Alexandra *mou*.' He placed an arm around me.

We watched my father walk up towards the house, head bowed, reading the most important love letter ever written. It was a letter that would decide whether my father accepted me as a daughter he hadn't known he had or continue living in bitterness for a woman whom he believed had let him down and discarded him as a plaything after a brief summer romance.

'I cannot wait longer,' said Vassilis. 'Let us go up to the house.'

My heart beat like a drum as we walked. The door opened and my father came to meet us, arms outstretched. He took me in his arms and kissed the top of my head.

'Alexandra. My daughter! I am so sorry to treat you like this.'

My body shook. That moment had been why I'd travelled all the way to Greece.

Vassilis beamed and shook my papa's hand until I thought it would go flying across the room. 'Your daughter, Stelios. Yours and Elin's.'

My papa stood back and looked at me closely. 'You look like your beautiful mamá but you have the Simonides colouring and … the famous dimple! How is Elin? She married the man she talks about in the letter, I take it?'

Vassilis looked awkward and spoke for me. 'She dies, Stelios. She has the horrible disease, like my Dimitra.'

My papa's eyes widened and he put a hand to his open mouth. 'No, not my beautiful Elin. Taken too young, too young.' His eyes were red along the rims.

I went to him and held him. 'Mam wanted me to find you. To find out who I am, the real me. I always knew there was something missing in my life. And now I've found you.'

We stood holding each other in silence and Vassilis left us alone.

'I wait for you, Alexandra,' he called.

My father took me by the hand and led me to a large, airy room. It had a high ceiling and floor-length windows along one side. Shafts of sunlight illuminated dark, antique furniture. The soft furnishings were made of dark, heavy materials in masculine colours.

'Come and sit down, Alexandra. We have much to say to each other.'

I'd dreamed of that moment ever since I'd first read Mam's diary yet I felt strangely awkward, not knowing where to start. It was then, looking around me, that I noticed there was something very familiar about the artwork displayed on the pale grey walls. Delicate, free brushwork, the colours of the sea, scenes of places I'd already visited on Péfka in the short time I'd been living there.

My heartbeat quickened. I stood up and went over to look more closely at one painting of Péfka harbour, the boats of the fishermen on one side in contrast to the gleaming schooners of the wealthy ship owners on the other. I was right. *E.M. 1969.* I moved to the next one. Another of Mam's paintings.

'Beautiful, aren't they? Your mamá was a very talented painter.'

'But … but how did you get them here? In her diary, she said they all sold in the exhibition, bar one. And Vassilis has that one.'

Stelios smiled. 'No one locally knows I survived the accident except for Vassilis. But I do have contacts in Athens. It's taken them twenty years to track these down for me.'

I thought how magnificent the solitary olive tree would look over the marble fireplace.

'I may never have forgiven your mother for leaving like she did, Alexandra, but I never stopped loving her. Having the paintings she put so much of her soul into makes me feel she is still here in a small way.'

It was time to show my father the diary. I turned to the last few pages where Mam described waiting for him under the olive tree. I handed him the diary. He was silent as he read and then gave out a moan.

'So she *did* come! I did not receive the letter, Alexandra. I swear … but I think I know who did, though.'

And I knew, too. The woman who shouted angrily at me, thinking I was my mother.

Stelios stood and paced the floor.

'To think how that woman made my life unbearable, always hinting I had something to do with my brother's death, always letting me know it should have been me that died not her precious Andreas.'

His voice rose.

'Because of my scheming mother, I lost the only woman I've ever loved and missed out on over twenty years of my daughter's life.'

He burst into tears. I put my arms around him. It was my turn to be strong.

'Look,' I said. 'The main thing is that we've found each other now. When I thought you were dead, I confessed to Thea that you were my father and she tried to explain to *Yiayiá* who I was. You must let Thea know you're alive. It's only fair. I'll leave Mam's diary here and you can read it on your own.'

By then, Stelios had calmed down and agreed. The first thing he had to do was make peace with his sister, introduce himself to his nephews and try to make his mother understand that he was alive after all.

'I'll come and see you again soon.' I hesitated, then added, '… Papa.'

He beamed at me.

'I love hearing you call me that. Alexandra, my daughter. Elin even picked a Greek name for you.'

I hugged him.

'Next time, you must tell me all about yourself. All about your early life with Elin.'

I put my arm through his and we walked together down the drive to the gates; father and daughter. The dogs no longer barked as if they'd accepted me as part of the Simonides family and the whispering in the olive trees was a gentle, soothing rustle.

Vassilis was parked near the entrance.

'You are very happy now, Alexandra *mou*?'

I smiled and felt that I wouldn't stop smiling ever again. I'd found out who I was; I'd found my father. Whatever happened, whether Sofia Simonides ever accepted she had a granddaughter or not, it didn't matter. Life would never be the same again. I couldn't wait to tell Yiannis my news and then I had to write to Nan and to Claire.

Chapter Thirty-Eight

It was Yiannis's day off and the wood turner's shop and studio was closed. It was over a week since I'd seen my father and told Yiannis that he was alive after all. The date of my return flight home was fast approaching. Just when I'd found my father, I was going to have to leave again.

'But you do not have to go, eh?' Yiannis and I had walked up to the old studio and sat under the pergola with our arms entwined. 'The season, it comes to an end. Zena does not have the guests booked into your room, perhaps … and of course, there is a bed at the apartment. I can persuade you?'

He pulled me closer and kissed the top of my head.

There was nothing I'd like more than to wake up each morning in Yiannis's arms, but I had to be sensible. This was a summer romance, I told myself. A lovely one but I'd only met Yiannis a few weeks ago. I couldn't make decisions to change my whole life in such a short time. Nan and Claire needed me back home. Especially Claire, after her row with Richard. I couldn't call him *'Dad'* again after the hurt he'd caused her.

'No, I have to go home and see my grandmother and sister. But I promise you, I'll be back. I tell you what. I'll see if I can stay another few weeks and get to know my father more. I'm sure they wouldn't begrudge me that. Let's hope Zena hasn't let my room.'

'*Ela*, Alexandra *mou,*' said Yiannis. He took my face in his hands and kissed me, his tongue gently probing through my lips and the familiar longing inside me returned. He dropped one hand and traced a finger down my neck and inside my T-shirt along the shape of my breast. I shivered and my pulse quickened. Saying goodbye to this man and the sensations he stirred in me was going to be the hardest thing I'd ever have to do. If his feelings for me were the same as I felt for him, our relationship could survive the distance between our two countries, couldn't it? I'd never felt like this before and I had to make it work.

We walked hand in hand back down to the village. The wood turner's door was open.

'What happens …? I *know* I lock it. I am sure,' said Yiannis.

We heard male voices coming from the sitting room up in the apartment. Yiannis placed a finger across his lips and crept up the steps with me following. The door was open and he barged into the room, talking rapidly in Greek.

Vassilis and Stelios sat either end of the sofa, glasses containing a milky liquid and ice cubes in hand. Yiannis reverted back to speaking English for my benefit.

'You make Alexandra and me very frightened. How do you get in?'

'I'm sorry,' said Stelios. 'It was my idea. Your papa still had my keys to here and the old studio on the hill. We thought we would surprise you. Since I met Alexandra last week, I wanted to come to Péfka but it's been a very long time and I asked Vassilis to come with me.'

'And I come back only one time after your mamá dies. Stelios and me, we need each other and some ouzo to help us to visit, eh? … Oh, and the time I come to see Alexandra.'

Yiannis looked at me. 'Ah, yes, she told me?'

I took his hand and squeezed it.

Stelios stood up and placed an arm around my shoulder. 'I'm ashamed I doubted her, Yiannis.' We all sat back down. 'The last time I was here on the island, I couldn't go anywhere without people looking at me, conversation ending once I went in a bar or a shop. Even though I'd been released without charge, it still felt as if people thought I was guilty. Today, no one bothered with me. I didn't see one person I know. All outsiders, I suspect.'

I smiled. 'That's what Zena and Filia said. Zena runs the taverna where I'm staying. She and Kostas came five years ago from Athens and they call themselves that, even now. And Filia.'

My father looked puzzled.

'Filia?

'She buys our taverna,' said Vassilis. 'The woman, she buys it when I move away. After I lose my Dimitra.' It went quiet again.

Yiannis broke the silence. 'It is more than twenty years. The people forget what happens, perhaps.

My father's face became grave.

'I never have. It's as clear in my mind as if it were yesterday. I still see Mamá's face when I arrived at the house the next morning. Haunted, like a corpse herself.'

'You must not be sad, Stelios. It is not right that your mama sees her son like that.' Vassilis filled the glasses with more ouzo and I watched as the liquid turned milky as it came into contact with the ice cubes.

Papa took a sip and then a deep breath. 'But they did find out who the murderer was. In the end. The Athens police have closed the case and newcomers will forget about it.'

'Anastasia?' I said. 'Didn't she go missing the day after he died? And Mam said the police had some leads.'

The two older men exchanged glances.

Vassilis started to explain, 'The police, they check. She goes from Greece with the Englishman. They hide for many years.'

'Ah, Tom Reynolds. I think that was his name. I remember reading it in the diary. Mam was right after all, then. He wasn't working for the port of Piraeus police,' I said.

My father explained how Interpol got involved and the pair were traced to Monte Carlo when they tried to buy a new yacht.

'But why would she murder Andreas if she had an affair with him? It doesn't make any sense,' I said.

'She had the motive and Reynolds was in on it. Her drugs were coming to an end and she wanted to frame me, seeing as I was the one who was trying to put a stop to it,' said Stelios. 'But in the end, Reynolds told the police everything, that he had nothing to do with the murder but admitted the drug dealing. They were brought back to Athens and she confessed after her fingerprints matched those on the knife. The Englishman was prosecuted for the drugs. That is all.'

'And there was the letter,' said Vassilis.

My father sighed. 'Oh, yes. A letter from Anastasia to Andreas was found at the Loukas Villa when the Captain and his wife moved in. It was about the same time as they were caught in Monaco. She got away with it until then. I was still under suspicion all those years. The letter explained why she did it, how she did it and how she wanted to frame me.'

'Why on earth would she write to Andreas if he was dead?' I couldn't take it in. Was it like a diary entry? Getting your thoughts off your chest, maybe?

'Justifying it to herself, perhaps. She never thought she would get caught.' He gasped for breath, his eyes misting with tears. 'Poor Andreas. He didn't deserve to die like that.'

'People, they say many lies. There are always the lies. First, they say the Englishman does it. Then they say her papa pays the money to police,' said Vassilis. 'Perhaps, eh? But it does no good. They have no daughter now.'

'What do you mean?' asked Yiannis.

My father explained, 'She was waiting trial and the prison warders found her dead in her cell. A drug overdose, they said. Just awful for her parents, very sad. But come, let us change the subject. I've some better news.'

Papa told us how he'd been to see Thea, the boys and his mother.

'I had Vassilis there to break the news to Thea first. I didn't think it was fair just to turn up on the doorstep. We eventually met at the old olive tree on the beach where Mamá found Andreas. She wouldn't come near at first. She was *very* angry with me.'

'I understand,' said Vassilis. 'She is right to be angry. I ask you for many years to tell her.'

My father took my hand and patted it.

'You, Alexandra, have been a big hit with your aunt and your cousins. They adore you already after only a few meetings.'

And Yiayiá?

He read my thoughts. 'Of course, Mamá was a very different matter. First, she thought I was my father, the husband she had lost when he was younger than me. Then when we got her to realise I was her son, she became angry and accused me of murdering Andreas again. In the end, she calmed down and I told her about you.'

'She'll never accept me. She thinks I'm Mam.'

I shuddered when I remembered how she'd attacked me when I tried to tell her I was her granddaughter.

We'd became so engrossed in our conversation we hadn't noticed that Yiannis and his father had left us alone. I went to the window and saw that the two of them were sitting outside in the sun where Yiannis was showing Vassilis his latest creations. The older man looked more contented than I'd seen him. Yiannis had his father back, too, perhaps.

Papa was talking again.

'I had such a shock. I was angry with her when I found out what she'd done to me and Elin but when you see her now, frail and lost, how can I be mad at her? She wouldn't understand and it would be me suffering the bitterness. I've done enough of that for twenty years. No, I'll do my duty and let it rest. I've made sure Vassilis has been looking out for her but from now on, I will call on her regularly.'

He was the good man Mam had fallen for after all. I should never have doubted him. I felt there was much more to my father than what I knew already and I was determined to find out everything I could about him.

Papa and Vassilis walked back to the harbour. We'd arranged that I would visit my father at his house in the olive groves the next day.

When I arrived back at Zena's Taverna, there were two letters waiting for me. Nan's was full of news and how pleased she was that I'd found my real father. It was clear, she said, how much Mam had loved him.

If only times had been different, Alexandra, and your mam had felt able to tell me she was expecting you. We would have managed. The tongues would have stopped wagging eventually. Your mam may have continued with her painting and become a talented painter here in her home country, too. But then, we wouldn't have had our lovely, Claire. I'm very pleased for you. I'd love to meet the man who made your mam very happy and it sounds as if your friend, Yiannis, is making you happy too (!!)

Dear Nan. You would love both the Greek men in my heart and you *will* meet them one day, I'm sure.

The second letter was from Claire. My heart raced as my finger slid under the flap of the sealed envelope. Whereas my letter had given Nan answers and filled in gaps about her only daughter, I hoped that the letter I'd written to Claire hadn't read like a rejection of the life we had. Richard was her father, after all.

Dear Alexandra,

I can't tell you how much I'm missing you. I'm counting the days until you come home.

I'm pleased you have found your real father. I wish you'd told me the real reason for your going to Greece. I was very shocked when Nan told me but I suppose it all fits. I wondered where you had your black hair from and why you hadn't inherited the lily-white skin that burns as soon as the sun comes out! Dad was always more lenient with me and I could never understand why he was down on you. But he's the only dad I'll ever have and I have to live with that. Not that I'm very happy with him at the moment! We had a massive row.

You were right about Sally. You could see it when no one else could. It's horrible there without you and Mam. They're all lovey-dovey now it's all out in the open – ugh!

Nan has been great. She's so lovely to me, explaining everything she knows about Mam's life before she had you and me. The one thing she keeps saying is that even though I don't have the same father as you – and it would appear that yours was the love of Mam's life! – she loved us both the same. And I believe her.

I visit Mam's grave all the time, talking to her. It makes me feel closer to her. A- level results are out next week. I don't know how I've done but hope I've enough to go to Bristol. I've changed my course from Accountancy – much to Dad's annoyance! – to do Psychology. I think I'll need it, ha, ha. And the hunky Adam Johnson is going to Bristol, too.

See you next week.

Lots and lots and lots of love,

Claire xxxxxxxxx

I folded the letter. Reading it had made me realise how much I was missing my sister. Mam was our link. Nothing could change our love for one another. I hoped that Adam Johnson was good enough for her and wouldn't break her heart. She'd had enough to deal with recently already. There was no way I could write and tell her I was staying on a few more weeks, could I?

Chapter Thirty-Nine

My father was waiting at the bus stop in *Poli me elyóthentra* when I went to visit him the next day. He wore a crisp white linen shirt and smart slacks, very different from the scruffy unshaven man I'd met the first time. His black hair was streaked with grey and the white at the temples contrasted with his tanned olive skin. I could see why Mam had fallen for him. His silver BMW was parked ready for the journey up into the hills.

He was a much more careful driver than Vassilis had been and I was able to take in the scenery as we travelled along the winding roads to his villa. In what seemed no time at all, we arrived. The electric gates opened automatically and his four dogs bounded alongside us.

'I'd have come to get you from Porto Nikos, if you'd let me, you know.'

'No, I didn't want to put you to any trouble.'

'Just like your mamá. She was independent, too. I read her letter many, many times and I don't understand why she went back to your father. Richard, is it? It sounds as if she knew he'd control her. That wasn't the Elin I knew.'

I thought sadly of what Mam had given up. If only she'd confided in Nan.

'You have to understand that back then to be an unmarried mother was still frowned upon. I suppose she didn't want to bring shame on my nan. My grandfather had just died. Even now, it's such a small village where everyone knows everyone else's business.'

Papa thought for a moment. 'It's the same here, especially on the island, I suppose. Do you know about Lyra, Yiannis's sister?'

'Yes. He told me her mother was only a teenager when she had her and Vassilis and Dimitra adopted her.'

'I don't suppose he told you who her real father was? He most likely doesn't know. It was Andreas. Mamá begged Dimitra's mother not to say who the father was. She saved him from yet *another* scrape.'

'So *Yiayiá* has another granddaughter … and she *is* all Greek.' *I now understood what Thea had meant.*

'Not that she acknowledges her, either. Anyway, I've prepared lunch for us already so I don't have to stop for any cooking. We can spend the day getting to know each other.'

We walked through the house and onto a terrace, reminiscent of the family home at *Ee Eliés*. The huge terracotta pots were ribbed in traditional Greek style. Pangs of wishful thinking about handling soft malleable clay and the pleasure of transforming lumps of it into pots on a potter's wheel under the pressure of my fingers came to mind. I loved trying to improve my painting here in the places where Mam had painted but I was a potter at heart.

'You're deep in thought, Alexandra *mou*. They're fabulous, aren't they, those urns? I'd always admired the ones all along the quayside in Ermione and at Mamá's house and I asked Vassilis to commission a local potter to make them for me.'

'Are they hand coiled? I'm sure they're too big to have been thrown on a wheel.'

'Hand built,' he said. 'You know something about pottery, eh?'

For the next hour, I told him all about how pottery had been my specialist subject at art college. How the thrill of creating beautiful pieces had been my passion. How the excitement when a new glaze revealed unexpected results in a firing had been exhilarating. I told him about my exhibition and its theme of interlocking shapes. Just talking to my father about what had driven me before Mam's illness made me realise that my dreams of opening my own pottery studio were still there. The events of the last few months had only dulled them temporarily.

Papa rose to pour another iced lemon water for us. 'So you inherited your mamá's passion for creating beautiful things, eh? I must take you to some galleries to look at the local potters' work. There are some very good ones on the Peloponnese.'

I realised I'd done all the talking and my father had just listened.

'What about you? I feel I know you from Mam's diary but tell me everything about your life after she left.'

'I will but let us have our lunch first.'

He wouldn't hear of me helping so I sat in the sun marvelling at the fact that I was there at my father's beautiful home about to eat our first meal together.

'I hope you like moussaka, Alexandra. They are my own aubergines and the lamb is from a butcher in Kranidi. It is a treat for me to go and shop for it myself now. Poor Vassilis would have had to do it for me when I was "dead".'

I shuddered at such a strange thing to say but until a week ago, that's what he was to the outside world … and me.

‘I love it, *efharistó*. I wasn’t sure about the aubergines when I first arrived but I’ve had it so many times at Zena’s – along with Greek salad – that I love them now and the olives!’

He swept his arm over the olive grove to the side of the terrace. ‘You’ll have to taste some of these.’ He kissed two fingers. ‘I wish you could be here for the olive harvest in a few months time. You could help me and Vassilis gather in the fruit and then come with us to the olive press and see how the oil is made. It is the best virgin oil in the world,’ he said, grinning.

The olive trees were silent that day. I didn’t know if it was because Mam wasn’t there or whether she was happy to let me have time with my father without interruptions. How was I going to leave so soon after finding him? And then I remembered Claire.

‘What did you do when you found Mam wasn’t on the ferry?’

‘I raced back home and got into the motor launch and went across to Péfka. It was Manos, a friend of hers, who said she had left on the hydrofoil from there and not on the ferry like Mamá said. He knew the time she was leaving, so why didn’t I? I convinced myself she did not care. What I should have done was question Mamá about the message she had given me about the Ermione ferry. Because of her …’

I leaned across and touched his arm.

‘It’s too late now. Tell me about the accident.’

‘Living with Mamá became unbearable. At first, she did not believe her son could murder his brother but after a while, she hinted that I wasn’t upset enough. Perhaps I had done it after all. All she did was complain. Everything I did was wrong and I moved back to Péfka. It was not much better there. Sales of my work slumped and when the weeks turned into months and still no one had been charged with the murder, all suspicion fell on me again. People said I had paid the police not to charge me. The Simonides have the money, they said. An anonymous note posted under the door at the wood turner’s said that no one on Péfka was safe while I was still free.’

‘That’s horrible,’ I said.

He pulled his mouth taut and took a deep breath.

‘I kept myself to myself. My only pleasure was going out in my boat, fishing for octopuses. The best place was to the south east of the island and the nearest spot to the mainland where there was only a narrow strait of water. I was nearly on dry land when a violent thunderstorm blew up and I lost control of the boat. I was thrown overboard. My dry clothes and shoes were where I had left them in the cove. I managed to get ashore but that's when I decided to disappear.'

Papa told me how he'd travelled on foot in his wet swimming clothes and, at night, as far along the coast as he could. He had no money and was desperate for food and water. He'd waited until the occupants of a house he was watching went out. He'd broken in, eaten food and used the phone to ring a college friend in Athens. The friend came to collect him and fixed him up with clothes, money and somewhere to live low in the city.

'It sounds like a crime movie,' I said, once he'd finished. 'Surely, people on Péfka would be searching for you?'

'The local newspaper, *The Peloponnese Patris*, ran the story for weeks. It implied I had done it deliberately to avoid being charged with Andreas's death. In the end, it died down when authorities pronounced me missing, presumed dead. I was free.'

My father had help from his Athenian friends to set up home on the coast, not far from his mother. In spite of the problems between them, he felt duty bound to keep a watchful eye on her and that was when he contacted Vassilis.

'And that is all. I am happy with my own company and my beloved dogs. I have a lathe in one of the out-buildings and I continue to make bowls and the ever-popular honey twizzlers out of olive wood. At busy times with the olive harvest, I employ a few men from the local village but they have no idea who I am – some grizzled old Athenian, eh?'

'You're not grizzled and you're not old,' I said. 'I'm surprised you haven't found someone to love and make you happy.'

'A nice Greek girl, you mean, like my mamá always wanted for me. No, after your mamá left and Anastasia betrayed me, killing my brother, I thought I was happy here on my own. Until now. This is *real* happiness.'

Papa beamed at me. We cleared away the plates and then he made coffee. He brought out a small tray of baklavas, dripping with honey and coated in finely chopped nuts.

'You'll be getting me fat,' I said, laughing.

'Nonsense! Let us drink this inside. I have a surprise for you.'

The wind sprung up through the trees and I could swear there was a recognisable lilt to the way the whispering sounded. My father led the way into the large sitting room where we'd talked on my first visit.

On the wall over the pink marble fireplace, just like the one in his mother's house, there was a large imposing painting; a new focal point in the room. I gasped. Mam's magnificent painting that had been bought by Stelios was hanging in its rightful place, alongside all the other paintings of hers he'd acquired.

'How did it get here? We found it stored in the outhouse at Yiannis's place.'

Then I remembered seeing Yiannis and his father deep in conversation in the courtyard the evening Vassilis and Papa came over to Péfka.

'It is all your friend Yiannis's idea. He and his father brought it here last night. I wanted to surprise you.' He swept his arm around the room. 'I have every one now. Only the lighthouse one owned by Vassilis is missing. And he will never sell it. I would not ask him to. I thought I had lost this one, too. After Elin left, I could not bear to look at it so I stored it in the outhouse with all the other paintings I owned.'

I placed my cup and plate down and hugged my father. I could never have wished for a better ending to my search when I stepped off that Flying Dolphin a few weeks ago.

'*Efharistó*, Papa. Thank you. I'm very lucky to have found you.'

He kissed the top of my head. 'You do not know how good that sounds.'

I hugged him tighter. 'You've made this room a tribute to my mam and her paintings. Now I want to see what your creative talents are. I have this already.'

I touched the silky wooden heart that always adorned my neck. My papa took my hand and we walked to the end of the garden, under a wooden arch draped in summer jasmine like the one at *Ee Eliés*.

'Do you know this was Mam's favourite flower?' I said, breathing in the sweet smell of the little flowers.

'I remember her perfume used to smell something like that, eh?'

I nodded.

'*Diorissimo.* That was Lily of the Valley.'

I'd sprayed every last drop of it on my clothes after she'd died so I would feel she was still close to me. But, there in Greece, I didn't need her perfume. I knew she was close by.

Papa opened the door to a light airy room. Shelves, adorned with bowls of every size and shape, lined the opposite wall. Just like the ones in Yiannis's studio, the range of olive wood colours was beautiful. There was a smell of fresh shavings and sawdust that lay under the lathe and a large piece of wood was fixed ready to be turned and carved.

'So you see, Alexandra *mou*, you and I have something in common. We start with a lump of wood or clay and we transform it into a thing of beauty.'

He was right. *Both* my parents were creative people and I knew then I had to follow my dreams.

'They are works of art, Papa. No less than Mam's paintings are.'

'*Efharistó*. Now, what are your plans for the future? You cannot waste that remarkable talent. You have to continue with your craft. To have one artist not fulfilling her potential is bad enough but I cannot let that happen to my daughter, too.'

We walked back arm in arm to the terrace and found a place to sit in the shade.

'I always dreamed of having a studio and selling my own pots,' I said. 'Mam was keen but Richard said I wouldn't make a living from it. There was no way he was going to support me.'

Papa frowned. 'But you do not need his help, now, Alexandra. You are *my* daughter. I shall run you back to Porto Nikos now and give it some thought. '

The ferry across to Péfka was crowded that evening and I stood at the back, looking in the direction of my father's house, mulling over the day I'd had with him. Would it be possible to open my own studio like he said? Where would be the best place and how would it work if we were thousands of miles apart? And then there was Yiannis. I wondered what he would say when I left for home. Would he wait for me to come over for a visit? Was it even fair to ask him to wait?

From feeling euphoric about the possible plans made with my father, I knew I had a choice to make and I'd have to make it very soon.

Chapter Forty

I didn't sleep much that night. I read Claire's letter again and one minute, I'd decided to return home as planned, see my sister off to university and settle back living with Nan. Then I thought about my papa and how my life would never be the same now I'd found him and a Greek family I didn't know existed. And there was my lovely Yiannis to consider. What was I going to do?

I looked at the clock. It was getting light and I'd not slept a wink. I wrote everything down – reasons to stay and reasons to return. It didn't help but I must have dropped off after that because the next thing I knew Zena was knocking on my door.

'Alexandra, there is someone here to see you.'

I dressed and went downstairs.

Papa was sitting in the cool of the bar with an empty coffee cup in front of him.

'Here she is,' he said, standing up as I crossed the bar.

'Papa. I didn't know you were coming over to Péfka today. Zena, this is my father, Stelios Simonides.'

He shook Zena's hand. '*Kaliméra*, Zena, and *efharistó*. Thank you for looking after my daughter during her stay here on Péfka.'

'Kýrios Simonides.' She smiled at him. 'It has been a pleasure. You have a lovely daughter. I am pleased you have found each other.'

Papa beamed one of his now familiar smiles and his eyes crinkled in the corners. He placed an arm around my shoulder. 'So am I, Zena. So am I.' He turned to me. 'I have something I want to talk to you about, Alexandra. You have some breakfast and join me up at Andreas's old studio when you're ready, eh?'

I walked along the cliff top towards the studio. There was hardly a murmur in the trees and the air was warm and still. I thought of Mam making this journey every morning to attend classes here and tried to imagine the building before it had fallen into disrepair.

The shutters along the front of the building were raised and Papa had opened up the glass doors, or what was left of them. No wonder Mam had written about the magnificent sea views they had painted from the studio. He waved as he saw me approach.

'Come in. What do you think, eh?'

I'd only been around the back of the building with Yiannis as it had always been locked up. Going inside, I was drawn to the open windows and looked no further.

'What a view! No wonder Mam painted those sensational seascapes. Some of them had to be from here.'

'I know. No one has been in here since the murder but I thought I'd see what sort of state it was in. The metal shutters still worked – just about – but I'm afraid it's pretty run-down.'

I looked around the room for the first time. Shards of glass were strewn over the floor. The ceiling was partly down where rain had seeped in. You could see daylight where the roof tiles had been dislodged and there was damage to the floors where the wood had rotted. Plants and foliage were growing through the floorboards and there was evidence of vermin by the gnawed wooden legs of the benches. Even though the open doors had brought in some fresh air, there was no mistaking a stench of damp and mustiness that settled in the back of my throat.

'It's a bit of a mess.'

'More than a bit. That is why I do not know what you are going to think about my proposition now.'

'What proposition? Papa, tell me.'

He led me back outside and we sat under the pergola. I breathed deeply, welcoming the sweet smell of the summer jasmine.

'I have been to see Thea – she acts on behalf of Mamá now – and she agrees.'

I still didn't know what he meant.

'How would you like to open your studio here, eh? Your own pottery. You can make your pots and have a shop area to sell them.'

'But … I couldn't. I have to go home soon. It's a lovely thought but …'

Papa smiled at me and took my hand.

'I know what you are thinking. How can the mess in there become habitable again? But you have to look past that, Alexandra *mou*. You imagine what it will be like when all that is cleared, the roof and floors repaired. The internal walls will be re-built and decorated. The right place for you to start up on your own, eh?'

This was exactly what I'd been afraid of. I didn't want to leave him, the island or Yiannis but I felt I owed it to Nan and Claire to go back. Papa was getting more and more animated as he tried to convince me what a good idea he'd come up with.

'This way, the studio stays in the Simonides family. You can choose everything yourself. You can add living rooms for you to make this your home as well as your work place. What do you think, eh?'

I stood up and walked around to the front where the room was open. The space was generous, and I could imagine my wheel and work bench facing out to sea. What prospect did I have of opening a pottery back home in Wales? It could take me years to get enough money to even rent premises and there I was with a father offering to set me up in a business in the craft I loved. Papa followed me round. He said nothing else and waited for my reaction.

'It would be lovely but I can't let you do that for me.'

'I can do anything for my daughter. I've a lot of making up to do.'

He picked up a wooden sign resting against the side of the building.

'I took this down when I arrived here. It was hanging on one hook, anyway. You can just about make out "Simonides Painting School". Can you imagine a freshly painted sign saying "Simonides Pottery"? Maybe when you are ready, it will become "Simonides Pottery School", eh? Promise me you will think about it.'

'I'll think about it, Papa, but I'm afraid the answer's always going to be "no". I'll come and visit as often as I can but I have to go home. And you can come to Wales to visit me and meet Nan and Claire.'

He started to close the shutters and lock the doors. We walked back down into Santa Marina and sat at Xante's overlooking the harbour.

'I am going back home now, Alexandra. You take your time, eh? Perhaps you ring your Welsh *yiayiá* and talk it over with her? Is coffee all right for you?' He called over the waiter.

Later on, I phoned my nan. 'Hello, Nan?'

Hearing the soft lilting voice so far away made me realise the seriousness of what I was asking my grandmother to consider. Ever practical, Nan worried about me spending so much on phone calls.

'It's all right. I can chat. I know it's only a couple of weeks until I see you but I need to talk to you.'

My heart thumping, I explained what Papa had offered and assured her I wouldn't give him my answer until I'd spoken to her.

'What do you think? I could be at the opposite end of the country from Wales anyway if I go where the work is. I could pop on a plane anytime.'

I waited and the silence went on forever. There was an intake of breath at the other end of the phone.

'Yes, of course. I know I've sprung this on you but I want to know what you think. Papa says he knows it will be a shock for you and Claire if I move here so he says he won't ask again until I've made my decision. I'll ring again in a few days. Yes, I'm having a terrific time … Yiannis? Oh, yes, Nan, he's a good friend. You'd love him.'

I smiled to myself. *I know I do.*

'Tell Claire I'm sorry I missed her. And wish her good luck on results day. Bye, then I'm very grateful you encouraged me to come here.'

Papa was true to his word and never mentioned opening the pottery again. I didn't tell anyone, not even Yiannis, in case nothing came of my father's offer. It helped that Yiannis was very busy with several commissions for his bowls but we managed to see each other in the evenings. Making love, eating meals together in the balmy evenings, enjoying being together and never admitting that in twelve days it would all be coming to an end. It was as if neither of us wanted to burst the bubble and make plans for how we could keep seeing each other in the future.

Nan must have written the letter as soon as she'd put the phone down after our chat. Zena knocked on my door, and seeing the air-mail envelope, my hand shook as I took it from her.

'*Efharistó*, Zena. It's from my *yiayiá* by the look of the handwriting.'

My pulse raced. I had to have my grandmother's blessing if I was to stay. I took a deep breath and slid my nail under the seal.

My dear Alexandra

Your phone call came as a shock. When I heard your voice, I panicked thinking something had happened. But then, it has, hasn't it, cariad? You've found the man who loved your mam and made her happy. You've found your father. What he's offering you is very generous. The family must be very wealthy for him to be able to do that but I'm sure the main reason is he wants to make up for all the years he didn't know he had a lovely daughter.

Your postcards and letters have convinced me how much you love being there, close to where your mam was happy and fulfilled. It would be selfish of me to insist you come home just because I'm going to miss you ... and I will, cariad, more than you'll ever know. But I don't want you to end up like your mam. She was not able to tell me why she changed. And I never asked. Afraid of upsetting her. I can see now how silly that was of me. Her own mother and I didn't know anything about her summer in Greece.

Well, hard as it is, I'm not going to make the same mistake again. Follow your dreams, cariad. Become that famous potter you've always wanted to be, stay close to your father and your Greek family. I've told Claire – she's made it up with Richard and Sally, by the way. She was very upset at first but we talked it through and she agreed that she wouldn't see you much when she goes to university, anyway. She came up with an idea and we hope you'll like it. How about we come out to Greece for a holiday before she leaves for uni in September? I'd love to meet your father. And I think from a few hints, that we need to meet your friend, Yiannis, too. Claire knows more than she's letting on! We both need to meet the young man who's made such an impression on my granddaughter.

This is a long letter, Alexandra, but I want you to know I would never stop you following your heart. If it doesn't work out, there will always be a place here for you and I've told Claire the same.

I'll look at flights for us and if you find us somewhere to stay near you, Claire and I will be with you in a few weeks. It will be good for me to see the country Grampy loved so much, too.

Lots of love, Nan xxxxx

I held the letter close to my chest. Tears streamed down my face. *Nan, thank you. Thank you.*

Chapter Forty-One

The next few weeks flew by, but on the day Nan and Claire were due to arrive, every minute seemed to last a lifetime. In the end, I couldn't wait any longer. The Flying Dolphin wasn't due in for another hour but I had to get down to the harbour. I'd asked Zena if she would put Nan in my single room and let me share with Claire. The rooms were ready, my papa was with Yiannis at the wood turner's and there I was, unable to settle. My stomach somersaulted every few minutes and I'd been to the bathroom again and again. I couldn't wait to see Nan and Claire so why did I feel like I did?

Zena hugged me as I left. 'They do not come any quicker. But it is not good you being like this. You must go down to Xante's and get yourself a coffee and a baklava. I cannot wait to meet them.'

'*Efharistó*, Zena.'

I walked out into the shimmering heat. As I headed up from the taverna, the flowers in the terracotta pots outside each doorway appeared to be more vibrant and the whitewashed walls of the cottages gleamed more brightly. If there had been olive trees along the street, I was sure they would have whispered their approval.

At the bar, I sat under the blue parasol facing the quayside, remembering events that had happened since I arrived. Taking my time sipping coffee and eating the sweet pastry, I looked at my watch every few minutes. I stood up and wandered around the colourful gift shops and boutiques. Claire was going to love them. *I wondered what she thought about me staying? I've only Nan's word she's happy about it. But what does she actually think?*

It wasn't long before I'd be able to find out for myself. The blue and yellow hydrofoil approached the quayside and I saw Nan and my sister standing at the back of the boat, waving their arms. I ran down the steps and moved to the front of the passengers queuing to return to Piraeus.

'Nan, Claire!' I shouted. 'Over here.'

Claire ran down the gangplank first and I gathered her up in my arms. Nan followed her, tears forming in her eyes.

'I'm so excited you're here. Let's stand here in a bit of shade while they unload your cases. How was the airport? It's always busy. How did you find the taxi ride to the port? Awful, wasn't it? But you're here now, that's the main thing.'

Claire looked at Nan and they both laughed.

'Do you think she'll let us get a word in edgeways, Nan?'

I grinned. 'Sorry. It's just I've such a lot to tell you.'

Back at the taverna, after introducing them to Zena, we went up to our rooms for them to unpack.

'When you are ready, I have the food for you. You are hungry after your long journey, eh?' she called, as we disappeared up the staircase.

'*Efharistó*, Zena.'

I showed Nan to my room and then went with Claire along the corridor to ours. We didn't have the distant view of the sea that Nan had but the room was light and airy, and because it didn't catch the afternoon sun, also refreshingly cool.

'Bagsy, I have the one by the window,' said Claire, bouncing on the beds. It was like turning the clock back to when we were children, staying at Nan's. It was what she always said and a lump formed in my throat.

'Oh, go on then. You always get your own way.' I laughed. It never bothered me. She was my baby sister and nothing would change that. 'What about your results, then, brain-box? Off to Bristol, no problem. And Adam Johnson?'

Her eyes sparkled. 'He got his grades, too. I expect I'll see him around.' She grinned and coughed. 'I haven't told Dad or Nan about him, though. I don't want to jinx things. Just see how things work out. Anyway. What about you? You have so much to tell us. Starting with the divine Yiannis.'

Typical of my sister not to want to know about the life-changing events of the last month but be more interested in my love life.

'There's not much to tell, yet. But he *is* divine. You'll meet him later … and Stelios. We've booked to have dinner in a restaurant in the harbour. They can't wait to meet you and Nan.'

Claire still didn't mention my papa. Over lunch, when Nan asked about him and mentioned how she was looking forward to meeting him later, Claire kept changing the conversation back to Yiannis. How did we meet? What does he look like? What does he do for a living? But not one question about Papa and no mention of Mam.

'She'll come round, *cariad*,' Nan whispered to me as we went up to our rooms to change for dinner.

Yiannis had invited his father to join us as he thought it would be nice for Nan and Claire to hear from him about Mam's time at the taverna. The three men were seated at an outside table when we arrived. They stood up.

'Nan, Claire, I want you to meet Stelios Simonides, Vassilis Guikas and his son, Yiannis.'

Papa spoke first and took my grandmother's hand.

'Kýria Morgan. It is wonderful to meet Elin's mother.' He looked across at my sister. 'And to meet her other beautiful daughter, too. You both have Elin's smile. I remember it as if it were yesterday. Your mamá lives on in you, Claire.'

Claire's smile didn't reach her eyes. 'Thanks.'

'Yes, thank you, Mr Simonides,' said Nan.

Papa put up his hand. 'Stelios, please. You must call me Stelios.'

Nan smiled. 'Then, I'm Sadie.'

Vassilis introduced himself and explained how Mam had stayed with him and Dimitra and that she was there when his son was born, leaving Yiannis very embarrassed.

'It is honour to help your daughter stay in Greece, Sadie. She is a very good artist.'

Claire spent the evening chatting to Yiannis. Papa tried hard to include her in the conversation, asking her about her plans for university but she replied with short minimal answers. This wasn't the bubbly sister I knew, and I wondered if arranging the meal had been a bad idea. Once it was over, I suggested we head back to the taverna making the excuse that Nan and Claire would need an early night.

Papa stood as we went to go. 'It has been lovely to meet you both. Perhaps when you are ready, you will come to my home and I will give you a traditional Greek welcome.'

'Thank you. That would be wonderful. You've been very kind to me and my granddaughters already this evening.'

'Yes, thanks,' said Claire.

We walked along the quayside to begin the walk back to the taverna in silence.

'Well, what do you think?' I said. 'Neither of you has said a word since we left the restaurant.'

'Stelios is a very charming man, Alexandra. I'm just finding it hard to think of him as your father, that's all. I'm pleased you've found him, of course I am. Now I'm here, it's hard to take in that's all.'

Claire had marched on ahead. I caught her up. 'What about you, Claire? You were barely civil to him.'

Her cheeks were red. 'What do you expect me to say? Where have you been for the last twenty years? What about the man who brought you up? Doesn't he count?'

My heart raced. So much for all the encouraging words in their letters.

I lowered my voice. 'I shall always be grateful to Richard.' *But he never loved me like he did you. Now I know why!* I thought to myself.

'Now, girls. It will all look different in the morning. We're on holiday, don't forget? We're going to make the most of this week, Claire. Get some sun and enjoy being the three of us. Alexandra will show us all the places your mam went to and if we get time, I'd like to visit some of the ancient sites your Grampy used to rave about.'

She threaded her arms through ours and we walked together down the centre of the road to Zena's Taverna.

Lying in the twin bed alongside my sister, I thought about the decision I'd made. I was planning my future with the family and friends I'd just met and they were losing a member of theirs very soon after Mam dying. Perhaps I should leave it for a while, go back with them and return to Péfka next year.

Thin early morning light was peeping through the curtains when I awoke. When I came to, I realised that the quiet sobbing was coming from the bed next to me. I shot out of bed and placed my arms around my sister.

'Claire. Whatever's wrong? Don't cry. Tell me.'

She sat up and rubbed her eyes.

'I'm sorry, Alexandra. I hate being a cow to you. I just can't bear to lose you. All I keep thinking is that because Stelios is your father and Mam loved him so much, then she couldn't have loved me as much as you.' She sobbed uncontrollably. 'And now I can't ask her if she really loved Dad or was he second best?'

For all her bravado and pretence to be grown up and independent, what I saw in front of me was the vulnerable baby sister I'd always protected and looked out for.

'You silly sausage, of course Mam loved you. She adored you. Didn't she always go out of her way to treat us exactly the same?'

'That's what Nan always says.' She blew her nose.

'Look, I don't know if Mam knew for definite she was expecting me when she came back. She would have told Richard when she found out, I'm sure of it. He gave me a good life, Claire, and I shall always be grateful. And he loves you very much. Everyone rows with their parents at some stage, especially when you get to our age.'

Claire nodded. 'He's been lovely since I've gone back home to live. And Sally has been very helpful helping me get things for uni.'

I prickled at her name but tried not to show it.

'Look, what if I put off staying out here until next year? That will give you and Nan time to get used to the idea.'

I felt as if all air was being squeezed out of my body as my sister gave me the biggest bear hug ever.

'And I think I owe it to Richard – I mean Dad – to thank him for all he's done for me.'

'Would you do all that for me, Alexandra?'

Writing to Richard would be no problem. I *was* grateful to him for the opportunities he gave me while I was growing up. I sat holding Claire, looking out to the peach-pink streaked dawn, and wondered if I should have made that promise to return home. My heart sank.

Later that morning, we walked along the cliff top towards the old studio, stopping to admire the views across to the mainland. The sea sparkled like a faceted aquamarine jewel, glinting in the bright sunshine. There was hardly a murmur in the olive trees and the air was hauntingly still. *No whispers today, Mam? Surely you're happy I'm sharing your story with Nan and Claire?*

'See over there.' I pointed in the direction of the Simonides' family home. 'That's where Mam did the painting of the olive tree that's hanging in the attic bedroom, Nan.'

'Can we go and see it?' asked Claire. No mention had been made of our early morning talk and she was back to her bubbly self.

'If there's time. We can take the ferry boat across and you'll love the shops in Porto Nikos. And Nan, Mam won the gold award with a painting of the same olive tree but in oils. It's huge.'

'Will we be able to see that one, too?'

'You certainly will but not yet. I'm going to keep it as a surprise for you both'.

I smiled. Nan and Claire were coming round to the idea that Papa was part of my life. If Claire had told Nan about my offer to delay moving to Greece, no one mentioned it. I was determined to make their visit a memorable one. We'd called to see Yiannis on the way up. At least, Claire approved of my boyfriend, even if she didn't say much about my papa. 'He's gorrrgeous!' she'd whispered as we left the workshop.

'See in that direction. That's where Papa lives and just along to the right that row of buildings is the town of olive groves where Vassilis has his house.' I took them around the back of the old building and we sat on the bench under the pergola.

'The views are amazing. I can see why there was a painting school here – an artist's paradise, I'm sure.'

'This is where Mam came everyday to improve her painting. You can't see now as the shutters are down but the whole of one wall on the other side was glass doors that opened back and the students painted the views from there.'

'And this belongs to Stelios now?'

'Yes, his brother died and it belongs to the family. This is where my studio will be. He's offered to do it up and convert it to a pottery for me.'

I stood up and walked to the side of the building and beckoned my nan and sister to follow.

'And here is where there'll be an extra bedroom for when you two come to stay. That was one of the conditions. What do you think?'

Nan hugged me.

'I'm sorry I was less than enthusiastic when I arrived, *cariad*. I can see how much it means to you. This is your future now. I'm not going to be selfish. Of course, we'd love to stay here. Try stopping us, don't you agree, Claire?'

'Yes, I'm sorry I'm being such a baby. I told Nan about our talk in the night and she's made me see sense. You must stay. And she says we can come out in the uni holidays and you'll come home as well. Can we have the room with the best view?'

I laughed. 'They'll all have the same view, stupid,' I said pushing her. We began to play fight and Nan took out her camera and took a photo of us.

I grabbed both their hands and said, 'Oh, thank you. You two are the best. Wait till I tell Papa.' I jumped up and down like a little girl again.

'And the divine Yiannis!' said Claire.

A breeze sprung up and the leaves in the olive trees whistled and shook. Mam was there after all and I knew she'd be smiling!

Chapter Forty-Two

The rest of the time flew by and Nan managed to visit Epidaurus: one of the places Grampy had told her about. In the ancient amphitheatre, she and Claire sat on stone seats while I ran into the centre and whispered the lines of 'The Sun Has Got His Hat On', one of the rhymes Nan used to recite to us when we stayed at her house. It seemed appropriate in the midday heat.

'We could hear every word,' said Claire, when I rejoined them. 'Amazing!'

'I'll take you to one of Grampy's haunts every time you visit, Nan. That way you'll have to keep coming back.'

On the last evening, we travelled to Papa's house. We hadn't seen him since the disastrous meal in the restaurant. I'd rung him to tell him how my grandmother and sister had come round to accepting I was going to stay in Greece. Together, we decided it would be just the four of us and it would be a very low-key visit, just chatting and no formal meal. I wanted Nan and Claire to feel at ease with my father and realise he wasn't going to take me away from them.

He was waiting at the bus stop as he'd done when I'd visited for the first time on my own and then walked us to the parked car.

'*Kalisperá*, Papa.'

He bent and kissed me on my cheek. He held out his hand to my nan.

'Sadie, welcome. And Claire.'

He held open the passenger door for my grandmother to sit beside him in the front and Claire and I piled into the back seat. On the journey there, I pointed out the landmarks of interest and Papa stopped at the same viewing spot Vassilis had done for me.

'The sunset is spectacular tonight, isn't it?' said Nan. 'That will be what I'll have to remember when faced with the grey Welsh skies over the next few months.'

We all laughed but I knew Nan hated the next few months and their dark early evenings. October was when she'd lost my grampy all those years ago but it was still a gloomy part of the year for her, she always said. I reached over to the front and patted her shoulder.

The electric gates opened as if in slow motion onto the drive and closed behind us once the car was clear. Papa's magnificent villa came into view at the end of its long drive.

'I was not sure if you are happy around large dogs so I have put them in an outhouse. They are – how do you say? – big softies, but they look fierce.'

'No we're fine. We always had dogs when you were little, didn't we girls?'

'Good, I will let them come and say hello when we get there.'

As promised, Papa kept it very informal and we sat on the terrace outside the house. He brought out crisps, pistachios and olives and we drank chilled wine. The Dobermans were a big hit with Nan and Claire, and lay sprawled at our feet in the late warm sunshine. The intense perfume from the jasmine climbing over the pergola settled in the balmy evening air and reminded me again of Mam who would be pleased we were all getting along.

Claire relaxed, chatting to Papa as if she'd known him for years.

'Did Alexandra tell you she had a first at art college? I bet she didn't. She's the most modest person I know. Mam was so proud and even Dad said he didn't know how talented she was.'

Papa looked at me. 'No, I did not, Claire. All she said she had done a pottery course and that that was what she wanted to do. I had the impression she would be happy throwing a few pots.'

'She got the highest mark in the whole year!'

Papa stood up. 'Come with me.'

I knew what was coming. He led us inside, into the large room where he'd hung all of Mam's paintings.

'And from what I hear from Alexandra, you did not know how talented your mother was either, eh?'

'Oh my word,' said Nan. 'Are these all Elin's?' Her mouth dropped open.

'I didn't even know she could paint.'

'Neither did I, Claire,' I said.

My grandmother and sister wandered around the room, examining each of the paintings.

'Look at this, Claire. That's where Alexandra took us yesterday. Your mam's captured it perfectly.'

'And this one. The fishermen's nets – they look real.'

Then Nan noticed the painting above the fireplace.

‘There it is! The one you were telling us about that won the award. No wonder!’ Nan turned to Stelios. ‘I have the small version of this but in a watercolour.’

The next time they visited, I planned to take them over to the beach and see the old olive tree for themselves. Time had run out and their holiday was almost over.

‘The olive tree painting, it is my favourite. To think it is the very place she waited for me and I did not show up,’ said Papa.

I looked at Claire and put my arm on her shoulder. ‘It would never have worked, would it, Papa? Mam wasn’t Greek, for a start, and if she hadn’t have gone back to Wales, I would never have had this lovely sister of mine.’

‘I am sorry, Claire. That was thoughtless of me to say it. You mean so much more to Alexandra than I ever will. I hope you will treat me as your old Greek uncle, now. My home is open to you and your grandmother every time. I mean it.’

My father stood between us and placed an arm around each of us.

‘It’s fine. I’m sorry I was rude to you when we met,’ said Claire.

We followed Papa back outside and had another drink before he drove us back to the port.

‘Before you go, you must pick a painting each. You do not need anything to remember Elin but they are my presents to you. I can remove the canvases from the frames and I will roll them. Then it is easy to take them home, eh?’

We didn’t talk much on the ferry back to Péfka and it was nearly dark when we arrived in the harbour. The lights of the bars and restaurants dotted around the quayside gave the place a holiday feel and there was a buzz of tourists enjoying themselves. It dawned on me that whereas the holiday was coming to an end for Nan and Claire, for me life on Péfka was just beginning.

‘Alexandra, you come here. *Ela*.’

A beaming Yiannis was sitting at a table in Xante’s waiting for us. When I saw him I knew I’d made the right decision.

‘You have everything, eh? You must stay here anytime. It is going to be much time before Alexandra’s place is ready.’

Two cases were placed by the door of the bar and Zena had come to see Nan and Claire off.

‘Thank you, Zena. It’s been amazing. Our first holiday in Greece and it certainly won’t be our last.’ Nan shook her hand.

‘Yes, thank you, Zena. Look after her for us, won’t you?’ Claire smiled at me.

The Flying Dolphin was already in the harbour and, in a way, it made saying goodbye easier without a long wait. Claire hugged me tight, fighting back the tears.

‘Good luck next week. You’ll have a great time in freshers’ week. Send me some photos of that Adam Johnson and I can decide for myself how fit he is,’ I whispered. ‘Say “hi” to Dad and Sally for me.’

Claire walked up the gangplank without looking back, her shoulders shaking as she entered the boat.

Nan kissed my cheek. ‘Don’t worry, *cariad*. She’ll be fine. You’re doing the right thing, I know it. That’s why I made room in my case for all your Mam’s mementos of her time here. I knew you wouldn’t be coming back.’

‘Oh, Nan. Thank you. I shall treasure every one.’

‘Your mam would approve. We’ll be back before you know it.’

We both tried not to cry and Nan rushed onto the hydrofoil as the siren hooted.

‘Write as soon as you get home,’ I shouted.

I waved until the vessel merged into a dot. I turned and walked away, my heart thumping as my new life on Péfka began.

Epilogue

Alexandra
The Peloponnese, Southern Greece
Six months later

I've been living at the studio for a week now, Mam. I still can't believe it. There's nothing here to remind me of the dirty, dilapidated place Papa showed me. The room is bright and fresh, with gleaming white walls. The air coming in from the open wall is lovely and cool and I have stunning views out to sea without having to leave the sofa. While all this work was going on, I spent the time learning Greek and working at a pottery near Ermione. I've been working on a new collection – plates and bowls in sea colours, semi-matte glazes in muted shades of turquoise and teal, cobalt and ultramarine. Most will form the first pieces in the pottery shop but I've hung some of the plates on the walls. I think you'd approve, Mam. They were your favourite colours, weren't they? Your olive tree painting hangs in pride of place opposite the open doors. Papa's house-warming present to me.

The workshop is ready, my wheel and kiln have arrived along with bags of clay and glazes and I start work in the morning. Things are waking up on the island after the winter and the tourists will be arriving shortly. Wish me luck, Mam! I want to make you proud.

This will be the very last entry in the diary. It is time to look to the future. Things are looking good for Yiannis and me and who knows? Times are changing. At least, Papa will like the nice Greek boy I've fallen for!

I closed the diary and locked it with its tiny key. I ran my fingers over the soft supple leather one last time. I'd put it in a safe place with all the other treasures belonging to my mam that Nan had brought over for me. There would be no more whispering in the olive trees, I was certain of that. Mam would be happy with the decision I'd made. It was time to move on.

* The End *

Thank You!

Dear Reader

Thank you for reading my first novel, *Her Mother's Secret*. I hope you enjoyed Elin and Alexandra's stories and finding out about the special mother and daughter relationship they shared. Both of them visited Greece for the first time but for different reasons and I hope through their eyes I have captured the beauty, its people and colours of that wonderful country for you.

It's both exciting and nerve wracking to share with you the characters with whom I've formed a very close bond. Until now, very few people knew about why Elin cut her travels short and why Alexandra had to make the same journey as her mother to find answers to things she didn't fully understand. Now you do too. I'd love to hear how you enjoyed *Her Mother's Secret* and would really appreciate you taking time to leave a review in order for the book to reach more readers. Thank you.

My contact details appear at the end of my author profile and I'd love to hear from you. I'm fascinated by family secrets and the bond between mothers and daughters so look out for more novels in future.

Love Jan x

About the Author

After retiring from a career in teaching and advisory education, Jan joined a small writing group in a local library where she wrote her first piece of fiction. From then on, she was hooked! She soon went on to take a writing class at the local university and began to submit short stories for publication to a wider audience. Her stories and flash fiction pieces have been longlisted and shortlisted in competitions and several appear in anthologies both online and in print. In October 2019, her first collection of stories was published. Her stories started getting longer and longer so that, following a novel writing course, she began to write her first full-length novel. She loves being able to explore her characters in further depth and delve into their stories.

Originally from mid-Wales, Jan lives in Cardiff with her husband. Having joined the Romantic Novelists Association in 2016, she values the friendship and support from other members and regularly attends conferences, workshops, talks and get togethers. She is co-organiser of her local RNA Chapter.

You may find out more about Jan here:
Twitter: @JanBaynham
Facebook: Jan Baynham Writer
Blog: www.janbaynham.blogspot.com

More Ruby Fiction
from
Jan Baynham

Her Sister's Secret

How far would you travel to find the truth?

It's the 1960s and Jennifer Howells is a young woman with the world at her feet, just on the cusp of leaving her Welsh village for an exciting life in the city. Then the contents of an inconspicuous brown envelope turn Jennifer's world upside down. The discovery leaves her spiralling, unsure who she is. Overnight, Miss Goody Two Shoes is replaced by a mini-skirted wild child who lives for parties and rock'n'roll.

But Jennifer's experience with the excesses of sixties' culture leaves her no closer to her true identity. She soon realises she'll have to travel further – first to Cardiff, then across the ocean to Sicily – if she wants to find out who she really is ...

Her Nanny's Secret

How far would you go to save the person you loved the most?

It's 1941, and Annie Beynon has just become the first stable girl for the most powerful family in her Welsh village. Whilst her gift for working with horses is clear, there are some who are willing to make her life very difficult on the Pryce estate, simply for being a girl.

There are other – secret – ways Annie is defying conventions, too. As the war rages, and when Edmund, the heir to the Pryce fortune, leaves to join the RAF, it seems that it's only a matter of time before Annie's secret is exposed. That is, until she makes a shocking decision.

It's 1963 before Annie is able to face up to the secret she chose to keep over twenty years before. Justifying that decision takes her to Normandy in France, and an outcome she could never have expected …

Visit www.rubyfiction.com for more details.

Introducing Ruby Fiction

Ruby Fiction is in imprint of Choc Lit Publishing.
We're an award-winning independent publisher, creating a delicious selection of fiction.

See our selection here:
www.rubyfiction.com

Ruby Fiction brings you stories that inspire emotions.

We'd love to hear how you enjoyed *Her Morther's Secret*. Please leave a review on the store where you purchased this novel or visit www.rubyfiction.com and give your feedback.

Ruby novels are selected by genuine readers like yourself. We only publish stories our Tasting Panel want to see in print. Our reviews and awards speak for themselves.

Could you be a Star Selector and join our Tasting Panel?
Would you like to play a role in choosing which novels we decide to publish? Do you enjoy reading women's fiction? Then you could be perfect for our Tasting Panel.

Visit: www.rubyfiction.com/join-the-choc-lit-tasting-panel

Keep in touch:

Sign up for our newsletter for all the latest news and offers:
www.spread.choc-lit.com

Follow us on Twitter: @RubyFiction and
Facebook: RubyFiction

Ruby
FICTION

Stories that inspire emotions!

Printed in Great Britain
by Amazon

42401460R00148